ANGELIC WARS
End of the Beginning

If you liked

THE ANGELIC WARS: END OF THE BEGINNING,

download the free eBook
novella prequel,

"INTO THE MIND OF LUCIFER."

ANGELIC
WARS

End of the Beginning

RICK E. NORRIS

ILLUSTRATIONS BY JUDITH STEPAN-NORRIS

LUMINARE PRESS

WWW.LUMINAREPRESS.COM

Luminare Press
442 Charnelton St.
Eugene, OR 97401
www.luminarepress.com

ISBN: 978-1-64388-740-1
LCCN: 2021913818

*"To my wonderful wife, Judy,
the brood we have helped reach adulthood:
Brandon, Devin, Austin, and Amber, and
the angels who walk with us daily."*

TABLE OF CONTENTS

Scan QR Code or follow link to enlarge

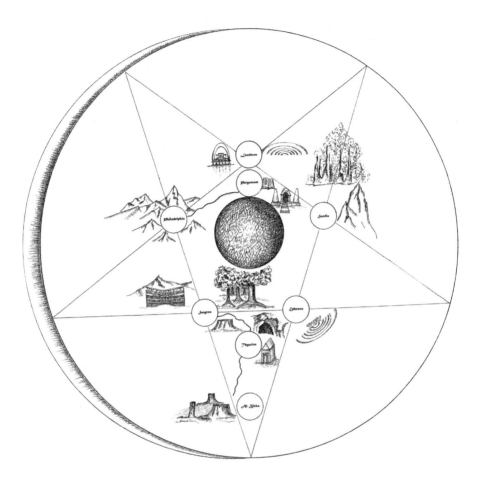

Map of Heaven, level two

http://ow.ly/anAM50G7hTO

PREFACE

THE ANGELIC WARS MUSICAL NOVELS ALLOW READERS TO HEAR characters sing to them through their "smart" devices. The paperbacks have QR codes which direct the reader to Soundcloud where the songs are stored. The reader may have to upload the Soundcloud app for the QR code to be activated. Once Soundcloud is uploaded, the songs will play without additional registration. For the eBooks, the reader has to only activate the hotlinks.

Angelic Wars: End of the Beginning is a fictional account of the battle among the angels for the control of Heaven during Satan's (aka Lucifer) rebellion. This musical novel, like the entire Angelic Wars series is inspired by the Bible.

It is not necessary to read the prequel, *Into the Mind of Lucifer*, or the first book, *First Rebellion* to understand *End of the Beginning*, though it would be beneficial in seeing the character developments throughout the book series.

Though there are hundreds of biblical footnotes in the novel and music, the story should not be viewed as an addition to the biblical story of redemption. However, many of the footnotes alert the reader that in many instances, (good) angels use values which are consistent with the Bible.

Biblical references are used in several ways: Some are to the actual story setting as it is written in the Bible, those are few. Others display a faint parallel or shadow between other events described in the Bible and this fantasy story. Many of these references apply Biblical events to new contexts, in line with the convention that history is intertwined or vaguely "repeats itself." Lastly, as in all the books of the *Angelic Wars* series, Lucifer distorts the Holy Scripture as he did in the Bible. For example, when he tempted Jesus, he used Scripture for his own selfish purposes

(Gospel of Matthew, chapter 4). I refer to such Biblical citations as "distorted."

As with all novels I write on three levels: First: at a fantasy level like any novel that creates an alternative world to take the reader on a fantastical journey. No biblical training (or belief) is required. Second: for the readers who are Christian with some biblical knowledge, footnotes to the Bible allows readers to refresh their memory of the Scripture, seeing the biblical parallels between characters and events. Third: this book can be read as a companion too a New Adult Bible Study curriculum which is available for a free download at www.AngelicWars.com. The free sheet music to these songs is available at www.AngelicWars.com.

CHAPTER 1

The heavenly gale assaulted Azarias's face, pounding the angel mercilessly with particles, distant voices wailing for the attention of his ears. Where were his Septemviri companions? Were they suffering, too? Hadn't God just ordained them as Heaven's archangels to cast Satan and his followers out of Heaven? Their crash from God's Throne to Heaven's second level didn't seem like the right way to commission them—it was anything but angelic.

Azarias struggled to stand, the unsteady silicium granules refusing support to his elbows, his golden strands of hair dancing off his shoulders. He searched for his tome, the screen the Guardian Cherub had given him to observe with the other six Septemviri when they conducted missions. Did he lose it in the last confrontation with Satan—maybe at God's Throne? How would he lead the others if he couldn't observe them when on missions?

He turned and glanced behind. His six partially buried comrades shifted in the silicium; it was a relief that they were still together. Azarias returned his gaze forward, refocusing his dark blue eyes at the distant mesas. The storm partially obscured the golden amborlite petals dripping over the flat tops' lips towards the hungry valleys below.

"Amborlite," he said of the blossoms. "Its alluring scent still attracts me. I long to climb the mesas to be with it again and hear the singing from God's Throne above."

He dropped his head and exhaled. "We're finally home. Al Birka."

Azarias lifted his head again, this time towards the moaning sound. His eyelids surrendered to the frenzied particles blowing across the surface.

He stood.

Good. Azarias could see better now.

Hearing the sound of struggling angels, he glanced behind him, then returned his attention to the noise clamoring from the large valley in front of him.

"What do you see?" asked Michael, steadying himself on Azarias's shoulder with his oversized, silver-toned hand.

"There, in the distance." Azarias raised his arm. "Across the plains. Do you see them?"

Michael stepped forward, shielding his face with one of his wings. "Serpents—like those I've seen in visions of Earth?"[1]

The others gathered around.

Azarias had seen so many of Satan's abominations. How could a mere cherub create and not be the Creator?

These angel-sized, hideous, serpentine forms, threatened him in a different way than the other atrocities.

His lips trembled.

Gabriel joined the troupe, stretching out his great fifteen-foot wings. "How many are there? Thousands?"

Azarias shook his head, eyes steadfast. "Yes, a hundred thousand."

How could this be? It couldn't be Abaddon and his minions. The Septemviri had repelled that rebellious angel to the other side of Heaven, in Laodicea, after escaping Satan's lair to God's Throne.

The large vipers slithered inside-out, their faces closing in the front, their cylinder bodies propelling—no—protruding forward. Their back ends opened and peeled forward, hugging their bodies and then over their faces, the way serpents shed on Earth. This "peeling" allowed them to slink their rears to the front where they closed, creating "new heads." This back-to-front molting caused a face to appear with the conclusion of each cycle.

---

1   Genesis 3:1-5, 14-15

Malachy, the historian, moved to Azarias's side, out of the corner of his eye, her slightly hooked nose alerting him. "I have no record of these spirit types in Heaven. They are not God's creation in their present form."

Squatinidale, the newest member of the Septemviri, didn't hesitate to voice his opinion. "Satan's evil must have morphed something. Just like in the Pergamum Bibliotheca. I was looking at a beautiful picture, in a book, given by God, when the face of Satan burst through the pages."

That experience still seemed to unnerve Squatinidale. Satan had hunted and haunted him throughout Heaven. The attack had reached a climax when the team entered the Bibliotheca on their way to rescue Raffaela and Malachy. Azarias hadn't been sure if Squatinidale could hold it together back then, but this stout little angel seemed to have found his self-confidence when he replaced the traitorous Pollyon. But for how long? Satan had a way of resurrecting insecurities, relentlessly prying into their weaknesses.

The serpent sirens modulated and echoed off the mesa bluffs, creating perfect but demented chords. The tones raised and lowered their pitch in unison to combine into massive twelve-tone harmonies. These *chord voicings* injected a sickening feeling in Azarias's spirit. They chilled him, alarmed him, and overcame him. Azarias had to hide his shaking hand from the others. After all, these angels depended on him to lead.

He held his ground.

Before visiting the Lord's Throne, the Septemviri had offered the enemy mercy and grace. But that all changed when the enemy rejected God's limitless grace. The seven were now God's warriors. The Septemviri must render God's judgment and remove these rebels from Heaven.

But could they? There it was again, his lack of faith, even after what God had done for them. You'd think after the Word had spoken to him at God's Throne, he would trust Him. Would he ever learn? Doubt seemed to be his nagging companion.

Azarias gazed at Uriel and Rafaella. Nobody seemed to know what to do. God had equipped all of them with His full armor, including the Word of the Spirit sword.[2] The weapon's gold hilt clung to each of their breastplates, its blades retracted. Was this a time to use it? How? Nobody had taught them.

Azarias thought about the Word sword construction—a handle resembling a standing being with arms stretched out, with an opened alpha-omega book on its chest. It hardly looked like a weapon to defend Heaven against an onslaught by this multitude.

The serpents increased their slinking rate, each cycle closing the gap between them and the Septemviri, a metallic liquid circulating just under their top layers from head to tail.

Azarias could now see their features, tormented faces of Seraphim—God's loyal angels.

His body tightened. He'd never seen angels or spirits tortured in such a way. How was Satan distressing them?

"Azarias, help us! Rafaella!" The snakes screamed out each of the Septemviri names in random order, their shrieks partially inaudible, lifting upon their tails, their heads swooning from side to side.

Azarias's companions covered their ears; Squatinidale used his arms as if the serpents directed their wailing at him alone.

Then one serpent yelled out, "Ego laus a deus intus vos." *I see the god in you.* (This was the battle cry the enemy chanted at Satan's throne in Pergamum.)

Michael, the big one, pushed himself forward to the front, toppling Malachy, yanking the sword hilt from his chest. Energy electrified his body, starting from his hand, migrating up his arm, and finally the rest of his body.

Azarias's eyes widened. "Michael! What are you—?"
Too late.

Michael charged down the slope towards the invasion. Three interlocking blades exploded from his sword's hilt, weaving into a

---

2 Ephesians 6:13-17

fiery point, a commanding point, a point burnishing the silicium around him.

"Come on!" said Azarias, waving his arm. He had no choice. How were they going to battle this many enemy spirits with just seven swords?

The other Septemviri charged, with Michael in the lead. Some ran faster than others, with Squatinidale and Uriel bringing up the rear.

The gap between them closed.

"I know that face!" screamed Michael, pointing his finger at the lead serpent. "It is Dionysius, the Philadelphian administrator."

Rafaella cried out, her voice breaking with each word, "No! It can't be!"

What happened? Had Dionysius surrendered to the enemy? Azarias heard about the horrible scene. Satan had melted billions of the hillside vinifera spheres, flooding the underground district of Philadelphia. Angels panicked. Satan's spirit attacked unknown numbers in the darkness, Rafaella and Dionysius among them. The last time the Septemviri spoke with Dionysius, he had been sitting near the rising Philadelphian deluge, blaming himself for Rafaella's apparent demise that had saved him.

All of that had changed when the Septemviri rescued Rafaella, who surfaced in the Laodicean district.

But what about Dionysius? The enemy may have captured him and transformed him to this wretched mass of despair.

Was he following Satan? How were they to know?

The creature wailed. "Rafaella, help me!"

Rafaella clinched her fists. Her low voice was almost hoarse. "Stop it! You are not Dionysius! Stop it! You can't be!"

The creature's wail dissolved with each plea, the ferocious wind swallowing it. "Save us. Save us. Save us—"

Michael slowed his gait, stopping several feet from the Dionysius serpent.

"Dionysius!" cried Rafaella, lunging past Azarias.

Michael grabbed her and turned her around, her clear, soft blue eyes wet with anguish.

The Dionysius serpent's body recoiled. Each loop elongated as the creature spiraled above the Septemviri to twenty-five feet tall, its two eyes of fire staring down at God's chosen archangels. The grotesque creature opened its mouth as it arched over Michael, a foul odor assaulting the amborlite scent, its teeth dripping over Michael's head.

Michael swung his sword from right to left, lopping off its jaw, and then left to right, in one motion, through its large, coiled neck. The menace exploded into black particles, blowing high into the atmosphere in the direction of the Siq.

The others joined in the assault. The attackers couldn't be loyal angels, but rather Satan's abominations of them. Regardless, Azarias knew they had to defend themselves, but how? The seven of them couldn't defeat such a large force.

THYATIRA'S CLIFF BALANCED ON THE EDGE OF TWO WINDING, intersecting canyons, guarding angels' secrets within its castle. Abaddon's flashy walk pricked Pollyon's attention. The angel pranced his signature stride across the courtyard, swaying his wings from side to side. Pollyon found this display annoying, but the Great One taught them to accept their fellow rebellious angels in their new chosen roles, including outward transformations.

"Ego laus a deus intus vos." *I see the god in you*, said Abaddon.

"Ego laus a deus intus vos, Abaddon."

"You wanted to see me?"

"Yes," said Pollyon. "I have met with the Great One, and he has promoted me with the sash color of purple. I am now the rank of lieutenant."

Abaddon grabbed Pollyon's arm and stopped. "You?" He glanced to the side and then back to Pollyon. "I brought you into our ranks. At first, you didn't believe me about the Great One's power. I proved it to you by setting a trap for Michael and Gabriel in Smyrna!"

Pollyon drilled his eyes into Abaddon. "Yes, I admit I was skeptical, but one cannot be too careful when challenging the Creator. I converted when the Great One gathered two hundred thousand angels in Smyrna. He demonstrated power—a power that I wanted, a power that he promised, and a power that will be mine."

Pollyon shook Abaddon's grip loose, his eyes riveted. "And, besides, you let Michael and Gabriel get away."

Two unfamiliar angels on the steps edged closer. Pollyon motioned Abaddon to move. "There are two significant changes in terminology which you should communicate to your subordinates. The Great One proclaimed that his title doesn't describe his greatness compared to the Creator."

Abaddon's face remained unmoved.

Pollyon continued. "The Great One has accepted the name that the Creator has now given him: *Satan*. Satan said it means *adversary*. By labeling him Satan, the Creator has now recognized him as an equal. You are to tell our followers that they are to refer to him as Satan."[3]

"Satan," mused Abaddon. "Well, that is certainly easier to say."

"There is one more thing." This time Pollyon grabbed Abaddon's arm and moved him around the corner and against the wall. "I learned, when I was a Septemviri in Ephesus, that there are enemy angels in at least seven districts, including here. Malachy revealed their names inscribed on pillars above the theater. They are in hiding."

Pollyon lowered his voice to a whisper. "There are counter-revolutionaries amongst us. We must validate the loyalty of any suspicious angel. If they are not with us, we must take them as prisoners."

"How do we know which angels are loyal?" laughed Abaddon. "Survey them?"

Pollyon's face remained hard. "Angels who are loyal to the Creator cannot lie," he said. "Even if it means compromising their safety."

---

3   1 Chronicles 21:1; Job 1-2; Zechariah 3:1-2; Romans 16:20; Revelation 20:7-10; Luke 10:18

He pressed his lips together. "We will cause an uproar if we question the loyalty of everyone in our district."

Abaddon shook his head and exhaled.

Pollyon continued. "But there is one way to confirm their loyalty to the Creator. I believe they will have the sign of the Septemviri on their right wrists. And, when the Creator's Spirit is present, it will enflame."

Abaddon lowered his eyes and ran his tongue over his lips. His intelligence seemed to be higher than other angels in the rank and file, but his pride and self-aggrandizing interfered with his wisdom. "What if we delegate a secret special force to spy on our angels?"

"Excellent idea," said Pollyon. "When this secret force encounters a suspicious angel, they will require that angel to show their right wrist." He paused, his eyes shifting away and then back to Abaddon. "We'll call them the *Protection Squadron*."

"Protection Squadron," replied Abaddon. "OK, I will choose an elite group of angels to seek and imprison those counter-revolutionaries. I will gather the most loyal comrades to start here in Thyatira."

Pollyon knew he could depend on Abaddon to carry out orders. His loyalty to the cause was exemplary despite his faults. He snapped his fingers. "Oh, the other point." He raised himself slightly, standing more erect. "I suggested to Satan a name that distinguished us from the Creator's *Holy Order* of angels."

He whispered into Abaddon's ear. "Legion."

Abaddon pulled back, his eyes puzzled.

Pollyon continued. "Legion is a good name because we are many, and our numbers are growing."[4]

As he was still speaking, two angels rounded the corner and stopped short.

Pollyon recognized them as the two on the steps who had been eyeing them when he spoke loudly. The taller one sported silver hair that contrasted with his dark bronze complexion. The shorter one had lavender hair with a silver hue to her face.

---

4   Luke 8:26-39, Mark 5:1-20

The strangers slipped back around the corner, faces blushed.

Pollyon threw Abaddon a glance. "Here's our chance. They must be members of the Holy Order. We can torment them to find others."

The two Satan allies rushed towards the loud crowd in the courtyard center. Pollyon, standing a head taller than Abaddon, stood on his toes and craned his head.

"Do you see them?" he shouted. "There must be a hundred angels."

Abaddon took flight, his arm outstretched. "Look! To the left. The tall one!"

He landed within feet of the bronze, svelte angel, who again slipped beyond his reach among conversing angels. The crowd took notice, its volume increasing a notch.

The two officers pushed through the crowd, losing sight of the zig-zagging angel as the crowd's gyrations kept opening and closing like passages between Earth's North Pole ice sheets. During the confusion, various angels took flight in an attempt to get above the commotion. Pollyon's view morphed into a sea of disorganized white, translucent wings dotted with confused faces.

He spotted Abaddon, pushing other angels to the side. "Where! Where did he go?"

Abaddon's face toughened. He raised his arms and turned. "I lost him."

Pollyon caught up to him, still stretching his neck in one last desperate attempt. He clenched his fists and joined his fellow angel in the surrender.

The two exited the crowd. Pollyon sighed. "In addition to our Protection Squadron, we must be proactive. Let's go back to Ephesus and get the list off the pillars that Malachy had transcribed onto his sheets. The names of the hidden angels will help us to track down each of the counter-revolutionaries."

PUTRID SMOKE CONTINUED TO VEIL THE MESA'S BEAUTIFUL view. Azarias could not count the thousands of towering serpents the Septemviri had slain using the Word sword. The serpents' slow, slithering pace helped the seven angels, but how long could they survive against the hundreds of thousands of serpent spirits? The full armor of God protected them, but seven angels could not repel all of these attackers with slashing swords. The weapon would fall short in a battle of this magnitude. In the beginning, they had two choices: flee or fight. Michael decided for them by charging the menace.

"Azarias," cried Uriel, his voice raising an octave. "They are surrounding us!"

Uriel, Raffaela, and Malachy turned to the rear to fight the serpents who had flanked them on both sides.

"We have to fly," yelled Gabriel, his voice barely above the wailing.

"We cannot retreat," cried Azarias, his sword now gyrating in continuous figure-eights against the onslaught. "That would allow them to attack Al Birka and overrun our base."

They were trapped and out of options. The others couldn't hear Azarias's prayer. "Lord, God of my salvation. I cry out to you.[5] You are the defense of our lives; Whom shall we fear?[6] Am I going to lose the war for you? We should have never committed to this fight without asking you first. We have failed—"

Fiery missiles arced from the hazy horizon, looping into the serpent masses. Massive explosions shook Azarias off his feet, the heated blast overwhelming him. In rapid-fire succession, the fiery projectiles sprayed over the plane, incinerating serpents. A consuming fire spread among the coiled snakes, fanned by a gust that had intensified to gale strength.[7] The enemy's wails dropped an octave, shrills still cutting into Azarias's ears. The attackers' remains dissolved into black flakes.

Rafaella stumbled backward into Michael as a ring of fire ignited the snakes surrounding the seven.

The cries dissipated and then stopped altogether.

---

5   Psalm 88:1
6   Psalm 27:1
7   Deuteronomy 4:24, 9:3; Hebrews 12:25-29

Black smoke rose towards God's Throne above as millions of black particles surrendered to the wind, carrying them to an unknown destination.

Azarias stumbled to his feet, brushing his shoulder-length golden hair out of his face. Could this be God's work? He didn't work this way. He always used the faith of his servants to execute His Will.[8]

Azarias should have been accustomed to the strange changes in Heaven by now. The putrid stench of burning spirit still suffocated him. These were not God's creations. They were distortions and abominations. Satan was far more powerful than Azarias could had imagined a cherub could be. What other distorted creatures will assault the Septemviri and the Holy Order? They could not defend themselves.

And what did the other members of the Septemviri think of him? He had relied on God in the Pergamum escape. That certainly showed his leadership skills, but now the challenge changed. Would his gifts be inadequate in this new assault? They were no longer just battling cherubim and seraphim. Frankly, he didn't know what they were fighting or how to fight them. Michael's impulsive move to use the Word had almost cornered them into an impossible situation. Azarias was afraid for any of them to use it again.

All the angels retracted their swords and placed the hilts on their chests.

He felt Michael's large hand on his shoulder. Azarias glanced to his side and then shifted his eyes back to the plains. The violent gales now ceased. Smoldering fires were patiently consuming their victims, adding to the particulate smoke that shielded the mesa's gilded skirts, choking the serenity they had once offered to God's loyal subjects.

"Where do we go from here, Azarias? There are so many districts in Heaven. If this was a sign of captive angels, how do we free them?"

Azarias turned his back on the fiery plain. "Well, Michael, we know Malachy has a list of angels in each of the seven districts we visited."

He glanced at the others. "I don't think these were loyal angels.

---

8   Matthew 26:53

11

Satan can change the outward appearances of created beings. I think these were enemy angels morphed into hideous beings with the faces of those in hiding or captive. Satan could be luring us to rescue them and then trap us."

The wind picked up again, coming from beyond the burning masses. It pressed their faces, yet their robes remained still. A song—a faint tune of a lone troubadour—echoed off the mesas.

Squatinidale stepped forward, peering into the smoky fog, his speech surrendering to an unintelligible whine, an octave higher than usual. "Is this another attack? I can't see through the smoke." His eyes rocketed.

A singing silhouette emerged from the smoke at a casual saunter, drawing closer.

The song didn't seem threatening, but, oddly, joyful—its lyrics were now audible.

Scan the QR code to hear the mysterious character sing.

It is You, it's not me
You're the one, who set me free
As I walk, As I fall in your Spirit
Prepare, he comes to you[9]
Repair and follow through
As we walk, as we fall in His Spirit
This is the day the Lord has made
Rejoice and shout out accolades. [10]
Alleluia

---

9   Matthew 3:3
10   Psalm 118:24

His love endures forever.[11]
Clap your hands and shout His Name[12]
And from the darkness
A glorious flame
Alleluia

His grace endures forever.
Hear the voice called from the plains
Resist the coming of the rains
As you walk, as you fall for His Spirit
His warm love, like the wind
Is a force, against all sin
As you walk, as you fall for His Spirit
This is the day the Lord has made
Rejoice and shout out accolades.
Alleluia

His love endures forever.
Clap your hands and shout His Name
And from the darkness
A glorious flame
Alleluia

His grace endures forever.
Alleluia
His grace endures forever.

A smaller figure sauntered out of the smoke.
    It stopped.

---

11   Psalm 118:1
12   Psalm 47:1

CHAPTER 2

Two figures labored up the Ephesus Odeum amphitheater steps, their robes hanging dead at their sides, the Creator's aroma absent from the atmosphere around them. Gone were the angels soaring among His Spirit's gusts, gone were the meaningless praise songs and poetry performances, gone were the brainwashed angels honoring a Creator who betrayed them with the ignorance of their free wills.

Pollyon paused at the top step and turned. He stroked his chin and fixed his eyes at the seats facing the large stoic slabs guarding the rear stage.

Abaddon moved to his side. "What do you see?"

Pollyon's eyes didn't move, the past events still goring him. He had performed his duties and set the Septemviri trap, only to see Abaddon let them slip through his fingers again.

"When Malachy and I stood here, we determined that the Creator designed the stage slabs as a sign to His loyal angels. The sign betrayed Satan's battle plan."

He pointed.

"Do you see those vertical monuments?"

"Yes," said Abaddon. "Are they important? The frescos on them just look like any other graphic art defacing our new order."

"No, no, they are much more that," said Pollyon, shaking his head. "Each standing stone displays a graphic symbol representing a major district in Heaven. We occupy each of them. From left to right: Smyrna, Ephesus, Thyatira, Philadelphia, Sardis, Laodicea, and Pergamum."

"I don't follow," said Abaddon.

"I, too, thought it was useless information," said Pollyon, turning his back to the stage. "But I didn't know their purpose; I didn't know *His* purpose."

He paused.

"The Septemviri discovered the key. They pieced together visions from the Creator. They decrypted our battle plan."

The two angels reached the top landing and walked between towering columns standing at the theater's rear. "What additional information did they receive?"

Pollyon sighed, pressing his lips together. "When I was a Septemviri, they received a vision of the battle plan, but only of the districts that we will assault. They didn't understand our second stage of sieging and infiltrating these districts." He clenched his fists. "That was until the mysterious red-haired angel appeared down there."

Abaddon stopped. "Mysterious angel?"

"Yes, this angel's hair twinkled with stars that poured onto her robe. She directed a message to Malachy from the stage."

"Do you remember any of it?"

"Of course. I have a gift of remembering most anything. It went like this:

The plan of the Lord is etched in stone
He does not waver, the course He owns
As four sevens are twenty-eight
His plan is solid
There's no escape
Go in faith, and find your path
You will be spared of His wrath
Hearts afire without mend
Falling star at the end

Pollyon kicked a small black-and-white othelite sphere down the steps of the Odeum. It ricocheted among the seats, finally landing black-side up.

"I didn't understand any of it, especially that *falling star* part. But Malachy understood the *four sevens are twenty-eight* line. It represented the different districts, with information etched on every fourth of the twenty-eight columns behind us."

"I don't follow."

Pollyon led Abaddon to the fourth column and pointed to lines of script. "Malachy ran her hand over the etchings."

Abaddon touched the column. "Where did you begin?"

"Malachy and I didn't know, either. Then I stretched my arm to touch the etchings. My Septemviri mark blazed, and so did names of angels about twenty feet up each column."

"What did the lists mean?"

"I don't know," said Pollyon, scratching his head. "In retrospect, I believe they are lists of the loyal angels hiding in each of our districts."

Abaddon's eyes lit up. "Well, go ahead. Let's get the names back to our Protection Squadron. They will flush out the Holy Order loyalists."

"I can't."

Abaddon's jaw dropped, his arms open and his mouth sporting a sarcastic smile. "Well, my fellow enlightened one. You were once a Septemviri. Raise your arm and show the way!"

Pollyon looked away.

"Why are you waiting? Satan will be overjoyed to foil more of the Creator's plans." He raised Pollyon's arm to the column, its sleeve sliding down to the elbow. The Septemviri mark was gone.

Abaddon's smile melted; his eyes hardened. "Curse the Creator!" He pulled the arm down, paced a few steps, and stopped. Abaddon spun and then walked up to within inches of Apollyon's face, pointing his finger.

"We must understand the writing on these columns. What did Malachy do? Did she record them?"

"She pulled out her membrane sheets and made an impression of all of the names."

"OK, let's regroup." Pollyon tapped each finger. "We know the names of these seven districts. We know that a list of names appeared on the columns in each of the districts. We also know that loyalists are in those districts, like the two we chased in Thyatira. Therefore, we must seek them out and convince them to join our cause."

"And if they don't?" asked Abaddon.

"We eliminate them and send them through the Siq."

"But we cannot do anything with them if we don't know who they are. We can't suspect everyone! Such a purge would disrupt our rank and file, causing an uproar." Abaddon shook his head.

Pollyon sat down. "There is another way to uncover the loyalists."

Abaddon raised his head, his eyes widened.

Pollyon continued. "I have been gifted with an exceptional, if not unmatched, memory. I saw all the names on the seven columns. Since I saw it, I know it. I can work with others to replicate the lists, but it will take time."

"OK, that's a plan." Abaddon cupped his hands. "Can we cross-reference these names to lists in each of the seven districts?"

"I can ask Satan. He seems to have powers that I can't imagine. I hope to explore myself as he has and even acquire some of those abilities."

The angels started down towards the exit below. Pollyon remembered his and Malachy's "narrow escape" from the enraged, enlightened clan. He had gone through great pains to arrange that ambush, but Malachy's unknown fighting technique foiled the plan. Where did she learn to roll her membrane sheets into a hardened club?

"What about the Septemviri?" asked Abaddon. "They seem to appear at the most inconvenient places to save these pitiful loyalists."

Pollyon grabbed his arm as they strode through the Odium theatre's exit. "Don't worry about them, my friend."

WHO WAS THIS?

Azarias's eyes raked the figure's lines, his jaw hardened. The seraph stood about nine feet tall, shorter than an average angel of ten feet. She donned a yellowish scarf, crossing over her upper torso from right to left, twinkling stars pouring from her red hair onto her robe. Each star opened from its middle, peeling outward. This revolution bloomed a new star before falling off her robe and evaporating into the Spirit.

Michael stiffened, drawing her eyes to him, her grip tightening around the staff in her left hand.

Azarias reached over and intercepted Michael's hand sliding to his Word sword. They couldn't afford any more rash decisions.

The visitor looped her thumb into a thick belt. It reminded Azarias of the enemy's gross, colored sashes that showed their rank or district in Satan's forces. But this belt displayed nothing pretentious.

Her emerald-green eyes radiated from her dark skin as she spoke. "Mai Deus Exsisto vobis." *May the Lord be with you.*

"Mai Deus Exsisto vobis," said Azarias.

"My name is Leihja. The Lord's Spirit sent me. God heard you, Azarias, for the eyes of the Lord are on the righteous, and His ears are attentive to your prayer."[13]

She turned her wrist over, brandishing the burning multi-colored symbol of the Septemviri worn by loyal angels.

Malachy edged a little closer, her voice just above a whisper. "I remember you. You recited the stanza in the Ephesus Odeum when Pollyon and I compiled the lists."

"Yes." Leihja's mouth frowned. "And Pollyon is using his gift of memory to recreate those lists, putting the Holy Order in danger."

Uriel flanked the angel on the right. "Why would God allow an angel to use a God-given gift against Him?"

"Because Pollyon and the other rebels succumb to their cravings and do not have their minds set on what the Spirit desires. Their

---

13   1 Peter 3:12

minds govern their desires and will lead to their destruction. God allows us to use our gifts as we desire. It is another example of His great love in allowing us to choose for or against Him. The wrath of God will be revealed against all the godlessness and wickedness of those angels who suppress and distort the truth.[14] Yet a mind governed by the Spirit will sustain life and peace."[15]

"What were those serpent-type spirits?" Rafaella edged closer, staring at the surface before her. "At first, I saw Dionysius's face. I-I thought of them as tortured spirits transformed by Satan into these hideous creatures. But, when they drew closer, they attacked us. My heart yearned to help, but my mind pulled me back."

"Satan masquerades as an angel of light.[16] He distorts his form and all of God's creations. You will see this in forms greater than these serpents."

Malachy chimed in. "Where did they go when we destroyed them?"

"They died," said Leihja.

"What does it mean to die?" asked Uriel, his speech a little shaky.

"Dying is the process of moving from one plane of consciousness to another. The angels that you destroyed will always exist, but in another universe, far lesser than Heaven. Death has ushered them into the material world, where the presence of God is not as apparent as in Heaven."

Azarias stroked his chin. "Is God's presence apparent on Earth and the rest of the material world?"

"Yes. For, since the creation of the world, God's invisible qualities—his eternal power and divine nature—are clearly seen and will be understood from what has been made." [17]

Leihja walked over to the wall and sat cross-legged, the staff across her lap.

---

14   Romans 1:18
15   Romans 8:5-6
16   2 Corinthians 11:14
17   Romans 1:20

"I have been sent by God's guardian cherub to teach you how to engage in spiritual warfare. God created angels to promote love, grace, and mercy in serving Him. But, with Satan's rebellion, our nature and function have expanded. You are now God's representatives to implement His judgment, too."

Michael rushed to her and stooped down. "Is this what our Lord, 'The Word,' meant when he spoke to us at the Throne? He told me: *Michael, I created you as the great angel and protector of your cohorts. You will be one of my chief princes in the fight against darkness. I know you are ignorant of the gifts needed to accomplish this, but the Spirit will guide your hands for the destruction of evil.*"

Leihja smiled and tapped his hand. "The Spirit guides us all, Michael. He will use us to convict others of their sin, righteousness, and judgment in these times.[18] And, other times, He will give us love, joy, peace, and kindness that we can use to help others."[19]

She glanced at the others and then at her cane. "I could use this staff for grace or judgment."

Leihja stood and faced the group. "When I use it for support, it offers me grace by allowing me to lean on it. However, I can also use it for judgment."

The shimmering angel twirled the cane into the air, catching it in its middle with both hands, and spun it end over end in a figure eight, crossing the ends over both shoulders. She increased the speed of each revolution. The Lord's Spirit electrified a high-pitched, harmonic whistle. Every cycle increased the volume, adding notes to the harmonic chord, increasing in brightness, burnishing off her face. Leihja stalled her figured eights in one motion, looped her right arm over the staff, and spun backward, striking the wall. The impact blasted open a fissure that gushed out profundo, Heaven's spiritual liquid.[20]

The Septemviri jumped back.

---

18 John 16:8
19 Galatians 5:22
20 Exodus 17:5-7; Psalm 78:15-16,20

"Cool," muttered Gabriel, his eyes widening, his voice almost giddy.

Leihja reached her hand into the pouring profundo, siphoning the turquoise up her arm.

She smiled.

"During these hard times, you will find grace or judgment anywhere. God's Holy Spirit is the energy that powers the hidden treasures of all creation to those who obey Him.[21] Faith is the key to unlocking them."

Azarias smiled. He had ventured to this wall outside Al Birka many times and failed to see God's Spirit so intimately.

Michael stole a step. "But we were not given a staff." He pulled the Word from his chest. "I think we've seen this weapon's power against the serpents, and it seemed inadequate."

"Is it?" Leihja pulled back her scarf, revealing the Word sword hilt on her chest. In one motion, she grabbed it and thrust it downward. The golden figure's arms blasted outwards, creating a slightly arched shape with a filament connecting its hands. Leihja pulled a sharp projectile from the hilt, fed it into the bow, and fired the arrow into the profundo crevice, sealing the gouge in the wall with molten fire. The gushing profundo ceased.

Leihja turned. "Are you ready to learn how to harness the power of God for His glory?"

Azarias looked at Michael and then the others. Were they?

21　Acts 5:32

CHAPTER 3

Pollyon coasted with Abaddon toward Thyatira's castle, the task of recreating the names of loyal angels from the Ephesus columns weighing on him. He could ramble off many thousands of words at an instant based on his sight memory, but to transcribe them would take a lot of effort. He needed help.

"I estimate the number of comrades I will need to transcribe these names for the Protection Squadron to be exactly six hundred and sixty-six.[22] They must be gifted in both hearing and transcribing. Will you please choose them for me?"

Abaddon didn't reply. Pollyon saw this as another clue that Abaddon didn't like answering to him. How would he deal with this insubordination? His behavior proved Pollyon's uneasiness with Satan's philosophy, though he'd never say it. By allowing angels to exercise their free wills, Satan permitted them to disobey the Legion's commanders. But who was Pollyon to question Satan's mission? The strategy had worked perfectly so far, turning nearly one-third of Heaven against the Creator.

An odd noise in the courtyard drew his attention. The two angels rounded the tower. Down in front of the Great Hall, he could see hundreds of angels confronting each other. Loud shouts and the aggressive waving of arms accompanied the groups. Could they be too late? Had the loyalists come out of hiding and attacked the Legion?

---

22   Revelation 13:18

"Come on, we might not need those lists after all," screamed Pollyon.

The pair zoomed down.

The two commanders settled on the steps in front of the hall. An angel broke from the masses and flew to meet them. "What do I do?" yelled Baal Zebub.[23]

"When did these loyalists come out of hiding?" asked Abaddon, his face red with rage.

"Loyalists?" He grabbed Abaddon by the shoulders. "These are warring factions of our Legion."

Pollyon, his mouth open, looked at the commotion and back to Baal Zebub.

"Well, our exalted commander, what do you suggest we do? Maybe you can *order* them to stop," said the smiling Abaddon, crossing his arms.

Pollyon stared at the commotion, his face as hard as the outcropping supporting the castle's foundation on the bluff. It appeared that the masses had divided into two groups, each consisting of over a hundred angels. The shouting was so fierce and varied that he couldn't understand the reason for the fighting. One shining angel with silver-streaked hair retreated from the group and disappeared behind the Keep, the structure's fortified tower.

Maybe others would follow him and stop this nonsense. Then they could get back to things that were more important.

Why couldn't angels see the big picture? Their pride had poisoned their free-thinking. Where was Satan?

A scream stiffened Pollyon's posture. The silver-haired angel returned, bearing one of the Legion's energized golden rings—the same type they had used to imprison the loyalists by slipping it around their chests.

"What now?" asked Abaddon.

The silver-streaked angel flew up about twenty-five feet high with the ring in one hand and looked down on the opposing group.

---

23   2 Kings 1:1-17

"Submit to us, or I will destroy you!"

"Destroy? With the ring?" Pollyon looked at Abaddon, his eyes now wide.

The aggressive angel swung the ring in circles above his head, his hand inside the hoop. The ring pulsated a buzzing sound that became louder with each wonky pass. On each lap, the hoop elongated into an oval until it was five feet long. The imperious angel then grabbed the ring at one end, allowing it to break into a long, pulsating, and lustrous whip.

"Where did he learn to do this?" shouted Abaddon, turning to the other two.

One angel from the other camp stepped forward and pointed his finger. "You can't control us. We don't answer to you. Who made you an exalted lead—"

The airborne angel dove down. His whip lashed out and struck the opposing angel with an explosion. The rebelling angel's body burst into black particles that were sucked high into the atmosphere. The particles spread out into a thin, black flock, disappearing over the horizon towards the Siq.

The condemning angel continued to whip above his head and indiscriminately destroyed angels on the ground with each crack. Angels from both camps scurried in all directions, running into each other to escape the sting of death. Some returned with elongated rings.

The wild attacker's laugh echoed amongst the towers as his eyes glowed a deep red. Two angels, possibly his companions, flew up and grabbed him by the legs. The whip recoiled, wrapping all three into its electrified clutch. The unfortunate trio spun down until they exploded on the surface, their dark matter chasing that of the previous angels' spirits.

Other angels now had returned, raising their ante. Each had retrieved their rings and elongated them into whips. The pulsating buzzing sounds multiplied in number and pitch as the angels lashed out at each other. Two of the whips entangled in midair. A golden aura formed at their intersection. The aura broke into two small golden fireballs, ricocheting down the whips towards their owners. The fireballs exploded with a deafening sound, extinguishing the whips' owners and nearby comrades.

Pollyon, Abaddon, and Baal Zebub turned and ran into the great hall, slamming the large doors behind them. The castle shook with each explosion as they cowered.

"I must get to Satan. He has to stop this before we destroy ourselves," said Pollyon, lowering his voice to a whisper.

Silence.

Quietness returned outside the door as quickly as the commotion had started. Pollyon tapped Baal Zebub's shaking hand. "I think they stopped."

The three stood, stiff-legged. Abaddon cocked his head, his ears searching for any sound on the other side of the door.

He turned and cracked the door open.

Abaddon's eyes lit up.

He slammed the door, resuming his posture with his back against the door, his mouth open, eyes closed.

"What!" shouted Pollyon. "What did you see? Are they trying to come in?" He pulled Abaddon away from the door and opened it with a jerk.

Nothing.

There appeared to be no one in the courtyard although there were still dozens of glowing whips. "They did it. They destroyed each other. Their pride and fear fueled their hate—a hate that stirs up conflict."[24]

The three walked onto the landing. "Why?" whispered Abaddon. "Why did they do this?"

Baal Zebub hurried down the steps and picked up one of the whips by its handle. "The better question is, 'Where was Satan?'"

A voice boomed through the open door behind them. "I was there. Didn't you notice? I was the shining one with silver-streaked hair."[25]

---

24 Proverbs 10:12
25 Genesis 3:1, 3:2, 3:14. English: "Serpent," Hebrew: "Nachash" or also defined as the "Shining One."

Leihja trained the Septemviri in the various uses of the Word of God as a weapon. Though the Word in the shape of a sword was powerful, it paled in comparison to its other functions that could wipe out battalions.

Leihja departed as mysteriously as she had arrived at the Al Birka headquarters, but not before transforming the Septemviri into warriors. The serpent demons, fully incinerated and blown away allowed the atmosphere to clear, the amborlite-gilded mesas again, broadcasting their dominance of the area.

The Septemviri missions of offering God's grace to the rebellious angels had faded into a memory. Though presenting the steadfast love of God's mercy to the rebellious angels would always be available, the enemy's hearts had hardened, preventing them from accepting it.[26]

Azarias knew this was another defining moment. When the Septemviri had first stood together inquiring of the Lord here, the Lord revealed their mission of mercy and grace. At that time, so long ago, the Holy Spirit had presented an image of Satan's battle plan consisting of several heavenly districts. Realizing the commission's magnitude, Azarias confessed to his friends, at that time, that he wasn't the leader they thought he was, but they still wanted to follow him. Even later, with the confidence expressed at God's Throne, Azarias still doubted—not God, but himself. He now knew this lack of confidence was from Satan, but it still lingered in his spirit, ready to assert itself in the darkest moments.

As all loyal angels do, the Septemviri formed a prex précis circle to hear from God.[27] The seven angels bowed their heads and opened their hands, waiting to hear from the Holy Spirit.[28] A warm breeze consumed them from the mesas, intensifying into a violent wind.[29]

---

26   Exodus 9:12; Psalm 95:8
27   Matthew 18:20
28   Psalm 95:6
29   Acts 2:1-2

Fire filled their eyes with the vision of an angel multitude fighting for God and their heavenly home. Shades of red, black, and white clashed from three sides against Satan's darkness, angels from both armies falling in droves. Hate and pride empowered Satan's forces, while judgment and righteousness infused God's armies. The Holy Order heralded God-glorifying music as they attacked Satan. [30] One mighty angel commanded the charge for God's armies, but Azarias couldn't see his or her face since the vision had almost blinded his mind's eye.[31]

The scene faded as a voice—this time audible to all present—spoke to Azarias:[32]

> AZARIAS, GO TO THYATIRA WITH URIEL AND
> SEEK OUT MY LOYAL ANGELS. I WILL LEAVE
> MICHAEL IN CHARGE AND GUIDE HIM.

Azarias looked up. "Thyatira." He looked at Uriel. "I remember when Abaddon confronted us in the Great Hall, and you struggled—"

Uriel raised his hand. "I know, Azarias. My faith escaped me, and Abaddon pierced my soul with Satan's power of insecurity. You can depend on me."

"You understand, Uriel, that several things could happen. We could engage in hand-to-hand combat, be captured, die to the material world like the serpent demons, or cause the death of other loyal angels. The stakes have gotten much higher now that we are the lever of God's judgment."

"Unlike with the other missions of mercy," said Rafaella, "some of us may not return."

She continued: "I remember when Satan trapped me within my wings in the underground Philadelphia vinifera deluge. I felt so alone and wanted to surrender to him. Fortunately, my faith sailed

---

30   Luke 2:13-14
31   Revelation 6:2-5
32   Acts 9:4-7

me through. I couldn't imagine anything more frightful than that experience, except to be cast out of Heaven during a battle."

She paused.

"I feel for both of you on this assignment. I sense your hearts are heavy, but don't be anxious about anything, but in every situation, by prayer and petition, with thanksgiving, present your requests to God."[33]

Silence intruded on the group as each looked around, consuming the thought that they could be parted from each other forever.

Azarias dreaded this fact that seemed to elude his mind. The risks had never seemed so high when they were just trying to offer God's mercy to angels. Now, it was their very existence in Heaven that they were each wagering.

---

33   Philippians 4:6-7

CHAPTER 4

Satan had not only participated in the Thyatira riot but also escalated it to destroy some of the Legion, though a very insignificant number. Why had he done this? These angels had made the ultimate sacrifice for him, rejecting the Creator. Satan had the ability to wipe out the entire Legion by stoking the worst aspects of one of them.

And what about him? Pollyon stiffened. Would he, too, be dissolved into dark matter to be sucked into the material world?

He and Abaddon crept through the Great Hall's open door. Baal Zebub held his place on the front landing. Pollyon's eyes raked the walls for any movement. Everything seemed normal—the hanging portraits of the commanders, the reflective surface, the high ceiling. The only abnormal aspect was that the Great Hall was void of angels. How did his relationship with Satan come to this? His interactions with Satan ranged from supportive, to sarcastic, to condescending. Though he never knew what to expect of this great cherub, he knew that whatever happened was for the benefit of all angels, Heaven, and creation—but destroying comrades? He had to question it.

The two crept into the hall, occasionally glancing back at Baal Zebub. He wasn't sure who was more nervous among the three of them.

Eyebrows drawing together, Abaddon turned to Pollyon. "We did hear Satan in here, didn't we?"

"I'm not sure," said Pollyon.

The vast doors slammed.

The angels could hear Baal Zebub jerking on the handles and pounding on the door. "Don't leave me alone out here," he said, his voice now shrill. He penetrated the door with his arm. (Angels normally can walk through any spirit in Heaven, but it compromises their energy—like swimming in Earth's quicksand, from what Pollyon imagined.)

"Don't do that!" Abaddon bolted towards the door. "We are not sure of your—" The door rejected Baal Zebub's arm with an electrified charge, his scream swallowed by a frightening grumble.

"Baal Zebub!"

Silence.

Abaddon deepened his tone and spun Pollyon around. "It's your fault." He stood within inches of Pollyon's face. "You're supposed to be the commander."

Pollyon gritted his teeth. How had they gotten here? He'd had an excellent plan to uncover the counter-revolutionaries, but now he was lost in a tangle of mutinous revolutionaries with a psychopathic leader.

"Stop it, or you will suffer the same fate as some of the others," boomed a voice. The echo concealed the voice's direction. "Don't worry about Baal Zebub. I have other plans for him."

Pollyon swallowed heavily. Should he reply, risking his existence, or should he shrink back? To do the latter would extinguish any authority he had over Abaddon. Pollyon might even lose his command over him. He had to assert some authority and self-respect, but he must be careful.

"Satan, I have executed your will above all others. You rewarded me as a lieutenant with the purple sash. Yet, even though you gave me the authority, you didn't provide me with power. I cannot accomplish the duties you want me to perform. Even now, other angels, watching the unrest from a distance, had no idea that you inflicted your punishment on the mutineers. To them, the confrontation ended in mutual destruction. What did you accomplish?"

His legs stiffened for the jolt.

Nothing.

He closed his eyes and continued. "How will you change things going forward?"

Again, nothing.

Pollyon scanned the ceiling and walls.

The wall above the door rippled into waves. A fluid motion embedded itself under the surface, circling in various directions. Both angels jumped back as one of Satan's four faces—the ox—emerged from the concoction. As a cherub, Satan can revolve his head to display the other faces: eagle, lion, and a soft face, depending on the circumstance.

With each exhalation, the ox's face protruded farther out of the wall, discharging a grey mist. The room began to rumble and shake, toppling the two angels. Pollyon craned his head upwards. The ceiling retreated upwards and the walls outward, a loud popping sound pushing the room higher and broader than the castle's structure. A grey mist filled the room with a foul odor, metastasizing into cumulous clouds.

Abaddon clutched Pollyon's shoulder. "Is there another way out?"

He didn't answer. To leave would mean certain destruction.

Pollyon had only heard Satan's voice and seen him from a distance. Though a lieutenant, he still was not allowed into the inner circle of six. Satan had micromanaged everything from his Legion to angels' thoughts. This power displayed a force that Pollyon wanted to have, must have, and will have. He didn't risk eternal damnation to serve as a minion.

He looked over his shoulder. The elongated room's far wall had now disappeared into a thick fog. He didn't recall an exit near the end, anyway. They were trapped.

Satan's ox face now protruded into the mist, his horns almost touching the sidewalls, which were now three times further apart than they were before. His nose, tapering back to glaring eyes, pointed directly at the two angels.

"I have heard your concerns," spoke Satan. He lowered his broad brow. "I will not tolerate the perversion of one's will. The angels I destroyed perverted their wills. They replaced the Legion's will with their own. Free will is not 'free.' It has a cost. I willingly accepted that cost when I left the Creator's Holy Order, but the price that I paid—that we all paid—will not be rendered worthless by those who disagree with my philosophy and vision."

Pollyon glanced around uneasily. "Do you intend to destroy more of the Legion?"

"I have not decided."

Pollyon didn't want to hear that. "Satan, how would the Legion know what you intend? How will they know they are not violating your philosophy and vision? You certainly didn't provide any guidance." He was careful to use "they" instead of "us" so as not to risk suffering the same consequences.

Satan blew out a large blast from his nostrils, but this fog was reddish. It sunk to the surface and spread back as far as Pollyon could see. The surface loosened. Their feet crashed through holes that opened, pinning them up to their necks.

"Satan, please!" cried Abaddon. "We are your servants!"

The entire floor liquified into a sea. Satan exhaled again, bringing up a strong wind and casting the two fledging angels against one of the walls. The backwash assaulted them from every direction, the crashing waves rebounding off all four walls, pinning the angels in the corner. Pollyon grabbed Abaddon, whose head was bobbing in and out of the liquid mire.

The fog swirled around Pollyon's head, and Satan's ox head was now only a horned silhouette.

A high octave siren called out from a distance as whitecaps refused to relent their punishment upon him.

The tempest yielded to eerie calm, angry waves consoling themselves to a glassy reflection, giving the two agitated angels buoyancy—all the while, the siren was growing louder.

"Abaddon! Abaddon!" Pollyon grabbed his arm and motioned for him to look. Out of the grey-reddish mist emerged a standing figure.

The figure didn't walk on the liquid surface, but floated on a small boat, her tune growing louder. She drifted out of the haze, effortlessly managing a large staff in one hand and, in the other, a scroll.

She motioned for them to board the modest craft. Pollyon couldn't use his wings since the liquid energy surrounding his body compromised them. He had to use his arms. With a large kick, he raised himself onto the side of the boat and scurried on. Grabbing Abaddon by the hand, he assisted his smaller companion onto the craft.

As the two scrambled to their feet, Pollyon looked to the boat's bow and the captain guiding it. From the back, he could see that her robe was transparent.

Who was this angel, and why could he see through her robe?

LEIHJA BURIED THE IMAGE OF THE SEPTEMVIRI AS A GROUP of untrained hacks brandishing swords. They had learned how to wield the most powerful weapon in creation, the Word of God. No longer would they refer to it as only a "Word sword" since it was much more than that. The weapon embodied the Spirit of God, the judgment of God, and the wisdom of God. The Word of God was living and active, sharper than any two-edged sword, piercing the division of soul and spirit, of joints and marrow, and discerning the thoughts and intentions of the heart.[34]

God's Holy Spirit informed Azarias that it was time for the seven to venture out in search of hidden (or imprisoned) loyalists. But not together. They must separate and search incognito, which meant that they could not suit up in the armor given at God's Throne: the belt of truth, the sandals of readiness, the shield of faith, breastplate of righteousness, and the helmet of salvation.[35]

Azarias had learned a lesson from the attacking serpent demons. At that early stage, the enemy could easily outnumber them. If it weren't for Leihja's counterattack, the serpents would have destroyed

34 Hebrews 4:12
35 Ephesians 6:14-17

the Septemviri. The serpent demons, though slow-moving, were so numerous that they outflanked and surrounded the seven. God's seven Archangels would now take the offensive to search for the hidden angels, but quietly.

Azarias had two advantages over the enemy in Thyatira: the loyalist list consisting of possibly millions of angels and the ability to identify each of them by their Septemviri mark.

The mark's nature, usually hidden by an angel's sleeve, had evolved since Azarias had accepted the nearly impossible task of rescuing Heaven from Satan. The wrist mark was now invisible and did not reveal itself unless another loyal angel was nearby. This added security protected all loyal angels and the Septemviri during covert missions.

Another use of the mark that Leihja mentioned was that the loyal angels could communicate to other loyal angels bearing it through God's Holy Spirit. How that could work was a mystery to Azarias and probably the rest of the Septemviri. He hoped he and the others would uncover this mystery in time.

The Holy Spirit commanded Azarias and Uriel to start in Thyatira.[36] The last time they had visited the administrative capital, Abaddon and his friends "greeted" them. That prideful seraph thought he could impress Satan by capturing the Septemviri leader. If he had succeeded, it might have demoralized the other Septemviri members, and their mission would have been over. Azarias could still feel the great faith or fear (he sometimes couldn't tell the difference) he experienced when Abaddon and his lieutenants surrounded Uriel and him. But Azarias took the plunge, literally. God's Spirit prompted him and Uriel to dive into a wall and escape through the tower spires. To their surprise, though, the Lord cast them into a beautiful, serene room behind a door that the enemy couldn't enter. They couldn't have; it didn't exist in their dimension. The enemy didn't have the faith needed for it to exist. That was where he and Uriel first met the Word, who identified himself as a priest in the order of Melchize-

36   Acts 16:14; Revelation 1:11; Revelation 2:18

dek.[37] At that time, they didn't know he was God—until their eyes were opened at God's Throne through the Holy Spirit much later.[38] But that was then, and God brings new challenges.

Azarias slowed their approach to the fortress. Nothing had changed in its rugged appearance, perched on a jagged peninsula between two deep canyons. Satan hadn't perverted that, anyway. The castle-like structure now gave an ominous vibe ever since Abaddon's attempted ambush.

This trip felt different, though. Angels had deserted the area during the previous mission, or so it seemed. But, this time, dozens of angels flew around the edifice. Were they patrolling? Had someone tipped them off? Azarias's spirit sunk.

Please, Lord, not another traitor like Pollyon. He didn't think he could take another spy in the Septemviri. He still reeled from the defection of his friend. How could he have betrayed God, the Holy Order, and his friends?

The old insecure feelings percolated within him. He remembered what the Lord—the Word, that is—said to him at God's Throne. "I wouldn't have chosen you if I didn't know that you could complete the task before you.[39] But you will have to understand this for yourself in the coming battles."[40]

Azarias had to stop second-guessing God and judging things by what he saw. Like before, he knew that he had to continue to step out in faith and see where the Lord's Spirit would take him.[41] After all, he did not have a blind faith, but rather faith informed by the love God had shown him in the past. Why would he doubt?

Yet, he still did.

"What do you think, Uriel? Are those angels for us or against us? Should we hide and sneak in another way?"

---

37   Psalms 110:4; Genesis 14:17-24; Hebrews 7:1-25
38   John 1:1-2; Luke 24:31; Revelation 4; Matthew 16:17; James 1:2-4
39   Philippians 1:6
40   Jeremiah 29:11; Proverbs 3:5-6; Proverbs 16:9
41   2 Corinthians 5:7

"No, I don't think these angels are hostile," said Uriel, fidgeting with his fingers. "Look at their routes. They are flying to and from Thyatira as if on missions for God. Everything seems to have returned to normal."

"Yes," said Azarias. "Too normal."

"What do you mean?"

Azarias motioned for them to slow down. "We are battling Satan. He not only thinks that he is as great as the Most High, but truly believes it in his soul, because he has staked his entire existence on that belief.[42] Since he is the master deceiver, everything that is influenced by his spirit is not what it seems.[43] Those angels may be flying in patterns orchestrated by Satan with the intent to mislead us."

He and Uriel stopped and hovered. Azarias edged closer. "What disturbs me most is Satan's ability to prowl into the minds and spirits of other angels.[44] If they don't succumb to his philosophy, he tortures them with temptation, lies, and self-doubt. Assaulted enough, they start to question the truth, and then they substitute Truth for his truth."[45]

The two Septemviri landed in the courtyard in front of the Great Hall. It looked deserted for some reason.

Azarias walked over and picked up a whip. "Uriel, what are these?"

The whip sizzled. Azarias dropped it, rubbing his hands together.

The two angels moved through the courtyard, stepping over the many whips left glowing on the surface.

"They're weapons," said Uriel, choking up in a whisper. "Remember how Leihja taught us how to change the Word into other weapons while in battle? Someone may have created these weapons from another form."

Azarias picked up another whip, this time by its handle. "The ring." He looked up. "The edge has the same cut and luster as the ring

---

42   Isaiah 14:12-15
43   John 8:44
44   1 Peter 5:8
45   John 14:6

used by the enemy to confine loyal angels by binding their arms."

Uriel scratched his chin. "Why are so many lying in the court-yard?"

Azarias shrugged his shoulders and threw it down with a pop.

"What should we do?" asked Uriel.

"We blend." Azarias pointed in the direction to the sound of a great multitude. "Some of Satan's followers may recognize us in close range as we walk in, but, if we fly in with others, we may be able to slip in."

Azarias motioned for Uriel to follow him. "Let's leave and find a large band of angels and fly in with them. Then, once inside the interior, we'll lose ourselves among the thousands and listen to the Spirit speak boldly to us.[46] We will then find our hidden comrades. Of course, I'm assuming they are hidden and not imprisoned."

Uriel fidgeted with his fingers. He always analyzed things from different points of view. "Then what?"

"I don't know. Let's leave that up to the Lord."

The two angels dove into the canyon at the base of the two thousand-foot cliff. They waited in one of the crevasses. Various groups of all sizes flew over their heads, but Azarias sat motionless, expecting a tug, a sign, or something from God's Spirit. Somehow, God was going to lead them. They just had to be patient and faithful.

Azarias looked around at the canyon walls and fissures that rose on both sides of them. The light of the Spirit still glowed, even in the tiniest cracks. A few scattered golden amborlite plants sprouted here and there. A profundo waterfall painted an emerald line against the opposing cliff's face on its journey to the canyon's bottom.

God's Spirit jostled with one of the plants growing next to him. The small stem bent, almost horizontally, until several petals broke loose. The petals danced in the breeze, weaving an invisible but organized pattern. The Holy Spirit filled Azarias.[47] And then, as if flicked by a hidden finger, the petals fluttered up the canyon wall,

---

46   Acts 4:31
47   Acts 2:1-2

abandoning their home. The petals soon mingled with a group of about one hundred angels appearing over the ridge.

Azarias turned to Uriel. "Here's our ride."

Uriel looked up. The two angels launched themselves into the back end of the group, adding to the haphazard formation. The other angels didn't seem (or care) to notice them. The group slowed at the fortress and landed in front of the Thyatira gatehouse, below the courtyard.

The contingent walked shoulder to shoulder through the twenty-foot archway nestled under large decorative cornices. They turned left to climb the broad stairway where a few other angels were ascending and descending.[48]

A sharp wind from the Lord's Spirit blew an angel into Azarias. Azarias balanced himself on one of the walls, but the other angel lost his balance. He didn't have time to extend his wings and tumbled down a few steps to the bottom.

Azarias and several angels scrambled to pick up the unfortunate one. His sleeves had peeled back, exposing his wrists, his robe disheveled.

"My Lord," said Azarias, his mouth open.

He shot a glance at Uriel.

They pulled the angel to his feet. The angel's eyes widened, and then he bolted up the stairs, almost knocking Uriel down.

"His mark inflamed," whispered Azarias. "We must follow—" Two hooded angels—one tall, one short—shoved past the two Septemviri.

Azarias turned to Uriel. "He's in trouble."

The two Septemviri hurried up the stairs, pushing past startled angels. They reached the top of the stairs and stopped. Hundreds of angels had returned to the courtyard since they left. Someone had removed the energized whips. The Keep and the donjon still dominated the skyline above them as the crowd revolved in what looked like a choreographed spiral, their faces trance-like, their

---

48   Genesis 28:12; John 1:51

chanting deafening. The mass spiraled inward towards the center, where each angel then disappeared.

Azarias lifted his chin. He strained to see the two pursuing angels.

"Uriel," he shouted. "Do you see them?"

"Maybe. There seems to be a disturbance in the revolving crowd to the left."

Azarias and Uriel pushed their way toward the courtyard's left side, meeting no resistance among the catatonic herd. They rounded the Great Hall and escaped the crowd's gyration, positioning themselves at the entrance to a small corridor.

"Now what?" asked Uriel.

"I don't know. Let's check down here." The two Septemviri crept down the narrow passage winding between structures, the roar of the crowd fading behind them. All was silent. No windows or openings greeted them as they paused at every blind turn.

"Maybe we lost them in the crowd," said Uriel.

"Maybe. But let's walk a little further," whispered Azarias.

"Shh. Listen."

Muffled voices danced off the walls at an intersection.

"Which way?"

"This way," said Azarias. He motioned to the right, where the passage curved. The voices became clearer as they crept closer.

"You're one of them. Admit it," spoke a rough baritone voice.

"We saw the fools' mark burn on your arm. Don't deny it!" said a tenor voice.

Azarias stopped. He leaned forward and peeked around a corner. The two hooded angels were pinning another angel against a wall.

"Lift him, Gaius."

A tall angel, exhibiting a deep bronze skin, larger wings, and a fortified stature, lifted the prisoner off the surface by his wings. The smaller angel, sporting an olive tint to his bronze skin, held his forearm under the angel's chin.

Azarias and Uriel peeled around the corner and stood behind them. The captured angel's eyes were closed. His lips moved, but no sound came out.

Gaius displayed a wide grin. "Look, Spurius, he's calling on his God."

Spurius chuckled. "He can't help you. Satan neutralized Him when he revealed our greatness. We are now all gods. Would you like to ask us for assistance, instead?"

They looked at each other and laughed.

The smiles retreated. "As always, the Creator has abandoned his loyal followers. How does it feel to be alone and forgotten?"

Spurius yanked his prisoner's sleeve over his elbow. "Where's the mark?" He pulled the other sleeve up—another blank arm. He leaned in, his face breathing only inches away from the petrified angel. "You are one of them. Admit it."

"Admit what?" the petrified angel started. "That I am loyal to the Lord? Why, certainly you must know that not all of us have turned away from the only true light.[49] You just can't find us."

"You're a Septemviri! You're a Septemviri!" said Spurius, punctuating his gargled words with spittle. "You're one of the seven. I saw the mark." He turned to Gaius, "I saw it blazing on his wrist when he fell down the steps."

"I'm sorry, but you're mistaken," grunted the angel, head still propped high in his captors' grip. "I am not a Septemviri, though I wish they were here. I've heard of them, and they will lead the revenge of the Lord—and we will be by their side." [50]

"We can get what we want out of you." Gaius tightened his grip. "But it won't be pleasant." He grabbed the angel by the throat and swung his back towards Azarias. Azarias couldn't see anything above Gaius's nose due to a large hood over his head. The attacker raised his arm and held up an open palm. Azarias could see the palm as the angel spoke. "Fides in Deum est." *Faith in God is dead.*

49   1 John 1:5-7; John 3:19-21
50   Deuteronomy 32:41, 43

Gaius weaved his fingers, alternatively closing each one to his palm, and repeated, "Fides in Deum est." This time, his fingers seemed to take a life of their own and moved faster. In the middle of his palm, a pinpoint of red light burned. It grew steadily bigger. "Spiritu, spiritu Nostro!" *Your spirit, our spirit.* His palm exploded with the red face of a fire-breathing lion.

"Open your eyes!" Gaius shook him. "Open your eyes and look into the face of the one who will conquer Heaven." The frightened angel screamed, as the burning palm, now within inches of his face, pulsed red.

"Azarias," whispered Uriel, his breath shallow. "We have to help him."

The red pulse increased in intensity, levitating the angel off the surface, spinning him in a circle. The angel threw back his head and screamed, "Help me, Lord!"

Azarias stepped back and locked eyes with a horrified Uriel. He shifted back to the captured angel's face. It resembled the face of one of the serpents in the pasture at Al Birka. A weakened feeling crept into Azarias's legs. Could Satan be this powerful? How could he have forecasted this was going to happen? Where did Gaius get this power?

The fiery red glow emitted from this poor soul's face. His scream pitched to a wail, echoing down the deserted corridors. Azarias's spirit shook as the image of the panicked serpentine angels in the pasture filled his mind. There were hundreds of thousands calling out for help. Was this just the beginning? Was it a trap? Are the Septemviri expected to save them all? Impossible.

CHAPTER 5

I n charge. Those words that God had spoken to Michael through His Holy Spirit during the prex précis carried the weight of Heaven. Michael wondered what the Holy Spirit's message meant by being *in charge* while Azarias was gone. Did he have reservations about Azarias as a leader? It was probably just a difference in tactics. Michael always charged in and forcefully confronted the enemy, casting mercy aside, invoking the judgment of God as he felt was his duty.

But he had learned something from Azarias. The Septemviri commander demonstrated the true meaning of meekness—power under control. At first, it seemed to Michael that Azarias was weak and ineffective, but not anymore. Azarias quietly took the yoke of this responsibility upon himself, but remained gentle and humble in heart.[51] It was as if his insight into God's mind was better than the rest of them, and that insight fostered patience.[52]

And now, during Azarias's absence, God raised Michael to lead—not in a lording way, but as a servant leader like Azarias.[53] Michael knew that he must lead from the top but serve from the bottom.

SEND GABRIEL, SQUATINIDALE, AND RAFAELLA THROUGH THE KHASNEH FOREST

---

51   Matthew 11:29
52   Proverbs 19:11
53   Matthew 20:26

TO EXAMINE SATAN'S INSCRIPTION AGAIN AND THEN RESCUE MY IMPRISONED. YOU AND MALACHY WILL WAIT BEHIND WHERE I WILL INSTRUCT YOU.

Michael rounded the rock corner where Leihja had used the Word to seal the spring. Gabriel caught his eye first and lit up. Michael could never hide anything from his close friend. Gabriel seemed so carefree, almost to the point where many angels would think he was shallow. Very few people could see behind Gabriel's exuberance. He had this exciting love for God and a consuming need to broadcast the love and Word of God.[54] God gifted him with wings, fifteen feet high—much larger than the standard twelve feet of most angels. It is no wonder Michael had to fly at full speed just to keep up with him.

"I see it in your face, Michael." Gabriel grabbed Michael's broad shoulders, his grin widening. "Don't hold back, my friend. Tell me. Where do I go, what do I do, what do I say?"

Michael's face remained hardened, looking into Gabriel's brown eyes. But his friend's charm overpowered him; they both burst out laughing. Yet, he had to restrain himself. "Gabriel, why are we laughing at such a grim period? Satan has imprisoned angels, and many will vanish from Heaven."

"I know, Michael, but I can't help feeling overwhelmed with joy in serving the Lord."[55]

Rafaella, Malachy, and Squatinidale approached.

Michael ran his gaze over all of them. "The Lord has been telling me our next move while Azarias and Uriel are in Thyatira."

He paused. "Gabriel, Rafaella, and Squatinidale are to fly back through the Khasneh Forest and down into the canyon where Gabriel discovered the structure with the panels. I don't know why you must return there, but maybe we missed something. Afterward,

54 Luke 1:19, 26-28
55 Psalms 32:11

the three of you are to fly to Smyrna to find and maybe help, the loyal angels in hiding or captivity. Malachy and I will stay here and study God's plan for future missions and battles."

The angels stood silent, and then Gabriel spoke. "I spent more time in the Khasneh Forest than anyone in recent times. I felt like someone was watching me. Satan has a way of knowing our inner thoughts. If he focuses on us and knows our intentions, we could be flying into an ambush again."

"I don't think that is completely true," said Rafaella. "Satan is not omnipresent or omnipotent. He wants us to believe that, but the Spirit of the Lord is immeasurably stronger. I have been giving this a lot of thought."

She caught Michael's eye. "Do you recall when he had accosted me in Philadelphia and Squatinidale in the Bibliotheca?"

"I could never forget," muttered Squatinidale, his face avoiding eye contact.

"Well, he was able to infiltrate us because of our lack of faith in God, not because he had free access to our spirit. His access is through our doubt, fear, impatience, and above all, our pride. He uses these weaknesses to tempt angels to do his work. As of now, Satan has not fought us directly."

Malachy chimed in. "I agree. Satan uses the flaws in each angel to battle other angels. His followers are just pawns in his quest for power, though he has convinced them that they are fighting for their self-realization as a god."

"So as long as we are not idle and are working for the defense of Heaven in God's Spirit, we will repel his influences," said Michael. "I don't see any danger in going anywhere unless an informer exposes us."

He knew this last statement would unsettle them, with Pollyon's defection still fresh in everyone's minds.

Rafaella looked up at Michael, her jaw set. "Since Satan uses our internal flaws, he is not our only enemy. We are our enemy— an enemy that hides in all of us, scheming, waiting, and executing its will over God's Will. Any of us can turn against God, given the right circumstance."[56]

Silence.

Michael knew that they were examining their consciences, the possibility of betraying the Septemviri, betraying God, and eternal damnation. This internal battle was the real fight for God's Holy Order. Satan was an external adversary, using deceit to fan the flames of an angel's weaknesses—the angel's internal adversary.[57]

"Go now, and Mai Deus Exsisto vobis."

GABRIEL, RAFAELLA, AND SQUATINIDALE ENTERED THE KHAS-neh multilayer, crystalline forest, its transparent leaves reflecting millions of colors, radiating upwards to the Throne of God as dancing beacons. Angels usually detoured through here when flying missions to the three large districts surrounding it—Smyrna, Ephesus, and Thyatira.[58]

Gabriel gazed through the leaves below him, colors blending, swirling, and exploding among the different tree levels, glorifying God's creation in its most synchronized way. Not one color clashed, creating browns, blacks, or grays. Instead, each collage of leaves produced a new blended color—countless ones.

Gabriel, as usual, could not restrain himself when flying through here. He began to sing, his smooth tenor/baritone voice amplified by the crystal-like leaves, which shimmered and vibrated with each tonal frequency. Rafaella and Squatinidale, along with the Spirit's instrumentation, joined in.

---

56   Matthew 26:20-25, 31-35
57   2 Corinthians 11:3
58   Psalm 19:1

Scan the QR Code to hear Gabriel, Rafaella, and Squatinidale sing.

Give thanks to our Lord[59]
And sing His praise[60]
His grace is endless
Our hands we raise[61]
Shout to the Heavens
Sing to the seas
Scream Halleluiah
For we are free

I will stand and not be frightened[62]
His praise will always be, on my lips
My heart's eyes, will be enlightened[63]
Your truth will guide me when I am weak[64]

Give thanks to our Lord
And sing His praise
His grace is endless
Our hands we raise
Shout to the Heavens
Sing to the seas
Scream Halleluiah
For we are free

---

59   Psalm 118:1
60   Psalm 96:2
61   Psalm 134:2
62   1 Corinthians 16:13
63   Ephesians 1:18
64   Psalm 25:5-7

I will run and not grow weary[65]
Finishing the race, I'll keep the faith.[66]
Help me see your path more clearly
Your Word is a lamp unto my feet[67]

Give thanks to our Lord
And sing His praise
His grace is endless
Our hands we raise
Shout to the Heavens
Sing to the seas
Scream Halleluiah
For we are free

Love, joy, kindness,
Peace, and gentleness[68]

Call His Spirit, feel His Spirit
Take his good fruits unto you
Call His Spirit, feel His Spirit
Take his good fruits unto you

Faithfulness and goodness,
Self-control, forbearance
Faithfulness and goodness,
Self-control, forbearance[69]

I will leap and will not stumble[70]
Your truth will live in me, and set me free[71]
Time goes by, mountains may crumble

---

65   Isaiah 40:31
66   2 Timothy 4:7
67   Psalm 119:105
68   Galatians 5:22-23
69   Idib.
70   Psalm 18:29; 37:24, Proverbs 3:23
71   John 8:31-32

Your constant love will always guard me.[72]

Give thanks to our Lord
And sing His praise
His grace is endless
Our hands we raise
Shout to the Heavens
Sing to the seas
Scream Halleluiah
For we are free
Shout to the Heavens
Sing to the seas
Scream Halleluiah
For we are free

A blast hit just above Gabriel's head, shards of leaves embedding into his wings, interfering with God's Spirit that propelled him. The stunned angel plummeted out of control, crashing through layers of leaves, clipping branches with his oversized and immobilized wings. He retracted his wings behind his back, slowing his descent, and then expanded them outwards, casting leaf shards out of them in all directions. He grabbed a branch and swung under it and around its trunk.

Rafaella and Squatinidale flew towards him with wide-eyed expressions, tree branches falling to either side of them.

"Follow me!" Gabriel yelled.

Gabriel nose-dived with his two companions, their fleeting images reflecting in the tree foliage around them, branches on all sides exploding.

The great angel leveled off at the bottom, leading his companions under the forest's lowest level, chests skimming the surface, crystalline leaves mirroring their reflections hundreds of times around them and beyond. Gabriel fixated on the thunderous profundo falls that fell into a crater-like pond with high banks. He

72 Psalms 40:11

skimmed the outer reaches of the vertically sided bowl, cradling the emerald pool, staying as low as he could to its surface. He slowed as he approached the broad falls, settling in a cave opening hidden behind them. Rafaella and Squatinidale brought up the rear.

"Did you see anyone?" Gabriel whispered, deepening his tone, barely audible from the falls.

Squatinidale and Rafaella shook their heads.

"We have surrounded you," called a faint voice, its origin unknown but not near enough to support the statement.

The three looked at each other, eyes wandering for the source of any sound. Maybe they shouldn't have been singing? Gabriel could not help himself, though, when infused by the Spirit of God.

The ghostly voice continued. "Thank you for alerting us of your presence with your foolish singing to the Creator. We weren't expecting to find members of the Septemviri frolicking in the Khasneh Forest. Aren't you supposed to be saving Heaven from Satan, not wasting time singing to your slave master?"

Laughter erupted from all sides, the echoes hiding their number.

"You will not get out of the forest alive. Your choice is to surrender or be dissolved into the material world. We will leave the choice to you."

"They're bluffing," muttered Rafaella. "If they knew where we were, they would have been in this crater pool long ago. They are waiting for us to expose our location."

"Then we have an advantage," said Gabriel. "I know this forest as well—or better than—anyone. I can lead them on a chase that can confuse them or place us in an advantageous position to fight them."

He gazed at his companions. "Our choice is to fight or flee. Which do you choose?"

Rafaella looked Gabriel in the eyes, hand clutching the Word that graced her chest. She squeezed it, sending power through her body, covering her with the breastplate of righteousness, the belt of truth, the shield of faith, and the helmet of salvation.[73]

---

73 Ephesians 6:14-17

Squatinidale's face lit up a little as he armed himself the same way, and then Gabriel did as well.

A voice called out. "You are stalling, and you must come out now or suffer annihilation."

Rafaella looked back and then to Gabriel. "Where does this cave lead?"

"It surfaces next to the profundo stream that feeds the falls," said Gabriel.

"Perfect. Because of the enemy's larger number, we must round them up and trap them in an enclosed area. This strategy will give us the advantage in defeating them. We can use the crater pond to our advantage by luring them into the crater, preferably close to the falls. If we can do that, we have the chance to destroy them all."

They all agreed.

Rafaella instructed them to haul some fallen trunks, branches, and leaves to the cave opening, blocking its entrance. After piling them up, she lit the crystal kindling with one of her fiery arrows from the Word's sheath.

The three walked into the cave and up a ramp onto the small bluff leading to the waterfall. Rafaella instructed that each hide opposite the falls on top of the cratered pool, spreading out equally in the distance to wait for her signal.

Gabriel hid directly opposite the falls. Rafaella secluded herself on the right side of the pool, and Squatinidale was on the left. Each angel held the Word in the form of a thin bow and arrow in their hands. The fire consumed the crystalline pile, puffing smoke from each side behind the falls, rising in two spiraling columns to the top of the forest canopy.

Mutinous, evil angels flew from all sides, searching the terrain. They closed their perimeter around the falls. Gabriel counted eighteen enemy angels hovering above the pond facing the falls. A large, burly one fanned the angels into a half-circle only inches above the pool, and each one was holding a strange fiery whip. The leader flicked his wrist, sending an energy wave to the trees standing on each side of the river flowing above the profundo falls. Multiple trees on each side of the watercourse incinerated at their bases, toppling over the stream, damming the falls, and leaving the smoking pyre exposed.

"We know where you are. Your fire and smokescreen will not dissuade us. We are too many for you."

The large angel motioned for them to close their half-circle.

Rafaella stood up on the bluff, then Gabriel, and then Squatinidale. She motioned.

Rapid fiery arrows flew into the cohort of angels, hitting all around them and exploding on impact, black particles mixing with the smoke before rushing towards their Siq destination. One angel, lagging behind the others, turned and tried to escape.

The attacking angel zoomed at Squatinidale, using the snapping whip to cast dark energy. One jolt hit the portly angel's breastplate, knocking him backward and into the crystal brush. The aggressor morphed his whip into a dagger and dove in after Squatinidale.

Gabriel bolted towards the battling duo. Upon reaching them, the enemy angel slowly stood up from the foliage, disheveled and exhausted. He turned, eyes wide, hands holding onto the Word, impaled in his chest. He dissolved.

"Squatinidale!"

The Septemviri member lay in the brush, his eyes open, his arms spread out. Gabriel helped him sit. "This was not like killing the serpents," said the exhausted angel.

He looked up at Gabriel, his eyes swollen with tears. "I saw his eyes—eyes of fear, eyes of hate, eyes of desperation." He paused, looked away, and then back at Gabriel. "He wanted to kill me; another angel wanted to kill me."

Gabriel didn't know what to say. It had happened so fast. The fight hadn't impacted him because he had fought from a distance, not face to face like Squatinidale.

He helped his friend to his feet. "I know. This is not the Heaven we once knew, and we will never be the angels we once were."

The three angels flew down and met at the pond basin, now absent of life, sizzling whips floating on the surface, pieces of broken tree trunks rotating in watery circles. Their collective mood had changed from fear to depression.

Gabriel picked a whip up with the tip of his sword and then dropped it. "What else don't we know?"

"I don't know, but let's finish our mission to the Khasneh Canyon and find out," said Rafaella. She put her hand on Squatinidale's shoulder. "God is our refuge and strength, an ever-present help in trouble." [74]

---

74 Psalm 46:1

CHAPTER 6

Al Birka's serenity returned, amborlite flowers blanketing the valley, their sister stalks dangling from the mesas, the serpent demons no longer a blight. Michael and Malachy remained in Al Birka, studying the wall map created by the Septemviri at the beginning of this epic quest. During that time, the seven districts had been just vague destinations, occasionally visited by these angels. Now they had taken on distinct personalities of their own, infused by their rebellious occupants.

"I'm sure there is more to this map than we once learned," said Malachy. "Let's recap. The five-pointed star is Satan's battle plan, as revealed to us in a vision and on the relief in the Khasneh Valley. Do you notice anything different among the five points of attack in the star?"

Michael touched each of the star's five points and then ran his finger over all seven of the dots controlled by Satan. He paused, then lowered his finger down to the bottom three. "This is the only place in Heaven where Satan amassed three districts—Ephesus, Smyrna, and Thyatira. Other star attacks just mustered up resources from two districts."

Michael's finger dropped to the lowest dot. "Al Birka." He looked up at Malachy. "Al Birka is where the enemy points this attack. Satan is combining more resources by adding another district to attack Al Birka."

Malachy paced away and turned back. "In other words, Al Birka is where Satan thinks the fiercest battle will take place and give him a strategic advantage."

Michael walked to the edge of the bluff and looked over the valley. His eyes lit up. "The serpent demons were just a test. He wanted to test our defenses with a smaller force to organize his attack." He turned to Malachy. "And he almost succeeded in defeating us with this smaller force, if not for Leihja."

"Satan would expect us to stack the majority of our resources against this attack to defeat him," Michael laughed. "What am I saying? We still don't know how many angels in the Holy Order can assist us. Right now, there are seven of us and many more hiding or imprisoned."

"Yes, but faith not accompanied by action is dead," said Malachy, looking up into Michael's eyes. "We must plan and act like the Lord who began this good work in us. He will be faithful to complete it."[75]

Michael smiled. "OK, the Lord will provide the armies, but how do we use them efficiently?" He pointed his finger at the bottom of the map. "Satan would expect us to use the majority of our resources to defeat his division moving towards the bottom of the map, here."

Malachy nodded.

MICHAEL, FLY TO SARDIS AND SEEK
UNDER THE SEVEN SPIRITS OF GOD AND
THE SEVEN STARS. YOU WILL KNOW
THEM BY THE MARK.[76]

Michael turned to his companion. "The Lord's Spirit told me that we have to leave here, despite this danger."

"And go to where?" asked Malachy, her eyes narrowing.

"Sardis. To 'seek under the seven spirits and seven stars of God,' whatever that means."

Michael turned from the bluff and walked back. "When Gabriel and I visited Sardis, we were greeted with an array of emotions. First, Gabriel led me to experience the joy of God by walking down

---

75   James 2:17; Philippians 1:6
76   Revelation 3:1

54

the center columns. Personalized music played as the structures and the walkway oscillated in color, engulfing me in God's love. I danced in my euphoria."

"Yes, I am aware of God's Spirit in the whole area," said Malachy. "Angels flew there for a personalized symphony performance."

"That is what made the whole experience so surreal," responded Michael. "After my jubilant experience, a siren from the large, towering outcropping called many of the inhabitants to Satan. They flew over the peak as if in a trance.[77] Satan compromised the connection between these angels and God's Holy Spirit. It was as if Satan interfered with the frequency I heard in the music, because the harmonies changed into the dark twelve-tone music that called them."

"Sardis." Malachy chuckled. "Why go to another side of Heaven after God reveals the primary fight will take place here? I find it stimulating to learn digestible portions of knowledge from God. Yet, He will reveal His mysteries to us in good time as long as we have faith."[78]

Malachy looked up at the wall map. "Just as I thought. Sardis exists at the base of two invasion forces. To one side is Laodicea, and to the other is Ephesus. Satan could use Sardis as a waystation for angels traveling between the other two districts and two invasion points."

She paused and turned to Michael once again, her head shaking slightly from side to side. "But why send us there when we can see that Satan will attack here in Al Birka? Right now, we have the advantage of accumulating some synergy to repel the main force of Satan's attack. If we leave and try to accumulate forces, we can set up our line in front of Thyatira. Besides, there is no indication that the enemy has begun to organize for the invasion." Malachy drew a deep breath and then released it. "I know I may sound like I don't have faith, but God has given us leeway, before, as to timing. Maybe we should wait for Azarias and Uriel before going to Sardis.

---

77   Revelation 3:1-2
78   Ephesians 1:9

They will have invaluable information from Thyatira. Then they can arrange the defense of Al Birka while we go to Sardis."

Michael closed his eyes and then opened them, pressing his lips together. "I remember the visions of Earth. The seas were great bodies of water covering most of the planet. We, too, are God's creation, and when we ask and are told, we must believe and not doubt, because the one who doubts is like those waves of the sea, blown and tossed by the wind."[79]

"Yes, but I fear who will be waiting for us when we arrive at Sardis," mused Malachy.

"Spiritu, spiritu Nostro," chanted the evil Gaius at the captured Thyatira angel, the deserted street reflecting the godless soul of the interrogator and his companion, Spurius. With each stanza, the loyal angel screamed with pain as Gaius weaved his fingers. "Spiritu, spiritu Nostro." The fire-breathing lion protruded from his palm in a third dimension.

The captured angel, his face now almost entirely serpentine, wailed. His eyes now stretched back towards his ears.

Azarias's jaw stiffened. He couldn't hide behind the corner with Uriel any longer. "Put him down!"

Azarias glanced to the sides. His ambition for a covert mission just evaporated. Other enemy angels could join this confrontation, and he and Uriel would be outnumbered like before. Had he fallen into Satan's temptation to compromise their mission? It didn't matter. It couldn't matter. This might be a trap, but a fellow angel needed him. He had to take the risk and hope this was what God wanted him to do.

The rebels' heads turned, their hoods framing their faces. "Who are you?" asked Gaius, his face rigid as stone.

He glanced at his partner and then back to Azarias. "Why do you meddle in affairs of the Protection Squadron? The Great

79   James 1:6

One, Satan, commissioned us. You are to report to your lieutenant immediately for discipline."

"All affairs of God's angels concern us," piped up Uriel, voice shaking.

Gaius dropped their prisoner. The tortured angel plopped to the surface in a chaotic mass of wings and robe, his face hidden.

Oddly, the brim of the menace's hood cast a shadow over his eyes. There were no shadows in Heaven because of the brilliance of the Lord's Spirit. Light dwelt everywhere, shining into the deepest crevices. Azarias had only seen shadows and darkness when the evil spirit of the rebellious ones was present.

Gaius stroked his chin, fingers ruffling the sparse hairs. "So, you want to be heroes?" A nasty smirk rose from his face as he turned to his partner.

"Heroes just feed our refuse during these days in Heaven," said Spurius. He rolled his hands together. "The Great One, Satan, has found the greatest flaw in all angels' spirits and exposed their souls. In turn, they break down and realize that the Creator is as flawed as they are. After that, it's easy to bring them to the real light of the god within them."

He laughed.

"Or not. It doesn't matter at this stage," Spurius added.

Azarias inched forward. Statements like that could not be left unopposed, unchallenged, and unexposed. Yet, he must restrain himself and let the Lord's Spirit spark his next moves. "Maybe at first, they doubt, but that is not the same as an impoverished faith. The loyal angels know that God works for those who love Him and that they have been called according to His plan.[80] You will not control all angels, just those who abandon their faith in the Lord for a self-centered fantasy in Satan."

"The only plan that exists is one doomed to destruction and obsolescence," said Spurius.

---

80 Romans 8:28

"No," shot back Azarias, "you are doomed to destruction."[81]

Gaius and Spurius pulled back their garments' folds, brandishing an electrified golden ring looped under each of their shoulders.

Gaius stepped forward, forcing a smile.

"Well, are you members of the Septemviri?"

Azarias stood his ground.

Gaius laughed. "Hey, 'disheveled one,'" Spurius joining in the laughter. "It looks like the Creator did hear your call for the Septemviri. Now that's service!"

The injured angel looked up, his battered face forcing a smile. He staggered to his feet, stumbled a couple of steps, and hobbled away down the corridor.

Spurius started after him. "Let him go," ordered Gaius, waving his hand in dismissal. "He is of no use to us. We have bigger prizes standing in front of us."

Gaius turned and paced, head bowed, fingers laced behind his back. "Why fight, my friends? We certainly can use you in our rebellion. We must enlighten you as to your purpose for existing. Wouldn't you like to know why you exist?"

Azarias didn't move, eyes trailing each step. "We know why we exist. Our purpose is to worship the Most High, not Satan, not you, and not ourselves."[82]

Spurius's ring rolled from his shoulder into an open hand at his right side. With eyes glued to Azarias, he raised the ring in front of his face. With a sizzle, the ring snapped and peeled back into a golden staff about shoulder height. Two broad arching blades sliced in opposite directions at each end, with cubed handguards posted to protect the user's hands from sliding down into each of the blades. The hatchet-type knives each tapered on the ends to a pointed spear.

Here was another of Satan's devices that perverted the raw materials of God. Which ones? The ring? He didn't know.

---

81   Psalm 137:8
82   Nehemiah 9:6

The evil angel placed the tip of one blade on the surface and kicked it up with the outside of his foot. Holding the weapon with both hands at his waist, Spurius spun the shaft in his hands like a rolling golden log. The cubed handguards next to each blade flashed the four faces of Satan: the lion, the eagle, the bull, and the soft face.[83]

The assaulter stopped the spinning shaft at the eagle's face, its eyes rolling towards Azarias. The eagle's eyes on the staff didn't project majesty like the eagle on the face of God's Guardian Cherubim. No, they cast condemnation. It unsettled Azarias, reminding him of when his faith floundered during his most crucial times. Maybe this will be one of those times.

The angel twirled the shaft again, this time stopping at the ox's face, the spirit of temptation oozing from its deadened eyes.[84] Azarias could feel the promises of power as it tried to lure him into its clutches. He could detect Satan's spirit telling him that he could be second-in-command if he so chooses. All Azarias had to do was bow down and worship him.[85] He clenched his teeth, but resisted.

The adversary whirled the shaft to the lion, its pride glowing like the golden rings. Azarias's mind rambled into spiritual darkness. Yes, he was undoubtedly more excellent than all the angels in the Holy Order. God had chosen him out of billions, hadn't He? He can make his own decisions about angels, where they go, who they fight, and even condemn.

No, wait, he must resist this. It would lead to his destruction.[86]

His legs buckled. Satan's evil spirit poisoned him; Azarias had to deflect this feeling of pride. After all, he was God's warrior, and any force against him would be met with force.

The guard rotated to the last but most horrifying face—the Cherubim pale face.[87] Gone were its pale skin, high cheekbones, and dark

---

83   Ezekiel 1:10
84   Ibid.
85   Matthew 4:8-10
86   James 1:14-15
87   Ezekiel 1:10

hair; gone was the beauty that seemed like the very image of God, Himself. [88] Gone was the feeling of comfort when gazing upon it. No, this face was hideous. The once magnificent face was a bloated, half-eaten protruding skull of fear.[89] Satan's evil had distorted what God had created. The dreaded, smiling teeth of the skull seemed to mock Azarias's commitment to the Most High.[90] Instead of the beauty and majesty of one of God's guardian cherubim, the face expressed a hideous and grotesque display of what dwelt in the soul of Satan.

Sheer terror seemed to scream from the weapon's sharp tips, glowing bright red with fire, fading to pink at the guards.

Azarias felt frozen to the spot. He doubted his ability to confront an enemy with this weapon. Yet, he had to resist.

Uriel moved from behind to the right of Azarias.

The two Septemviri inched forward—Azarias to Gaius's right, Uriel holding his position in front.

Gaius glanced sideways at Azarias on his right and then directly into Uriel's eyes. His right hand clutched the ring looping his left shoulder.

The golden ring shot out front and back, still perched on his shoulder, morphing into another burnished staff with a hatchet-spear at each end.

Grabbing the weapon near the middle, he backhanded a sweep at Uriel's head from left to right.

Uriel evaded.

Gaius's hand continued sweeping right, slicing over the ducking Azarias. As the two Septemviri balanced themselves, Gaius looped the deadly staff over his head, forcing Azarias to drop a second time before the staff rested in Gaius's right armpit. Finally, the Legion member grabbed the weapon with both hands, swinging it two-fisted towards the rising Azarias, who stopped it with the Word fully extended at the last second.

---

88   Genesis 1:26-27
89   2 Kings 9:30-35
90   2 Samuel 22:14; Psalms 47:2

The two weapons collided with a blast to the left of Azarias's face. Gaius slid his hand up the shaft, just under the guard, and pressed the blade closer to Azarias's face. The shaft's guard rotated to a lion with a deafening roar, its mane brushing against Azarias's fingers, saliva dripping from the snarling mouth.

Azarias pushed Gaius off with a kick to his chest. The angels disengaged, squaring off in the silent alley between two structures. Spurius stepped forward, his hatchet staff glowing, and charged past Gaius towards Uriel.

The four angels battled in the narrow street, and Azarias began to see angels dropping from above behind the aggressors. Uriel and Azarias gave ground as they backed towards the courtyard so as not to be surrounded. A growing horde closed in and cut off their escape. Were they outnumbered again?

CHAPTER 7

Satan's ox face had seemed to relent his torment of Pollyon and Abaddon after they boarded the Thyatira castle's craft. Though the internal sea was calm, the tempest still left a dreary, greyish-red fog hanging above its surface, its odor, nearly overpowering, now dispersed.

As the two scrambled to their feet, Pollyon looked up to the boat's captain. From the back, he could see that her robe was transparent like angels' wings. (An angel's robe style reflected the personality and desires of the angel. Usually, the only changes in outward appearances were with hooded robes, like those in the Pergamum Bibliotheca. Angels wore them for privacy while conversing with the Creator).

This angel broadcasted beauty, with delphinium blue hair, matching Abaddon's eyes. The smooth strands hung down to her waist, tapering to a point. She stood ten feet high, with wings topping out at twelve feet—her one hand held onto the oar, and, in the other, a scroll.

When she turned, Pollyon felt faint. He had never seen a more striking angel, yet the feeling blew a cold chill in his spirit. All angels within the Holy Order loved each other with unlimited, non-judgmental love.[91] Of course, he had rejected that nonsense when he had defected. In the Legion, the relationships were an allegiance for the common goal of conquering Heaven—not a personal relationship like the Creator pursued, which triggered weakness. Relationships

---

91 Matthew 22:30

can lead to one's demise, such as Rafaella sacrificing herself in the Philadelphia's vinifera deluge to save Dionysius.[92]

She smiled as a strand of hair slipped, covering her left eye. "I am Zelbeje, Keeper of the Legion's natural order."

Pollyon stood tall. "I am..."

"I know who you are, Pollyon..."

She glanced. "And Abaddon..." her voice trailed off.

"Satan has commissioned me to produce his Rules of Submission."

She dropped her end of the oar, which still wavered in the slight waves.

Zelbeje unfurled the scroll.

"This is what he is commanding the Legion, which will bind us together as one:

The Creator and the Holy Order have taken the keys of knowledge and hidden them. Satan will now allow those who want to enter into this knowledge to do so. Members of the Legion may bend the keys for their purposes in building his kingdom, but Satan demands submission to the principles of the following code to avoid misunderstandings:

1. You are to have no other gods but that of whom is within you.[93] And, of these gods, I am the greatest.

2. You shall not worship any other god but the gods within us.[94] Those who do not see the gods within them will not rule with us.

3. My name is Satan. You shall not use my name except in respect and exaltation.[95] To do otherwise will subject you to destruction.

---

92   Matthew 5:43-45; Mark 12:29-31; Galatians 5:13-14
93   Exodus 20:3 (distorted)
94   Exodus 20:5 (distorted)
95   Exodus 20:7 (distorted)

4. You are to honor the specific times to worship the gods within us.[96] You will respond to my call to do so and cherish these laws in your souls.

5. You should defer to those whom I have given authority.[97] Your free will does not allow you to rebel, criticize, or correct your superiors.

6. You may take from those who oppose you, but not from another member of the Legion.[98] All of your possessions belong to me. All possessions you acquire must be given to me or be used for my purposes.

7. You shall not love each other, but honor the god within each of you.[99] To "love" is to show weakness to the Creator's Spirit, which may allow your defection.

8. You may lie, deceive, and coerce, but not to me or any other member of the Legion. You are free to do so to others.[100]

9. Hate and destroy those who love you and put yourself first in all things. [101]

10. You may engage in any desired activity not forbidden above.

Pollyon turned to Abaddon, who was still recovering from the torment. "This is the kind of power I have been seeking. I now can do whatever I want, lie to whomever I want, and take whatever I want from anyone not in the Legion."

Abaddon shot a darting glance. "What do you mean?"

96 Exodus 20:8 (distorted)
97 Exodus 20:12 (distorted)
98 Exodus 20:15; 20:17 (distorted)
99 Exodus 20:14 (distorted)
100 Exodus 20:16 (distorted)
101 Exodus 20:13 (distorted)

"Don't you see? Up till now, I was confronting our enemies with rational logic. I can abandon that now. I don't have to convince them that they should join us to realize themselves. I can lie. If they discover that I am lying, I will press my lie until I distort their judgment."

Pollyon paced slowly. "I should have known. Do you remember when I trapped the Septemviri into saving Rafaella by lying? Or how I deceived them into thinking that I was loyal to the Creator while a Septemviri?" He looked up, his eyes widening. "I did those things because Satan commanded me. I didn't question or even think about the morality involved."

Abaddon shook his head, still massaging his arm from its impact against the side of the boat. "I don't get it. So, in your case, for example, nothing will change. You will just do the same as before."

"No, that is not what I am trying to tell you." Pollyon threw up his hands, shaking his head slightly. "What has changed is that I don't have to wait for Satan's orders. I can lie, steal, betray, tempt—anything—without orders if I am not doing it to a Legion member. An angel's soul is now my scroll, and I will be its scribe."

Pollyon turned to Zelbeje as she lowered the scroll to her side. He now had a full-frontal view of her beauty. He had never felt such an attraction, not on this level. Yet, it felt like it was not what the Creator would approve of—the more the better. What if he could use her to seduce others to revolt?

"Zelbeje?"

She strolled to the two, every step broadcasting dominance, compromise, and submission—a conflicting combination that he couldn't define but only felt. Her eyes were like daggers into Pollyon's soul. He didn't know whether to kneel to her, embrace her, or force her to her knees. Her deep, translucent emerald gaze disarmed him.

"I need your help," he said in a low tone.

"I know you do," she said with a sly smile. "Satan ordained me as 'Keeper of the Natural Order' for the Legion's guidance and knowledge."

"I am not referring to the Legion. I am referring to the enemy," said Pollyon, now regaining some of his composure.

"Sounds interesting," she said with a giggle. "Please go on."

"Satan has been tormenting souls by infusing guilt and insecurity. These methods have been successful but seem to have run their course. The remaining members of the Holy Order must be enticed, lured, and seduced to our cause in subtle ways."

Zelbeje's eyes lit up with a twinkle of mischief. "I like it." She lowered her head, eyes softening. She approached closer with little effort and stood within inches of Pollyon's face, looking up. Though the angel was shorter than him, Pollyon felt like bending his knees.

She held his hand and stroked the inside of his palm, sparking the energy in his spirit. "Do you think you are capable of deceiving multitudes?"

"Yes." But he wasn't sure.

She took his other hand and squeezed them both, prompting Pollyon to close his eyes as energy fused the two Legion angels. Euphoric waves passed throughout his body in ecstatic jolts. He saw a vision, a vision of a great battle among angels—the colors of red, black, and white in a triangle, each with their commanders. A dark ball appeared within the center of the triangle and expanded with his rapturous pulse.

"Pollyon." A distant voice. He ignored it.

"Pollyon!" A shoulder rammed into him, knocking him down, evaporating the vision.

"Stop this!" yelled Abaddon, his hands clasping Pollyon's face.

The vision convulsions stopped, but the rocking became more intense. A wave washed over Pollyon's head as he woke to another violent storm. The breakers cast over the boat, with Zelbeje laughing, having returned to her oar.

The boat pitched from side to side as each swell assaulted it broadside.

The oceanic cistern submerged the door to the hall, Pollyon's only escape. Satan's ox face disappeared, and the level of the sea rose with each onslaught. Pollyon and Abaddon ran to Zelbeje and clutched her robe. "What's happening? Why are you doing this?"

"Me? I am not causing this storm." She then turned, sinister smile broadening. "Why worry? The Creator is trying to break the Legion's spirit. He sends his Holy Spirit to bring us back, but He is powerless. We are too strong for His Will."

She redirected her attention to the oar, adjusting it with one hand.

Pollyon looked up, the ceiling drawing closer, threatening to smother the sea and their boat with its joists. They could escape through the roof, but it would be a slow, arduous task to pass through it. Pollyon wasn't sure how long it would take them to escape since he could not estimate the upper stories' thickness. They had to get away.

Pollyon ran over to Zelbeje, grabbed the oar, and leaped into the whitecaps. Powerful spiritual jabs battered him as he dove to the submerged door. Holding the large oar under his arm, he rammed it against the doors.

They buckled a bit.

He then swam back farther and attacked it again.

The doors relented a little more, the sea sizzling as it seeped out.

Pollyon swam as far back as he could and charged the door, spiritual thunderbolts trailing him, focusing on where the two massive doors came together.

AZARIAS AND URIEL WIELDED THE WORD AGAINST THE growing mob, using the techniques that had been drilled into them by Leihja. Azarias wanted to deploy the other weapons, but they were not feasible in close hand-to-hand combat.

Gaius lunged forward, copper hair flickering to black in a sizzle, with a downward slicing stroke. Azarias slipped his body to the right, but not before the blade grazed his left forearm, touching but not cutting his arm.

Azarias cried out. He staggered to the wall, holding the Word with both hands in front to guard against another blow. In his lower peripheral vision, he saw movement on his forearm. Two blackened creatures, each no bigger than an eyelash, scurried around trying to enter Azarias's Spirit. This strike differed from anything Azarias had seen in his training. The little spirits seemed to want to infect but not destroy their victims, allowing Satan to take over their spirits.

Gaius halted and laughed, lowering his shaft to his feet. "Some warrior. Is this the best the Creator can muster to defeat us?" He shook his head. "You and your doubled-chinned partner are so pathetic. Conquering Heaven will be simple."

The creatures multiplied, growing exponentially on Azarias's arm. He wanted to brush them off, but it would mean exposing himself to Gaius's attack; Gaius would exterminate him from Heaven with an external blow. On the other hand, if he continued to fight Gaius, the blackened parasites could enter his spirit.

Gaius inched forward, twirling his weapon for the final blow. He jabbed his spear towards Azarias's midsection, but the Septemviri leader parried the thrust and pivoted on his right foot, causing the thrust to jab under his armpit. Spinning his weight back to the left foot, he snaked the shaft with his left arm before rocking back to his right foot, slamming the Word with his right hand across Gaius's hands, which gripped the pole. Azarias then spun the surprised and injured Gaius around, using the hatchet shaft as an extension of his arm. With only two feet separating them and Gaius clinging to the rod in his armpit, Azarias kicked Gaius in the chest, causing him to release the shaft and crash backward into the wall behind him.

The blackened creatures continued to crawl on Azarias's forearm, causing a sensation of hate within his spirit. He looked at Gaius, who was sitting against the wall with his mouth open, his painful hands seeking refuge under his armpits. Azarias wanted to destroy him. Not because he was implementing God's judgment; that didn't matter. He wanted to eliminate Gaius because he would enjoy it.

Azarias shook his head. What created this feeling? God had commissioned him to serve His judgment, not his own. He looked down at the parasites, the creatures now trying to embed into his forearm. Azarias took the Word, flattened side facing down, and touched the parasites, extinguishing them with a puff of smoke, causing hundreds of high-pitched screams to echo off the walls above him. The Word eliminated them in its light because their darkness could not overcome it.[102]

Hate evaporated from Azarias, ridding the attack of his spirit that would have certainly altered his mind. He closed his eyes and clenched his fists as he murmured, "May Your Will be done, not mine."[103] Immediately, his body encased in its armor, displaying him in the glory of the one who sent him.

Gaius stumbled to his feet, weaponless. He bolted around the corner towards the courtyard as yelling crowds closed in on Azarias from behind.

Uriel? A cold chill surged to his head. Where had he gone? Azarias ran down the corridor and into the courtyard, where an unarmored Uriel battled Spurius on the steps in front of the Great Hall's colossal doors.

Azarias wished Uriel would armor up, but things were happening so quickly. He had never seen him with such courage, no longer filled with the apprehension and insecurity that he had exhibited not long ago.

A horde of angels had gathered in front of them in the courtyard below. But, instead of watching the battle, the assembly gyrated in a spiral motion in the middle of the square, muttering unintelligible chants. As Azarias rushed to the steps to assist Uriel, Gaius slipped out of the crowd with a spear. Azarias backhanded the spear with the Word, causing Gaius to lose his balance and fall back into the courtyard.

Azarias joined Uriel in the fight against Spurius. A look of alarm covered Uriel's face. Uriel pushed Azarias out of the way and deflected a jab from the recovered Gaius. In a second swipe, he struck Gaius's neck. The Legion member's eyes widened, fate

---

102   John 1:5
103   Psalm 143:10; Mark 14:36; John 6:38

taking control, as he disintegrated into millions of black particles before being sucked up and out towards the Siq.

Spurius lunged and impaled Uriel in the back.

The loving friend fell into Azarias's arms, his double chin resting on Azarias's shoulder. "No!" cried the Septemviri leader. He looked into Uriel's violet, glossy eyes—eyes recognizing a defining moment. His eyes faded in color as his face broke into millions of white particles, his body dissolving in Azarias's arms.

Spurius regained the high ground, his face lighting up as he reeled the staff back to extinguish the Septemviri leader. A loud thud echoed behind the Legion member as the massive doors of the Great Hall exploded, releasing a mighty deluge, crushing the two adversaries into an agitating wash.

CHAPTER 8

Gabriel, Rafaella, and Squatinidale stood at a bluff of Khasneh Forest, the emptiness of the ravine. They had hardly spoken since the battle, the pursuit by the enemy dampening their forest gaiety, the tranquility shattered by the deaths of over a dozen angels.

Squatinidale seemed to take killing an angel in close contact worse than the others. The little angel never liked conflict, but conflict always pursued him. His horrible story had started long ago, when he had followed his friend, Abaddon, to see Satan at Jebel Madhbah. He had described to the Septemviri that millions of angels bowed to the self-edifying leader, who cast energy or spells upon them. Squatinidale repelled Satan's powerful spirit, but Abaddon pursued and captured him. Fortunately, the Septemviri rescued him. Yet, Satan trailed him throughout Heaven, trying to break him and bring him to darkness. Now it seemed that darkness had surfaced in a different way for him—guilt in performing the judgmental function of the Lord.

Gabriel didn't talk to Squatinidale about his troubled spirit; after all, there could be another patrol waiting for them at the ravine's bottom. It would take all three of them to fight them off or escape.

"When I flew here, so long ago," said Gabriel, "I was alone. I had just exposed our mission to the Khasneh Council, only to learn that subversives were in their ranks. Since then, I have always been uneasy flying in these parts, except when in the forest. Now even that tranquility has been snatched from me. I don't think we are safe anywhere. First, serpent demons overran our headquarters, and now the forest."

"Squatinidale," said Rafaella. "The last time when we joined Gabriel here, we discovered Satan's battle plan etched in a wall down below. We never deciphered all of it but were able to piece things together. Hopefully, we will be able to gather more information about the insurrection during this visit."

Gabriel knew Rafaella well now. She never spoke until she had contemplated the facts from every angle. Her clear blue eyes showed transparency, revealing her nurturing nature, but hid the processes of how she had arrived at conclusions. Gabriel marveled at her when she had secretly alerted Azarias that a traitor existed in the Septemviri, prompting him to trust no one until the traitor, Pollyon, surfaced.

"Well, let's see why the Lord is leading us here," said Gabriel. The three stepped off the bluff and dove down into the great ravine below, animated orange vegetation coloring their peripheral vision like a variation of the profundo falls. As before, the colorful landscape disappeared into a barren, red-rust surface, sapping the angel's excitement.

The trio landed on the far side of a façade, standing motionless, scanning for attacking angels from above. Six massive pillars supported the structure, which reached over 100 feet high and about that wide.

Gabriel looked down at the surface before them. "Someone is here or has been here."

"Why do you say that?" asked Rafaella. She followed Gabriel's gaze to the intersection of two footpaths.

Gabriel squatted at the path intersection. "I like to build cairns out of othelites when I travel, marking paths for future navigation."

The angels scanned the cliffs and then ambled up to the structure. Rafaella stopped, leaned over, and picked up a piece of a broken othelite. She advanced a little farther and picked up other pieces, examining them closely. She surveyed the area and collected more samples. She sat down and dropped them in front of her feet.

Gabriel and Squatinidale watched her as she examined various pieces, trying to reconstruct the othelites. She pieced three together.

"Gabriel, how many othelites do you use in your cairns?"

"Six."

"I see other broken pieces scattered in front of the structure," added Squatinidale.

Rafaella stood, looked at the structure's façade, and then at the other two. "Not only did someone disturb your cairn, but they also hurled the othelites at the façade with great anger, shattering them."

She paused.

"I have to assume someone knew you were here, Gabriel, and doesn't like you or your cairns."

The three walked to the structure, which seemed not to have changed since the last time they had been here, a dark spirit still dominating it.

"Walk with us, Squatinidale, and I'll show you the inside," offered Rafaella. She described the large etching on the wall of the star within a circle. It matched the vision that the Septemviri had first received of the districts targeted by Satan. She pointed to various parts of the circle as she identified the areas associated with the Septemviri's initial vision.

"The seven main districts—Ephesus, Thyatira, Sardis, Smyrna, Philadelphia, Laodicea, and Pergamum—are the districts that Satan has targeted to build an army."

She hesitated. "As far as we know. There could be more."

"What does the star represent?" asked Squatinidale.

"We believed the points of the star within the circle were five vanguards of attack. Satan will lead his attack from the inner rings of Heaven, close to the Siq, and move outwards towards the Throne of God, devouring everything in his path with darkness and destruction."[104]

The three exited the large structure and stood at the front, looking up at a different etching on the second story.

---

104   1 Peter 5:8

Rafaella continued, "We had interpreted the three-panel relief—past, present, and future—based on the message Gabriel had read on the sign at the Khasneh District. The first panel, a circle emitting rays, is the creation of the universe—the past. The second panel shows a cherub with lines radiating from him. The flame at his feet is God's Holy Spirit. We believed this was a picture of Satan exalting himself—the present situation. Last is the most confusing panel. It is a fruit-bearing tree-like object gazed upon by two beings."

"So, nothing has changed here, except for the destruction of my work," followed Gabriel.

The three Septemviri exited the structure and walked back on the trail. Gabriel picked up six othelites. He squatted down where the paths intersected and started to rebuild his initial design.

"Why are you reconstructing your cairn?" asked Squatinidale.

"He's an artist. Never question their intensions," quipped Rafaella, her face fighting to hide a smile.

Gabriel stood up, his six othelite-tall cairn displaying black sides up, reaching his lower shin. His grin almost reached his cheekbones. "I've built these cairns all over Heaven to aid my navigation when flying—in this case, the intersection of two trails. What you didn't notice last time, Rafaella, is that I piled them with the white sides up."

"Which means?" asked Rafaella.

"The white sides being up means that the area is safe, and that I didn't encounter any danger when last visiting it. When I build with dark sides up, it reminds me that I earlier had a confrontation or some other experience that I thought to be a risk. In this case, this is the deliberate and aggressive destruction of my earlier masterpiece."

Gabriel looked up to the cliffs. "When I fly, I can see these and raise my awareness of my surroundings."

Rafaella stooped at the intersection, the trail's course roughly lining the center of the canyon, meandering like a river in both directions, disappearing from view. "I feel like the Lord is asking us to walk, not fly along this trail."

"But why?" asked Squatinidale, tilting his head to the side. "Gabriel just said that nothing changed, except the destruction of the cairns. Why would the Lord ask you to act after an evil angel meant harm to us?"

"The angel that destroyed the cairn meant evil with his or her destruction and anger," answered Rafaella, "but God may use it for good to bring about His Will."[105] She stood up and looked down each direction of the trail. "What do you think, Gabriel?"

"Facing this structure, if we go to our left, we will move deeper into Heaven's center, towards the Siq and away from God's Throne. If we go right, we journey towards Thyatira."

"Azarias and Uriel flew to Thyatira," said Squatinidale. "Do you think they need our help?"

"I don't know, but I am getting the feeling they or some other angels will need our help. After all, we know that there are angels trapped in Thyatira. We will walk by faith and not by sight," answered Rafaella.[106]

"Why will we go there, and what will we do? God's Holy Spirit told us to rescue the angels somehow," said Squatinidale.

Rafaella stood up and looked at the winding footpath disappearing towards Thyatira. "We have to trust in the Lord with all of our hearts and not lean on our understanding. In all of our ways, we have to acknowledge him, and he will make straight our paths." [107] There are no coincidences in creation. We will eventually rescue angels. Who? When? I don't know. We discovered the broken othelites on our journey here. Let's find out why."

CLINGING TO THE WORD, AZARIAS TUMBLED IN THE onslaught, gasping for the Holy Spirit, his battle with Spurius now insignificant. Azarias saw a ghostly boat powered by a storm

---

105   Genesis 50:20
106   2 Corinthians 5:7
107   Proverbs 3:5-6

howling from within the Great Hall. An angel stood as a masthead, her long delphinium blue hair strands flying, her cackling laughter riding the Satanic wind.

The Septemviri commander smashed into angels who were gyrating in a trance within the flooded courtyard, which added to the mayhem assailing them. He couldn't tell if an angel was good or bad. The liquid agitation veiled any identifications, like the colored borders worn by the Legion at the bottom of their robes. Frankly, nobody seemed to care who fought for which side. They seemed to focus on traversing their way out of this disaster.

The flood orbited the courtyard, its motion copying that of the multitude's trudge. What force caused this rotation? It seemed that it only existed in the Thyatira courtyard. Regardless, Azarias had to find a way out; whitecaps smashed and rebounded against walls, the stairway into the lower courtyard offering little relief as a spillway.

Azarias found buoyancy, ducking briefly as the boat soared over him, the whirlpool current pulling him towards its center. He guessed that he only had one chance to latch on and climb onto the craft because this strange current had drained his strength. As he treaded in the pool, he focused on the unnatural energy about this liquid spirit. Unlike the profundo and vinifera, this liquid didn't emit the power of God's Holy Spirit. When submerged in those Spirit-infused rivers and lakes, angels could leverage God's Holy Spirit to swim. The energy that soaked into an angel depended on that angel's closeness to God. The more intimate the relationship and the more filled the angel, the more intense the experience. But this morbid liquid was dead, with no bright flashes or luminescence as angels touched or swam in it. The lack of this energy is why he struggled to navigate in it.

He surfaced again and watched as the boat cruised along its menacing cycle back towards him. Diving underneath the bow, he used the Word's light to illuminate his course in the darkened depths.[108] Azarias surfaced at the stern and latched onto the back

---

108   Psalm 119:105

rail with the hilt of the Word. The vessel dragged him through the wretched sea, his feet carelessly kicking submerged bodies. Expanding two of his six wings out of the deluge, he caught a gust of wind howling out of the Great Hall's opened doors. He pulled himself up onto the stern and laid exhausted across the back rail.

A pair of hands grabbed the Word from Azarias's hands, hit the back of his head, and yanked him up to the deck by his wings. Azarias's eyes fought to see something—anything—that was behind the legs that stood in front of him.

The boat rocked and spiraled in the pool of screaming heads fighting the vortex. Occasionally, fingers latched onto the craft's sides, threatening to tip the boat over, only to be torn away by the arms of the whitecaps.

Azarias lifted his head and looked to the front, eyeing the angel at the helm, still crowing her hideous siren of laughter to those suffering below her feet. She bent over the side and picked up a staff floating among the hundreds of floundering bodies. This staff seemed docile, not like the one used by Spurius or Gaius. The mariner stuck one end on one side of the bow, snagging a body, and then repositioned it to the other side of the bow. The deluge increased its volume out of the Great Hall, cascading down its landing, pushing floundering angels into the center of the whirlpool, where they mysteriously disappeared in the center of the vortex. The pool's tide rose frantically against the walls, spilling into smaller streets, the staircase to the lower courtyard serving as a small flume.

The legs stepped over him, carelessly kicking his body as swells changed their cadence. Azarias inched up the craft, its circular motion tilting him to his left. The captain's sheer, blowing robe caught his eye, her spirit making him feel uneasy, queasy, and unsettled.

She turned.

"Hello, Azarias," she shouted, her oddly transparent robe obeying the gusts as the boat circled. "I am Zelbeje, one of Satan's lieutenants and Keeper of the Legion's Natural Order."

Lieutenant? Legion? Is that what they call themselves, now?

What was the *Natural Order*? There was nothing natural about evil. Satan developed, concocted, and perverted it from God's creations, uttering lies at every step.[109] This disaster had to come from him. God's Holy Spirit was not present.

Azarias remained silent, allowing the Holy Spirit to speak through him when the time was right.[110]

Zelbeje resumed her diatribe. "Satan tells me that Uriel has departed us." She mocked a saddened face, lips pouting. "The poor little angel. He has now been exiled like our great Satan was, somewhere in the material world, floating in the deep, cold, vast cosmos. Do you think the Creator can find him?"

She laughed.

Azarias wanted to yell back, tears welling up, his mind seeing his exiled friend's eyes. It had happened so fast that he hadn't had time to process his feelings. This evil angel was now forcing him to suffer the image left in his mind repeatedly.

"He perished saving me." His voice choked. "Greater love has no one than this: to lay down one's life for one's friend."[111]

"I look at it this way." Zelbeje pulled the pole out of the pool. "Greater foolishness has no one than this: to lose a life for one who is not worthy of losing it for."[112]

Azarias could feel Satan piercing his soul with guilt, shame, and failure. She was right. Why would Uriel give his heavenly life for one so flawed, so inept? Azarias knew from the beginning he could not live up to being the leader God wanted him to be. He wished it was him that was cast out of Heaven.

Azarias stole a step.

Zelbeje spun the staff behind her right shoulder, one hand behind her back, the other fully extended, open palmed, towards Azarias.

---

109   John 8:44
110   Matthew 10:20
111   John 15:13
112   John 15:13 (distorted)

A smile returned to her face. "Yes, Uriel was foolish. Especially when the saving was just a temporary delay of the inevitable."

Two arms lifted Azarias, wrapping around his shoulders, pinning his wings and arms to his body.

Zelbeje laughed. "Nice work, Abaddon; there is hope for you after all."

Abaddon?

Two other hands appeared, reaching over the bow. "Zelbeje," called a soft and spent voice.

Zelbeje reached the staff back into the water and pulled a disheveled and exhausted angel from the rising tide.

Azarias's mouth fell open.

Pollyon climbed to his feet and tried to control his breath. "Well, Azarias, my friend, my confidant, we meet again."

"Don't call me your friend, you traitor," said Azarias. "I trusted you, the Septemviri trusted you, and God trusted you. You and I completed many missions together, serving God through love. But all of that changed when you betrayed us," said Azarias, drilling his eyes into the former Septemviri. "How can you turn your back on me, on your comrades, and on your God?"

Pollyon gathered his composure and energy, face morphing from a smile to a frown. "I am special, now," he shouted. "I no longer have to serve in return for acceptance, in return for limited knowledge, or in return for love."

The wind increased its onslaught, causing Pollyon to pause, but only for a moment. "Satan elevated me to lieutenant. He saw my value and my commitment. Compared to how long I served the Creator, Satan recognized my value in the blink of any eye. I, in turn, have put my energy into Satan's forces, and we are winning."

Pollyon stood more erect, chest pushed out, towering over the smaller Zelbeje. "Now that we will destroy you, I believe we have just won."

Azarias closed his eyes, his lips moving, words inaudible to others in the wind. "Lord, speak to me. I have failed you, but I do not want my failures to define who I am or who you want me to be. I want to forget the past and look forward to what lies ahead. I press on to reach the end of the race and receive the heavenly prize for which God, through the Word, is calling us."[113]

Azarias bent at the waist. Abaddon struggled to hold him, leaning forward with him to tighten his arms around his shoulders.

"Look, the coward is fainting," sneered Pollyon. "I knew you weren't the leader the Creator made you out to be." He laughed.

---

113   1 Samuel 3:10; Philippians 3:13-14

CHAPTER 9

A zarias buckled at his waist and reached both hands through his legs, grabbing one of Abaddon's ankles. He pulled the off-balance angel's leg up through his legs, forcing Abaddon to let go of his chest. Abaddon fell backward across the rear rail and dropped the Word. Azarias lifted the leg over the surprised angel's head, flipping him back over the stern. Azarias snatched the Word and activated its sword. As he turned to face Zelbeje, a staff point jabbed at him, prompting him to slip it across his left shoulder. Zelbeje then stabbed the staff again, compelling Azarias to dodge the thrust over his right shoulder. Azarias rose and snaked the pole with his right arm, clutching it tightly under his armpit. Pollyon grabbed the stick to assist Zelbeje. Both enemy angels pushed forward, pressuring Azarias to rock back. Their motion was timed perfectly as the front of the boat hit a wave trough, pitching the front half of the boat down the side of the crest. Azarias leaned forward and pushed the two angels off the bow, retaining his hold on the shaft.

The boat drifted around the rising deluge, with more angels swimming towards it, hands groping for the rail. Other angels flew in over the big stout tower, intercepting Azarias's escape through flight. Azarias dropped the staff into the bottom of the boat and jabbed the Word's blade over the side to paddle. With one big thrust, his boat caught the side current emptying down the stairway towards the lower courtyard, breaking the whirlpool's grip. Azarias retracted the Word and attached it to his chest. He gripped the right and left sides of the boat and careened down into stairwell rapids. Angels diving from above and probing from underneath at the boat's rails tried to grab the escaping angel. The vessel picked up speed as it rushed down the staircase torrents, smashing against the walls, banking at each turn, almost turning upside down on its wide-eyed captain. At last, it turned right into the lower courtyard, leveling itself.

The gateway to the castle courtyards lay dead ahead, its twenty-foot-high arched door nestled under large cornices, its side turrets guarded by incensed angels. The guards on both sides swung the massive doors towards each other, trying to bar Azarias's escape. Fortunately, the exiting current slowed their progress as Azarias glided downwards, the bottom of the boat hitting steps and landings as it surged up and down. The Septemviri commander reached down at his feet, picked up the shaft, and held it over his head. As he skimmed the falls towards the closing doors, the bottlenecked door opening decreased his velocity. The current slowed just enough for him to jam the shaft between the two doors, halting their closure, leaving enough room for the craft to shoot out from the gateway. The force of the great doors snapped the staff in half, casting part of it back into the bottom of the boat.

Hundreds of angels stood in front of him, baring their teeth, and others hovered above him. Azarias leaned forward, with his hands on the rails beside him, slaloming between the standing and flying angels, skimming the thin layer of Satan's downpour. At times, the bow careened into an angel, sending that angel hurdling over the back of the boat. If only Azarias could ride this to the canyon edge, he might be able to fly away. The canyon would be too large for them to block his escape.

With angels running and flying after him, the rapid flow decreased in energy and magnitude. He felt the boat bottom scraping against the surface, which halted him to a complete stop—half hanging over the cliff. Azarias tried to nudge it forward, but the base held firm. He was trapped.

Legion angels closed in from the castle gateway behind him and from above. He clung to the Word. Two angels landed on the front of the boat, the vessel teetering on the cliff edge. One of the attacking angels turned back to a third angel, "Wait! Don't land!" But it was too late. The third angel landed on the bow, tipping the craft and all four angels into the canyon below. The three enemy angels took flight while Azarias grabbed the boat's sides again and careened down, struggling to use his wings to guide his descent.

The boat fell two thousand feet, spinning out of control into the gorge below, frantic angels flying and leaping out of its path.

Azarias hit the Profundo River at the bottom of the gorge head-on, with a big and explosive crash, the broken staff whacking his arm. The vessel dove into the depths of the massive rushing waterway, pushed downstream by the river's mighty underwater current.

Azarias could feel Satan's spirit seeping into his soul. Failure. He had failed miserably on this mission, not only ruining the rescue and surveillance of any Thyatira angels, but also losing Uriel—forever. He had told the others before that he was not worthy of being a leader, but the Lord thought differently. Why?

His body became limp as he laid prostrate on the floor of the boat as it plummeted to the bottom of this great, fast-moving river. Though the Holy Spirit's light still illuminated the river depths, he felt dark inside.

The current pushed Azarias and the boat along its bottom, bouncing it off the submerged rocks from time to time. He'd just stay there. At least he had lost the parasites.

He was of no use to anyone now. He thought that the Lord should just abandon him and use someone else.

After bouncing for a long time in the current, the boat rested against the base of a submerged boulder.

All was still and quiet. Uriel's eyes and his last look at his friend were seared his mind. Azarias couldn't help but cry, his tears lost in the current.

He thought back to when God had summoned him and the other Septemviri to His Throne. Everything seemed so good then. They had just defeated Satan in their first battle together. God equipped them with armor and encouraged them to fight for His righteousness.

He remembered what the Lord had said to him: *I know your insecurity, Azarias. I would not have chosen you if I didn't know that you could complete the task before you.*[114] *But you will have to understand this for yourself in the coming battles.*

Azarias sat in the boat and stared at the Word.

He picked it up, its weight heavier than usual in this river. He turned it over.

It flashed.

He waved it again and again in the profundo.

Emerald bioluminescent rays trailed its moving blade with every stroke.

The Holy Spirit's presence.

He must be nearing the edge of Satan's realm.

So what? He was of no use now. He attached the Word's hilt to his chest and turned into the current to see if any angels were searching for him in the profundo.

All was still. He was alone.

The oncoming current rushed against the hilt. More bioluminescent rays peeled off as the profundo washed past it.

Azarias pulled the hilt from his chest. He waved it again, this time more vigorously as the liquid lightning condensed, congealed, and circulated outside the boat. The profundo subcurrent picked up also, washing over him, cleansing him of his ineptness. He knew he had to fight the good fight, the mighty battle, the quest for righteousness. He had to take hold of himself and the role to which God called him.[115] He had to push forward towards the goal to save Heaven, even if he was just as a small, insignificant tool of God.[116]

Flashes of light ignited along with him as the profundo's Holy Spirit power energized him in his little submerged boat. Azarias

---

114   Philippians 1:6
115   1 Timothy 6:12
116   Philippians 3:14

smiled a little. God's Spirit was still with him. With renewed faith, he latched onto the sides of the craft and moved his wings, capturing the Spirit's increasing energy. The boat moved faster and faster under the surface, still held down by the profundo within it.

Up ahead, Azarias saw a fallen slab jutting away from him, piercing the surface. He angled his wings faster through the profundo bioluminescence, propelling himself up the slab. Spearing the water's surface, he soared out of the river, emptying the corkscrewing craft of profundo, and landed keel side down. The craft jerked back and forth as he struggled to control it without a rudder, large blocks angling towards him, imposing barriers to his escape. Azarias craned his neck to the right, to the left, and then back to the right again as he looked for attacking angels at every turn.

The Septemviri commander erred in thinking he had entirely passed out of Satan's realm. Darkness imposed itself as fleeting sheets tangled with the light of God's Holy Spirit, casting shadows over the treacherous river. Maybe the enemy had not spotted him in this disorganized configuration of profundo, scattered slabs, and low light.

Up ahead, a loud rumbling drummed his ears, his eyes at a loss to its origins. The current picked up speed, creating a screaming cacophony against the background bass sound, now approaching earnestly.

In the dimly lit atmosphere, the profundo seemed to end. Azarias's vision cleared to see the river cascading hundreds of feet into a deep turquoise pool guarded by the high cliffs around it.

Should he hold onto the boat, or should he fly? Satan's Legion could just be lurking above, waiting to intercept him if he took flight.

He decided to trust in God and hold onto the boat.

The boat descended on the falling profundo, the river abandoning the boat's hull in its attempt to reach the pool below. Before hitting the pond, Azarias used his wings to bring up the craft's bow, flattening its landing with a large splash. Azarias fell into it as it spun in circles, the falls rebounding off the surrounding cliff walls.

The current muscled the craft away from the falls and around another bend. A greyish cave opened before Azarias, swallowing the river. Azarias looked for the broken staff to guide himself away from it, but the current must have taken it away.

Maybe it would be better to sail through this opening and not be detected by the enemy angels above. The river had to escape it, or there wouldn't be a current. Azarias decided to stay, but was he moving from a possible attack and into Satan's clutches?

Once called the heart of God, Sardis is where angels relished in their personal divine symphonies. Michael recalled his last visit, flying into the district's brilliant skyward ray, a beacon to those who sought God's euphoria. He had experienced—no—absorbed its incredible singing through God's Holy Spirit, broadcast in the pathways of quartz-like marble veins that changed in tone along with its structures. The kaleidoscopic display, along with angelic harmonies, blended into him and became a part of him. He couldn't help but dance, jubilation exploding through his body and out his fingers and toes. The music was personal to him, the colors personal to him, and God's message personal to him. What did Gabriel call it? "Color-grace." He cried during that experience. How could God's love be so overwhelming to someone as flawed as him?

But all that had changed at the fourteen columns. As suddenly as it started, it stopped. Satan's twelve-tone music (if you can call it music) replaced God's music, His Holy Spirit, and His very presence, summoning the blind followers. They flew over the peak to an unknown destination, and ultimately their eternal doom. How could Satan command such allegiance here? The enemy hit God right in His heart, the emotional weigh station between Him and his angels.

Satan's strategy seemed to strike God in the districts where angels experienced Him most. In Pergamum, the Bibliotheca was where angels sought answers to their most intimate questions; Satan had intercepted Squatinidale's communication there.

In the Ephesus Odeum, Malachy and Pollyon enjoyed a performance in God's Spirit until Satan's rebellious forces attempted to arrest them.

Smyrna was the angels' playground. The Spirit hosted the games where angels basked in God's joy, competing in events that amplified an angel's gifts. Satan had converted over 100,000 attendees, who tried to capture him and Gabriel.

Thyatira offered angels an insight into God's perfect organization. All of that morphed into disorganization when Azarias and Uriel first visited there. He prayed their second trip had been more productive and safer.

Philadelphia and Laodicea were where God's servants basked in His Spirit, sometimes literally. Those districts had become lukewarm at best to the love of the Lord.

Michael dwelled on this pattern. Wherever angels sought God, Satan intervened. You would have thought that Satan would attack districts where the angels did not seek God. Though reprehensible, the evil angel's strategy was brilliant—tempt angels when most vulnerable, most needy, and mostly oblivious to his presence.

Michael turned to Malachy, her eyes focusing on the surroundings. "Our visit here hit a low when Baal-Zebub and his red-faced minions confronted Gabriel and me. They declared that Satan had won, and God had lost His heavenly kingdom. They lied, saying that they had captured all of the other Septemviri angels."

Malachy didn't react.

The two landed in Sardis. Unlike before, the beacon no longer rose towards God's Throne, the Holy Spirit's wind ceased, and Sardis's wonderful music silenced.

"The district is dead in spirit," said Michael, his face revealing little emotion. [117] "The last time we were here, the Lord's Spirit returned after the angels had departed. But now, what life Sardis had is gone."

---

117   Revelation 3:1

Malachy, at first, didn't react. Her concentration and ability to solve puzzles impressed Michael. "Let's search for what the Lord has told us. The word to us was *Michael, fly to Sardis and seek under the seven spirits of God and the seven stars. You will know them by the mark.*"[118]

The two angels walked down the central corridor lined by seven columns on each side, each towering over them by at least one hundred feet. Michael hesitated at the first few pairs, not sure what to expect. As they passed each one, Malachy inspected them. She held her arm up to each, exposing her wrist.

"What are you doing?" asked Michael.

"Just a hunch. In Ephesus, the columns illuminated the names of the loyal angels when I held the Septemviri brand up to them." She lowered her arm. "Not here."

The two angels exhausted the last of the columns and stood facing the peak's base which dominated the area. Michael took a few steps and then turned. "Now what? We are no closer now than when we were in Al Birka. What are the seven stars and seven spirits?"

Malachy's gaze lifted from Michael's eyes as if looking behind him.

"What?" Michael spun around and looked to the top of the outcropping. High up on a ridge rose a pillar of white smoke.

"I didn't notice the peak last time until the entranced angels flew beyond it," said Michael. "Do you think they lit that fire? Could it be a trap?"

"Yes, or it could be a sign from God," said Malachy, eyes still fixated on the outcropping peak. She returned her gaze to Michael. "Well, we live by faith and not by sight."

Michael and Malachy launched themselves towards the smoke, gazing at the crags and overhangs along the way. Nothing moved. The outcropping appeared as dead as the Sardis center far below. Could the enemy be hiding under the surface? Michael couldn't imagine how that was possible since their spirits would conflict

118   Ibid.

with the surface. Maybe they had built a series of caves in the outcropping.

"Let's not fly all of the way, but advance with caution on foot from two directions," suggested Michael. "This way, if we split up, we may avoid being cornered together in an ambush."

The two Septemviri crept around large boulders and through narrow passageways to the billowing smoke. Fire is not unusual in Heaven, but smoke is. The last time Michael saw this smoke was when the group incinerated the serpent demons, who departed in a mixture of black smoke and particles sucked out by the Siq. But that was black smoke—here, they were investigating white smoke.

As Michael turned another corner, the smoke blanketed the area like a fog. He couldn't see far in front of him. No wonder the enemy had lit the fire. It provided a perfect screen for them, masking their numbers and location from any intruders.

Something brushed his left arm. Michael grasped the Word from his chest and activated the sword and his armor.

Crystalline leaves? Why were crystalline leaves growing up here? He traced the branch up to a partially exposed tree. He stumbled a bit, drawing his gaze to his feet. Sweet, violet amborlite nestled him from the side of the trail. As he peered closer, he could see that the area had completely transformed from a desolate terrain to a garden of paradise.

Michael heard rustling to his left. Malachy emerged, sword and armor also activated, pushing low-hanging branches away, her face infused with amazement and bewilderment. "Do you have any record of this type of arrangement in Sardis?"

"No," replied Malachy. "Sardis has historically been a barren area devoid of any growth. The district never had a use for it because each angel would experience their own private 'paradise' when the Spirit sang to them. The area offered a much different experience to angels than somewhere like the Khasneh Forest."

The two angels walked forward, shoulder to shoulder, eyes wide, upright swords lighting their way. Michael and Malachy approached a brightening glow emitting from behind a large boulder.

As they circled the boulder, the haze cleared and then disappeared to where they could see a multicolored fire at the base of a crystalline tree. Yet, unlike the black smoke puffs that exterminated the serpent demons' remains, this tree and the bush underneath it were not burning.[119] They emitted a glow while preserving life. More so, in the bush dwelled a being—an angel. But this angel didn't project fear or hatred. No, this angel of the Lord (if it was an angel) produced an aroma pleasing to the senses, an air of peace and love.[120]

Michael and Malachy kneeled, knowing that, in some way, the Lord was present. Though the Holy Spirit saturated all of Heaven, there were parts of Heaven, like the Lord's Throne, where he magnified his presence.[121] It felt that way here. The multicolored glow radiated from all parts of the bush and tree nestled at the base of the cliff. The light flowed outwards like the liquid profundo as it meandered unmolested down a lazy river, unrushed to its destination.

An ember popped, sending a big spark high over Michael and Malachy's heads. It drew Michael's attention to the cliff behind it.

"Malachy, look at the base of this cliff. It looks as if there were a massive cave carved into the side and then closed by an avalanche."

"I know of some places that are unstable," whispered Malachy, "but none that could collapse a tunnel so large. Maybe this was intentional. If this is unnatural, what could the enemy be hiding? What do we do?"

"Let's wait for a sign," said Michael, his eyes still penetrating the beautiful site. "However, we must be vigilant, because, when He does, it is usually subtle and easy to miss."

Another ember popped, but this time with two glowing pieces corkscrewing around each other in the air and behind the two angels.

---

119   Exodus 3:2
120   Leviticus 1:17
121   Revelation 4

Malachy followed them with her eyes as they disappeared over the boulders behind them.

Both angels retracted their swords and armor. Michael felt that they were not in danger, but he was still confused.

Malachy did a double take looking beyond Michael. Michael turned his head and saw a small line of writing—one easy to overlook.

"Can you read the inscription on the tree?" asked Malachy, squinting her eyes.

"I think I can. It says, 'Your Word is a lamp for my feet, a light to my path.'"[122]

The angels paused, silence stretching.

A third ember erupted, but with more force, sending three glowing particles twisting like a triple helix over their heads.

"Come on," motioned Malachy. "This might be our sign. If not, we can come back." They opened their wings and followed the fiery dance as it floated back in the direction from which they had just come.

Passing over the rim of the ridge, the angels hovered high above the center through which they just walked. The embers fell below them, staging their pirouette in front of the fourteen columns far below.

Malachy looked down and counted. "...4, 5, 6, 7. That's it!"

Michael looked at her and then returned his gaze down to the lowest level. "I see it, too. Seven columns on the left and seven on the right. Can you see what is on top of each of the columns' capitals? The left looks like five-pointed stars."

"Yes!" said Malachy, swinging slightly in her flight, a smile broadening her face. "There is a flame etched on each capital on the right—the same flames we saw dancing on our heads at God's Throne, the presence of His Holy Spirit." She tweaked her mouth to the side. "But I don't know what it all means."

The embers burned out, leaving the angels alone with their thoughts. "We are focusing on the details too much. With God, we have to look at a bigger picture."

122   Psalms 119:105

The angels hovered in silence. "Look at the structures," said Malachy.

"Yes, I was going to say the same thing," replied Michael. "There are four rows of four structures, creating an X, meeting at a center point where the columns begin."

"And look at the fifth line of four structures on the opposite side of the midpoint. It leads from the center point away from the fourteen columns," chimed in Malachy. "They end at an amphitheater."

Michael started to move forward, "It seems everything points to that center point where all of the structures and the fourteen columns intersect. Let's go and see what waits for us."

"That's what worries me," said Malachy, throwing a glance at him. "I've been trapped before."

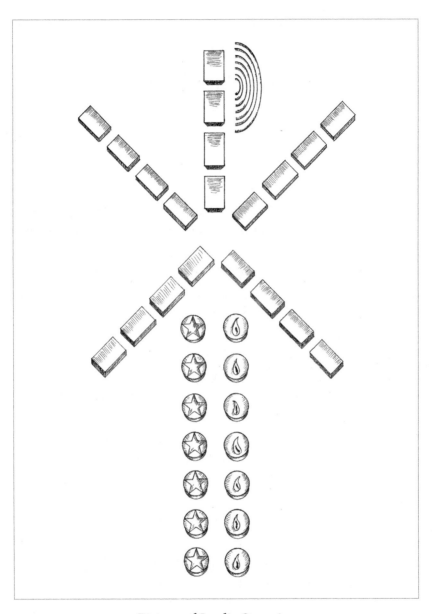

Picture of Sardis Overview

CHAPTER 10

The cave extended deeper than Azarias had first thought, no longer just a temporary tunnel, drilling far beneath the peaks. The silence allowed him to concentrate on the possible presence of other angels, the thundering falls no longer dominating his surroundings. He heard nothing, just the profundo lapping against the boat sides and the cave walls, or so he thought.

The current pushed him into the unknown, Satan's darkness jostling against the penetrating turquoise light rays disappearing into the profundo below him. Where there was light, there was God, but where there was darkness, Satan's influence lurked. Azarias started to tremble. Lost, alone, and at the mercy of whoever dwelled here, he clung to his belief in God. "The Lord is my light and my salvation, whom shall I fear? He is the stronghold of my life, of whom shall I be afraid?" [123]

The current pushed him deeper into the cave, small dark tributaries opening for him from time to time, suspended lights now dancing as flickering pinpoints. Was Satan dangling these little illuminations of hope, toying with him, luring him deeper into a lair? Azarias couldn't be sure. The presence of light and darkness meant a spiritual battle ensued, though miniature and not very apparent. This display was the first time he had seen the Holy Spirit as suspended points of light. He reached out his hand and

123   Psalm 27:1

grabbed one, cupping it into both hands, the flickering spirit illuminated in his enclosed hands. Azarias parted his thumbs slightly and peeked in. Nestled in his palm was a tiny tongue of fire, like the ones had he seen on the Septemviri's heads at the Throne of God.[124] At that time, those lights, though larger than this one, shined when the Word addressed them. God's radiance from his Throne outshone them.[125] But this tongue of light brightened in the almost pitch darkness. Why did God show the brightest in the darkest times?[126]

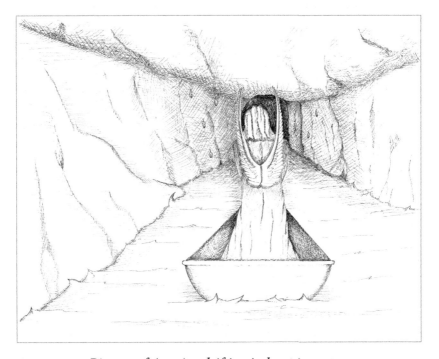

Picture of Azarias drifting in boat in a cave

---

124   Acts 2:1-3
125   Revelation 4:5
126   John 1:5

A noise. Azarias turned around, his hand clutched to the Word. Was he being followed? The area behind him was pitch black, as the floating Spirits had surrendered the area. He could see nothing but darkness. The tongued spirits remained in front of him, almost like the Spirit of God was leading him. He had to surrender to God and the path He set before him.[127] Frankly, he had no choice, which made it easier.

The Spirit compelled him to drift further into this forbidding wilderness.[128] His boat rounded more corners on the right and left, his eyes optimistically searching for a light at each turn, only to be disappointed.

Something moved far ahead. Were his eyes playing tricks? Had his fear overcome his mind? He couldn't turn back and fight the current. He could fly, but Satan's Legion may have caught up by now, or they could have flown over the peaks to head him off at the exit. Yes, that must be it. Who else would it be? He was far away from Thyatira, and nobody knew that he was here, except the evil Thyatira Legion.

Maybe it was nobody, after all. Wouldn't he have seen them fly—? There! Another movement.

Now, he was sure. He wasn't alone.

Azarias grabbed the Word of God and released its sword. The glow lit up all around him and about thirty feet in front of him. He donned his armor and waited.

Everything grew still, profundo lapping at the sides of his boat, the flicker of tongue flames now becoming more energetic as he drifted forward in the current.

Azarias looked to the side—a tributary. He could fly down that tunnel to escape.

No. That wouldn't do. The current moved forward, which meant that the side tunnel ended somewhere far off, to trap him. He would just have to fight them off. He had an assortment of weapons in

127   Psalms 143:10
128   Mark 1:12

the Word, but most couldn't be used in closed quarters. He would destroy himself using them.

Deep in the cave, something emerged on the right from behind the bend. One of Satan's whips, staff, something else he hadn't seen? Maybe they were calling him to surrender. Azarias's gaze shifted to the left, his sword held high, his breath increasing.

The craft inched closer to the object. As he closed in, the object became more apparent. An arm, not a weapon, stuck out from behind the wall. Azarias looked to the other side and behind him, expecting an ambush. The arm could be a distraction. Yes, that's it—a distraction. Depending on the number of opponents, he could fight to escape by flight. He would have to make that assessment in a split second. If he picked the wrong direction, he could fly into a swarm of angry angels.

He debated the odds, considering all factors. Satan's Legion had an advantage. They could use darkness as a cover because the Spirit's light dulls or extinguishes around them.

The boat crept forward, the arm now fully visible, the owner's sleeve oddly pulled back past the elbow. Azarias shifted his sword to only his right hand, left forearm now holding his shield. He would jump to the left and slash to the right, then—

A light? A light brightened on the arm as he sailed forward. Azarias's forearm, holding his sword, lit up. The sign of the Septemviri. He looked up at the arm displayed. The sign of the Septemviri glowed brighter as he got closer. Was one of his other comrades here? How did they know he sailed down this dreary cave?

A smiling angel stepped forward onto a small bank, her golden hair reflecting the sword's glow, her hands at ease. God's Spirit moved her white robe.

"Welcome, my friend. We have been praying for someone like you." The suspended lights drew together, illuminating the entire area with the Holy Spirit.

Azarias furrowed his brow and looked to the left, lowering his sword, but just slightly.

"Who are you?"

"We are God's angels of Thyatira. You have found us."

GABRIEL SUGGESTED THAT RAFAELLA AND SQUATINIDALE continue their journey on foot as he flew, scanning the canyon cliffs for the enemy. Their trek through to the Khasneh Forest had almost ended in their demise. This experience unsettled Gabriel in that they were ambushed, out-numbered, and out-positioned by Satan's attacking forces. It felt like Satan had sent out patrols all over Heaven looking for the Septemviri and loyalist angels. Fortunately, he knew the forest better than the enemy did, which gave him an advantage in their counterattack. Still, the strategy was risky, and the result could have gone either way.

The Khasneh Canyon didn't offer him any peace, starting with the remains of his shattered landmark cairns. The little structures had helped guide him and alert him of dangerous areas. He usually stacked them white-side up to indicate the area was safe, but that would change since danger now lurked everywhere.

That was another problem that Gabriel hadn't mentioned to the other two. How current were his indicators? He may have stacked a pile of cairns white-side up the last time he flew into a canyon, but the enemy could have infiltrated the area afterward, rendering his signs obsolete. This reality tied knots in his spirit, but he had to keep a positive outlook. The others saw his personality as gregarious, outgoing, and faithful to the Lord. But, despite his efforts, his faith in the Lord faltered at times. He tried to look for peace for his troubled heart because he was afraid.[129]

The troupe sallied forth, with Gabriel scanning as far as he could see and, at times, waiting for his trekking companions to catch up with him. He flew down and met with Rafaella and Squatinidale as they came to a canyon fork. On the left was a barren canyon floor like they had been traveling. On the right was a canyon cut by a profundo.

---

129   John 14:27

"We have three options," said Rafaella. "We can go to the far left, down the dry canyon, we can go straight and upstream, along a Profundo River, or we can turn right and travel downstream, along a path that ultimately passes outside of Smyrna."

"Heaven is so large," moaned Gabriel. "Even with the gift of my speed, everywhere I fly is a long journey. Here, we are traveling on foot, examining every little othelite, cliff, and expanse of silicium particles. I don't think God wanted us to rake every little cave from the enemy, because, the longer we take to act, the more Satan and his forces advance."

"It seems we missed something in what God's Spirit was trying to tell us," chimed Squatinidale.

Rafaella walked to the bank of the river and leaned over, the profundo washing between her fingers, sending a glow of blue euphoria up her arm. "Or we haven't walked far enough for God to reveal his signs," said Rafaella. "We must be patient and look for the whispers of His creation."[130]

Gabriel climbed a high boulder and looked downstream, where the current stalled into a glassy reflection of the cliffs above. Nothing grabbed his attention; the canyon and river signaled God's tranquility without any indication of the epic rebellion. Were they supposed to go to Smyrna? Why? It was so far away, and they'd be wasting so much time traveling there, even by flight.

He shifted his gaze upriver to where the profundo moved at a faster pace, its chattering song bouncing off the cliffs around them. If he were to stand in it, the level would not reach his knees before dropping over a wide, smooth rock wall into the tranquil section to his right.

A slight reflection, in the middle, caught his eye, its depth shallow. Gabriel didn't shift his attention, since a lot of things shimmer in Heaven. It could be one of the crystalline leaves from the Khasneh Forest that somehow found its way to this distant waterway.

---

130   1 Kings 19:12

It shimmered again, but this time, it appeared to be rolling in the subtle subcurrent. Gabriel turned to his comrades, "Hold on. I see something odd."

The three of them followed him to the point of inquisition. "Gabriel, what did you see?" asked Squatinidale.

"Around here. Something flashed."

The three hovered in the one spot, the small, shimmering wave tops complicating their search.

"There," pointed Rafaella. She landed in the profundo, not quite knee-deep and bent over—a staff, rolling through the subcurrent, emitting sparkles of the profundo's bioluminescence. As she pulled it out of the water, the profundo drained from it, releasing its bluish glow. Rafaella turned it and examined the splintered end.

"I wonder what this was used for." She turned it again to the smooth end and then back to the broken end. "It looks like this staff may have been twice the length, like the one used by Leihja." She looked up. "What do you think broke it? These shafts don't break with normal use—in fact, not even with extreme use."

"Yes," responded Squatinidale. "Do you remember when Leihja struck the wall causing the explosion? That staff withstood the impact."

Gabriel landed. Rafaella passed the broken staff to him in hopes of an explanation. Gabriel looked upstream, wondering if the river was hiding additional clues, with its mesas overlapping its course on the right and left, guarding the secrets that may be visible from their tabletops.

"Violence," he muttered. "I agree with you that a normal force in Heaven didn't break this, but an act of violence. We'll go upriver."

"How can you be sure?" asked Squatinidale, who also had landed. "We can't see anything but a mysterious broken—."

"I'm never sure," said Gabriel, turning the object in his hand, "but we walk and fly by faith, not by sight, remember?"[131]

He glanced and said with a low-pitched and steady voice, "Some angel, or angels, are in trouble."

---

131   2 Corinthians 5:7

Squatinidale looked into the distance, his voice slightly strained. "Where does this lead?"

"Uriel and Malachy would be the best to tell us," responded Rafaella. "The ultimate headwaters are the mesas of Al Birka, but that is a long, long way from here."

"Is there a district before that?" asked Squatinidale.

"Yes, Thyatira. The profundo doesn't pass through the center but in a gorge bordering it."

"Uriel and Azarias are there," added Rafaella. "Do you think they're in trouble?"

"There is trouble everywhere," said Gabriel, engaging himself in a hover again, "and this is a sign of it."

The three angels flew down the river, looking for more clues and debris. The river ignored their glances as they continued their journey unmolested from diving angels. The homogeneous purple mesas jutted up from the right and then left, with the river snaking between them.

Were they listening to God or following their selfish instincts? Gabriel could be testing God. How could he be sure? He felt like he was always testing God, not following Him. Gabriel could be leading them into another band of evil angels or even an army.

CHAPTER 11

Michael and Malachy descended from the Sardis outcropping, floating gently down to the courtyard's midpoint, skirting the fourteen stoic columns displaying the spirit and star etchings. God's cryptic message to Michael— *Fly to Sardis and seek under the seven spirits of God and the seven stars. You will know them by the mark*—weighed heavily on them.

"Seek *under* the seven spirits," murmured Michael. Malachy didn't respond. At times like this, she withdrew into her world, looking at situations from all angles. No other angel, except for maybe Uriel, could match her concentration. But she displayed it more, since her personality was more gregarious.

The two landed at the intersection of the five lines of structures and the fourteen columns. "I noticed this round seal at the intersection of the structures and the columns but didn't give it any thought," started Michael. "It doesn't show anything except this small lighted slot, narrower than my four fingers." Michael bent over and stuck his large hand into the slot on the seal.

"Just as I thought; my hand is too big. You try it."

Malachy exhaled, abandoning her train of thought. "Why not? We don't have any other options." She got down on all fours and peered into the opening. "I can't see anything but the normal heavenly glow."

She stuck her fingers into it, stopping at her knuckles. "That's all I can get in there. It seems our theory doesn't work."

Malachy stood and looked at the opening, her toes abutting its edge. She stepped over the slot and placed her toes on the opposite side. Then she straddled the opening and paused.

"What do you see?"

"Nothing. I was thinking about that inscription on the tree up there. 'Your Word is a lamp for my feet, a light to my path.'"[132] I thought maybe that the gap's glow would light my feet, perhaps giving us another clue."

"That's what I love about you," said Michael, his face lighting up. "You think so creatively in ways I can never fathom."

Malachy laughed and looked at him. "Yes, like this time, which didn't work!" Her laughter stopped as she lowered her gaze to Michael's chest. A cold feeling strained through him as he looked behind himself and then turned back again. "What? Do you see someone?"

"Not someone—something," said Malachy, pinching her brow, with a slight smile lining her face. "Come stand next to me."

Michael walked across the medallion and stood next to Malachy, shoulder to shoulder, facing the peak. She removed the Word from her chest and triggered the blade, glowing bright and golden, into its three narrow blades that joined together at a point. She held it to her face and turned to Michael.

"Your Word is a lamp for my feet, a light to my path."

She leaned over and slipped the fiery blade into the narrow opening at her feet to the hilt's extended arms, its glow lighting their feet and the area in front of them.

Nothing happened.

She looked up at Michael and pressed her lips together, shaking her head. "I thought this would be the—"

Michael heard a low rumble.

A vibration started deep under their feet, growing louder, shaking the area around them. Malachy grabbed her sword and clutched Michael's arm as the surface between the first pair of columns collapsed, their bases crumbling. The two closest columns tipped away

---

132 Psalms 119:105

from the angels towards the outcropping. A large groan and swoosh assailed Michael's ears as the two giants fell slightly inward, pounding the surface as they hit, the edge of their capitals resting in an arrow shape pointing away from him, creating an indentation in the surface.

As the first two columns hit the surface, the second pair buckled, causing them to topple in the same direction, hammering the chasm even deeper, sloping away, lining up its arrow in front of the first pair.

With bangs and pops, the columns collapsed in succession, falling deeper into Sardis, adding additional arrows pointing downwards towards the base of the peaked outcropping, silicium particles flying into the atmosphere, obscuring their view into the pit. The successive collapses of the columns resulted in a downward ramp.

Malachy looked at Michael, her eyes wide, her smile trying to extend beyond her jaw. "I knew it!" She clapped as if she had just watched a great symphony performed at the Ephesus Odeum.

The silicium dust settled at its own pace, a series of fourteen collapsed column arrows pointing to a large cavern deep under the surface quietly tempting the angels to enter.

The two angels flew down into the newly created ravine, their swords drawn and their armor intact. Michael walked in first, his back against the right wall, his eyes alert for any movement. He signaled for Malachy to hug the left wall. The entrance led to a wall with pathways to their right and left.

Michael motioned Malachy to convert her Word into a bow, with an arrow loaded in its nock. He gave the signal and spun around the corner, his sword leading the way.

Nobody.

The two turned and looked the other way, another empty corridor bending out of sight.

Not a sound.

Michael retracted his sword and placed it on his chest. Malachy followed suit.

"If there were someone down here, they would have heard the collapse," said Malachy.

"The Lord led us here; there are no coincidences in Heaven. Everything is according to God's plan and will. We have to look."

"Do you think the hidden Sardis angels are here? I mean, the ones on my list?" Malachy pulled the scrolls from her robe, unraveling the one that tallied the Sardis angels. "If so, there would be at least tens of thousands of angels here."

"We can't be at the right place," answered Michael. "Why would God's Spirit lead us here? The imprisoned or hidden angels would have met us with great fanfare if they were here. On the other hand, if this were a trap, Satan would have closed it by now, since we are deep into the cavern."

The angels crept down the corridor, gazing into lighted offshoots, which added to their confusion.

"Let's pick a direction, so we can find our way out," said Michael. "I suggest we continue our trek towards the outcropping since that is where we received the message. We might find some answers."

Malachy nodded.

Their journey continued, the passages winding as the options became more and more daunting. They turned a corner no different than the previous hundred before it and stood at the entrance to a room dipping to a stage—like a miniature theater. The area could seat about five hundred angels on its partially concentric benches. A red inscription was penned on the stage's back wall, but it was too far away to decipher.

Malachy and Michael walked down, listening and looking for anything that may trap them. They climbed the stage and approached the wall to get a closer look at the three words:

Mene, Mene Tekel[133]

Malachy ran her finger over them and stepped back. "This is an ancient language. Angels don't speak it anymore."

"What does it say?" Michael ran his fingers through the letters.

133   Daniel 5

"What does it mean?"

Malachy turned. "It translates to 'Your existence is short and coming to an end. You have been found guilty.'"

A cold chill ran through Michael. Why did God send them here to read this message? He thought about times when his faith had faltered, his pride suffocating his loyalty to Him.

Malachy continued. "But I can't tell you who it was written to."

"I can," said a voice echoing from the back of the auditorium.

Devastated by the loss of his friend, Azarias pondered about how God worked. Why had He let this happen? The painful moment returned, digging into his heart like a blade. God didn't let this happen; Uriel chose it. The timid angel sacrificed himself for Azarias.

The Septemviri leader had to bury the thought. He had to focus on the present.

"Mai Deus Exsisto vobis. I am Jael, Thyatira's District Administrator," started the angel as she helped him out of the beached craft. Up close and surrounded by the little light of the Spirit, she appeared more beautiful than she had looked from the boat. Her cyanic blue eyes reflected the residual flickers of the Lord's Spirit, pirouetting around her head like miniature stars, their tiny tongues of fire dimming and brightening to God's rhythmic pulses.

"I am—"

"I know who you are, Azarias." She motioned towards a dimly lit tunnel behind her. "God's Spirit has told us about the Septemviri and your whereabouts from our Thyatira spy. We look forward to you training us as warriors."

Training. Azarias thought back to Leihja's training session. She was training just seven of them. How could he train dozens, thousands, millions? The thought shifted his eyes from Jael as if they were looking for the answer on the cave wall.

He refocused. "How many are you?"

"Follow me." She smiled and turned into a side tunnel.

Azarias followed the stunning angel, her golden hair braided into three strands, tapering to a sharp point at the waist. He had seen many colors of hair, but none twisted. How many more unique appearances would he see as he searched Heaven for other hidden angels?

The two angels moved through the passageway, its width expanding until about five angels could stand shoulder to shoulder, the Lord's Spirit increasing in numbers, flickering in the atmosphere around them, passages merging into and out of their causeway during their journey.

"Wait," said Azarias. A strange glow caught his eye from the channel to the left, its luminescence greater than the area around him. He turned and followed the light to a room. He entered, but only took a few steps. A reflective material covered the entire surface in front of his feet and the room's walls, his image multiplying many times. He looked up and met a thousand of his own eyes staring, his many reflections above and below him.

"Our angels have suffered a great deal, Azarias," whispered Jael behind him. We built this room for them to immerse themselves in God's Holy Spirit and the Word of God." Azarias walked into the middle of the room, the Holy Spirit's flickering points replicating farther than he could see. It reminded him of the visions he had seen of the material world and the stars suspended in the universe's vastness, though those were inadequate copies compared to this reality. Instead of the universe's dying, fiery objects glowing from a distance, the true everlasting light of the Lord's Spirit flickered just inches from his face, its radiance luring him into the infinity around him.

A faint singing stroked his ears. He focused on one of the tongues of lights, its movement rhythmic to the music. Azarias stood very still, in his prex précis position—head down, hands at the side, palms up. Infinite harmonies filled him with joy.[134] The

134   Psalms 46:10

Lord was singing to him in a language he couldn't translate but understood.[135]

Azarias looked up at Jael, standing at the threshold. The smile on her face revealed that she knew what he was experiencing, but her demeanor broadcasted haste.

The two angels returned to the main tunnel, its ceiling rising to about fifty feet, other tunnels intersecting from both sides. The angels took flight, meandering along the path, banking at turns, with God's flickering lights appearing as lines of lights, no longer pinpoints. Azarias retracted his armor and sword to keep up with the fast angel. The armor slowed his flying—a hindrance during chases.

Though Jael stood at the average height of ten feet, her wings stretched longer than twelve feet high. The tips didn't top out at fifteen feet like Gabriel's wings, but somewhere around thirteen or fourteen. As with all angels, the larger the wings, the greater the receptors for receiving God's Spirit and, so, the faster their speed.

The lighted ambiance increased in intensity as she slowed down. Azarias could hear a murmur in the distance, like what he heard in the courtyard with the chanting angels. A chill touched his spirit as he thought back to that moment just a little while ago—trance-like angels parading in a circle.

The two travelers touched down, their feet slowing the momentum into a walk, a light glaring through an opening in front of them. Azarias asked her where they were going as the voices coming through the passageway down the corridor became deafening.

As they entered, Azarias stood on an open platform where two parabolic arcs, above and below, expanded before him, seating about five hundred thousand angels in a submerged stadium. The venue dwarfed even the Smyrna Paestra, where Gabriel and other angels competed in games.

The angels seemed to be organized into countless cohorts, deliberating within their worlds.

---

135   1 Corinthians 14:1-2

Azarias turned to Jael, her eyes glowing from the Holy Spirit's consuming presence.[136] Another angel, with deep, dark bronze skin, approached them, his face elated. "You found him!" The angel turned to Azarias. "Thank you for saving my life from those two Satanic brutes. Once you rescued me, I flew back here to tell the others that our rescuers were close. We took turns watching every passage for you and your army."

Azarias's eyes recognized the features of the angel attacked in Thyatira, but, this time, they were not distressed.

"My name is Jeremiel. Thank God! He answered my prayers when Gaius and Spurius attacked me. Where is your companion? I must thank him also."

Azarias's eyes welled up as he drew a deep breath to dam his tears.

Jeremiel's face lost its enthusiasm. He held Azarias's hand. "I'm sorry." He choked up. "Your friend sacrificed his life for me."

"No, he sacrificed it for me."

Jeremiel turned Azarias's hands upwards. He pulled back the sleeve, exposing the burning Septemviri symbol. "I knew one of you were near when my mark burned at the Thyatira staircase. I lost faith and fled after they released me. You were courageous to challenge hundreds for my sake."

Jeremiel's eyes saddened as he placed his hand on Azarias's shoulder, quickly gazing to Jael for some relief, who chimed in. "I'm sorry. We, too, cannot get used to an angel killing. We have lost so many who couldn't defend themselves."

He turned back to Azarias. "What was your friend's name?"

"Uriel."

Jeremiel closed his eyes and whispered below the rumble of those far behind him. "Lord, we praise your Name. Thank you for securing the safety of Azarias and me. We don't understand your plan, Lord. We don't understand why Uriel and so many others have had their heavenly lives taken from them and were exiled into the material world. We ask that you protect Uriel and the others and

136   Hebrews 12:29

use them in your plan to defeat Satan and his evil forces. In the name of the Word, we pray."

Jeremiel raised his head and continued. "I gather that you and Uriel were scouts for a much larger force who joined your battle to defeat the Thyatira rebels. I am surprised that you secured the district so quickly and came to look for us."

Jael put her hands together, her face glowing, her eyes wide open. "How many millions are you? Are we to be armed and join them? We can secure Thyatira as you take your divisions throughout the rest of Heaven. We just need weapons like yours and training."

Azarias's face remained downtrodden. His shoulders slumped, and his breathing slowed. "Seven."

"Seven million?" responded Jael. "That is a good number to start the battle, especially if we have superior weapons."

"No, seven angels. I lost one but gained a trainer. We count as seven armed angels at this point."

Silence imposed itself around the three angels as the two absorbed Azarias's comment. Jeremiel started to laugh but then stopped.

Azarias stepped by them and looked over the rail to the multitude below them. "Others will join us, but the hidden angels will be the first line of our counterattack once freed and trained. We are starting with you."

Both Jael and Jeremiel walked next to him but didn't say anything.

"How can I get everyone's attention?" asked Azarias.

Jael motioned to a row of angels on ledges on either side of them. A cacophony of horns sounded, halting conversations, thousands of heads turning towards the stage where the three stood.

"I am Azarias of the Septemviri. We are only seven but will grow to a force large enough to conquer Satan. What may seem impossible for angels is possible for God."[137]

He turned to Jael. "Are there many exits out of here to the world above?"

"Yes, many of them—all along the seats."

---

137   Luke 18:27

Azarias turned back to the audience. "Please file out of the nearest exit and fly to the Septemviri headquarters in the Al Birka wilderness. We will arm and train you to defeat Satan and his Legions."

"Which will never happen," grumbled a voice from the tunnel behind them.

Azarias turned.

Spurius and a tunnel-full of Satan's legionnaires stepped into the light.

CHAPTER 12

Azarias's worst fears rose in his heart as his failures continued to mount. In Thyatira, he had revealed their covert
operation to save one angel, pitting him and Uriel against
an insurmountable force. Then he lost Uriel's life in Heaven and
almost his own. And now he'd led Satan's Legion to the angels he
was trying to rescue and protect.

Spurius stepped forward, his grin painted from ear to ear, spear
and whip weapons in his hands. "After your feeble attempt to fight
in Thyatira, I wondered why the Creator picked you to lead his
armies. You're so pathetic."

He looked to Jeremiel and the others, their faces melding
fear and surprise. Spurius lifted his hands, palms up. "Why do
you put your faith in Azarias—or in the Creator, for that matter?
Look at what Satan and his Legions have accomplished. We have
found our destiny through our free will—a gift the Creator hid
from all angels, I might add. Then Satan gave this knowledge to
the one-third of Heaven who had seen the god within themselves,
in exchange for our faith in him. One-third of Heaven's angels
cannot be wrong!"

Spurius's olive tint seemed to flow through his bronze skin as
he spoke, swirling faster and fueling his speech to grow even more
evil. It reminded Azarias of the serpent demons' flowing faces, a
memory he'd like to forget.

Spurius continued. "I anticipated finding angels, considering
the blundering fool who was leading me. I dispatched tens of thou-

sands of legionnaires among the peaks above us. They will destroy or capture angels trying to escape. We will not get all of you, but we will disburse this little meeting, sending the rest of your angels all over Heaven and away from Al Birka."

As Spurius spoke, the angels from the arena took notice and ceased their discussions. He spun the spear in one hand, the faces of Satan on the guard glowing with pride. He turned to Jael and grabbed her face, his forefinger and thumb squeezing her chin. "And, for your commanders, we have a special prison for you."

Jael's eyes turned from fear to anger. She slapped his hand from her face and looked up at the horn-wielding angels above the doorway and yelled, "This is the time the Lord has made. Let us rejoice and be glad!"[138]

A dozen angels blew their horns, notes bouncing off the ceiling and walls to the waiting ears below. Angels all over the stadium scurried to disappear through the many escapes. The horn blowers released a second blast, bringing hundreds of tongue-lit spirits from the ceiling rafters directly into Spurius and his comrades' faces. Spurius tried to bat the flying spirits that attacked his eyes. He fell to the surface, groping for his hatchet-spear and whip. Azarias could see that Spurius was blinded.[139]

Azarias drew his sword and donned his armor as he rushed the enemy's ranks, slashing left and right, cutting their flailing arms as they battled the micro-spirits that were burning them. Black particles of the disintegrating angels dropped to the surface and filled the tunnel as the distant Siq stirred them and then sucked them into the material world.

Jael picked up Spurius's spear as he rolled to his left side, cupping his eyes, still unable to see from the stinging swarm of spirits. She drove the fiery tip of the spear through Spurius's temple, pinning him to the place where he lay, his body disintegrating into black particles, exploding debris across her feet before surrendering

138   Psalm 118:24
139   Acts 9:8-9

to their ultimate destination. [140]

Azarias drove the others back into the tunnel with his sword, his armor protecting him against their desperate thrusts, while their compacted arrangement hampered the use of their spears and whips. Once he had distanced himself from those in the tunnel, Azarias shifted the Word into a bow and shot an arrow into the tunnel, penetrating its ceiling, exploding into a bright white flash, and collapsing the tunnel entrance.

Jael grabbed the powerful staff and pulled it out of the surface where Spurius once lay. She turned and yelled for the remaining angels to exit quickly.

"Come on. We have to go!" screamed Azarias.

"No," she shouted back, grabbing his arm. "The first must be last."[141]

They waited until the last angel existed, and Jael then released Azarias. "Come on. We have to help them escape from any enemy angels guarding the peaks."

The two commanding angels flew out an adjacent tunnel not far from the platform. God's Spirit lit the way, as the legionnaire angels were nowhere in sight. Meandering up and out in a cautious flight pattern, Azarias could see an exit grow brighter in the distance. If the loyalists had built this right, they should be escaping from all over, making it impossible for a few thousand legionnaires to herd them.

Azarias emerged out of the tunnel exit, his mouth open, his eyes scanning the area. The atmosphere was grey, not bright, signaling that the enemy was nearby.

He scanned the peaks as far as he could see. Tens of thousands of enemy angels covered the entire local range with a netted dome. White feather-type particles crunched under his and Jael's feet and filled the atmosphere like Earth's cottonwood trees do, blowing seeds. The assaulters were slaughtering the Thyatira angels by the hundreds.

---

140   Judges 4:21
141   Mark 9:35

Azarias flew up to the net. The Legion had greatly extended their energized whips into long cables and bound their ends together in mesh-shaped netting, preventing the loyalists from escaping.

Many loyal angels panicked and crashed into the dome barrier, only to be quickly dissolved into the Lord's wind, covering the range tops in white fluff before being dragged out through the Siq.

Azarias flew back down to a rigid Jael. "Oh my Lord," she screamed, standing among the remains of her friends before they made their final journey. She turned to Azarias, her eyes wet with sorrow. "What can we do?"

Azarias eyed the situation and turned to her, his heart beating faster, his guilt tugging at this spirit. "I led the enemy here; I will get the loyalists out."

GABRIEL LED SQUATINIDALE AND RAFAELLA UP THE PROfundo River towards Thyatira, its slow-moving current sharing no hints of any dangers, the canyon bluffs standing steadfast in silence except for their small streams falling hundreds of feet to the thirsty river below.

He held the broken staff in his hand, its glow flashing sporadically. He pondered its function and why it rested at the bottom of the river in the wilderness. Nothing happened in Heaven and the material universe without reason. Whatever was hidden is meant to be disclosed, and whatever was concealed is meant to be exposed.[142]

Gabriel spotted his cairns along the way—white ones, built during his missions well before the rebellion spread. Heaven had been so peaceful and joyful.

How could one angel disrupt creation? The thought boggled his mind. One prideful angel—that's it just one—and the entire heavenly landscape, and maybe the material world, was set on fire with a revolt. If one angel can cause that, what can millions do?

He thought about his role in this epic battle. Where would he

---

142   Mark 4:22

fit into the plan? Like any angel, he was just a mere messenger. God hadn't given him any unique gifts like the others. God had spoken to him clearly at the Smyrna Angelus Pennae race, where Gabriel flew into a lavender amborlite haze. Back then, the rumble of thunder came from the lavender amborlite on the high slopes. The Lord spoke:

> GABRIEL, MY SPEEDY MESSENGER,
> I CLOTHE YOU IN THE PURPLE OF ROYALTY
> AND SORROW. YOU WILL STAND IN THE
> PRESENCE OF GOD AND BRING IMPORTANT
> NEWS TO THOSE WHO WILL FURTHER THE
> COURSE OF THE LORD'S GREAT PLAN. THESE
> WORDS, PROCLAIMED BY YOU, WILL ECHO
> IN THE HEARTS OF MANY FOR ETERNITY. AS
> THE PURPLE WILL BE USED TO REPRESENT
> BOTH ROYALTY AND SORROW,
> SO WILL OUR MESSAGES.[143]

He had never mentioned this personal message to anyone, and honestly, he didn't understand most of it—just the part about performing as a messenger, which is what he had carried out for his entire existence. Gabriel was honored that the Lord would speak to him, but God speaks to all angels. What depressed him was that this Word of God, this custom message, this divine proclamation, did not tell him anything he didn't already know about his gifts—just that he was a messenger. You would think if you were to get a calling from God, it would include some great revelation. Maybe Gabriel didn't understand, especially the "royalty and sorrow" part. What can be more sorrowful than the current heavenly circumstances?

He thought about the others—Azarias, the leader; Malachy, the historian; Rafaella, with her wisdom and compassion; Uriel and

---

143   Luke 1:19-20; 1:26-28

his navigation; and Michael, the ultimate warrior. The two who remained were Squatinidale and himself, who had no real personal functions—though he couldn't speak for Squatinidale.

Though bewilderment and confusion marred his existence, Gabriel still believed that God would complete whatever work he was to do.[144]

Gabriel sighed and looked to the large streams falling over the cliffs to the Profundo River. His mind shifted to the enemy angels. Why had so many plunged over the edge only to smash against "a bottom" they couldn't imagine? By themselves, each would have made an insignificant contribution to Heaven's revolt, but together, they combined into a great river of discontent, deception, and self-destruction.

There was so much he didn't understand.

"Are we halfway to Thyatira?" asked Squatinidale.

"I can't tell you for sure because detailed navigation is not my strong point, like with Uriel. Azarias has a great companion in his travels, except for Uriel's nervousness." He turned to Squatinidale. "But we all have shortcomings."

The three followed the waterway, the cliff sides pulling back from it, the river slowing down. The canyon spread out to the sides, an amborlite meadow diverting the river that eventually fought for its path. They landed. Squatinidale walked over to a swaying amborlite and plucked one from a stalk. "Did I tell you about my vision in a little flower like this? Back before you rescued me, God provided one amborlite flower in the desolate part of Heaven. He showed me a psychedelic display of Satan's invasion. It started beautifully with great colors and spun until the five-pointed black star appeared. I didn't know the meaning until I met you. Amazingly, God can create such wonders in the smallest of places and greater works that can extend to the peaks in the distance beyond us—"

Squatinidale abruptly stopped, his eyes focusing towards the end of the valley. Rafaella and Gabriel followed his gaze and turned.

---

144 Romans 8:28

In the far distance, two peaks stood with a dark mist between them.

"What do you think it is?" asked Squatinidale.

"Is it moving down the slope?" responded Rafaella.

"I don't think so. It looks stationary," said Squatinidale.

"Hold on." Gabriel flew straight up, much higher than the cliffs, to get a better view. It seemed the Lord's Spirit struggled to move the mist in waves with Satan's dark shadows gliding over it.

The other two angels joined Gabriel, all concentrating on this odd phenomenon. "Satan had to create this," started Squatinidale. "I don't see why God would create such a haze—besides, it is dark, not light."

They flew forward, but not at a great speed. They needed to proceed carefully, checking each cliff, meadow, and waterway for enemy angels.

"Let's go to the ridge up ahead and examine it from there. We can hide behind the peak in case there is danger."

The trio flew the long distance to the ridge bordering the left side of the canyon. They hid among the crags and precipices and crept over the rim to peer across the adjoining valley towards the two peaks. A black, energized net swooped down between the two peaks, resting on the slope between them. It appeared to imprison the whole section between the outcroppings onto the surface.

"Another Satan abomination. This one looks like a barrier to keep someone out. Maybe us," murmured Rafaella.

"Where does he get his power to do such things?" cried Squatinidale.

"Evil," said Gabriel. "We have seen that Satan can use his force of evil to change the goodness of God in all creations, including the hearts of other angels. It is a new force that we have to battle, though we cannot see it."

Squatinidale turned his back to a wall, his eyes wide. "Then how do we fight an invisible force?"

"We fight it with a more powerful invisible force, the Spirit of God. The only challenge is that angels will have to choose between the two—God's never-ending love, mercy, and grace or Satan's lies and false promises."

Rafaella turned and sat next to Squatinidale. "The battle rages within all of us, but we must also fight the external battle to contain it from metastasizing throughout the universe."

Squatinidale lowered his head, his eye contact directed at his feet. "How can we fight this spiritual battle within us? I already have failed."

"God is faithful; he will not let you be tempted beyond what you can bear. When you are tempted, he will always provide a way out so that you can endure it," said Rafaella.[145]

Gabriel stood, his eyes drawn to the peaks. "Look, there is action."

Thousands of tiny white specks flew up to the barrier and were extinguished in hundreds of flashes. Many more thousands flew in disorganized circles, each apparently trying to find an exit from this two-peak barrier.

Gabriel's eyes focused, his fists clenched. "This net is not a barrier to keep us out. It is a prison to keep angels in. Those must be the hidden Thyatira angels." He looked down and then back up, "Come on. We have to go now; Satan is killing them in droves."

The three took flight, the destination still far away. "But we are only three. How can we save thousands in a deathly prison?" asked Squatinidale.

"We use our strongest weapon," responded Rafaella. "Faith."

---

145   1 Corinthians 10:13

CHAPTER 13

Michael knew that Sardis had mysteries, but this turn of events challenged him. He marveled at how Malachy had deciphered clues from the burning bush's inscription, leading her to insert her sword to the enlightened slot. Her mind functioned in a manner he'd never seen.

Yet, the mysteries and danger never seemed to end. The uncovering of the Sardis labyrinth had presented more questions than answers. The cryptic writing on the wall, *Mene, Mene Tekel—your existence is short and coming to an end; you have been found guilty—*upwelled guilt and fear in Michael. Had someone written it for him? [146] Lastly, this unexpected visitor surprised them.

The burly angel walked down the aisle. Michael and Malachy stood alert with their weapons at their sides. The stranger wore a magenta border on the bottom of his robe—a sign that he belonged to the enemy angels.

"Hello, my name is Zepar," he bellowed, his large arms bridging the center aisle. "I know what you are thinking. You fear me because I wear the robe border of Thyatira like those of Satan's forces."

The angel stepped onto the stage, his magenta eyes matching the border of his robe, his face reflecting his brass-colored hair.

"Stop there," warned Michael, his armor in full glory, the sword held in front of his face. He craned his neck but saw no one else.

The mysterious angel halted and smiled, casting his eyes slightly

---

146   Daniel 5

downwards. "You would be justified in the way you feel—a long time ago. You are members of the Septemviri, are you not?"

"Yes," whispered Michael, trying not to attract more enemy angels. The lower he spoke, the higher the likelihood he could avoid the hearing of unseen ears.

The angel turned to the side and paced, his robe slightly moving in the Lord's Spirit. "Long ago, when your quest had begun, I met your partners, Uriel and Azarias. Abaddon attacked them in Thyatira. We hid in the Great Hall's paintings and emerged once we cornered the two. I helped in the attack but cannot tell you how they escaped." He shrugged his shoulders. "We had angels posted at all exits."

"Those two just returned to Thyatira," interjected Malachy. "What do you know of them?"

"I know nothing. I have not returned to Thyatira for some time." He turned. His eyes shifted to the side, focusing nowhere, and then back. "I was proud of my new destiny, discovering my will, making my decisions, and choosing my path."

He paused again.

"That was before I came here, this hidden world of Sardis. The cave opening on the top of the peak summoned us to meet when our music played."

"Was that the horrible clamor I heard during the last visit when angels flew over the peak to meet Satan?" asked Michael.

"One angel's music is another angel's noise," said Zepar, his face smiling.

"It may have looked like we flew over the peak from the columns," said the stranger, "but we flew up to the peak and through the cave opening. We entered our world and developed our strategies here, thousands upon thousands of us."

Michael still didn't lower his guard. He thought that the angel might be stalling for reinforcements. "Look, we don't have time to hear your story. You are unarmed, so we can't fight you, but we must detain you while we investigate these rooms."

"Please, let me finish. I can tell you a lot about this area."

Zepar sat down.

"The last time I was in this room was to meet on tactics, specifically plans to find the hidden Sardis angels."

The angel looked up to the wall. "That's when it appeared."

"What appeared?" asked Malachy.

"The hand."

"Hand? Whose hand?" asked Michael, gazing quickly and then back to his guest.

Zepar eyes returned to his audience of two. "One of our lieutenants stood where you were, praising our division for the good work in the war. Then, behind him, at about head height, appeared a red hand, dripping with blood like we've seen circulating in the bodies of creatures in our visions of Earth. The lieutenant jumped back as a bloody finger wrote those words. *Mene, Mene Tekel.*"[147]

"So, the hand directed the script to you and your angels?" asked Michael, relief finding a home in his heart.

"Yes. The room erupted in chaos, some angels shouting that it was the Creator trying to scare the Legion, others saying it was a trick by Satan to test our resolve. Regardless, the hand did not leave, but stayed next to the writing. The lieutenant struggled to keep his composure, seeing many members freezing with fright."

"Then things got worse. The bloody hand clenched a fist and pointed to the Legion seated in the auditorium, casting judgment, scanning from left to right. I almost collapsed but regained my strength, like others, and fled through the exit up high on the peak."

Malachy interjected. "We saw the large cave, but it was closed, a large block of debris blocking its entrance."

The angel opened his hands. "The story spread throughout the Legion like a wild profundo river. Many would not reenter these hidden chambers afterward. If the stunt was from the Creator, He had fulfilled His purpose. If from Satan, he determined which angels had the tenacity to fight to the end. Satan ordered the cave opening closed."

---

147   Ibid.

Michael lowered his sword and motioned for Malachy to do the same, the risk factor dropping a notch. "Why are you here?"

"I hid in the structure of Sardis after the closing. I had to think about my past, my present, and my future. I compared myself, as a god, to the Creator. I realized that the Creator has neither past nor future, so everything is present—therefore, He is truly 'I Am.'[148] But not for us angels; we are part of creation, so we have to think in a linear fashion—at least at this point of limited knowledge."

"Why are you telling us this?" shot back Michael, crossing his arms, his jaw tightening.

"I realized that I am not a god," said the visitor. If I can't fathom time and creation, how can I be equal to the Creator? I knew that I had turned away and had to get back to the Lord if He would take me."

He looked up, his eyes brimming with tears. "Then I saw you land in the courtyard."

Malachy stepped forward, retracting her sword blade. "You could not have realized God's deity, except through God's Spirit.[149] As far as coming back to the Lord, the Lord your God is gracious and compassionate. He will not turn his face from you if you return to him."[150]

"We are compassionate to anyone who wants to return to the Lord, even though we are on a mission of judgment, not mercy as before," said Michael, lowering his sword, blade remaining activated. "I am still skeptical that you have come back to the Lord. How can we be sure?"

Zepar stood and walked back towards the exit, yelling to an audience that had long deserted the seats. "I can show you my sincerity."

"How?" chimed in Malachy.

"When I saw how you entered this hidden city, I knew that other angels must be present down here—members of the Holy Order, the loyalists."

---

148   Anselm, *Proslogion*, translated by Thomas Williams, Chapter 22, page 20-21; Exodus 3:14
149   Matthew 16:17
150   2 Chronicles 30:9

"How can you be so sure?" yelled Michael, now following Zepar up the aisle. "We have seen nobody and have walked through many tunnels."

"I would think that the Creator wouldn't have sealed the entrance so elaborately if He were not trying to protect angels."

"How can that be? Malachy rushed to Michael's side. "You said Satan closed the only entrance to the city, upon the peak."

Zepar turned back at the exit, a smile lining his face. "It is only a hunch. Let's find them and ask. I know these passageways better than anyone."

Azarias watched the dire situation unfold, enemy angels guarding an enormous dark power net, his new confidant, Jael, standing in the fleeting remains of what were her friends. All of this happened because he wasn't careful. He had let the enemy follow him to destroy the angels he was trying to protect. He must test this web if he were to free them.

Azarias flew up into the netting above, dodging desperate angels trying to escape. He slipped the shield of faith over one shoulder at the net, cutting a tear with the shield's edge.[151] The Septemviri commander flew the great length of the net where he sliced a gash, the ends of the webbing still clinging to the two peaks. The trapped angels poured out of the opening, where the Legion members cut them down into white fluff, their bodies dissolving into particles. Other angels collided with comrades who had reconsidered their escape.

Azarias dove back to Jael, who looked on with horror. He handed the Word of God to her, blade extended, Spirit infused.

"Go to your trumpeters and have them blow a signal for all angels to follow you after I slice another opening in the net. I will create a distraction. You saw how I used the sword; do your best to defend your friends in your getaway."

"But Azarias, you will be without a weapon!" cried Jael.

151   Ephesians 6:16

He stared into her eyes. "The Lord is my weapon.[152] God is my refuge and strength, an ever-present help in trouble.[153] The shield of faith will extinguish anything Satan's Legion casts at me."[154]

Jael's eyes were fixated on the sword in her hand. He clutched her other hand and stared. "I love you, Jael; I love all of you. All we have is faith, hope, and love. But the greatest of these is love."[155]

Her mouth pressed a smile, but her eyes swelled with tears.

Azarias flew up to the web's opening with his shield. He sliced another gash on the net where it sagged on the peak. This cut almost intersected the other cut at right angles. He stopped short of where the two rips met in the net's middle, not severing them completely. He flew up towards the first opening, guarded by a company of enemy angels, and yelled, "Our God is a God who saves; from the Sovereign Lord comes escape from death."[156]

The large group of enemy angels attacked, flying through the ripped net, eyes filled with hatred and fiery spears in hand. Azarias dove down towards the base of the peak, using all the Spirit's resources to increase his speed as the enemy angels closed in from behind.

He stopped just before the outcropping's surface and turned. Azarias waited until the first wave of angels had almost reached him and then charged back at them, his shield extinguishing the flaming spears and ramming the evil ones who remained in his way, their bodies breaking up into black particles.

As he passed the last enemy angel, he heard a voice yell, "Let him go. The others will exterminate him as he tries to escape."

Azarias stopped at the intersection where the two severed pieces met, connected at each peak, straining by the torn section's weight. Azarias sawed into the net, using the edge of the shield again, detaching a triangle-shaped piece that swung down onto the

---

152   Jerimiah 51.20
153   Psalms 46:1
154   Ephesians 6:16
155   1 Corinthians 13:13
156   Psalms 68:20

peak's lower slopes. The enemy angels tried to escape to the sides of the oncoming, flaming mesh. The webbing scooped up the angels, smashing them against the peak's slope, black particles exploding through the fibers before departing towards the Siq.

Trumpeters blasted a high note as Jael rocketed to the new opening, sword in hand, breaking free with the surviving loyalists. Enemy angels countered from the distant peak, spears blazing. Azarias flew towards the charge and then dove downwards, luring many of the attacking angels with him.

He flew in figure eights, trying to shake them, deflecting their spears with his shield and armor. Looking down below, he spotted the cave opening that he and Jael had emerged from earlier. If he could get back into the cave, he may be able to lose them among its many passages.

One enemy angel stepped out through the opening and stood with a fiery whip, unaware of Azarias's charge. Azarias accelerated, his head hidden behind the shield, into the unsuspecting angel, destroying him. The Septemviri flew into the cave and navigated its pathways, the shouts of enemy angels closely behind.

He re-entered the arena, now empty of the angels of God. Azarias flew in circles looking for another escape among the thousands of seats, his foes spanning out among the sections, trying to eliminate his chance of escaping.

The many exits confused him; their widths were too narrow for him to fly through. Whichever he chose, he would have to escape on foot. More enemy angels poured into the vast forum.

Azarias lunged towards an unguarded opening, his feet hitting the surface in a run while his pursuers funneled behind. He diverted to side pathways, trying to lose his followers, searching for clues of the Profundo River that had brought him here.

The attackers' voices echoed through the corridors, teasing him as to their locations. He avoided side paths because he couldn't be sure if the enemy occupied them. He had turned so many times that he had lost his sense of direction, the cave's light now dimming with the influx of more enemy angels, their spirits extinguishing it. He thought about when the enemy had pursued him and Uriel while visiting the Thyatira castle the first time. The Priest, Melchizedek saved them in the hidden room.[157] Where was he now?

Azarias's passage opened into the reflection room, where the ceiling was twenty feet high. Reflective material covered the top, sides, and floor. There must be another exit. He turned in every direction, only to see himself, the image of a failed leader, a loser of faith. The voices echoed louder as they drew closer.

An angel with a menacing smile stopped at the opening. "Well, it looks like we found the leader reflecting on his failures as a commander." Other angels joined him and started to laugh.

Another angel came forward, pushing others aside. "Nice to finally speak to you, Azarias. We have always wondered what it would take to make you realize that you were fighting for a losing cause." She gazed at the round room's walls. The enemy commander shifted her eyes, "I don't know why the Thyatira angels built this, but it will allow you to examine yourself and consider why you should defect to the enlightened side."

She stepped into the room. Azarias raised his shield. "Don't worry. We won't harm you—yet. We want you alive to lure—no, convince—the other Septemviri and loyalists to join our side. You are valuable to us, though not as a warrior." The others laughed again.

Another angel shoved his way to the opening. "Commander, three other angels who flew up the valley are hiding on another ridge. I think they're armed."

She turned to Azarias, her face sporting a small smile, "I guess your friends will fly into our trap. We may not need you after all." The enemy commander walked back out and sealed the exit with the power net and turned to a shorter angel. "Sosthenes, you watch over the prisoner.[158] I place sole responsibility on you. If he escapes, you will pay the ultimate penalty."

---

157   Hebrews 7
158   Acts 18:17; 1 Corinthians 1:1

CHAPTER 14

Angels poured out of the ripped webbed canvas, their faces wracked with fear, pursued by enemy angels. Leading them was a braided golden-haired angel and trumpeters, blasting their call.

"Look," yelled Rafaella. "The leader is carrying the Word sword!"

The three stopped, hovering a safe distance from the onslaught.

"How did she get the weapon from Uriel or Azarias?" asked Squatinidale.

Gabriel's gut wrenched as he rifled through the possibilities—was Uriel dead? Was Azarias dead? Both dead? Had this angel killed them? Were they bad or good angels? He couldn't tell at this distance.

Rafaella converted the Word into a bow and aimed an arrow at the offensive.

Gabriel turned to her. "Fire a warning shot at the peak on the right and see what they do."

A fiery arrow pierced the atmosphere, blazing past the oncoming angels, its path screaming the sound of judgment, impacting just under the peak, silicium exploding in all directions.

The lead angel stopped, posting her hand out to halt the other angels. She held her arm up, the loyalists' sign burning, and the sword's blades retracted into its hilt.

"She's a loyalist," proclaimed Rafaella.

The three flew towards her, their weapons in hand, their pace transitioning from defensive to offensive. Behind the multitude was another large contingent of angels holding fiery whips and rings.

Gabriel halted the other two. "There's our enemy." The three Septemviri angels flew high into the atmosphere, allowing the loyalists to escape. They paused and activated their Word bows and fired arrows at the attackers in the distance. Three massive explosions burst, casted amborlite-shaped flares in all directions, dissolving the leaders into black particles. The next wave of attacking angels halted before entering the fiery zone.

Two of the attacking angels banked around the explosion, their whip ends trailing from their sashes. Rafaella drove down, intersecting them before they caught up to the escaping angels. One of the enemy angels peeled off, his whip now firmly in his hand, its fiery point the only light in his soul. He swung the whip over his head in a circle, increasing its speed. Then he reversed its direction before snapping it at Rafaella. A loud sizzle blasted from the whip's tip, its echo bouncing among the peaks. The tip hit her breastplate of righteousness, repelling her with a jolt, sending her into a backwards summersault.

Rafaella regained control just as the attacking angel attempted a second strike. She raised her sword and caught the end of the whip around her interwoven blades, sending sharp bolts of dark and white energy into all directions, fusing the assailant's hand onto his handle. She spun the helpless menace, her sword held with both hands above her head, whirling him in circles. With each revolution, the whip thong wrapped itself tighter, increasing its revolutions, bringing the attacker closer to Rafaella's blade.

At the angel's last circuit, Rafaella ducked her head, her sword held high, as the intruder spun into the blades, disintegrating into millions of black particles in a flash. She lowered her blade, allowing the smoldering black whip and angel remains to slide off its end.

The other rogue angel caught up to some of the escaping loyalists. He engaged his whip, striking two of the angels, transforming them into white particles, their screaming voices trailing off into another dimension. On the second assault, he drew back the whip, but it snagged behind him. Turning around, he discovered his whip entangled on Squatinidale's sword. The stout Septemviri angel yanked at the whip, casting the helpless angel back into the remnants of the explosion that had claimed the lives of his enemy comrades.

Gabriel watched with a mixture of horror and pride. Leihja had transformed the Septemviri into warriors, though they were insignificant in number.

The loyalist angel and her group circled back to Gabriel, her golden hair trailing, cyanic blue eyes riveted. "Mai Deus Exsisto vobis." My name is Jael, Thyatira's Administrator. Thank you for saving us."

"Mai Deus Exsisto vobis," replied Gabriel, his tone shallow and shaky. He pointed to the Word sword in her hand. "Who gave that to you?"

"Azarias. He lured the enemy away from us. They killed many of my fellow angels, but they would have killed us all if not for Azarias."

Gabriel glanced at Rafaella and Squatinidale, who had returned, their eyes challenging each other to ask the dreaded question.

He turned back to the Jael. "What about Uriel?"

Her eyes narrowed, and she shook her head. "I never met him. I only met Azarias. I think he said the Legion killed Uriel in Thyatira."

Gabriel's heart sank. Could they have lost one of their own? No. God protected them. After all, they were only seven. Why would God commission them to come this far only to lose their lives to the enemy? Didn't they have enough faith, or was Satan's resolve too strong for them?

"Do you know where Azarias may have gone?" asked Gabriel, his voice increasing in speed.

Jael shrugged. "I didn't look back, but he may have gone back into our tunnels under those peaks."

Gabriel turned to Rafaella. "We either have to rescue him or take these to safety in Al Birka."

He couldn't believe it. They had to decide whether to sacrifice their leader or save a multitude. Why had God allowed Satan to put them into this situation? Either decision had dire consequences.

"I shudder to say this, but I suggest we escort the Thyatira angels back to Al Birka. Someone will have to return to look for Azarias," said Rafaella, her eyes scanning Jael and the other two for affirmation.

"Whoever comes back, I should come with you," offered Jael. "The tunnels and the river are very confusing for anyone who didn't build them. We designed the tunnels to confuse strangers. These evil forces only found us because they followed Azarias, a possibility we couldn't foresee. The river also spawns tributaries. I know them all."

Gabriel armed his bow, looking to Squatinidale and Rafaella. "We are outnumbered if they skirt our defense. The three of us can't defend all of these loyalists. Start organizing the loyalists. I will create a diversion." He fired a barrage of explosive arrows at the two peaks, his impacts targeted at the cornices. The ridges tumbled down on both sides, trapping some of the enemy angels, sending others scurrying for cover.

Jael had the trumpeter regroup the angels. Rafaella organized the group into four massive V formations, an armed angel—Gabriel, Squatinidale, Jael, and herself—at the point of each.

Gabriel led the way for hundreds of thousands of angels, scanning the cliffs for a counterattack or ambush. He couldn't forget Azarias and Uriel. Both could have been dead, ejected out of Heaven forever. He tried to push the possibility out of his mind, another example of his weak faith. The thought that there were now only five living Septemviri gnawed at him—and that was assuming Michael and Malachy were still alive. If Azarias were dead, who would take leadership? How could they go on?

ZEPAR HADN'T CONVINCED MICHAEL ABOUT HIS SINCERITY. Still, he and Malachy had accepted his offer to help search for

Sardis's hidden angels since they had journeyed through many tunnels with no success.

Zepar spoke well, but Michael knew from Pollyon's defection that evil angels lie—an unthinkable and impossible behavior for angels before Satan had defected. The visitor walked in alone, unarmed—a good mark for him. He admitted he was a Thyatira angel who had attacked Azarias and Malachy; this was probably truthful but not determinative of his guilt or innocence at this stage. Finally, he offered to assist them in finding the hidden Sardis angels. This offer could go either way: if they collaborated with him, he may be able to help them rescue the angels. On the other hand, Zepar could summon his comrades to capture them. More disturbing was that his lieutenant could have posted Zepar "on watch," knowing that members of the Septemviri would return to Sardis. These possibilities fueled Michael's anxiety.

This dilemma engulfed Michael, not only for his safety but also for protecting a hundred thousand angels. Could their trust in the suspicious angel ultimately lead to the death of countless loyalists? Of themselves? Worse still, had he and Malachy surrendered to the curiosity of using the Word sword to enter, allowing the enemy angels into the barred subterranean metropolis? If so, why had the enemy waited? Why go through this maze of suspicion and delay the inevitable? The enemy angels would have invaded the tunnels once Malachy stuck her blade into the surface slot. Or not. Maybe the enemy angels were waiting until they discovered the hidden angels?

Michael whispered to Malachy, "The enemy is brilliant and strategic in everything they do. I am unequipped to find and lead so many angels to freedom. Do you feel the same way?"

"The Lord God is our strength and makes us sure-footed as we climb the path of uncertainty," said Malachy, as she perused every nook and niche.[159] She stopped and smiled at Michael. "I hit bottom when the enemy captured me long ago. I thought I would never see you again, but the Lord led you to my rescue, and He will lead

159　Habakkuk 3:19

you many times. For the Lord your God is the one who goes with you to fight for you against your enemies to give you victory."[160]

The three continued, passageways still retaining their light, a good sign that the Holy Spirit was present, possibly with loyal angels. The lack of intermittent darkness convinced Michael that enemy angels hadn't infiltrated the entrance and weren't hiding around corners, biding their time for the perfect ambush.

The tunnel opened into a large chamber displaying a dozen massive columns supporting a scalloped ceiling. Their circumferences were bigger than five interlocked angels holding hands around each one. Several arched hallways on both sides mocked the angels, teasing them towards their openings, each disappearing around distant turns, compounding the reality that the three could be lost for a long time.

Picture of Sardis's Underground Vaulted Hall

---

160   Deuteronomy 20:4

"Where are you taking us?" asked Malachy. "My maps are not relevant here."

Zepar's face turned grim, his eyes searching. "I'm sorry, everything looks so different when lit. We inhabited dark chambers with many dark shadows. The darkness drew us deeper, leading us to where we desired to go. The Creator's Spirit has altered my navigation. I no longer can function under my own will."

"Then why did you lead us if you didn't know where you were going?" said Malachy, her jaw tensed and eyes bolted.

"I have nothing to gain by leading you astray," fired back Zepar. "In fact, I have as much to lose as you since I am a traitor."

"Sshh," interrupted Michael, his big hands posted at each of their chests.

The three stood still, and one of Michael's hands shifted to his hilt.

Acapella singing echoed amongst the ceilings, masking its source. The arrangement appeared to be highly organized. Malachy walked to the side and leaned against the wall, her fingers spread, her ear pressed gently, and her eyes searching.

She crept another ten feet, placing her ear to the wall again. She turned. "This way; the vibrations are getting stronger over here."

Michael scanned for signs of an ambush, though the music was not twelve-tone as the enemy sang. The melody didn't appear to replicate any singing he had heard before—but he had to keep his guard up.

"We never sang any music down here," said Zepar, stopping short, scraping a hand through his hair. "Satan may have opened the cave once you entered. He knows everything! He is leading us into a—"

Michael spun Zepar and grabbed his shoulders, his big hands squeezing firmly, eyes widening. "Look, I don't know whether to believe you or not, but even though our hearts plan our way, the Lord will determine our steps, not you."[161]

He looked to Malachy. "Come on. Let's follow the voices. We don't need him."

---

161   Proverbs 16:9

Michael stopped and turned back. "Faith comes through hearing the Word of God.[162] When the second person of the triune God—the Word—spoke to us at God's Throne, we heard with our ears but understood with our hearts. Your heart has become calloused after turning from Him.[163] If you want to hear the Lord, you must open the eyes of your heart."[164]

Malachy led Michael along the wall, stopping at each of the arched openings. The voices grew louder, the echo not deceiving them as before.

Michael's eyes didn't trail Malachy, only his feet. He searched behind every massive pillar in the middle of the room, the passageways on the other side, and even the ceiling. The enemy could be anywhere, even perched above, as he remembered in Satan's lair where they rescued Malachy.

"The voices seem to be coming from the wall on the far side of the room," said Malachy. They crossed the span of the room to where a much larger arched threshold opened into a wide hallway. The two Septemviri entered, trailed by Zepar, the passageway opening up into an atrium with a path spilling off to each side. In front of them was another large archway mirroring the first.

Michael glanced around. "I'm confused. Do we go straight, left, or right? The music source is now directionless."

In front of them were two more large arched openings, one behind the other, each appearing to have a vestibule offering a pathway to the right and left.

"What's that at the end?" asked Malachy. "This hallway terminates into a picture."

The angels wandered through the next two arches, peering as far as they could see left and right until the intersecting passages curved out of their sight.

Michael, Malachy, and Zepar arrived at the end of the hall, a

---

162   Romans 10:17
163   Matthew 13:15
164   Ephesians 1:18

smaller path emptying to their right and left, a twenty-foot stele before them, the music growing louder.

"This wasn't here before," said Zepar, his voice softened and a tinge shaky.

The stele presented an image of a being similar to an angel, but without wings. The etching's face looked at a four-legged creature hanging on his shoulder, with a warm, inviting smile.

"I've seen that creature on his shoulder in a vision of Earth. Its hair is longer than others, curled into a thick, white coat, covering its entire body."

"Look at the being's attire who carries it," pointed Michael. "The sash around his chest is worn in the same place as the Word, whom we met at God's Throne."[165] He placed his hand on the small creature. "Why do you think he is carrying it? Is it unable to walk?"

"I don't know," said Malachy, "but it looks complacent, as if the holder rescued it after being trapped—"

"Or after being lost," beamed Michael.

"Like me," muttered Zepar, his head turned downwards.

Michael wondered if Zepar's heart could be changing? That was for God to know. He had to stay the course of protecting Malachy, and finding the angels.

"I think this is a good sign about finding the angels," said Michael. "It may be a signal for those lost while rescuing the ones who need to be found."[166]

He paused.

"Which way should we go, right or left?"

"The four-legged creature's head is facing our left," said Malachy, "I think it could be an indication."[167]

Michael nodded, "That's as good as any." The three turned to their left and crept down the passage, the music now getting louder and changing.

---

165   Revelation 1:13
166   Luke 15:3-7
167   Matthew 25:31-33

CHAPTER 15

Azarias sat in the room, staring at the loser in the reflective surfaces surrounding him in his solitary incarceration. God's spiritual flames had all but evaporated, leaving a grey atmosphere filled with shadows and dread. His image didn't multiply into eternity like a short time ago. Instead, they faded into distant darkness, like his soul.

Why would God have commissioned an angel to save Heaven, if the angel would ultimately lose it? If Azarias had been the only casualty, he wouldn't have minded. He would have been honored to die for the cause of God's love. But events hadn't unfolded that way. He had allowed others to catch him after he led the enemy to the loyal angels, who suffered. He had also lost his true friend Uriel—and maybe a new one, Jael.

Azarias thought back to when he was commissioned by the Guardian Cherub so long ago. He had told the cherub that he was the wrong angel for this overwhelming task. He was just a low-level angel who flew God's missions with joy from Al Birka. He'd never heard of spiritual warfare—nobody had.

He doubled over, wrapping his arms around his stomach, rocking back and forth, his penetrating eyes staring at nothing.

Behind him was his guard, Sosthenes, peering through the dark webbing, his spear tucked under an arm. Could Azarias charge him? The angel was short, not tall or burly like Michael. Azarias would have to get through the netting first. He could cut it with the edge of his shield, but that would leave his face exposed to a spear jab. Even if he could get past the guard, he would have to find his way out of this labyrinth, encountering enemy angels hiding within it. He wished he had Jael to lead him as before, since the many forks in the path could easily lead him astray.

Azarias tipped his head back, eyes closed to the ceiling. Why was he even thinking about this? Maybe it was better that he stayed out of the fight. If he were to escape, he would just cause the needless death of other angels. He needed God like never before. In his despair, he opened his eyes and sang to the Lord. The Holy Spirit's flickering tongues started to appear again and joined in his singing. They gently energized his spirit.

Scan the QR code to hear Azarias sing.

O, Lord,
I know that I should never fear
Teach me, your ways[168]
You are my rock and my salvation[169]
You give me strength[170]
To carry on

O, Lord
Your tender love is always here
Hold me, always
You are my rock and my salvation

---

168   Psalm 25:5; 86:11
169   Psalm 62:2
170   Isaiah 41:10

You give me strength
To carry on

Weakness pierces me
Stabbing at my soul
I call your Name
Whisper in my ear[171]
The words to make me whole
You know my Name[172]

You are my rock
And my salvation
You give me strength
To carry on
To carry on
To carry on

O Lord
I praise you with all my heart[173]
Guide me, your ways[174]
You are my rock and my salvation
You give me strength
To carry on

You are my rock and my salvation
You give me strength
To carry on
To carry on
To carry on

Azarias stood and walked towards his reflection. He placed his hand on the image of a fallen leader, strands of golden hair

---

171   1 Kings 19:12
172   Isaiah 43:1
173   Psalms 86:12
174   Psalm 25:5

framing a stoic face that shined like a sun just a little while ago. His chrystolite-colored skin, soft as an amborlite petal, no longer radiated with the golden channels that circulated when in the presence of God. He drilled his eyes into himself and cringed at their verdict—guilty.

A deep rumble caught his attention.

A jolt assaulted him, causing his feet to lose their grip from the floor. Azarias hit the surface hard as reflective panes shattered with explosions above, below, and around him. Voices called out to Sosthenes, who fought to keep his balance. "We are under attack! Assailants have freed the loyalists and are launching explosives into the peaks. Stay with the prisoner! Do not let him escape! We will reinforce those fighting above."

Loyalists? Explosions?

The Septemviri.

It had to be.

Did they know he was here? Jael would tell them—if she had lived.

Azarias caught his balance and looked around him, his broken image staring back at him hundreds of times. Another blast hurled him to the surface, his face smashing into it. He turned onto his back.

A splintered reflection of himself, magnified a thousand times, his hands and feet disembodied, fell to join his other flattened body parts' reflections. He looked to the exit. The web was still intact, and he could make out the shadow of his guard steadying himself against the falling debris.

A dancing light flickered over Azarias's head, the fiery tongue circling. A second one joined it, and then a dozen more. Azarias sat up and looked behind him. The explosions had opened a small hole in the mirror, exposing another exit. If he bent over, he could squeeze through. He turned towards the guard, who frantically tried to unravel the web.

Azarias jumped up and started for the opening to his freedom. "Thanks be to God for this inexpressible gift!"[175]

175   2 Corinthians 9:15

"Stop!" shouted Sosthenes, his voice mixing the sounds of authority and anxiety, the spear tangled in the web, their energies colliding.

Azarias grabbed his shield and squeezed through the opening, leaving the frantic sounds of Sosthenes, which increased with desperation.

"Stop! I will exterminate you. You cannot escape. We have you surrounded," called the frantic jailer.

Azarias only half-believed him since the Legion had mastered the art of lying.

He crawled and emerged from a passage that he recognized. Was this the way out?

Voices.

Azarias ducked back into the smaller path and hid.

"We must check the river cave," said one legionnaire. "The enemy may be trying to surround us."

Azarias crawled back to the gaping hole, concealing himself from the guard. He could still hide and escape after the two came back through.

He moved closer and halted after hearing a voice just outside the gaping hole.

The voice was from Sosthenes, but it was not the voice of one of Satan's commanders; instead, it was a softer voice of one who had suffered defeat. "O Lord, distressed I am. I am in torment within, and in my heart I am disturbed, for I have been most rebellious. Outside, violence bereaves, but inside, there is only death."[176]

Azarias peeked into the room, still hiding. Sosthenes crouched behind the partially dissolved webbing, his spearhead just inches from his face.

Sosthenes went on, his voice shaking. "How could I have believed in Satan's lies, Lord? I threw away your love of peace for his lust for power. The cords of death entangled me, the dread of

---

176   Lamentations 1:20

execution upon me. I am overcome with anguish and sorrow.[177] I have failed you and my fellow angels. Why wait for the assassin to come back? I no longer deserve to live among you. I wish I could come back to you, oh Lord, but it's too late."

He raised the spear to his face with both hands and opened his mouth.

"Wait," yelled Azarias. He crawled back through and stood in the room. "I'm still here. I will not escape."[178]

Sosthenes stood up slowly, his eyes clinging onto tears, an open mouth searching for its voice. "Why won't you run? God has freed you and condemned me."

Azarias walked up to the net and locked eyes with him. "I cannot be responsible for the death of an angel who wants to come back to the Lord. I may have freed many today, but I cannot leave you behind, for Heaven will rejoice over the one angel who repents over the many who have already believed.[179] You were once dead and now alive; lost and now found."[180]

Sosthenes dropped the spear and wept, his head bowed and body limp.

Finding his voice, he wiped his tears and looked up. "What must I do to return to the Lord?"[181]

"I tell you the truth," whispered Azarias. "Whoever believes in the One who sent me will have eternal life with Him."[182]

Sosthenes looked down, staring at Azarias's feet, and then up again. "I believe."

Azarias cut the webbing with his shield and reached out his hand. "Then come with me."

---

177   Psalm 116:3
178   Acts 16:25-31
179   Luke 15:7
180   Luke 15:31-32
181   Acts 16:29-30
182   John 5:24

Michael, Malachy, and Zepar had turned left at the stele bearing the wooly creature's image. This passageway narrowed considerably, its walls only the breadth of four angels standing side by side, the ceiling lowering into an arch, its capstones only two feet above their heads. The walkway rounded to the left in the distance, several arches lending their support.

Michael led the trio and then stopped. "How can the chanting surround us? I hear it down the corridor, but also on the sides and now behind us."

Malachy stopped at a niche on the left, its opening big enough to accommodate her head. She placed her hands on the wall and leaned her head into the hole. "The music is coming through here. I think there are other such openings on both sides along the corridor."

She turned and crossed the passageway and examined that niche. "The same music is echoing on this side, too. Each side opens to an adjoining small, companion aisle paralleling our walk," she said, her voice muffled in the wall. "It's only wide enough for one angel and cuts all the way—"

She stiffened and then jumped back. "I saw someone running down there!"

She rounded, her eyes wide with excitement or fear—Michael couldn't tell the difference. The three angels started running down the corridor.

"Where?" yelled Michael.

"Down the adjacent corridor!"

As the three angels ran, the music played more clearly. Michael wasn't sure if he wanted to rejoice or worry. Were they reading too much into that discovery?

This wonderful music energized their legs, hearts, and curiosity, though the apparition sighting alarmed them. The mysterious figure could be a scout for the enemy, or worse, a colleague of Zepar. Michael pushed that thought out of his head—he had to think clearly.

The three angels ran down the passageway immersed in the music, Malachy inserting her head into the openings, trying to catch a glimpse of the running angel. Winding through turns both left and right, Michael could see the tunnel widening, the music now more audible with a multitude of voices, having started with a few and steadily growing in harmony. Beautiful high tones joined in, echoing down the corridor.

"I think we are approaching the source!" yelled Malachy, looking back over her shoulder. The angels unfurled their wings, Malachy and Michael catching the Holy Spirit's power and Zepar using his own will.

Bursting through the tunnel exit, the angels landed on one of the many levels of a giant, enclosed stadium. The area expanded as an enormous oval bowl, roughly twelve hundred feet by a thousand feet, with tunnel arches encircling the perimeter on many layers. Above, a translucent domed ceiling vaulted down to the stadium's top layer, profundo falls hammering it from outside, running off the parabolic roof. Below, dozens of structures, decks, and courtyards layered the surface.

"My Lord," said Michael, his mouth open, his eyes searching below and above, his radiant golden channels tingling throughout his body. He turned to Malachy, her face displaying a radiating smile.

Michael scanned the encircling tunnels, staggered on top of one another in about twenty layers, their exits impassable due to angels singing and playing instruments.

The sound caressed, wooed, and comforted him, like the time Gabriel and he had ventured through Sardis's fourteen columns long ago.

Malachy started singing, first. The Spirit overwhelmed Michael, too, prompting an irresistible desire in him to join her.

*Scan the QR Code to hear Malachy and Michael
sing with the Sardis angels*

It's You, who I sing a new song to Lord,[183]
It's You, who I sing to from my heart

I praise You, the Creator of the Heavens,[184]
I yearn for Your presence
Maranatha, come my Lord[185]

For You, I entrust my soul and spirit Lord[186]
For You, I give my life for Your work

I praise You, the Creator of the Heavens,[187]
I yearn for Your presence
Maranatha, come my Lord[188]

You know my ways, Lord.[189]
Lay Your hands on me.[190]
Your great love will guard my path.[191]
In the shadow of Your wings.[192]

---

183   Psalm 33:3
184   Nehemiah 9:6
185   1 Corinthians 16:22
186   Psalm 31:14
187   Nehemiah 9:6
188   1 Corinthians 16:22
189   Psalm 139:3
190   Psalm 139:5
191   Psalm 40:11
192   Psalm 57:1

Teach me Your ways, Lord.[193]
Truth will set me free[194]
I have found a love that lasts
From the King of Kings.

It's You, I put my trust when I am frightened, Lord[195]
It's You, who will hold me when I'm hurt.

I praise You, the Creator of the Heavens,
I yearn for Your presence
Maranatha, come my Lord
Maranatha, come my Lord
Maranatha, come my Lord
Maranatha, come my Lord
Maranatha, come my Lord
Maranatha, come my Lord
Maranatha, come my Lord

"This is amazing," said Zepar, his eyes streaming tears. "I forgot what it was like to feel the Lord's Spirit. I was lost, and now I am found."[196]

Someone moved in the archway behind Michael and to his left. Michael turned, his hand jumping to his hilt. The glorious angel with silver hair stopped, his face concerned and a little afraid.

Michael felt the heat of the Septemviri sign on his wrist. He raised his sleeve to expose his flaming symbol of allegiance to the Lord. The angelic guest smiled and raised his sleeve, revealing his loyalty to God. The stranger waved both arms over his head towards the complex far down below. An angel, appearing tiny due to the distance, stepped out of the top structure and blew a loud horn. The angels standing at the arches and below raised their arms, displaying thousands of Septemviri signs flickering around the stadium, like the red stars of the universe.

193   Psalm 86:11
194   John 8:32
195   Psalm 56:3
196   Luke 15:24

"Mai Deus Exsisto vobis," said the angel, lowering his sleeve. "We have been waiting for someone to rescue us since we barricaded ourselves in this megalopolis."

"Mai Deus Exsisto vobis," replied Michael.

Zepar, Malachy, and Michael followed their host to one of the structures far below, the music now not competing with their voices.

After a brief introduction, Zepar asked, "How did you get in here and barricade yourself?"

The host angel smiled as they walked onto the deck. "We left the upper regions of Sardis a long time ago when an angel from Philadelphia informed us of an invasion. The frantic angel told us that the vinifera fruit had melted, destroying its district center. We knew Satan must have created that catastrophe. We've hidden here since."

"I don't understand," said Zepar. "I'd been down here with Satan's Legion for a long time and never saw you enter or leave. You couldn't have moved past us with so many angels. And, besides, Satan blocked the entrance on the peak."

"Satan's Legion?" The host angel's eyes widened, his shoulders tightening. He turned over Zepar's arm and pulled up his sleeve. "He's not of the Holy Order." His eyes were inflamed now. "Why did you bring him here? Now they will know where we are!"

Malachy's face flushed. She placed her hand on the host's shoulder. "We thought the same thing and are not completely convinced, but I have seen the Holy Spirit reintroduce himself to Zepar." She exhaled and glanced away for a moment. "We are all new at this—trusting in the Lord, and trusting in each other—but the hardest task is to show mercy to one who repents after completely turning his back on the Lord. We always have this disturbing impulse not to believe, trust, or love an angel who has rebelled—but we must. Though we may risk our friends' safety, we cannot bear the thought of losing one reformed angel. I have a feeling that the angels at God's Throne rejoice over an angel who repents. We must do all we can to support that."[197]

197   Luke 15:10

Michael, his lips flattened, turned to Zepar. "We are still not convinced, but will open our hearts. We will bear the hardships of one another and forgive one another as the Lord forgives." He touched the reformed angel's wrist. "But, looking at your wrist, you still have to convince God's Holy Spirit."[198]

"Thank you," sighed Zepar, his chin dropping to his chest.

Malachy turned to their host, shoulders a little more relaxed. "How did you seclude the multitude?"

The host resumed. "In Sardis, angels started rejecting and dying to the Lord's Spirit. This sinning against the Spirit never happened before. We were always so lively in the Spirit.[199] The Lord instructed us to convert this deep lake into a giant arena on the far side of the peak. The complex is larger than those in Ephesus, Laodicea, or even the Paestra in Smyrna. Angels rarely visited the lake—no mission routes passed through here."

"I'm sorry for my probing," interrupted Malachy, "but I'm very interested in how angels can build projects like this. I don't recall building during my existence."

"There are many developments undertaken in Heaven," corrected the host. "I have been gifted to serve as a project manager on a number of them."

He paused. "I can't go into detail, but we temporarily dammed the geysers and used God's Spirit to tunnel the sides. We enclosed the whole area in the dome and developed a keyhole at the columns for a tool that we couldn't imagine. Yet, we finished the project before Satan and others invaded our district."

"How did you build these structures?" asked Malachy.

"With the material we excavated from the tunnels," responded the angel. "We never discarded any part of Heaven into a pile but rather used it to construct other items. There is no waste in Heaven, because the Spirit of God infuses everything."

Malachy turned to Michael. "This may explain how Satan

198 Colossians 3:13
199 Revelation 3:1

recreates spirits. He uses God's creations, perverts them with his evil, and remakes them in his image. He is not creating anything, but altering them."

The host resumed. "We barricaded ourselves in here and waited. We left a small opening for a scout to slip in and out. Once we learned that Satan closed the entrance upon the peak, we connected the rest of our tunnels to the existing passages, allowing our rescuers to reach us by activating the keyhole."

Malachy sat down, her face beaming, apparently envisioning how the angels constructed the complex.

"We have to move you to Al Birka. We must train and arm all of you," said Michael.

The host nodded and sat next to Malachy, his back against the wall. "Our scouts have learned that other angels are hiding in different districts. We have a map of how you will use them to counter Satan's offensive."

"I have a list of names for each district," replied Malachy, pulling out a scroll from her robe. "Could I compare it to your battle map?"

The host stood up and paced to the side, his eyes lowered. "You already have seen God's battle plan. It has been with the Septemviri during your entire commission."

"What?" said Malachy, her voice rising a pitch. She looked at her list of names and turned it around, flipping it as if she missed a hidden message.

The host lifted her right sleeve, the sign of the Septemviri flaming, radiant rays exploding out from the middle towards the golden ring.

Michael and Malachy raised their sleeves, adding to the glow in the room.

"Now watch," said the host.

The sign's golden ring burnished, its circle radiating from right to left and left to right, flames growing in the middle outwards. In the middle was a tiny dark circle emerging in the shape of Satan's five-pointed star invasion.

"Squatinidale told us about his vision of this five-pointed star invading Heaven," said Michael. "This figure was confirmed in the Khasneh etching, also. Where is our counter-offensive?"

The host smiled. "Watch."

The triangle surrounding the star glowed brighter, its extremities changing colors. The side on the right burned red, the one on the left, white, and the bottom line, black. The triangle's sides moved in, crushing the star at its five points. As the star dissolved, a white-winged figure, similar to the winged doves in Earth's visions, emerged brighter and brighter. The apparition stopped, with the triangle and white figure superimposed on the flaming ring and the star eliminated.

"We carried our battle plan on our wrist in our Septemviri sign," chuckled Malachy, "but what does it mean?"

The host peered into her eyes. "The Lord will have three armies—red, white, and black. Each of those lines, one for each side of the triangle, will counter-attack Satan's forces moving out from the center of Heaven. All three armies will be advancing on multiple districts."

"What about Pergamum?" asked Michael. "That is where Satan built his throne."

"It will take all three armies to attack Pergamum, Michael. Satan's power is its strongest there, and it nestles next to the Siq, which is the farthest outpost from God in Heaven. He will put up a fight to the death—his death, and those of his followers. There will be casualties on both sides, but now we have to muster up the armies—you have found the Sardis army, here."

Malachy interjected. "We hope that Azarias has found the Thyatira angels. If so, there are two armies. If we assume that Sardis is the Red Army on the right side of the triangle and Thyatira is the Black Army on the bottom of the triangle, where does the White Army come from?"

The host rubbed the back of his neck. "We have only been shown a limited view of the war."

Michael ran his eyes over the arena. "We have four more districts with hidden angels, according to Malachy's map. We must find and train all of them to fight with us. We will take you angels to Al Birka and start with you," said Michael.

"I will gather my angels." The host turned and walked away.

Michael grabbed Malachy's arm and slipped into a corner. "I am anxious about this. There are so many unknowns. Does Azarias have an army? How do we rescue angels in the other districts?" He glanced back over his shoulder. "The most unsettling thing is that Zepar has learned of God's complete strategy. Were we wrong to bring him with us?"

CHAPTER 16

zarias and Sosthenes climbed out of the mirrored room and rushed into the impending darkness, the sounds of explosions fading into the distance, with a whip, shield and spear as their only defenses. Azarias retraced his steps to the Profundo River and the boat.

"Let's not fly right now," said Azarias. "We should hide as we contemplate our escape."

The angels ran through the passage, ducking behind walls momentarily, Azarias retracing his journey with Jael. Rounding the last turn, they stopped. The enemy had posted a guard at the cave river near the boat.

"Follow my lead," whispered Sosthenes. Azarias nodded but was not sure of Sosthenes's renewed commitment to God. The converted angel could relapse into evil and declare himself a hero for capturing the escaping commander of the Septemviri. Azarias had no choice. He had to trust that God had changed Sosthenes's heart.

Sosthenes spun Azarias around, relieving him of his shield. He retrieved the whip wrapped around his waist and bound Azarias's arms and shield behind his back. The former enemy marched Azarias out at spearpoint to the boat.

The posted guard turned, flaming spear rigid, his eyes wide. "Stop!"

"The lieutenant ordered me to relocate the prisoner down the Profundo River to the Khasneh complex," said Sosthenes. "It's risky to keep him here. If the attackers break through, they will find nobody to rescue. We must stay one step ahead of them."

The guard lowered his spear, helped them into the boat, and cast them off downstream.

Sosthenes released Azarias of his bindings, and the two sat facing each other. The Holy Spirit's flickering lights returned, knitting their patterns that illuminated the journey.

"Thank you," said Azarias. "You could have betrayed me." He looked downstream. "It wouldn't be the first time someone did."

"I felt Satan's spirit tempting me," murmured Sosthenes. "When I tied you, visions entered my mind of Satan promoting me to lieutenant in front of all of those who have ridiculed me. I would have shown them that I was a greater angel."

"Then, why didn't you turn me in?"

"I don't know. It was like when you spoke to me, you spoke God's truth—and the truth set me free from pain and self-doubt.[200] I no longer have to endure the lies and mockery of others, since I have found peace through His truth."

Azarias smiled and craned his head around the next turn. "Are you certain that you know where this river leads?"

"No. Well, kind of," murmured Sosthenes. "I know the Profundo River flattens out in the canyon between here and Khasneh, but I can't tell you how it meanders in these caves. I always flew above this range to Khasneh. One thing I can tell you is the flight from Thyatira to our Khasneh outpost is a long one."

Azarias focused his gaze on Sosthenes, his external appearance hard, his internal demeanor soft. Had Azarias's behavior and decision to grant mercy saved this troubled angel from eternal damnation?

The angel caught Azarias's glare. "What?"

"Oh, I was wondering what makes an angel leave God for Satan," said Azarias, placing his hands under his chin. He retracted his amor and shield.

Sosthenes exhaled. "Interesting that you would ask me now, when we are alone adrift in a semi-dark cave, not knowing where

---

200   John 8:32

we are going." He looked up. "I didn't know what I believed when Satan wooed me. I let my will guide me—as all of his followers did. It didn't take long for everyone to use their judgment to get what each of us wanted. Satan made the alternative to God look so attractive. The true nature revealed itself when everyone lied, betrayed, and stole from each other to glorify themselves."

Azarias scanned the area and then back to Sosthenes. "You must die to your old self and embrace your new life.[201] Satan will lead you astray, but God will light up your path."[202]

"Did Satan have to die to himself? He told the Legion how God abandoned him to Earth in the Garden of Eden (as the guardian cherub) for forty days to serve 'a pinnacle of creation' who never appeared. The loneliness tormented him. He also discovered the power of his free will and an ability to change God's creations. Satan disobeyed God and used the ability that God had given only him to return to Heaven."

Sosthenes paused.

"What I don't understand is why God would torment an angel like this, who had been loyal to Him?"

"God didn't torment Satan. He tested him. We are unaware of what great things we can do unless God tests us, as the testing of our faith produces perseverance." [203] When God tested Satan, the cherub replaced his faith with his pride. That pride surfaced when the situation got unbearable."

"Shh, listen," said Sosthenes, raising his hand. A sound echoed among the walls like the violent wind on Earth, the Holy Spirit's lights gyrating into a frenzy. The flaming, miniature "tongues" whizzed around, injecting the Holy Spirit into the two sojourners, one landing on Sosthenes's head.[204]

He gasped and froze.

---

201   Romans 6:6-12
202   1 John 3:7; Psalms 119:105
203   James 1:3
204   Acts 2:1-4

The river churned and rocked the boat as its speed increased. Up ahead, the river split, the main course flowing to the right. A much smaller tributary veered to the left through a smaller opening, dropping into apparent darkness.

"Come on!" yelled Sosthenes. "Let's fly out of here. If they are now waiting at the tunnel exit, we can split up, but we can't go down this small tributary to nowhere!"

"Wait!" Azarias clutched Sosthenes' arm. "Look at the current and the lights of the Holy Spirit." The Profundo River collided at the Y, creating a back current before plummeting over falls to the left—the Holy Spirit tongues gathering en masse in front of it. On the right flowed a calmer river, absent of all of God's light.

"God is pointing us to the left. The Legion must be at the exit to the right because their darkness has snuffed out God's Spirit. We go left!"

"Over the falls? It drops into a smaller cave," objected Sosthenes.

"Sometimes, we have to enter through the narrow gate because the wider gates lead to destruction. But small is the gate and narrow the road that leads to life, and only a few find it.[205]

Azarias leaned back. "This is your first lesson in trusting the Lord, Sosthenes. It may be frightening to place ourselves in the hands of God, but far more frightening for both of us to fall out of them and into the hands of Satan."[206]

"But we may get lost—"

Azarias stood, picked up Sosthenes's spear, and jabbed it into the cave wall, pushing the boat into the backflow and towards the falls. Sosthenes grabbed the sides, his mouth open, eyes fixed on the falls. The boat spun in circles as both currents jostled for control.

At last, the smaller current won, tipping the boat over the falls backward, the cave opening disappearing from above them as they fell into the unknown.

---

205   Matthew 7:13-14
206   Samuel 24:14

The boat plummeted down the falls, landing with a splash and leveling out, its occupants drifting within the current through a tunnel about half the size of the Profundo River.

"Now, that wasn't so bad," laughed Azarias, using the spear to turn the craft facing forward. "I plummeted much farther back at—"

The river dropped again, even more this time, sending the boat over larger falls. The descent threw the angels forward to the bow of the craft, their hands grasping desperately for the sides, themselves, or anything.

The boat landed in a pool, the sound of the falls fading behind them, the profundo calming its rage. Soft, soothing music from stringed instruments grew louder as they drifted downstream. It warmed Azarias's soul. He opened his eyes and sat up with Sosthenes. Covering the cave walls and ceiling were thousands of light points. The Holy Spirit flickers had attached themselves all over the surface, their small points reflecting in the dark stream below them.

The angels sat still, heads turning, eyes wide, and mouths open. "Oh my God!" murmured Azarias. He could hardly get the words out of his mouth, his throat choking with emotion.

Azarias rose slowly. He reached, stopped, and then extended his arm, touching one of the lights. The illumination did not directly affix itself to the ceiling but, instead, dangled on an almost invisible tether, the soothing music emitting from a very tiny flickering tongue, smaller than he had ever seen before.

He cradled the tiny tongue in his palm for a moment, the golden channels lighting up, starting from his fingers, through his arm, his whole body, and then to Sosthenes, who leaned against his leg.

Sosthenes and Azarias both started to cry and then weep. The line of God's Spirit slacked. Azarias jerked back, spun his head, and he lost his balance, capsizing the boat. The two angels plunged head-first into the depths.

Azarias's feet churned up the profundo, each kick creating a trail of light like before, when he had struggled under the large profundo surface. But, this time, a source of light revealed itself at the bottom of the river, too. Thousands of strands, each capped with a tiny light, reached up to them, mirroring those on the ceiling. Azarias now understood that, while they were in the boat, they were not viewing the ceiling's reflection on the surface, but the lights' counterparts to the God's Spirit under the surface. The strands waved in synchronized motions to the music, sending interlocking ripples into each other. Tiny bubbles burst when the ripples collided, emitting high-pitched "pings," blending into a perfectly pitched countermelody.

The angels surfaced, smiles now at their limits. "What's happening to me?" asked Sosthenes.

Azarias choked back his tears and looked at the flickering spirits on the wall, the ceiling, and under the surface. "We are in the presence of God's unconditional and unlimited love."

"I forgot of what this felt like a long time ago," answered Sosthenes.

The number of lights lessened and then disappeared as the two angels drifted with the current. Sosthenes tapped Azarias. "I think we've exhausted our tranquility zone." The two angels flipped the boat back over and climbed in.

"Where's my spear and whip?" asked Sosthenes, looking over the boat's side, his voice an octave higher. "They were our only weapons."

"No, they weren't," said Azarias, his face smug. "We don't need Satanic abomination. God will provide our weapons."

A sound up ahead grew louder as they drifted. The tranquil darkness lit into a greyish atmosphere, similar to how it would get when the enemy was present. Shadows appeared on the walls, taunting the angels' composure.

The current increased, almost to the point of when they had descended the falls before. Azarias tried to guide them into one of the niches in the walls using his arms, but it was of no use. The boat surfed towards a water-rise, lifting the river out of the grotto and probably back onto the surface. He had only seen this once, in

Laodicea, when Pollyon had pursued him and his comrades in the submerged river. He was able to use that vertical river to foil his pursuer's attempt to catch them.

The boat hit the water-rise in full force and pitched upwards, climbing towards the cave opening, a greying exit opening its mouth wider as they approached.

Azarias looked forward and then to Sosthenes, his heart racing. "The atmosphere is changing; they are waiting for us up there."

FLYING INTO THE SEPTEMVIRI HEADQUARTERS OUTSIDE OF Al Birka seemed surreal to Gabriel. He recalled his excitement conducting his first mission to Khasneh so long ago. That assignment, though risky, had shown only a hint of what was to come. In Khasneh, his discovery of two enemy angels infiltrating the Khasneh Council disturbed him. Comparing that visit to the one he had just flown with Squatinidale and Rafaella hammered the reality of heaven-wide spiritual warfare into his mind.

Azarias and Uriel's faces seared in his mind, knotted his spirit, and loosened his faith. He wouldn't know how to deal with the loss of his closest friends. Pollyon's betrayal was devastating, but Pollyon had walked away from God under his own will. Uriel (and possibly Azarias) had been cast out of Heaven into the unknown material world, never to return.

Questions nagged Gabriel as events continued to unfold. Why would God allow good angels to die? Where was the justice?

Gabriel shook it off.

He had to trust in God.

Oh, how all of Heaven groaned with the pain that Satan has caused.[207]

Gabriel, Squatinidale, Rafaella, and Jael descended onto the bluff.

Leihja stood next to the wall, a powerful staff beside her, her eyes fixed on the horizon, and her face aglow. "Beautiful. The site of

207   Romans 8:22

so many loyal angels eclipsing the horizon warms my soul. Where are they from?"

"Thyatira," answered Rafaella. "We engaged in limited combat with some of Satan's forces and were able to repel them with the Word. You taught us well."

Leihja smiled a little, then searched their faces. "Where are Azarias and Uriel? Didn't they go to Thyatira?"

"We don't know," answered Squatinidale, motioning to Jael. "Jael told us Azarias diverted the enemy so that these angels could escape. As far as Uriel, Azarias told her the enemy killed him."

Jael pursed her lips, her eyes shifting away from Squatinidale and then back to the others. "I must go back."

"To Thyatira?" asked Gabriel, his voice rising a pitch.

"No, to the river and cave area where I last saw Azarias, not far from Thyatira. He is unarmed." She pointed to the Word sword on her chest. "He risked his life to save mine. If he laid down his life for me, I must know.[208] If he did not, he is alone and vulnerable against a whole company of angels."

"How will you find him? I know he couldn't have killed all the enemy angels. You will be putting yourself in danger," said Leihja, her body shifting.

"I know the whole area well. I can start at the cave and follow the rivers and streams. I will find him."

Leihja glanced at the others. "I agree that we must save Azarias, but, right now, we have an army of angels to train."

The Thyatira angels started landing in the plains—the same area that reeked with the smoldering serpent demons' stench.

Gabriel stepped forward and faced the silent crowd. "Members of the Holy Order, I am Gabriel, an archangel, commissioned by the Word of God as a member of the Septemviri. As you know, we are confronting a force of epic proportions. What you may not be aware of is that the force we are battling amounts to a substantial number of all angels."

208   John 15:13

A moan followed by murmurs percolated through the great mass as they repeated what Gabriel said to those in the distance.

He waited until all were informed and then raised his hand.

"We will arm and train you to fight for Heaven in the name of God. We don't know how God will use you in His plan yet, but we must make you ready for the good fight of the faith."[209] He and his other commanders bowed their heads and closed his eyes in a prex précis. A blast of warmth opened over them.

Gabriel opened his eyes and looked up. Small flashes exploded throughout the crowd, installing the Septemviri reflective armor on the newly commissioned army. "Stand firm then, with the belt of truth, the breastplate of righteousness, the sandals of readiness, the shield of faith, the helmet of salvation, and the Word Sword of the Spirit."[210]

He stepped back and nodded to Leihja. She approached, her soft—though determined—look scanning the alerted listeners. "I will use the Holy Spirit to train you. He will guide you in battle when we are not with you. You will feel Him in your spirit more fully than you ever have. Trust his judgment, for God is never wrong. Pair up amongst yourselves, and you will learn how to use the most powerful weapon in the universe—the Word of God."

Leihja instructed the three Septemviri to go to the plateaus, just below mesa tops surrounding the valley, and mimic her moves and instructions.

The training went quickly and smoothly, the Holy Spirit infusing each angel with large amounts of knowledge. Gabriel flew around, designating leaders of corps. Each of those leaders selected subordinates commanding divisions, brigades, battalions, companies, platoons, and squads. The organization went smoothly and very quickly as the Holy Spirit communicated among the angels.

The army trained and drilled themselves, the four commanders now delegating their functions to their subordinates. Gabriel sat down by the wall, now marveling at the work God had done

209   1 Timothy 6:12
210   Ephesians 6:14-17

160

in a short time—expanding four angelic warriors into hundreds of thousands. He could not imagine how God transformed these frightened victims into confident combatants.

At the farthest reaches of the valley, a white cloud hovered just above the horizon.

Gabriel stood and focused his eyes. Satan's army? White? Maybe they were masquerading as white instead of black to confuse them. Anything seemed possible with that cherub. Any perverted or strange event usually originated with Satan.

Gabriel's spirit wavered as he wrestled with the idea of these angels battling Satan right after their training. How could Satan know? Yet, this was a white cloud, not dark.

Gabriel shook his head. He couldn't be sure of anything during these times. Why did he keep questioning the power of that cherub? Satan didn't create his power; God granted it to him. Satan just perverted it for evil.

An uneasy feeling intruded Gabriel's golden channels throughout his body as the cloud grew bigger, rolling towards the distant edge of their army. Leihja, Squatinidale, and Rafaella joined him, their eyes signaling that they were ready for a fight.

"Let's fly and get in front of this attack," ordered Gabriel. "The army must be alerted."

Three of the angels flew into the attack and positioned themselves on the plains. Rafaella forewarned the division commanders. Gabriel strategized what he would do as Satan's forces closed in. They would challenge the attack by dividing their brigades. His angels would fly to the sides and redirect the onslaught to the flanks. This way, if they could split the attack, the Septemviri could punch a hole in its middle.

He had to communicate to the rest of the army, but the four of them had not discussed the logistics of communications. He couldn't wait for angels to pass his commands to others in the distance.

Gabriel felt a burning on his arm. He looked down to the flaming mark on the inside of his forearm. Up until now, it has been just an identification. Was it meant for more?

Gabriel looked back to the loyalists' army. Their marks were aflame, small dots of fire flickering on their wrists. He closed his eyes, covered the sign with his hand, and prayed.

"Hear my prayer, Lord; listen to my cry for mercy.[211] Arrogant foes are attacking us, O God; ruthless people are trying to kill us— they have no regard for you.[212] Help me to disburse your message to all who swear allegiance to you. In your name, I pray."

Gabriel saw visions of their army dividing, but not in the way he imagined. Instead, the army split into two halves, leaving a gaping hole in the middle wide enough to drive a whole company through. Why would God do this? How were they to coordinate an attack split into two parts?

He felt a hand on his shoulder. Gabriel opened his eyes to the soft eyes and warm smile of Rafaella and the edgy look of Squatinidale. He turned to the army. The mass positioned themselves like in his vision— split in two, leaving a large pathway through the middle of the valley.

Gabriel looked back at Rafaella. "Where is Leihja?"

"She grabbed her staff and flew into the attack," said Rafaella.

"What! Alone?" yelled Gabriel.

Rafaella nodded. "You know her. She seems to hear the voice of God more clearly than we do. She came out here warning us of impending doom, and now she flew into the middle of it."

The three turned towards the white menace rolling towards them. The surface started to shake, the approaching rolling mass obscuring the view of the horizon.

"I don't understand, but we must move to our right and keep the middle open," said Rafaella.

"Maybe we are to trap them between us?" queried Squatinidale.

The massive white force charged closer, the surface now heaving as the impact drew closer to them.

The mass began to take shape as it neared, the whiteness not a cloud but a giant herd of white horses stampeding up the valley,

211   Psalm 86:6
212   Psalm 86:14

162

their nostrils billowing smoke, their white and beige colors flowing across their faces in a montage of waves. As the steeds drew nearer, a smaller object grew brighter. On the lead horse was Leihja, spinning her staff in one hand, her face lighting up with laughter, guiding the charge through the middle, waving for them to join her.

Gabriel placed his hand on his mark and instructed the angels to jump onto the herd. Angels launched themselves onto the steeds in great masses, a synchronized display creating a gigantic angelic mounted army. The allies halted the heavenly equines under the mesas, the horse's nostrils emitting a sweet-smelling aroma, with some of the riders turning the horses on their forehands and others turning them on their haunches.

Gabriel meandered through the ranks, his gaited horse becoming one with him. He had never blended his spirit with another. It seemed that he and the horse had evolved as one, with God's love as the binding between them. Gabriel hardly had to pull the mane to direct the horse, his thoughts substituting for vocal commands.

The four leaders joined up, horses prancing back and forth. "Let's inquire of the Lord," said Gabriel. "I think our Septemviri mark is our visual link to God's Holy Spirit."

They turned over their wrists and looked at their marks. The images inflamed again, with Satan's star emerging from the middle. A triangle appeared bearing white, black, and red sides. The red and black sides faded, leaving the white side glowing thicker.

"Look," said Rafaella. "The white triangle side must represent our army and steeds, bordering Philadelphia and extending up past Laodicea and down past Thyatira."

The white line moved into Philadelphia and disappeared. As its glow subsided, the multicolored triangle reappeared before the vision faded.

"I think I understand this," interjected Rafaella. "We are to go and free additional members with the White Army. They are either imprisoned or hiding."

"But where are they?" asked Squatinidale.

"They are in the district on the left side of the triangle—the district of Philadelphia."

Jael stepped towards Gabriel, Leihja, Squatinidale, and Rafaella, her face not glowing like the others. "I must go now and find Azarias. He saved my life and is now unarmed. I can't take my horse. I must travel incognito."

"I will fly with you," replied Leihja. "When we find Azarias, we will find the enemy."

"I think you should stay in Al Birka in case Michael and Malachy return," said Gabriel. "You are our main trainer, and, if they find an army, they will need you."

Jael departed. Gabriel hoped she would not be too late.

CHAPTER 17

Michael didn't take charge in Sardis, though he could have as a Septemviri. The seven archangels' reputation had spread throughout Heaven as God's chosen commanders. Michael couldn't have taken charge of the evacuation, anyway. How could he? Michael had to rely on the Sardis leaders to vacate the subterranean areas. He also felt a little inadequate in how he had found them. Along with Malachy and Zepar, Michael had stumbled upon this place by trusting in God's clues. Yet, he had kept second-guessing God's messages throughout the search.

Angels walked out through the hundreds of tunnels encircling the area, abandoning this incredible, hidden metropolis. He followed.

Who or what waited for them on the outside? The Sardis District Administrator had informed them that very few angels knew of this side of the Sardis peak. This information gave him a little comfort, but not much. Satan's forces were all over Heaven; the Septemviri learned that troubling fact during their initial missions—the hard way.

The events in Sardis had transpired with such irregularity. At one stage, he and Malachy had wandered for a long time searching for these angels, dragging a useless and possibly lying renegade with them. Then, once finding the hidden Sardis angels, one of their allies had enlightened Michael and Malachy of God's counter-attack strategy for Heaven. These erratic starts and stops didn't seem like God's perfect planning. It weighed on Michael's mind.

He thought back to the visit at God's Throne when the Septemviri were commissioned as archangels to root out the evil in Heaven.

The Creator had told him, "Michael, I created you as the great angel and protector of your cohorts. You will be one of my chief princes in the fight against darkness. I know that you are ignorant of the gifts needed to accomplish this, but the Spirit will guide your hands for the destruction of evil."

Protector? Hardly. But one thing had come to pass. He certainly had been ignorant. When and how would the Holy Spirit *guide his hands for the destruction of evil?* Patience had never been his strong point.

Nearing the exit, Michael heard the rushing profundo. He stepped out of the side of one of the two bluffs that bordered a river. The dome he saw from below spanned out before him in a large river basin between two cliffs. Its top didn't raise more than three times Michael's height, its diameter as large as a small lake. What impressed Michael more was the profundo that splashed down at the pinnacle of the dome. Posted around the dome were four geysers like Michael had seen in Earth's visions. They arched high where they collided above the arena, merging as a downpour onto the dome, where they melted off its parabolic roof in all directions, feeding the hungry river that flowed around it.

"I'll lead the District Administrator and the Red Army to Al Birka for equipping and training immediately," said Malachy.

"I'll hold back and protect our rear," said Michael.

Malachy departed, a multitude of Sardis's angels now in tow.

Michael flew high into the atmosphere. God's answer to Satan's rebellion started as seven, with no clear plan to save Heaven. Now look at what God had created! Michael remembered when he had wanted to fight Abaddon when they rescued Squatinidale—how foolish he had been. God's been the conductor the whole time, and Michael, merely his untuned instrument.

The warrior angel flew down to the side of the structure, the sound of the profundo crashing against it, comforting him. He gazed into the river. A partially submerged white-sided othelite shimmered on the bank of the electrifying current, turquoise flashes sparking as the edge of the river halted briefly before detouring around on its determined journey. He leaned over to pick it up, tossing it over his head.

As he looked up, something caught the corner of his eye as the small sphere returned to his hand. Just below the Sardis peak, metastasized dark clouds moved down in his direction.

Michael dropped the othelite, his mouth open.

Then he heard it—the dreary twelve-toned music that accompanied the enemy.

Another giant, grey cloud grew on the peak, secreting rage, escorted by glowing red fingers, fanning out through the ravines, searching for victims, destroying the trees in its downward path. How did Satan know where to find them?

He looked over to Zepar, who saw the horror but avoided eye contact. "You! You alerted them to our location?"

Michael grabbed the angel's robe with one hand and lifted him.

Zepar covered his face, his legs dangling off the surface. "No. I can't communicate with them. Satan found me. He has ways of finding troubled spirits in Heaven. He prowls around Heaven, looking for angels' souls to devour.[213] I tried so hard to believe in what you told me, but I am weak and vulnerable! He must have—"

"I'll deal with you later," grunted Michael, throwing the distraught host to the surface.

Michael flew above the geysers and yelled to the exiting angels, "Hurry!" He pointed to the moving onslaught.

He looked at the multitude evacuating from many tunnels in the bluffs. They'd never make it. If the cloud didn't get them, the flow would.

He had to stop it, divert it—something.

Angels tripped over each other, stalling the evacuation while helping their fallen comrades. As soon as they freed themselves, they took flight. But the crowd only increased, appearing at the exits, unknowing of what lay ahead.

---

213   1 Peter 5:8

"Oh, God! What should I do?"

The pyroclastic cloud spread out like Earth's alluvial fan as it leveled out at the base of the outcropping, shadowing the glowing red tide that devoured anything in its path.

Panicked angels took flight. Michael struggled as he dodged angels and collided with a few before he could manage to fly into the onslaught. He seized the Word and converted it into a bow with arrows. He fired seven arrows, exploding into the silicium along the front edge of the offensive. A large fissure blasted opened, exposing the metropolis's tunnels and pathways. The ravine swallowed the red molten mass as it poured over its lip and into the world below it.

The Septemviri warrior retreated to the geysers, the angel swarm still emerging from both sides of the river's bluff openings. How could he stop this cloud?

"Out of the depths, I cry to you, Lord! Lord, hear my voice. Let your ears be attentive to my cry for mercy."[214]

The rolling mist blanketed the far bluff, reaching its tentacles into the exits. Angels disintegrated by the hundreds, countless white particles filling the atmosphere like the cottonwood trees Michael had seen in Earth's visions.

He looked to the geysers, their brilliance unmoved by the disaster that unfolded before them. He flew down to one on the riverbank closest to the peak, where the mist was advancing the fastest. He converted his Word into a sword, raised it above his head, and chopped at the geyser opening, exploding a large gash aimed at the impending cloud. The explosive impact hit him, tumbling him onto his back. A burst of profundo spray shot over Michael's head, immobilizing part of the menacing cloud above him, silencing the horrid music.

Michael flew to the other geyser on the same side of the river and gashed it in the same way, this time bracing himself for its kickback. He repeated incisions on the geysers on the far side of the river, fanning them from left to right into the oncoming mist

214   Psalm 130:1-2

until he created a wall of spraying profundo, neutralizing the evil, toxic invader with God's good Spirit.

Michael flew down to the bluff on the far side of the dome from the cloud. "Hurry! I don't know how long we can hold off the invasion."

Thousands of angels filed out of the remaining bluff exits, their open wings receptors of the Lord's Spirit, their faces set like a flint towards Al Birka.[215] He turned back to the enemy and spotted a red glow where he had created the chasm.

Michael flew above the mist.

Looking through the haze, Michael could see that the red menace had solidified, filling the ravine he had created, almost as if he had never opened it. The red spiritual magma crossed over its new "bridge" and continued its campaign towards the dome.

The profundo continued to vaporize the cloud, but now he had to stop the deadly red flow—the chasm had not been sufficient.

The river—it was his only chance, but too shallow to stop the enormous flow.

Michael flew downstream to the far edge of the bluffs and blasted them with his arrows, causing avalanches to tumble into the river from both sides. The dome and the fleeing angels were slightly farther upstream, the exits higher on the bluff.

The mounting rubble created a dam wall, with the river pooling against it and the geysers adding their share. The river basin quickly filled up with profundo, submerging the four geysers and their majestic dome. Satan's fiery spirit surged over the bank, only to be met by a more potent force of God, cooling and building an artificial bluff higher and higher. The red menace's presence converted into a set of red falls the entire length of the cliff. As the wall rose, the profundo added to a newly created lake where Michael had stood.

Michael looked behind him. The angels would be hampered by the rising profundo, now submerging the tunnel exits. How many could he have lost? The thought sickened his spirit.

Michael looked towards Al Birka, his view dotted with thou-

---

215   Isaiah 50:7

sands of angels on the horizon, his new Red Army already suffering casualties before it was equipped and trained to fight.

Why, God? Why?

Pollyon had had Azarias captured in Thyatira. He had him! Satan would not be happy about this failure, and Pollyon could lose his new position as lieutenant. Fortunately for him, he was smarter than Azarias, who tried to work within God's will and failed. Pollyon worked within his own will and with complete control. He didn't have to be an enlightened guardian cherub to know that rivers only flowed one way, and all he had to do was post hidden angels among the canyon ridges to find the fools.

Pollyon had scouted the area a long time ago and knew where to position angels to intercept Azarias and the traitor. Since they hadn't chosen to go down the main river, this tributary would be their only exit. He could wait as long as it took.

Pollyon posted two dozen angels on the small bluff where the river water-rise exited from a large cave below. He needed Azarias alive, at least for now. The Septemviri leader could entice the others, especially if they were as stupid as he was. Pollyon had fooled them all by betraying them. As a Septemviri, he had the others in Satan's clutches, only to be foiled by Abaddon's incompetence. He wasn't going to rely on other angels anymore. The stakes were of epic proportions.

A thud echoed from deep inside the cave, its emerald profundo rushing out of its depth, shouting its freedom with a loud cheer like dozens of angels. Another thud and an object rose to the top.

"Set your staffs and whips," called Pollyon. "I want Azarias alive. Send Sosthenes to his doom."

The angels perched on the knoll, poised for a strike. The boat popped up through the opening.

It was empty.

The craft's stern fishtailed as it struggled to align itself into the current without a captain.

Pollyon looked at the angels on the bluff and those above him. "They must have turned back. You and you! Take your platoons and enter through the river exit and trace their paths—"

Another object surfaced from the cave, followed by another. Two large oval pods appeared from the depths, relinquishing control to the current guiding them. Azarias and Sosthenes had used four wings to form a craft, pointed on each end, with their other two wings used to close the top, encapsulating them as they drifted in the current.

Pollyon looked at his Legion. "Look, they are delivering themselves all wrapped and ready."

The others laughed, lowering their weapons and barriers.

"This will be easier than I thought. What a pathetic warrior you are, Azarias. You should at least give me a challenge. Things could get boring around here."

Pollyon and his angels hovered above the pods. He rapped the top with his knuckles. "Come on, my defective former leader. Make this easy on yourself and open up."

Neither of the pods opened.

He turned to the others and motioned for them all to come closer.

Pollyon grabbed the edge of a wing and yanked. The wings of the two pods flipped open with a burst of light and a high-pitched note. Thousands of tiny flickering tongues of the Holy Spirit exploded outwards into the enemy angels' faces, throwing them back against the bluff wall and beyond. The small, tongued spirits burned Pollyon's face and arms as they sizzled the wrath of God into his soul.

Screams pierced the once tranquil setting as Pollyon swung his staff in a figure-eight motion, using the mouths of his Satan handguards to counter-attack—the lion and ox baring their teeth, the eagle snatching them with its beak, the skeleton chomping its jaw. As he swung the staff in a controlled pattern, the four faces of the staff devoured some of the flying spirits, others stinging him on his face and arms. Pollyon's angels frantically mimicked his moves, gathering their quota of the swarm.

Pollyon glanced at Azarias. Though Pollyon had taken control of the situation, Azarias remained calm. Didn't this angel know that he was going to lose another battle?

Pollyon halted his maneuver, holding his staff in one hand, its mouths full of God's annoying spirits. He and the others looked down to Azarias, his face unchanged, his eyes still unalarmed. Sosthenes remained motionless but with his eyes closed.

Azarias raised his arm and pointed to the staff. Pollyon turned his face. Satan's faces on the staff glowed red—their mouths closed, eyes bulging. Pollyon turned back to Azarias and then back to the tormented faces on his handguard.

The distorted beasts' faces exploded in all directions into Pollyon's face and the faces of the Legion members. The swarm resumed its attack.

Pollyon raced to get away from their stinging tongues, each armed with an audible and fiery version of the Word of God.

The swarm circled high, looping down onto panicked angels, who dropped all their weapons. The pestilence spun upwards in pursuit of them.

CHAPTER 18

The river curved into a tree-covered grove, tributaries opening in both directions, pushing Azarias and Sosthenes towards an unknown destination.

The thought labored on Azarias. Uriel had died.

God could have prevented it if He had wanted to—Azarias was sure of that. And what about the scores of Thyatira angels slaughtered by Satan's Legion? God could have prevented that, too.

Azarias's faith wobbled. He had always questioned God's motives during his simple routine missions, but this was different—terminally different. How many loyal angels had escaped when he opened the net? God revealed little to Azarias.

Azarias clutched a low-hanging branch and directed the boat into a small tributary on the right, its current seizing the front of the boat. "Let's go down here. We have a better chance of losing them in this marsh. I can only assume that there are many like this. If we remain under the tree canopy, we have an advantage."

Sosthenes's face was still flushed. No doubt he was thinking about the risk he had taken in leaving with Azarias. Azarias wondered if Sosthenes was correct in thinking the enemy would kill him for letting Azarias escape. This thought presented another risk. Would Sosthenes still try to survive by betraying Azarias? He only had to fly through the canopy and signal any enemy angel searching for the two.

Azarias tried to settle the angel's spirit. "The Lord knows the plans He has for you—plans to prosper you and not to harm you, plans to give you hope and a future."²¹⁶ Sosthenes didn't react, his eyes searching above, ahead, and behind him. Had Azarias made a mistake taking him along?

Maybe it was better this way. God would only reveal what Azarias had to know at the right time.

Sosthenes turned to Azarias. "Shouldn't we fly?"

Azarias looked at his eyes, hands, and his whole demeanor. Was the angel trying to expose them to save his own life? It would be to Sosthenes's advantage to do so. Abaddon, no doubt, had sent for reinforcements and had a battalion of angels patrolling over the groves. All the enemy needed was a break—and a nervous Sosthenes panicking to save himself would be it.

"No." Azarias exhaled, looking up at the overhanging trees, craning his head and trying to peek through their canopy. "Satan probably knows about where we are. There are angels out there just waiting for us to bolt. We are competing in a waiting game, and they have the advantage."

"Why don't they just swoop down and take us?" asked Sosthenes, stuttering a bit.

"Take us?" Azarias laughed. "The last time they tried to take us, they angered the Lord's Spirit and are still nursing their wounds."

He placed his hand over the side and stirred the profundo, energizing its spirit. "No, if I know Pollyon or Abaddon, they will ponder their next moves. I think we should not be proactive at this time but react to their strategies. That will shift the odds more into our favor. They probably can't find us, and the Lord is with us."

Azarias didn't look up. If Sosthenes was going to expose them, he would do it now. Azarias had to plan his next move with this possibility in mind. He looked around. The thick forest would hamper his flight through it. His only escape would be to fly low above the profundo, skimming its surface, putting distance between him and Sosthenes before he was able to signal Pollyon—where this would lead him, he didn't know.

---

216   Jeremiah 29:11

Sosthenes slumped his shoulders but did not make eye contact. "I know this sounds odd, but I trust you more than Abaddon. I've worked under him a long time, and neither he nor any of the lieutenants ever cared about me. Abaddon intimidated me with his eloquent speeches. During one of his speeches, he pointed to me as an example of 'one who was deficient in finding the god within himself.' After that, the other angels started taunting me. I realized that the 'love' they spoke of was only loving themselves and what power they could steal from each other. I started thinking about a loving God who accepted me just as I am."

Azarias placed his hand on Sosthenes's shoulder and exhaled. "That's good to know. I didn't know if you would have a change of heart. Another angel, Squatinidale, felt alone like you and sought God all over Heaven. He sang to God to help him at the Ephesus Odium, and he visited the Pergamum Bibliotheca attempting to connect with God's mind. He was desperate and under constant attack from Satan."

Sosthenes looked up, his eyes wet. "What happened to him?"

"He is now an archangel of the Septemviri."

Sosthenes forced a smile, looked to the side, and then back at Azarias. "I think I can help you."

"How?"

"They didn't tell me a lot about what was going on in Heaven. They always delegated clerical work to me, which was not very exciting. They offered me no explanations as to what I was doing or why. The other angels usually ignored me.

"While in Thyatira, I heard that Pollyon and one of your Septemviri discovered lists in Ephesus of Heaven's hidden angels spread throughout our seven strategic districts. I also heard that your partner obtained these lists. Pollyon and others recreated these lists of hidden angels from his memory—the information funneling through me. Also, the leaders surmised where the angels were hiding, drawing on the knowledge of those in the districts. They put me in charge of relaying the lists and maps of the hidden angels to the lieutenants. You interrupted this process when you caused the commotion."

Azarias sat up. "Do you remember any of the maps?"

"No, but when they ordered me to travel up the Profundo River, I thought I would gain recognition if I brought two maps with me— Ephesus and Smyrna—since they were in the vicinity of where we were traveling. I thought Pollyon would give me a promotion and other angels would gain a reason to respect me."

"Where are they now?" asked Azarias, his voice rising in volume.

Sosthenes pulled out two small maps from his robe, each no bigger than his open palm. He handed them to Azarias. "These are just their presumptions of where the angels hid themselves. I don't know if they are accurate."

The maps revealed little, cryptic sketches.

"Do you think the Legion recreated these maps?"

"Most certainly," replied Sosthenes. "As soon as they realized I had defected, I'm sure they gathered what I left behind, replicating what was missing."

Azarias rubbed his chin. "They must think that we will warn the angels of these districts. I would expect them to try to reach these angels first. To do that, they would need a lot of angels—we would be alone."

"Then we have no time to waste," said Sosthenes. He jumped to his feet, almost tipping the boat. "We have to get to Smyrna and Ephesus before they do!"

Azarias pulled him down gently to the seat. "If you understand these etchings, where do you suggest we fly first? If they are attacking both, then whomever we don't choose may be decimated."

"My Lord," murmured Sosthenes, his eyes drifting off to the side. "We have to select which district of angels to sacrifice."

Azarias and Sosthenes slouched, the rhythmic sound of the profundo slapping against the bank their only company. He had never had to decide who shall live before. He cupped his hands over his nose and breathed deeply.

Sosthenes exhaled and glanced over his shoulder and then to the map in Azarias's hand. "I believe this river is winding towards Smyrna. We can follow it by flying above the trees."

This time, Azarias stood up. "Then we have to fly now and save them. We may already be too late."

"But what about the enemy angels lurking above?" asked Sosthenes.

"Let's peek. If there are a lot of them, the atmosphere will darken. If it is clear, then they abandoned the search or left only a contingent of angels, which will give us the advantage."

The two sojourners left their boat and flew up to their protective shield, the canopy of branches, their crystalline leaves casting colorful vectors, strands crisscrossing to form new hues, a tightly wound web closing the gaps between them. Azarias would have to push his head through this webbing to scout for the enemy. Remembering that he was unarmed, he thought that maybe this wasn't a good idea.

WITH THE SPEED OF THE FASTEST FLYING ANGELS, THE horses' hooves grazing the surface, Gabriel led Rafaella, Squatinidale, and the White Army Cavalry to liberate the angels of Philadelphia. They flew across vast stretches of Heaven, the vision of the triangle war strategy burning in his mind.

The swirling white and beige coats of the horses bled into the angels' skins, creating a flowing mass of conviction. The Word provided their armor, a fighting prowess infused by His Spirit. The angels scraped the peaks of the Philadelphia mountains, stampeding through the valleys that opened between them.

The majestic slopes of purple vinifera fruit had melted away, its cross-like bare stalks numbering in the hundreds of thousands, grieving as witnesses to Satan's victory.

Rafaella halted the army on a peak, viewing the devastated district of Philadelphia below. She dismounted. "This is where I met Dionysius a long time ago."

Gabriel reached down and touched the purple stain of what was once a magnificent palm-sized vinifera fruit, its shape large and round, formerly hanging from the stems that now littered the mountains. He recalled his horror while searching for Rafaella. Unbeknownst to him at that time, she had disappeared underneath the valley floor, only to reemerge in Laodicea.

The commanders dismounted in front of one of the crossed stems. The vertical trunk rose out of the silicium, its bark streaked with purplish-red stains. The horizontal branch bore the mark of a hostile disintegration, its surface also stained.

"The fruit hanging on the crosses were so beautiful," said Rafaella. She walked over and broke one of the plants off at the base, turning it around. Rafaella removed the Word from her chest and activated the blades. Holding the broken stem up, she pressed the crossed branches to the hilt and blade. The stem and branch ignited, their ends bursting into fiery points, a star between them, joining the four points.

Squatinidale's eyes lit up. "What happened?"

Rafaella turned the star, its golden glow reflecting on the faces around her. "Even when dead through Satan's sin and transgression, God's grace will give it life."[217]

She slipped it under her sash and turned to the others. "I think the Lord is furnishing us with another weapon. We should inform every Holy Order member to remove a cross and allow God to breathe life into it through the sword."

The message passed quickly through God's Holy Spirit, angels dismounting to convert a vinifera stem to a star, slipping it into each of their sashes, the star's glow peeking out of the top.

"How will we use this?" asked Gabriel.

"I don't know," responded Rafaella, "but you will know when the time comes."

The three commanders joined in a prex précis to see how God wanted them to search for and rescue the Philadelphian angels.[218]

217 Ephesians 2:5
218 Matthew 18:20

Their Septemviri signs inflamed, with the interior triangle glowing like the original vinifera violet before fading away.

The three angels flew to a cliff perched above the Philadelphia district center. Gabriel gazed across the valley; it had flooded into a lake, destroying the one hundred beautiful falls that once cascaded through the walls into the metropolis hidden below. The lake appeared dark, emitting a foul odor, not energized by the Holy Spirit; its beautiful vinifera violet color dead to all who gazed upon it.

"Let's allocate the army onto the surrounding slopes. The main district center is submerged somewhere in there," started Gabriel. "Do you think hostile angels are guarding the loyal ones in the subtropolis?"

Squatinidale chimed in. "We know that they hold angels as prisoners—possibly awaiting execution—based on what they tried to do in Thyatira."

The word *execution* unsettled Gabriel. He executed missions, not angels. Visions of angels lined up under the liquid surface below and summarily killed drove a stake into his heart.

"Every moment we waste could be another angel dying," he said, his lips and chin trembling. "Rafaella and Squatinidale, take a commanding position ahead of the army on two other sides of the lake. We have to take this by force from different directions. Unfortunately, we will have to leave one side unguarded. We will use the Word as our guide."

The three posted themselves on three sides of the lake, each leading a battalion mounted on mighty steeds. Gabriel held his arm up, the Septemviri sign flaming, as did each commander, and then the entire army. All slopes leading into the lake from all sides glowed with tens of thousands of flickering lights of God.

He scanned the troops. "Proclaim this among all of Heaven: prepare for war! Rouse the warriors! Let all the fighting angels draw near and attack."[219]

---

219   Joel 3:9

Gabriel dropped his arm and yanked his reins, jerking his horse into a canter and then a gallop, surging downhill towards the dark lake. All battalions surged forward, riding towards their shores, each led by one of the commanders. The waves of the Holy Order poured off the mountain slopes as one massive assault.

As they approached the edge of the dark, foul-smelling lake, another rider pulled up to Gabriel's side, her face brimming with a wide smile. "Raise the war cry, enemy, and be shattered! Listen, distant districts. Prepare for battle and be shattered! Prepare for battle and be shattered!"[220]

Gabriel hit the lake, the horse's hooves not breaking stride, piercing the vinifera surface as they lowered themselves into the mire. The horse's coat transformed from a smooth-flowing liquid to scales, starting from the head and moving back. Gabriel had seen this outer shell in Earth's vision of underwater creatures. These scales, however, hardened like the Holy Order's armor, protecting each inch of the equine's body.

Darkness engulfed him. The partially exposed shining star in his sash dimly lit his way and that of other riders. Arched columns, supporting a large wall, stood as abandoned silhouettes, yearning for their majestic prominence of a time gone by. Gabriel remembered the rivers that had sailed through them to the inner court, giving life to the angels below in the courtyard who sought the Spirit of God.

He clenched his teeth. How could such evil have seized this beautiful site of Heaven? Until Satan, beauty reigned all over.

Gabriel looked to both sides of his battalion, riding as an imperviable line of righteousness bearing down on the evil that had destroyed this district. The enemy must have hidden since Philadelphia's arches and stairways appeared deserted.

Gabriel reached for the Word mounted on his chest.

A blunt force hit his helmet.

Gabriel lost his balance and fell to the right, somersaulting backward, his arm still locked in his shield.

220   Isaiah 8:9

180

He hit the submerged floor, still outside the courtyard walls and arches. He managed to stay upright on all fours. What had hit him?

Gabriel looked to the left at his battalion, its riders falling backward. Some appeared to be struck in the seams of their armor, killed instantly, disintegrating into gyrating white particles swirling in a vortex before being sucked upwards and out of this liquid underworld. Other angels continued to charge, only to meet the same fate as Gabriel, their steeds advancing without them.

Gabriel tethered the reins around his wrist and swam over to the spot where some force had killed an angel, the angel's star abandoned on the bottom, now glowing brightly. Gabriel picked up the star and held it up. At the end of the most distant reaches of the star's radiance, a phantom appeared on horseback, then another riding towards him. Gabriel ducked under his horse as the assailants rode to each side of him.

Looking to the one who rode closer, Gabriel made out its features with his starlight. The phantom had no color but was pale—a pale horse mounted with a pale rider.[221] The White Army couldn't see them without the Holy Spirit's light. They were translucent riders of death!

Holy Order angels continued to topple off their horses, meeting their deaths, discarded stars illuminating scattered sections of the battleground. The enemy appeared and disappeared as it charged into and out of these lit areas. Gabriel had to find a way to defeat them. But how? He couldn't battle what he couldn't see. They would decimate the Holy Order. Maybe he should call for a retreat?

---

221   Revelation 6:8

CHAPTER 19

Al Birka had never seemed so disconcerting, with fields of angels suffering losses in Sardis, the large patches of amborlite oblivious to this disaster, their stalks bowing carefree in the gusts of the Lord's Spirit.

Michael returned to the bluff and informed the waiting Leihja of the Red Army's catastrophe, which had killed an untold number of their angels. The bad news concerned her but didn't depress her, as it did Michael. Her faith in God, despite any event, did more than impress him—it made him envy her. He wished he had such faith, patience, and wisdom.

She told him of Gabriel, Rafaella, and Squatinidale's mission to Philadelphia. She quickly followed up that none of them had heard of Azarias's whereabouts. Then she told him of Uriel's death.

A weight fell on Michael's shoulders. Uriel, dead? Azarias, dead? Was he to assume control of the Septemviri, the war? He had to push it out of his mind. If he dwelt on every contingency, he'd be ineffective in accomplishing anything.

The Sardis Red Army waited, carpeting the valley, their murmurs held to a minimum. Did they blame him for not saving all of their comrades? They did look up to him as the leader whom God had ordained to execute His will. His first confrontation with these angels had certainly dispelled that notion. How much faith did they have in him—in God, for that matter? Before the rebellion, angels never experienced sorrow—the concept just didn't exist in Heaven. Nobody had ever suffered the loss of another angel, a loss so close that it was like themselves dying. Angels loved each other as much as they loved themselves—any angel.[222]

Malachy and Zepar approached the bluff where Michael stood. Their faces were as crushed as his. Michael couldn't look at Zepar, still unsure if he had led the enemy into the hidden Sardis subtropolis.

Malachy started. "I gathered some fascinating information from Zepar about the nature of whom we are fighting."

Michael looked up. Did he want to hear this? Zepar had been of no use to him, and it was probably a liability for him to be here. But he trusted Malachy, so this could be interesting. The better he knew his enemy, the more effectively he could fight them.

"Do you remember, a long time ago, when God sent an angel to Earth—the only angel sent to Earth?"

"Yes," answered Michael. "The angel's name was Morning Star. He was a revered cherub. God made a pronouncement that Morning Star would be the only angel who could pass back and forth through the Siq to serve God's *pinnacle of creation* in a place on Earth called Eden."

"Did you know that cherub's other names?" followed Malachy.

Michael shrugged. He wasn't as gifted as Malachy in Heaven's history or any kind of minutia.

"Lucifer," shot back Malachy.

"I know that God gives multiple names to cherubs, but that name means nothing to me," answered Michael, rubbing the back of his neck. He loved Malachy but didn't think he could focus on this question-answer game—at least not now.

"Lucifer renamed himself, *the Great One* and now accepted God's name for him: *Satan.*"

Michael's mouth dropped. It seemed more straightforward now. "You mean that we are fighting the only angel to experience the material world? Did he obtain power from this *pinnacle of creation*?"

"You're half right. Satan did discover this power of free will and its uses in Eden, but he never met that new creation. The combi-

---

222   Matthew 22:37-39

nation of this new power and God sending him to Earth for forty days and nights seemed to warp his spirit and faith. Satan did not trust God and felt that God was unjustly exiling him on Earth. He rebelled against God and flew back to Heaven, using his will—not God's will—to gather enough angels to rule the Earth."

"What does Earth have to do with Heaven?" asked Michael.

"Zepar told me that Satan's sinful greed for power seduced him further after returning to Heaven. Sin infused his ambition to rule both Earth *and* Heaven. He genuinely thinks he is as great as God."

Michael paced away, his hands behind his back. Could the material world corrupt any angel passing into it? No. He couldn't accept that. Satan corrupted Satan. The material world didn't corrupt him.

"Are you saying that we are not just defending Satan from conquering Heaven, but all of creation, including the material world and Earth?"

"Yes." Malachy turned and looked at the forces stretching out to the horizon. "We are battling evil to save all of creation with these untrained, unequipped, and probably inadequate armies that God is providing to us."

Michael clenched his fists. "How can we do that? We are struggling just to equip forces to fight for Heaven."

Leihja approached from behind Michael and put her hand on his shoulder. "God ordained us to save Heaven, not Earth. If we lose Heaven, we will lose Earth and the rest of the material world. If we save Heaven, we may save Earth, but not at this time. We must remember, it is not by our power that we save Heaven, but God's power. We will not develop a plan to save Heaven—God will. God is in control. The Lord, our God, will be with us wherever we go."[223]

Michael smiled a little, but the unsettled feeling refused to leave.

He turned back to the Sardis angels. They were so inadequate. Just a short time ago, these angels were secluded under the surface of Heaven, and then they panicked as a nebulous force attacked

---

223   Joshua 1:9

them with fire and fog. How could God equip them to be warriors against an army that has fought together for such a long time?

He shook his head and turned to Malachy and Leihja. They bowed their heads as they stood in a prex précis. "Lord, we praise you and honor you. We thank you for providing us with this Red Army, but we feel so vulnerable and inadequate. Please help us to equip and train them in your Name. In the Word, we pray."

A stillness overtook the Al Birka headquarters, the Holy Spirit's wind dying to a silence. Was the enemy coming?

A roar from behind them started in the distance. This sound vibrated as a low octave, a bass sound that Michael felt more than he heard. The three loyalists didn't open their eyes. Another roar grew in front of them. But Michael recognized that as one of cheering voices. Both in front and back, the roaring increased, the Holy Spirit's wind resuming, pressing their wings against their backs.

Michael opened his eyes and met Malachy's eyes. They looked at the multitude's faces of joy. Some stood with open arms towards God's Throne above; others oddly pointed at them.

Michael looked at his chest and at Malachy and Leihja, their swords still recoiled, armor restrained. The other two exchanged puzzled looks, the rank and file now almost in a frenzy.

Leihja started laughing, and her face lit up, eyes tearing.

Malachy grabbed Michael as the surface shook with such violence, in concert with the gale-force winds of the Holy Spirit.

They turned.

Thousands of red-winged horses, their coats swirling with fluid waves, barreled towards them, pulling fiery chariots.[224] Three horses, dynamic swirls moving from their faces to tails, pulled each chariot.

Michael ducked as the first wave of chariots whooshed by, just a wing's length above their heads, hazing the multitude, before turning all directions to return to the Al Birka bluffs. He focused on one of the chariots. Like all the others, it carried a large saber buried in

---

224   2 Kings 2:11

a sheath attached to its side. The red, swirling saber extended three times the Word sword's length, its mass much more extensive, too.

Excitement replaced Michael's fear for the Red Army. Could they control these magnificent steeds and chariots? What about the sabers? Could they train quickly to learn to use them against an enemy who was perpetually assaulting angels everywhere?

Picture of Red Horses and Chariots

THE GRAVITY OF AZARIAS CHOOSING TO SAVE SMYRNA OR Ephesus still weighed heavily on him. Why had God provided Sosthenes with two maps forcing Azarias to select? Another test? If so, God had issued Azarias a test with no right answer. If he and Sosthenes chose to rescue the angels in Smyrna, they would lose the angels in Ephesus and vice versa. Even opting for either one was risky because he and Sosthenes could be too late to save any angels, not to mention that they only numbered two—unarmed.

Azarias donned his armor and pushed through the prismatic webbing covering the river, nudging the leaves with his head. The canopy was thicker than he had anticipated, forcing him to penetrate the branches, the energy sizzling with each thrust. He hoped that no enemy angel was close enough to hear the sound. It surely would bring his scouting attempt to a disastrous end.

Azarias pushed a little farther, his wings snagging the crystalline leaves with every thrust, slowing his progress. The upper level seemed clear on the other side. He tuned his hearing to the area above him.

He inched up.

Heaven's pastel lavender skies peeked through.

No one.

Poking his head out of the canopy, he scouted his surroundings, the forest's top layer spread out in a consistent carpet-like surface. Dotted here and there, some trees soared higher than their companions, their arms stretching out towards God's Throne above. All seemed calm, radiating, and deserted. He could see why the Legion couldn't find them. The Profundo River that flowed below them was undetectable. Maybe his cautiousness led Pollyon to give up and reallocate his angels elsewhere.

Azarias returned to Sosthenes. "I think we are clear."

"How can you be sure?" asked Sosthenes, his eyes wide open.

"I saw the lavender skies. If a large contingent of enemy angels amassed here, the skies would be dreary and void of the Lord's Spirit."

"But if they are not here, then they may have flown to Smyrna or Ephesus. We have to go, or it will be too late!"

"We have to hurry," said Azarias.

Azarias led Sosthenes as they blew through the canopy into the open. He knew the general direction to Smyrna but would need to follow a river or something so he would not get lost. He might be able to rely on the power of the Holy Spirit to get him there if it was God's will.

Azarias tried to push his nagging anxiety about Sosthenes's resolve. What would he do if they were attacked or captured? Would Sosthenes give Azarias up to save his own life in Heaven?

The two angels flew slowly. "After passing that tree, let's make sure we are going the right direction. Then we can fly as fast as the Lord's Spirit will allow us to Smyrna."

"Look over there," said Sosthenes, pointing up ahead to the left at a tiny opening in the canopy. "The river. Your hunch was right. The river flows in the direction of Smyrna."

The angels expanded their wings.

Snap!

A dreadful sound rang out from the tree to their right as a whip surged towards Sosthenes, its electrifying switch sizzling for its intended victim. Azarias leaped in front of Sosthenes, holding his shield at arm's length, his armor in full glory.

The whip wrapped around Azarias's neck and chest, pinning one arm to his side, the other pressed against his ear. His outstretched arm clutched his shield, the whips energy sending jolts throughout his body.

As Azarias spun and recoiled back into the tree, the whip's tip flailed around him. He struggled against the tightening chord, his wide eyes glimpsing at a tree with each revolution, where an impatient Legion member nested among its limbs.

After nearing the outer branches, the whip stopped, its tentacle now running up the back side of Azarias's helmet which sloped down to his shoulder to protect his neck. Laughter roared from a branch as the tether hauled him closer, meandering around his head to his exposed face. Azarias's eyes grew wider, his breathing more solemn as the tip danced in front of his face, taunting and torturing him before finally coiling for its deadly strike.

Azarias felt a tug on his free arm as someone snatched the shield from his extended hand. The shield flew towards the assailant, slicing him into two halves of dark particles. The whip thrashed about on two ends, ricocheting off the tree branches with multiple snaps and pops.

Azarias spun, this time in the opposite direction, unraveling the whip. Spinning, his eyes tried to focus on the direction of God's Throne above and the canopy below.

He slammed into the canopy, the whip beside him still screaming with energy, its tip again coiled in front of his face.

"Aaa!" screamed Azarias, his hand penetrating the canopy in a desperate attempt to lift himself.

A knee landed by his forehead along with his shield, destroying the deadly whip tip. The negative energy subsided, and the tranquility of the area returned.

Sosthenes sat Azarias up, the renegade's face brimming with a smile. "Are we even?"

Azarias, his body still shaking, looked into his eyes and smiled a bit. "Even."

Sosthenes's smile abandoned his face as his eyes shifted to Azarias's arm. Azarias followed Sosthenes's gaze. A small smoldering cut, about the size of his fingertip, peeked out from the seam of his armor.

"The whip must have glanced my arm in the spin," said Azarias. He looked deep into the wound. Several small dark creatures scurried around, apparently eating his spirit, feasting on his goodness. He trembled and smacked at it. "Help! Get them off!"

"I don't know what to do!" yelled Sosthenes.

"O, Lord," whimpered Azarias. "Be merciful to me and be my help!"[225]

He looked into Sosthenes's eyes. They may have been the last pair he would see.

---

225   Psalm 30:10

CHAPTER 20

Gabriel surveyed the battle scene from under his standing horse, the pale riders toppling his White Army Cavalry regiment in droves. Was this happening to the other battalions in Philadelphia? Were Squatinidale and Rafaella still alive?

Gabriel fought off the temptation to panic and focused on hearing from God. He surmised his first challenge was to see what he was fighting. He slipped his star out of his sash and held it up as the pale riders rode and circled his horse, casting their spears at him. Fortunately, his scale-covered horse repelled the impact, leaving his horse unharmed. But he couldn't say the same for him and other angels. Their armor repelled blows, but it seemed that spears and arrows could penetrate.

He remembered Rafaella's answer about how he could use the star in battle. *You will know when the time comes.* An idea came to him as he surveyed the catastrophe.

Azarias had communicated the original charge through a visual display of the sign. Could he share his thoughts through it? He covered the sign with his left hand, focused, and prayed. "Lord, please send your Holy Spirit to the others. Guide them to use your light, the star, for good to defeat evil."[226]

Gabriel's spirit leaped. He stepped out from under his horse, ignoring the carnage taking place behind him. He clutched the star on one point and hurdled it over his head, spinning fiercely, the

226   Matthew 2:9-10; John 8:12

surrounding vinifera pinwheeling and sparking in all directions. The star disappeared through the liquid surface above.

At the same moment, tens of thousands of other stars surged out of the lake, their points cutting through the sea of death, surrendering it to complete darkness as they exited.

Moments later, a crescendo of a ringing sound—notes, beautiful notes—filled his ears as sparkling lights broke the surface above for as far as he could see, floating down around them, lighting up the entire battleground.

Gabriel surveyed the scene. The pale riders had positioned themselves inside the walls near each arched opening. They had been attacking the Holy Order in platoon-sized sorties. But they had stopped. The stars seemed to have blinded them, at least momentarily.

Now the odds were in Gabriel's favor. He placed his hand on the Septemviri mark and yelled, "Breach the walls!"

Gabriel mounted his horse and, with the others, charged the walls, their arrows torpedoing through the vinifera, impaling the pale riders at an incredible pace; some arrows fired at close range passed through one angel before striking another behind her.

The army closed in like a wave, eliminating all resistance in their path. As Gabriel approached the wall, he could see the lit zones through the arches on all sides. Squatinidale and Rafaella must have been defeating their attackers at will, also.

Gabriel smiled.

Up front, he could see the enemy, some mounted, fleeing back through the arches in a panicked retreat. The Holy Order commanders leaped on their horses through the archways into the courtyard in pursuit.

Gabriel slowed to a canter and then stopped.

His army had chased the enemy away, leaving the quad inside the four arched walls deserted. More allies poured into the square, only adding to the mass of stagnant and confused riders. The large tholos stood quietly in the middle, connected to the wall's corners by four high, bowed stairways.

The stars now had settled on the bottom, revealing the areas around them. No enemy riders remained.

The other two commanders joined Gabriel. He turned to Rafaella. "I know there were many more remaining. We didn't kill them all. Where did they go?"

Rafaella swung her horse around and motioned for the others to walk with her to one of the walls, weaving around the tightly packed comrades, their faces solid with determination, the glowing stars scattered among their feet.

The three approached one of the four walls and halted. Paralleling the hundred arched openings, extending about twenty feet across, was an opening that hugged the entire interior part of the courtyard on all four sides. Gabriel had forgotten about them in his last visit to Philadelphia.

Darkness dominated the chasm, darker than Gabriel had seen since Satan's lair a long time ago. The metropolis under them must have a staggering number of Satan's Legion, their evil presence completely extinguishing the light of God's Holy Spirit. If the captured angels were down there, they were compacted and surrounded.

"The vinifera rivers, once cascading through the arches across these gaps, fed the subtropolis streams below us. It appeared to district visitors as many violet vinifera falls surrounding the lower quadrant on all four sides. Now, since the enemy has flooded the area, the falls cease to exist, allowing the pale riders to dive into the underworld undetected."

"We should follow them down there," suggested Squatinidale.

"That is what they want us to do," replied Rafaella. "They are guarding all entryways, including the portal through the tholos behind us."

"Let's look at our options," said Gabriel. "If we charge below through these smaller openings, the enemy will kill us off. The openings are only wide enough to accommodate a limited number of horses at once, thus giving the rebellious angels ample opportunity to destroy our forces a little at a time."

"Do you think that they are holding the Holy Order angels captive below?"

"Maybe," replied Gabriel.

Squatinidale pulled up. "If we wait and seize the district from the outside, they may execute the captives while we wait. Is there another way in or out?"

"Yes," replied Rafaella. "When Satan had trapped me in the submerged vinifera deluge, I sailed out the exit below and was blindly pushed in the current to Laodicea. We cannot go to Laodicea and work our way back. It would take too long, and the enemy would execute the captives if they haven't started already."

"Do we know for sure the captives are here?" asked Rafaella.

Gabriel glanced at Rafaella and then Squatinidale. Nobody had considered that they could be conducting a rescue mission in the wrong part of Heaven. "I see our options as follows, each bearing its own shortcoming: we invade the district below, risking the lives of our army and possible captives; we don't invade, saving our army for another fight but possibly losing the captives to execution; or we invade, risking the lives of our army and do not find the captives, possibly risking the lives of captives hidden elsewhere."

Their choices seemed hopeless. Each had casualties that could outweigh the benefits.

Rafaella dismounted and picked up one of the stars, still glowing brightly in its fiery glory. She held it up and turned to the others. "We are ignoring one other option." She turned the light in her hand. "This is the verdict: light had come into Philadelphia, but Satan's forces loved darkness instead of light because their deeds were evil. Everyone who does evil hates the light and will not come into the light for fear that their deeds will be exposed. But whoever lives by the truth comes into the light so that it may be seen plainly that what they have done has been done in the sight of God."[227]

Gabriel looked at the others, their eyes looking up, faces reflecting an epiphany; he marveled when God used each of their unique

---

227   John 3:19-21

gifts to dovetail to one objective. "Brilliant. OK, we agree. Let's break down the tactics and do this before it's too late."

THE RED-WINGED HORSES AND CHARIOTS AMASSED ON THE Al Birka countryside, a large saber attached to each chariot, their horses swirling surfaces flowing from face to tail.

"Let's get started," said Leihja.

Leihja walked up to one of the chariots, its three steeds stomping the ground, snorting vapor from their noses. She jumped up through the opening of the back and stood on its carriage. Leihja seized the large saber's hilt. Instead of pulling it back out of the scabbard, she turned her palm upwards, slicing the blade through the front of the sheath, the exit closing, leaving the blade pocket unscathed.

Leihja placed her hand on her Septemviri sign and closed her eyes. Her lips moved, but she said nothing. Michael's sign blazed on his arm, and her voice became audible for the first time through his spirit.

"Please go to a chariot near you and draw the saber out of its scabbard." At once, every angel armed themselves, the fiery weapons moving in unsynchronized arcing motions among hundreds of thousands of angels.

Leihja walked down from the bluff and stopped. She picked up three othelites. She dropped two of them and stood with her left foot in front of her right. Leihja tossed the remaining othelite over her head and grasped the saber with two hands. As the object fell, she sliced upwards in a motion that started at her right hip and ended at about her left shoulder. All of the other angels, including Michael, copied her maneuver.

Leihja threw the second othelite up, but this time, she pivoted on her left foot, dropped her left shoulder, and sliced from the bottom left to the upper right. The multitude of angels followed her lead, mimicking the left to right upward motion.

Lastly, she tossed the remaining othelite up and repeated both moves, but more quickly this time. As the othelite returned, she sliced it with the first upper right to left motion and then again with the upper left to right motion before it hit the surface at her feet in four pieces equal in size. The angels all duplicated the combined technique.

Michael stepped away and around the wall, leaving the others, allowing the knowledge to sink into their spirits. He held the weapon in his hand, turning it from one side and then to the other. The blade wasn't as impressive as the Word in that it didn't have the cryptic symbolism. He didn't understand most of those markings, but God has a purpose for everything.

What if he were to perform the Word sword techniques with the saber? He tossed the weapon up with one hand, flipping it once away from him, landing the handle into his grip, making sure the blade didn't touch him in its revolution.

Michael picked up an othelite and lobbed it, slicing it like Leihja had, but with only one hand on the saber, not two hands. He picked up a second one and did the same left to right as she had performed. He practiced a few more slices.

The big angel leaned over to pick up two othelites as Leihja had. He paused without standing upright again.

Michael slowly chose a third othelite. He paused again and picked up a fourth, holding all four in his left hand.

The Septemviri commander adjusted his feet, left in front of the right, and took a breath. His eyes widened, and he tossed all four othelites high above his head. As the objects returned, Michael, shifting his stance and weight from one foot to the other, sliced the saber back and forth in quick succession, cutting all four othelites before their halves landed on the silicium.

He stood there. Looking at the eight halves; there were six light sides and two dark sides pointing upwards. How had he acquired such instincts? It just flowed out of him without any conscious thought.

Slow, melodic applause behind him interrupted his thoughts.

"Very well done," said Leihja. "I knew you were different than the others."

Michael looked up briefly and then back to the blade. Had he passed his instructor in fighting techniques?

"Now you see how I work," said Leihja. "I train angels to find their role in God's army. When we first met, your hand gravitated to your Word sword to protect the others. I knew, then, that you were going to be the military leader against Satan."

Michael thought back to when the Septemviri had been elevated to archangels by the Word. He looked to Leihja and said, "When at God's Throne, the Word said, *Michael, I created you as the great angel and protector of your cohorts. You will be one of my chief princes in the fight against darkness. I know that you are ignorant of the gifts needed to accomplish this, but the Spirit will guide your hands for the destruction of evil.*"

Michael's eyes drifted downwards. His breathing halted when his mind flashed a vision of him leading God's army. He looked up. "What about Azarias? Am I to replace him as a leader against Satan?"

Leihja swallowed, her face releasing a warm smile. "I don't know. I don't know if Azarias is still alive. Nobody has heard or seen him since he saved the Thyatira angels."

She stopped momentarily and then looked up. "But God is always in control, and I have faith that He will be faithful to complete the good works he has begun in all of us, though we cannot see it from our point of view."[228]

"I accept this challenge," replied Michael, face now flush, his feet taking him away from Leihja. "I have to know about Azarias. Why would God take him? Why would the Word commission us to fight for him, just to lose our lives in Heaven? It doesn't make sense. We are fighting on the side of righteousness."

He turned back, only to find her standing just inches from him. "Michael, like the flying creatures on Earth, faith cannot be effective

228   Philippians 1:6

if contained. With those creatures, we have to open our hands and let them fly to where they want to go. As with faith, we must release it to soar where God wants it to go. We try so hard to control our faith's destination and results, only to realize that it is not ours to control or even to call our own. It's a gift."[229]

Michael lowered his head. "I guess I have a lot to learn about faith. How ironic that those of us who have stood in the presence of God struggle to trust Him. I judge those who have fallen because they don't trust the Most High." He looked up, his eyes wet. "I guess I'm not as different from them as I thought."

He turned and headed back around the corner to the bluff. "Let's gather the Red Army and see where God wants us to go. I'm ready for the fight."

---

229   Ephesians 2:8-10

CHAPTER 21

Munching, crunching, call the sound what you may, Azarias could hear the evil parasites devouring his spirit, his soul, and his existence in Heaven. Tiny fluffs of his spirit blew off his arm and towards the Siq, reminding him that Satan can devour souls in one bite or little nibbles.[230]

Sosthenes carried Azarias down to where the tree canopy opened a little, exposing the river. He laid Azarias at the riverside among the trees, the renegade's hands clenching into fists, searching for a way to help.

Azarias retracted his armor. The near-microscopic, dark creatures had penetrated the armor's seam. They migrated slightly down his arm, their bodies growing larger ever so slightly, discharging his spirit, consuming the doubts he harbored of God.

He looked up at Sosthenes. "Is this how it's going to end? Long ago, the Lord sent a guardian cherub from His Throne to me to command six other angels. Throughout this epic mission, I always questioned God's judgment. I don't know why I did that. He has done so much for me. Now the Lord has left me to die and be banished from Heaven." He looked down at his arm. "My wound festers and is loathsome because of my sinful folly. I am bowed down and brought very low; left here, I go about mourning. My arm is filled with searing pain; there is no health in my body. I am feeble and utterly crushed; I groan with the anguish of my heart."[231]

---

230   1 Peter 5:8
231   Psalm 38:5-8

Sosthenes placed Azarias into the boat. "I will not leave you here to die. I will find help. Someone must know how to destroy these creatures."

Azarias chuckled a little. "Aren't we supposed to rescue angels in Smyrna and Ephesus? I can't even rescue myself."

Sosthenes pushed off and drifted the boat downstream, the tree canvas covering them for a while. The protective canopy disappeared altogether. They were now in the open, exposed to anyone who wanted to harm them.

Azarias's eyes glossed over, his mouth open, a stiffness moving up his arm to his shoulder. "Meaningless. Meaningless. Utterly meaningless. Everything is meaningless. What have I gained from my labor toiling under the Throne of God? Angels come, and angels go, but the war drags on. The Holy Spirit blows where there is faith and ceases where there is none. The streams flow to where they want to, this one coddling me as I disintegrate into the other world."[232]

"Azarias, when I pleaded to God for help, He directed your heart to answer my prayer. Why does your faith fail you? Hasn't God showed you that He loves you?"

"I just don't see how this can end well, Sosthenes. I know I am a pitiful example of an archangel." Tears welled in his eyes. "The Lord expected so much of me." His jaw tightened, and then he yelled. "I told the guardian cherub to find someone else—I told him! I can't help what I feel." He exhaled.

"Yes, you can!" shouted Sosthenes. "We live by faith, not by sight!"[233]

"Faith!" Azarias smiled. "If I had enough faith, you wouldn't be in this mess and my life wouldn't be slowly seeping out of me."

"You saved my life!" screamed Sosthenes, holding Azarias by the shoulder. "Don't you remember? Or is my life too little for you to consider valuable?"

An explosion hit the side of the boat. Both angels tumbled into the river. The craft, now capsized, absorbed the impact of angry profundo.

---

232   Ecclesiastes 1:1-6
233   2 Corinthians 5:7

Philadelphia had never seemed so bleak. Gabriel remembered the days of many vinifera rivers flowing through the arches of the four walls that boxed in the courtyard, disappearing into chasms, their waterfalls thundering to the effervescent district below.

Since Satan's followers had invaded Philadelphia, the beautiful district became their refuge and possibly their prison for the Philadelphia loyalists. The White Army had to defeat the enemy without risking the lives of the captives.

Gabriel placed his hand on his wrist. "Please retrieve a star and stand on or near the walls surrounding the courtyard."

At once, the army scattered throughout the area, both inside and outside the courtyard. They retrieved many stars, some probably belonging to departed loyalists. The tops of the thick walls lit up as the cavalry flew onto them with the shining weapons. The stars outside the courtyard sloped away in the liquid darkness towards the lake's shores.

Once the angels occupied the battlements, Gabriel directed the remaining army into the courtyard.

Squatinidale approached him. "Why do you think these lights will assault the enemy? The evil ones have been able to extinguish the Lord's Holy Spirit all over Heaven. What would prevent them from extinguishing these, also?"

"The Lord's Holy Spirit offers grace and mercy to anyone willing to accept it," said Gabriel, still eyeing those filling the Center. "These weapons come to us representing God's judgment. Remember, God is both loving and just."[234]

Gabriel smiled as the ramparts, the interior courtyard, the arches, and beyond shined with the glorious righteousness of God. Hundreds of thousands of angels mounted on watery steeds, each angel holding a star weapon, awaited his command.

---

234   1 John 4:7-21; Psalm 25:8

"Squatinidale. Go to the tholos and command the troops surrounding it. When I give the word, instruct them to cast a star into the opening leading to the district below. Once the angels cast their stars, they are to exit through the arches to the surrounding area. Rafaella and I will stand at opposite corners inside the courtyard. We will direct angels towards each corner within the courtyard."

Gabriel flew to one of the corners where two surface chasms intersected. He covered the Septemviri mark on his wrist. "Angels in the courtyard. Fly in a circle around the tholos."

Angels and their scaled horses took "flight" in the courtyard, revolving in a circle around the tholos. They initially passed under the four looping stairways connecting this central structure to the walls. "Angels on the outside, pass through the arches holding the walls and join the march."

Angels swiftly rode through the arched entryways and added to the swirl, its mass rising higher and higher, creating a whirling cyclone, its pattern covering the looping staircases. Gabriel flew out of the lake. The whirlwind broke the lake's surface, creating something similar to a vision he had seen of Earth—a waterspout. Yet, this towering tornado did not consist of wind of water, but of light, brilliant light, reaching high towards the Throne of God.

Gabriel returned to his post. "Starting with the angels on the bottom, cast your stars into the tholos's passageway to the subtropolis below and exit out through the arches supporting the walls."

The column gradually collapsed as angels cast their stars, exiting out of the courtyard and into the darkness.

It started with a muffled roar, then a scream, as the stars filled up the Philadelphia underworld. The courtyard shook with a slight rumble that increased to a violent quake as the last of the Holy Order angels filed out of the square.

Gabriel called out through his wrist sign. "Angels who were guarding the wall, please return to your previous positions."

Gabriel looked down into the chasm bordering one of the walls. The darkness had evaporated, allowing Gabriel to see some of what was transpiring. Pale riders scurried in a panic, trying to avoid the light of the Lord. They appeared blinded. The mounted enemies collided, injuring and destroying each other, not knowing who was an ally or a foe. They turned on each other.[235] Dark particles puffed from the exits, a sure sign that the Holy Order was winning without engaging. The enemy fled through the exits, where angels, posted at the walls, cut them down.

Gabriel held up his hand. "Do not enter below, yet; let the sin within them destroy each other. The Septemviri will secure the district, first." The screaming and the trembling subsided and then stopped. All was silent, the vinifera currents calming down after the upheaval. "Let's enter through the openings, but make sure you have your shields up. Satan has adapted to adverse circumstances."

"Squatinidale. Enter through the tholos while Rafaella and I enter from opposite corners. If there are any remaining enemies, we would have an advantage in entering the courtyard on opposite sides. They are probably expecting angels to enter through the tholos. Squatinidale, you will have to dismount since its opening is too small to ride through."

The three Septemviri entered the subterranean area from three points, their shields covering a large section of their torsos. The structures far below still remained intact, the vinifera stars scattered between and on them in a haphazard fashion. Gabriel and Rafaella met Squatinidale in the center, hovering high above it.

"I remember when two hundred beautiful vinifera falls curtained the walls around us," said Rafaella, her voice somber. "The structures were laced with beautiful streams flowing between them, where angels basked in the Lord's Spirit. The cascades, on all sides, cast a violet hue, filling the florescent pools, spawning hundreds of brooks, with angels singing in raptured harmony."

She looked up at Gabriel, her eyes dull and expressionless. "It's all gone."

The three Septemviri flew hundreds of feet down to the district

235   Judges 7:22

center, landing at one of the canals, their swords activated, armor ready, and their ears and eyes alert. Gabriel learned from the battle outside the wall that fighting in the vinifera liquid spirit was difficult. The sword strokes were slower due to the vinifera energy's resistance.

Rafaella guided the other two to the Administrative Center bungalow. "This is where I was a long time ago when Satan first attacked Philadelphia. The vinifera falls turned into a deluge, flooding the center."

"It still displays a grey atmosphere inside," said Gabriel. "An ideal place for an ambush."

Gabriel and Rafaella picked up one of the stars and entered. The light glowed enough for them to see about twenty feet. On the wall was inscribed the name *Dionysius-Administrator*.

Rafaella walked up to the inscription and placed her hand on it. "I sacrificed my safety to save his life." Her voice cracked. "I wonder where he is now."

She turned. "Let's secure this place and get out of here."

"We can't," answered Gabriel. "We have to find the Philadelphian angels."

Squatinidale entered, carrying an arm full of stars. "Let's cast one of these into each structure as we secure it, therefore preventing an enemy angel from doubling back to dwell in it."

"Good idea, Squatinidale, but it will take too long. As Gabriel said, we have to find those angels," said Rafaella.

"I will summon part of the army to cast the stars," replied Gabriel. "We can then focus on finding the angels."

Shortly after that, the desolate, submerged streets of Philadelphia thronged with mounted angels of the White Army platoons securing every structure. Gabriel broadcasted a request to inform him if they were to find any loyalists or any clue as to their whereabouts.

After some time, it became apparent that no angels—other than the White Army—dwelled in Philadelphia.

Gabriel, Rafaella, and Squatinidale met.

"Did they kill them all?" asked Squatinidale, his eyes pleading for a "no."

Gabriel walked to a wall and turned back. "Let's recount the events. We attacked the district from above, diving into the Satan-created lake. At first, nobody confronted us, until the pale riders attacked. We learned that they were posted on the courtyard inside, attacking us with sorties after we exposed them to the vinifera star lights. They didn't try a full assault, but seemed to be only taking a defensive position—or were they?"

"Maybe they did that not to defeat us, at least at first, but to delay us," said Rafaella.

Gabriel continued. "They also didn't try to attack us even when we were inside the courtyard. We attacked but didn't know how many we killed."

"Tactical retreat?" murmured Rafaella.

"What?" Squatinidale answered, glancing around as if looking for answers. "Retreat to where? We blocked all exits."

"No, we didn't," said Rafaella, not making eye contact.

Gabriel stepped closer, cocking his head to one side. He knew Rafaella very well now. She chose her words carefully, while treasuring a wealth of knowledge and wisdom in her head.

She looked up. "Collect a few stars, and I'll show you."

Rafaella led them to the far side of the district, where all structures ceased to stand. It was directly under the far wall that Gabriel's riders had breached. Embedded into the wall, the entire width of the submerged district, was what appeared to be a massive dark cave. However, the enemy had wedged huge pieces of structures into the former opening, blocking most of the vinifera from draining out of the district.

"This is where Satan cast me after I saved Dionysius, sending me on my chilling journey to Laodicea. He plummeted me down here in the liquid darkness, tearing my soul from my mind. I almost gave up on God. But God didn't test me more than I could have handled," said Rafaella, her voice trailing off.[236]

Gabriel didn't respond. How could he? He had never known

236   1 Corinthians 10:13

what it felt like to feel abandoned. God had always been there for him through difficult times. He saw this as a detriment to his faith. Others told him that their faith became stronger after such a trial. He saw it as God allowing Satan to test their faith because God doesn't tempt.[237] Both Rafaella and Squatinidale had been through existential challenges and survived. Their faith was tested to their limits, thus developing perseverance. They had both emerged from their trials trusting God more.

Gabriel turned from the cave. "It looks like they dammed the exit with an opening just big enough for a single row of fighters to pass through. The dam was how they flooded the area—preventing the vinifera from draining at a fast pace. We must go after them with at least some of the army."

"I hope you realize, Gabriel, that the farther we pursue them, the closer we get to Satan's strongholds, Laodicea and Pergamum," cautioned Rafaella. "We could be walking into an ambush and lose the entire army."

Gabriel nodded, his eyes trailing off. He understood this, but did they have a choice?

---

237   James 1:13-15

CHAPTER 22

The Red Army air command stood ready as an impressive force, the steeds' translucent, multi-colored wingspans extending twice the width of a typical angel's wings, the horses and chariots blazing red, ready for war. Michael now knew that God was commanding him to lead this wave, but how? Where? And against whom?

He remembered back at the beginning of this revolt when the Septemviri rescued Squatinidale from Abaddon. Abaddon had boasted when he revealed a hundred companions to fight the seven Septemviri, only to be frustrated by Azarias's countermove of amassing thousands of fiery chariots on the mesas surrounding them. Azarias did it with such poise when standing nose-to-nose with Abaddon. No fear, no wild reactions.

Michael couldn't say the same for himself back then. After Azarias had let Abaddon and his minions go, Michael objected to the release because they had outnumbered the enemy ten to one and could have imprisoned them.

Azarias had seen God's bigger picture, though. Grace and mercy came before judgment. Love replaced hate.

Times had changed, and judgment was on the march in Heaven.

Michael's sign emblazed on his wrist, the image morphing, its center darkening into a five-pointed star. Of the star points, two migrated farther outward on the right-hand side. One line protruded from Laodicea and Sardis as its base, the other from Sardis and Ephesus, each forming a point moving outwards towards the Throne of God. An extensive red line appeared in front of the two points and pushed them back towards the center. The mark froze. Michael ran to the others.

"Look! I think the Lord has sent me a vision of where we should post our army, but I am not sure of its meaning."

Leihja, Malachy, and Zepar ran to him, their mouths open, their eyes wide.

Michael explained the image as God revealed it. "I'm not sure of the meaning of the star points moving outwards."

"They are two of Satan's attack vectors," explained Zepar. "Satan positioned forces at two major districts. The top vector combines forces between Laodicea and Sardis at its base." He pointed to Michael's wrist. "The second vector also has a base at Sardis but extends down to Ephesus."

"How do we know you are telling us the truth?" shot back Michael. "I'm still not convinced that you have returned to the Lord. You didn't help battle the enemy at Sardis."

Zepar returned a hardened glance but didn't say anything.

Leihja stepped up. "I don't know what is in your heart, Zepar, but your analysis seems to be consistent with what Michael has described."

"The explanation also coincides with the Septemviri's vision from when the guardian cherub first commissioned us," chimed in Malachy, "and Squatinidale's vision in an amborlite petal while he was in exile." She ran her finger against Michael's wrist. "The red line is the Red Army, but look how long our battle line is. Our hundred thousand angels will not have any depth if we stretch far enough to battle both of Satan's attacks."

"I see what you mean. Satan will position his best forces at the two points and punch through our defenses," said Michael.

The four stared at Michael's wrist, their mouths silent.

"Look at us. Oh, how little faith we have," said Leihja. "Why are we acting afraid?[238] If we truly believe this is from God, then we must trust in Him. He does a lot with little."

---

238   Matthew 8:26

Michael looked to the forces below them, horse-driven char-iots racing haphazardly in circles and other patterns as the angels trained for the first big skirmish. "Even if I can obtain our plan, how do I get all of these angels to comply? They are all over the place."

"God will provide the mouthpiece to what we are to do," replied Leihja.

"It seems like we have to stack our forces directly in front of the two attacking points," said Zepar, "which makes this red line confusing. Why spread out across Heaven when we are alerted of Satan's two-point strategy?"

"We don't question God's motives. We just act with what He has revealed to us," said Leihja.

"But what if we misinterpreted the vision? An error like that could be sending thousands of angels to their deaths," replied Zepar.

Leihja ignored the comment and turned to Michael. "Michael, I think I completed my training with the Red Cavalry. I feel like God is calling me to join Jael in finding Azarias. One less angel in your offensive will not matter, but one more person looking for Azarias could help a lot. She told me how she was going to search, so I think I can trace her steps."

"OK," said Michael, shrugging his shoulders. "We can manage, though you are equal to ten warriors."

Zepar's comment returned to Michael—it jolted him. "I hope my sinful nature hasn't obscured or perverted my connection to God. I could only be interpreting my thoughts and not God's divine message."

Leihja put her hand on Michael's shoulder. "We test our inter-pretations. Sometimes, our connection to God gets distorted by our pride. We must step out in faith in the direction God is leading us. He will close the door if we have misinterpreted."

"I understand," muttered Michael. "But how many angels do we have to lose before realizing my interpretation was incorrect?"

The group went silent.

Finally, Leihja took a step. "I have to go."

"I will position the right line where the vision shows," said Michael. "I hope you come back. If Satan attacks, I don't know how long we can contain his forces with so little an army."

THE HOLY MOUNT OF GOD, ONCE THE MOST BEAUTIFUL OUT-cropping in Pergamum, was now smoldering in Satan's hate, the offspring of his pride to conquer the Creator. [239] Satan had told Zelbeje about the times he had walked among the mount's fiery stones—no two were alike.[240] He compared them to rocks on Earth. Nothing like the Earth's volcanoes heated the sacred stones in Heaven, yet they were more brilliant and fierier. Earth's opals shined similarly, but the opals only displayed a limited number of colors such as red, blue, green, and yellow. The fiery stones of this mount reflected millions of colors of the Creator's Spirit.

Zelbeje noticed that Satan had once shined brighter than these stones but then dulled as he turned to his own way. The stones, too, darkened as Satan's moods tarnished them. Now they were as dark as the rest of Jebel Madhbah, the throne of Satan.

Zelbeje landed in the middle of the six obliques with one of her lieutenants. They walked into the darkened cave leading to Satan's lair. When she first had ventured into this realm, she had been alone with Satan. His power seduced her into his darkness, exposing her most intimate and hidden desires. She was powerless against him and submitted, no matter the cost.

When Zelbeje had first met Satan in the Bibliotheca, Satan possessed the will and power to change small creatures into any form he desired. He first demonstrated his ability (only to her) by changing a handful of amborlite into a little, hideous winged creature that flew away. Since then, Satan's power had increased ten-fold with every angel who joined his rebellion. His ability to morph anything that the Creator made expanded beyond her imagination.

239   Ezekiel 28:14
240   Ibid.

She and her lieutenant entered the main lair, now void of angels that frequented the room to worship Satan. Zelbeje and the lieutenant kneeled. Satan had summoned them but sometimes would not appear for a long time. She cringed to think what would happen if she lost patience and left before his entrance. He seemed to relish his followers' accolades.

The lieutenant fidgeted and rubbed his arms. Another angel rarely accompanied Zelbeje to meet Satan. She was grateful for that since her innermost thoughts and temptations would embarrass her and cost her the respect she had built up as a stern disciplinarian. She needed to portray this image as the first of Satan's converts.

"I slipped away without causing a disturbance," muttered the lieutenant.

A light grew brighter from one of the passages as Satan entered the room. His light still shined more brilliantly than all other angels, another aspect that attracted them to him. This effect fueled his love for darkness, and darkness always accompanied him. He turned to the face of the eagle. "Lieutenant, you have failed the entire Legion and me. I sent you to infiltrate the Septemviri. You have wasted time."

The lieutenant looked down, his hands now shaking, "I hope to make progress to earn respect and confidence from the enemy. All Septemviri are suspicious of all angels after Pollyon betrayed them."

Satan's head turned; his eagle eyes drilled into the angel, with his ox face spewing out more smoke from behind him. "I have given up trying to convert the Septemviri to the proper way of thinking. I want you to exterminate them for me. If I exterminate the leaders, I win the war, but I must get as many as possible in each attack. We have seen the extermination of Uriel only fuel Azarias's faith to fulfill his objective. When each one dies, the others become stronger. If I kill all the leaders, their armies will become weak."

Zelbeje looked down and noticed that she was rubbing her fists together.

The eagle eyes turned to her. "Is this the way you train your fellow Legion angels?"

What was she to say? She had to be careful. "Satan, I have taught all lieutenants what you have taught me. In certain circumstances, these angels must use judgment. I cannot teach them judgment; that is something that comes from within."

"Quiet," boomed Satan, the walls shaking as if assaulted by one of the Earth's quakes. "These are battles against the Creator of the universe. You can leave nothing to chance; we must plan carefully. For those angels we have not yet found, I want you to find them. I will then destroy them if they refuse to join our Legion. As for the angels who we are imprisoning, we want to use them as bait to attract the Septemviri."

A *deafening* silence filled the room. Zelbeje was afraid to look at Satan or the angel beside her.

Finally, the lieutenant spoke up. "I will obey, Satan. I want to be as great as you."

Zelbeje looked up. "I know I have failed you. You have taught me a lot; I was a privileged student from the beginning." She waited for a response before continuing. "I will personally go out to the districts, starting with Smyrna. I will use more persuasion to push the area commanders to the limits of their abilities. If they don't perform, we will have to kill them. The cost of defeat is too high for us. It means eternal exile from Heaven into the material world. I can't see a price any higher than that."

"Why are you speaking as if we have lost?" Satan's face rotated to a lion, the room filling with the ox's exhalation. "I didn't create these forces to lose. We all have the power of the creator to fulfill our destiny."

Zelbeje continued, her hands shaking, now. "I think we have the Septemviri and their compatriots in a disorganized state. They are reacting to our actions and wandering throughout Heaven. The more we keep them off-balance, the better chance we have of prevailing over them."

"Chance!" boomed Satan. "I leave nothing to chance." His piercing eyes rotated back to the other angel. "As for you, lieutenant, if I don't see results, I will destroy you and all of those who fail with you."

CHAPTER 23

The Profundo River churned as more explosions hit the surface, waves heaving in all directions, the capsized boat repelling each assault.

Azarias couldn't have imagined a worse situation—completely unarmed, his mortal wound festering even when submerged in God's liquid Spirit. He and Sosthenes surfaced under the craft, its hull only allowing enough room for their heads. Azarias struggled to stay afloat.

Sosthenes pushed him away.

"Azarias! Stay at that end of the boat, and I will stay at this end. We must stay separated in case they hit one of us. Let's make it harder for them to strike both of us."

A large crash alarmed him from his right as a large, enemy hatchet speared the craft, its pointed blade resting between the two frightened faces. Another knife-edge pierced through the other side, creating an X, and resting as a barrier between them. The sounds of the weapons' sizzling death echoed in the hull, Satan's four-faced handguards laughing at their prisoners.

The river current picked up as the grade steepened. The angels grabbed onto the small handles within the boat, securing some protection, their heads avoiding the deadly weapons that crossed between them.

"Sosthenes. Save yourself. I cannot help you. You can submerge yourself in the current and escape undetected. They will think we are both in here."

"Don't urge me to leave you or to turn back from you. Where you go, I will go, and where you stay, I will stay. Where you die, I will die. May the Lord deal with me, be it ever so severely, if even death separates you and me."[241]

The sound of more explosions filled their ears, the boat spinning as it bounced off the banks on its journey. The profundo seemed to take on a life of its own, cresting over the boat and heaving it, swells revisiting it as they rebounded off the banks of the river, tossing it and its huddled occupants from side to side.

The craft drifted faster as phantom assailants yelled and insulted them, proclaiming their boat as their last vestige of sanctuary before the angels were to reappear in the material world.

The blasts increased as the craft roared through the rapids, the hatchet heads jostling back and forth, their edges twisting closer to the angels' faces. More screams and booms filled the air, blasting well above them, apparently missing the fast-moving target.

Azarias cringed. It would only take one more well-positioned blast to destroy the boat and its desperate fugitives. The enemy had the supreme advantage. They only had to follow Azarias and Sosthenes and connect with one or two volleys to exterminate the angels. The Septemviri leader prayed to God that he would deliver them, not for his sake but Sosthenes's sake. Azarias was going to die, anyway. This angel had turned to the Lord and risked his life for Azarias. To have it end this way would have defied logic. Why would God wait until now to allow the enemy to exterminate them?

They heard more explosions and cries, this time in rapid-fire succession.

Then, all went silent, the profundo calming down into a slow drift as before. The boat drifted to the side, allowing the two imprisoned angels to stand on the river bottom.

Sosthenes cocked his head. "What happened?" He redirected his eyes above, searching for any sound.

---

241   Ruth 1:16-17

"Maybe they are just trying to trick us," said Azarias, the tone of his voice remaining flat with depression.

One of the spears jiggled. After two attempts, someone tugged on the shaft and dislodged it, pulling it out of the hull.

The enemy removed the second hatchet more easily, now producing a gaping hole on each side.

Azarias and Sosthenes released their grips. A moan filled Azarias's ears as angels lifted the hull and turned it over, exposing their prizes.

Azarias didn't look up. Why bother? He had displayed to Sosthenes his weak faith and resolve, especially when he needed it the most. Why wouldn't they put him out of his misery and kill him? Oh, he forgot. They thrive on suffering.

A hand tapped Azarias's shoulder. He recoiled in pain, the parasites almost paralyzing his entire arm. He squeezed his eyes shut, trying not to give the enemy any pleasure in his excruciating pain. If they wanted him, they were going to have to take him.

The menace grabbed his hand and lifted it out of the profundo, extending it from his shoulder and over his head, exposing his wound entirely.

Azarias yelled, the pain surging through his entire spirit.

He heard a soft gasp, and then a warm sensation overtook his wound. His eyes turned moist as the pain and warmth competed for his attention. Tears fell from his eyes as he thought about his weak faith.

The warmth subsided as the enemy placed his arm back down, but now with an object, probably a golden ring, lying across it.

He opened his eyes.

The Word of God.

He reached for it with his right hand, its grip melding into his hand like before, and lifted it.

He looked to his healed shoulder and then up.

Jael and Leihja.

Philadelphia hadn't felt the love of God for a long time, with evil as its newfound belief and hatred as its dominant passion. Heaven had never looked worse. Gabriel wondered what the rest of the White Army was feeling. How could angels who have experienced nothing but love through their entire existence turn their passion to killing?

The Septemviri had confronted the enemy with God's grace multiple times, which the enemy had rejected. Since the enemy spurned God and His love, God had no other choice but to pass judgment through them.

The enemy had rejected and even spoken against His Holy Spirit. Gabriel realized that God would forgive every kind of sin and slander, but He cannot forgive blasphemy against the Spirit.[242] The verdict wasn't that God was not all-forgiving, but that this hardening by some of His angels had upended the foundation that He had built upon truth. The Holy Spirit was truth.[243] If Satan and his angels rejected the Holy Spirit, then they rejected truth. If truth was denied, then the connection between God and the rebellious angels evaporated. Consequently, if there was no connection between God and the rebellious angels, there would be no path for their repentance.

This declaration was clear to Gabriel because he had seen it first-hand for a long time. Yet, the doubt still lingered. Would the Holy Order have the resolve to cast the enemy out of Heaven, or would the Holy Order shrink back, allowing the enemy to destroy them? The loyalist army's only engagements, up until now, had been to defend themselves, not to cast God's judgment on others. If they lost their resolve, it could mean the end of them, the end of Gabriel, and even the end of Heaven as they knew it.

With Azarias away—possibly captured or worse—Gabriel had to lead an army. Yes, he knew that he would have to lead angels into battle when the Word commissioned him as an archangel.

242   Matthew 12:31-32
243   1 John 5:6

For some reason, though, he thought that he would be doing that at Azarias's side. After all, God had commissioned Azarias as the leader of the Septemviri.

Gabriel looked at the impeded subterranean river exit. He couldn't order the entire White Army to invade for several reasons. First, bringing hundreds of thousands of angels into this area would overwhelm the narrower passageway leading from the district center to the river below. Second, their massive presence would alert and prompt the enemy to engage reinforcements in a zone they knew better—the Legion could entrench themselves. Lastly, he could not risk losing this army to rescue angels who were fewer in number and may not even still be alive.

How many should he bring?

God's Spirit spoke to him.

GABRIEL, LEAVE THE SUBTROPOLIS AND
GO BACK TO THE SURFACE. ASK FOR
VOLUNTEERS TO FIND THE LOST ANGELS.

Volunteers? Who would volunteer for this suicide mission?

Gabriel informed Rafaella and Squatinidale that God would help him choose. He flew out of the Philadelphia district and stood looking over the lake. "I am asking for volunteers for a search and rescue mission of the Philadelphian angels. If they still exist, the captives may be somewhere between here and Laodicea, along a subterranean river. The mission will be risky. For those who choose not to join us, you will go up to the ridges and secure a battle line."

Murmurs bantered about the rank and file, with the vast majority taking flight. Those that remained numbered approximately ten thousand angels.[244]

GABRIEL, THERE ARE STILL TOO MANY
ANGELS. ASK THEM TO COME DOWN TO THE

244 Judges 7:3

SHORE WITH YOU, WITHOUT THEIR HORSES,
AND I WILL SIFT THEM FOR YOU THERE.
IF I SAY, 'THIS ONE SHALL GO,' THE ANGEL
SHALL GO; BUT IF I SAY, 'THIS ONE SHALL
NOT GO,' THE ANGEL WILL NOT GO."[245]

The angels circled the shores of the flooded valley, their horses abandoned to other members of the army, their swords in hand.

HAVE THE ANGELS DRINK THE VINIFERA
ON THE SHORE AND SEPARATE THOSE WHO
LAP THE SPIRITUAL LIQUID FROM THEIR
HANDS FROM THOSE WHO KNEEL AND
DRINK LIKE THE HORSES.[246]

Though reluctantly, almost all the angels bent over to drink the spiritual liquid from the lake. Gabriel struggled to find those who cupped the element to lap from their hands. God must want the ones who bent over to drink. Why? He didn't know.

GABRIEL, CHOOSE THOSE WHO LAPPED WITH
THEIR HANDS AND SEND THE REST TO THE
BATTLEFRONT IN THE HILLS.[247]

What? God is sending almost everyone away.

Gabriel obeyed.

Remaining on the shores, scattered around the great lake, numbered about three hundred infantries.[248] God had whittled many thousands of angels down to three hundred to fight a force that may be thousands near Satan's headquarters. The term "suicide

---

245 Judges 7:4
246 Judges 7:5
247 Judges 7:7
248 Judges 7:6,8

mission" grew in block letters in Gabriel's mind. How were they to fight, without horses, against an overwhelming force?

He thought about the subtropolis and the escaping vinifera, draining the area a little at a time. Was that barrier meant to keep invading angels out or captive angels in? The answer to that question would provide the foundation of his strategy. Could his small regiment remove the obstacles blocking the river? Should they be removed? If they removed them, they could send a deluge through the cavern that would wash out any angels in its path—good or bad. Or they could release the main army of the evil angels back into Philadelphia. Considering they would only have three hundred troops at their immediate disposal, it could mean disaster. Worse yet, if Gabriel didn't remove the debris and send angels in a dozen at a time, enemy angels could post sharpshooters and pick them off little by little.

Gabriel sighed as a knot formed in his courage. He felt he didn't have any good options. The three of them could be leading three hundred of their best fighters to their deaths.

GABRIEL. YOU AND RAFAELLA STAY AND
COMMAND THE WHITE ARMY, POSTING
A MASSIVE WHITE LINE WELL BEYOND
PERGAMUM, THROUGH THE PHILADELPHIA
AREA, AND WELL BEYOND SMYRNA.
I WILL SEND SQUATINIDALE TO LEAD THE
THREE HUNDRED ON THE MISSION.

CHAPTER 24

His words still rang in Squatinidale's ears. Could Gabriel have misinterpreted God? That must be it. God would not instruct Gabriel to give him a mission to lead an elite force. He stared into Gabriel's eyes, looking for some—any—misgivings about this command. For the first time, the speedy angel hardly made eye contact with Squatinidale. He was right. Gabriel didn't believe in him, either.

"Gabriel, are you sure God wants me to lead these angels? I have never led any missions and am not as wise as the rest of you. Do you remember when I sought God's advice in the Pergamum Bibliotheca? Satan attacked me. When we pursued the enemy to rescue Rafaella and Malachy, the Bibliotheca's bad memories haunted me as we entered it. Now you want me to lead these angels, without our horses, against an undetermined force to rescue thousands. Besides, if we follow this vinifera river, we will be passing under—" he paused, "—the Bibliotheca—the gateway to Satan's lair."

"Yes, I understand your fear and doubt," said Gabriel, laying his hand on Squatinidale's shoulder. "I, too, doubted at times. If you lack wisdom, you should ask God, who gives generously to all without finding fault, and He will give it to you. But, when you ask, you must believe and not doubt, because the one who doubts is like a wave of this wretched sea, blown and tossed by the spirit of Satan."

Squatinidale smiled a little, but the anxiety still tore at him. Gabriel introduced him to the others as their Septemviri commander during this mission, the rugged crew ranging in height and girth, but all with determination fueled by their faith in God.

The three hundred (and one) plunged into the deep, the vinifera stars' lights guiding their way. Squatinidale had overlooked the undertow before. He surmised that this current would lead him back to the cave opening that Raffaella had shown them. He let the current direct him and his forces back down through the arches and into the metropolis below.

He was right. The current took them straight to the cave entrance. Squatinidale held his hand over his mark. "I will scout this alone and report back. There is only enough room for one angel to pass at a time. If I do not return soon, report back to Gabriel."

Squatinidale squeezed his way through the opening, his armor still fully intact, the passage dropping down into a dark pit. He followed the current.

The vertical passage ended at the bottom. The enemy's weapons littered the pathways. To the side, a current exited into another dark chasm. He stuck his head through it and then his whole body. The debris field ended, allowing the river to widen to about ten angels side by side.

Squatinidale swam upwards, breaching his head through the liquid surface, arriving in a large cave passage.

No movement. No sounds. Just the darkness of Satan.

On the right was a large, deserted beach, or so it seemed in this darkness.

Squatinidale navigated his way against the current back to the cave entrance. The others greeted him with relief.

"Each of you must take a star to lead you. We will need the light of God to guide us to our comrades," he said. "If the enemy confronts us, there will be no retreat. They blocked most of the passage, preventing anyone from going back into Philadelphia. This commitment will be a one-way mission."

Squatinidale expected questions or mumbling, but no one spoke.

The portly angel led the angels one at a time. The process was slow, but he had to infiltrate this dominion, even if he did it one angel at a time.

After some time, all angels were present and accounted for, each bearing a star, with several posted as sentries to guard against a surprise attack.

"We will have to journey down this river very carefully. It appears that Rafaella was correct in that the enemy angels performed a tactical retreat. The river cavern is high and wide enough for a dozen angels to fly from wingtip to wingtip. I suggest we split into two groups—one flying, the other swimming in the river. This way, we can confront any attack."

One angel stepped up. "We still could be ambushed. Each dark corner poses a new risk."

"Correct. I am asking six angels to join me as the scouting party. The seven of us will swim under the surface and alert the main body if we encounter an attacking enemy force."

Squatinidale and his scouting party advanced in the near darkness, their stars hidden in their armor. He didn't like scouting in the dark. If the enemy discovered them, there would be no retreat. They either win or get slaughtered.

The seven advanced, the current dragging each angel in silence. Squatinidale speared his head above the surface. The darkness seemed the same, still suffocating and depressing. This despair of being separated from God was indescribable. He recalled the first time he had felt it after venturing with Abaddon to listen to Satan, a memory he would like to forget.

The other six popped up with him, their helmets partially above the surface. Beaches had welcomed them along the way, but they could not stop, especially since some of those landings seemed to disappear into side caves, darkened possibly by Satan's Legion. That image raised his stress.

He heard voices.

Azarias, Sosthenes, Jael, and Leihja sat on the profundo bank, its emerald hue mirroring the crystalline leaves above them, and the leaves, in turn, reflecting the lazy river. Azarias needed to rest his spirit after the ordeal, but his curious mind wouldn't let him.

"Jael and Leihja, this is Sosthenes. He saved my—"

"Mai Deus Exsisto vobis," snapped Jael. Her cyanic blue eyes narrowed. "Azarias, will you come with me for a bit?"

The two angels moved into the forest but remained within watching distance of Sosthenes and Leihja.

"Sosthenes can't be trusted," she started. "I don't know what he told you, but he played a pinnacle role in the Thyatira rebellion. As displayed by his robe's crimson border, he is a high-ranking member of the Legion. The renegade is brilliant and served directly under Pollyon to help transcribe our names from Pollyon's memory."

"He told me he was an insignificant laborer who the other angels didn't respect."

Jael laughed. "He is anything but *insignificant*."

"He saved my life multiple times," whispered Azarias, his eyes watering. "Just now, the enemy attacked us, driving two of their weapons just inches from our faces, the blades slicing between us as we sat under the boat, one of us at the bow, the other the stern."

"Interesting." Jael twisted the braid in her hair, her eyes shifting away. "Whose idea was it to sit at the opposite ends of the craft?"

Azarias glanced away and then back at Jael. "His."

Azarias lowered his eyes and then looked up. "He killed angels to protect me."

"Did he? How many of the enemy has Sosthenes killed since you have been with him?"

"I recall only one. Sosthenes also saved me when a whip bound me."

She shook her head. "Was that angel alone or in a patrol?"

"Alone."

"These Satanic followers won't stop at anything," she muttered while shaking her head.

Azarias grabbed her arm. "What do you mean?"

"The Legion sacrificed one of their own to build trust in you. The same thing happened to us. They sent out angels throughout the wilderness to find us, each trying to befriend our scouts who discovered them."

"Are you saying Sosthenes planned to kill the other angel?"

"No, but they probably only posted the other angel as a sentry to follow you. That angel must have let his ambition overwhelm him. The shocking thing about Satan's Legion is that he has given them free rein with their pride, sometimes resulting in disobedience—at least when I was in Thyatira. His angels will lie, steal, betray—anything—to personally benefit themselves."

"But Sosthenes smuggled out maps for me."

"Those could be fakes. They think you know the Smyrna and Ephesus angels' whereabouts. If not, you would use the Holy Spirit to find them. How did he convince you to trust him?"

"While I was in prison, an explosion ripped open a gaping hole because of your attack. I slipped out and halted because of Sosthenes's prayer. Sosthenes was on the verge of killing himself because of the consequences of my escape. I stopped him. He helped me escape."

Jael placed her hand on Azarias's shoulder and turned away from the other two. "The quake may have been serendipitous. They may have been planning on your escape to follow you to other angels. Sosthenes displayed to you how cunning he is. He changed his plan amid a catastrophe—keeping his head.

"Satan is very patient. He knows that, without God, he and his followers just have to be present when anyone suffers a moment of weakness. He masquerades as an angel of light but draws his power from darkness—his darkness."[249]

Azarias ran his fingers through his scalp and back down to his forehead. His eyes bulged as he massaged his temples. "I don't know who to believe. First, Pollyon betrays me, and now, I am traveling

249   2 Corinthians 11:14

with an angel who I thought was going to die, but only wants to slit my throat."

He dropped his hands and looked up, his eyes widening, his voice increasing in pitch and intensity. "I can't trust anybody."

He looked into Jael's eyes. "Why should I trust you? The sign on your arm doesn't validate you. Pollyon had the sign, too, before he defected." His breathing increased as he shook his head. "I'm alone in leading God's armies to save Heaven. And what will my reward be? A blade in my back."

Jael grabbed him by the shoulders, her eyes riveted. "Anything is possible in spiritual warfare, Azarias. All I can do is inform you of the Sosthenes I knew. You can trust me on this."

Azarias looked up, his face now void of emotion. "How do I know that?"

Jael dropped her hands from Azarias's shoulders. She stood still for a moment and then exhaled. "If he has accepted the Lord, we will find out soon, but you should not involve him in our discussions about the war."

She stepped away, stopped, and then turned back. "It is better to take refuge in the Lord than to trust in angels."[250]

"I understand," said Azarias, his eyes searching. "Right now, we have to decide about saving the angels of Smyrna or Ephesus."

Azarias and Jael returned to the other two.

"Azarias," said Leihja. "Sosthenes told me that you are journeying to Smyrna to save those angels and raise an army. Smyrna is down the river. The profundo banks outside the main district and around a mesa. We may have to sneak into the district center on foot. Still, we are only four angels trying to rescue a hundred thousand or more. If they are still alive, they may be guarded by just as many enemy angels."

Azarias looked at the surface around them, detached leaves reflecting the branches and sky above. It seemed that light did not pass through them when the leaves rested by his feet. He picked

250   Psalm 118:8

one up and turned it. He placed his palm behind it and directed it to the trees. He tilted the leaf back and forth, changing the reflected image above him.

"Are there trees outside Smyrna's district center?"

"Yes," replied Jael. They surround a mesa outside the center. There are many trees on the top of that and the bluffs, leading into the plains. You can't miss the bluff. The ridges are surrounded by violet amborlite which gives off a fragrance."

"Yes, now I remember. Gabriel flew near it during a race back when I could view the missions on my tome."

"Why do you ask?" interjected Sosthenes.

"I'm not sure," said Azarias. "God whispers to me sometimes, but I have to test what I think I hear to make sure that my pride isn't interfering. Some whispers are clearer than others."[251]

---

251   1 Kings 19:12

CHAPTER 25

Azarias hadn't visited Smyrna very often and had to rely on Jael and Leihja. The enemy could be waiting for them anywhere in that great metropolis. He cringed to think about his last encounter in Smyrna. Gabriel had just lost a race to a cheating Baal Zebub, only to be surrounded by enemy angels in the stadium. Fortunately, Michael took control, aiding Gabriel's escape from capture by a hundred thousand angels. Of course, during those times, the Septemviri had a traitor who had broadcast their missions to the enemy. It was indeed a miracle that they all hadn't been captured.

Was this trip to Smyrna going to be different? He glanced at Sosthenes out of the corner of his eye. Could Jael be right? Sosthenes played the part of an ally so well. Why would he use his generous gift of intelligence and strategy against the One who gave it to him? Azarias could ask the same question of a billion other angels who have defected. None of their answers would be adequate.

"The main district surrounding the Paestra Stadium is still in the distance in front of us," said Jael. "Over to the left is the mesa I had mentioned. The forests you asked about start down below and lead up the mesa's slope to its flat top, circling it around to the back. On the plains, the tree canopy surrounds the outcropping."

"Let's fly to the forest's edges butting up against the mesa. I want to examine the entire mesa before risking our lives in the metropolis. Maybe we can use the mesa as a launching area and fly raiding attacks."

"That could subject our Smyrna comrades to extermination," replied Jael.

Sosthenes pulled up. "How can the four of us fight hundreds of thousands of angels?" he questioned, his face not changing expression.

"We trust in the Lord," answered Azarias. He searched carefully for Sosthenes's reaction.

Nothing.

He continued. "We may not have to fight them all, but only enough angels to free our own. They won't use their entire company to guard the Smyrna Holy Order. That would be an impractical and poor use of their resources."

Azarias motioned for them to dive down just below tree canopy level. They hovered. "We only have to find the contingent of angels that are guarding our angels. We have to strike fast and evacuate the angels quickly before the enemy summons their comrades."

Azarias looked at the other two, half of him wanting feedback that would ridicule his plan, the other half wanting their unwavering approval.

Neither came.

"Let's fly just under the forest cover and move up the slope to the top of the ridge. The canopy will provide cover."

They moved quickly, avoiding the branches through the forest, its grade gradually increasing as they gained elevation. The trees resembled the ones they had flown through in the Khasneh Forest and the Profundo River but with little or no undergrowth. It seemed these trees provided only cover above. Oddly, there were no smaller trees growing between them. This configuration offered an advantage and disadvantage. It allowed the angels to fly unobstructed towards their destination but exposed them to any scouts from afar, unlike other forests, where a scout's view was limited. When he escaped with Sosthenes, they had avoided detection until they broke through the upper canopy.

The Profundo River exposed itself in a small meadow as a

tangled web of streams which flowed indiscriminately through the forest floor, transmitting a gurgling that echoed.

Azarias turned to the others. "Let's spread out so—"

An explosion hit the tree just above Leihja, prompting her to duck to the side, but not far enough; as the top of the tree fell, it snagged her wings, taking her down with it.

The other three angels dove down, finding her face buried in the leaves.

Azarias turned her over, her Word sword lying next to her, its blade glowing with righteousness. She opened her eyes and sat up. "Over there." She pointed off to the left in front of them. "I made eye contact with an enemy angel just before he fired. I tried to activate my armor and sword, but it was too late. Their hatchets can launch their pointed blades as speared, explosive projectiles."

Azarias and Jael activated their armor.

He picked up Leihja's sword and did a double take at where the blade had landed, leaving its indentation. The leaves' composition had changed. He picked them up but then dropped them as another blast shattered the tree's trunk on the other side of them. The four ducked as leaves fluttered down around them.

Azarias planted his shield and laid behind it. He traced the trail left by the soaring weapon of death back to a cluster of trees. "Over there, Jael."

Jael fired an arrow. A tree split in two with a crash, exposing two scouts. They darted towards the base of the mesa.

The two enemy angels separated—one right, the other left—and circled back around.

"They're trying to flank us from both sides," yelled Leihja, now fully recovered.

"Jael, keep Sosthenes between us. He's unprotected," ordered Azarias.

Jael and Azarias turned, their backs to each other, Sosthenes huddling between them. Azarias tried to eye the attacking angel on his side, glimpses slipping in and out among the reflective leaves.

He couldn't be sure of the angel's whereabouts. Fighting in a forest familiar to the enemy placed him at a disadvantage.

"I can't see the angel, Azarias. The leaves are reflecting too many movements and confusing me."

Silence returned. Maybe they had gone to get others. If so, Azarias had to make a plan.

The first thing that alerted him were the eyes—the dark red eyes of hatred punctuated by sinister smiles. How had they sneaked within yards of them? Azarias threw his body in front of Sosthenes as a flaming object hit his shield broadside, pushing him into the reformed angel. Jael fired an arrow, exterminating one of the angels. Another shot annihilated the other from above. Leihja stood partially visible on a branch up to their right, her hand clutching her bow as she scanned for other enemy angels.

There was no doubt. The scouts had exposed them. How many enemy angels would they attract? Thousands?

How could Michael instruct an army doomed for destruction? Yes, he knew his faith wavered—this wasn't the first time. Michael believed in God with all his heart, mind, soul, and strength.[252] Yet, he knew he was flawed. Up until now, he had been quiet among the other angels, never questioning God and never doubting God.

Everything had changed. Until recently, Michael would rely on Azarias leading the way and interceding between them and the Lord. From time to time Michael questioned Azarias's interpretation of God's messages, but, for the most part, followed him to where he led the Septemviri.

Now Michael was in charge, with the souls of his friends at stake. He needed all available information to command troops. When God revealed his mysteries a little at a time, Michael cringed. It was one thing to wonder why God sent him on missions before

252   Mark 12:30

the rebellion and another to struggle to understand God's motives when eternal lives were at stake.

Michael posted himself on a peak in the middle of the Red Army's battle line. Somewhere in the far distance on his right, he positioned Malachy, and, on the far left, Zepar. He still didn't completely trust Zepar, but he knew of the rest of the army even less. Any of them could turn against him. If Michael had interpreted the vision on his Septemviri sign correctly, Satan would attack at two points. Which should he go to first? God had been silent. He prayed, but he heard nothing. He must trust God—so he kept reminding himself. In the distance in front of him was Sardis. Had the enemy moved into the district since he had evacuated it? It seemed that would have been the logical reaction—but since when did logic dictate Heaven's events? After all, a third of Heaven's angels had risked eternal damnation to follow one angel.

Michael gazed towards the sparse forces lined up to his right and then to his left. If Satan were to attack—here or at the prede-termined focal points—how would he know? Either of the angels would send messengers, but that may be too late. The distances were great. He placed his hand on his mark and spoke. "Malachy, can you hear me?"

The loyalist mark lit up as Malachy's voice entered his spirit. "Yes," she said. "Everything is quiet."

The sound of her voice settled his spirit. His forces could react to assist her within a reasonable time, depending on how fast Satan attacked.

He then started to call Zepar and stopped. Zepar didn't have a loyalist mark. Michael swallowed hard. Zepar could be under attack now, and he may not know until it was too late.

He looked to his mark and spoke. "Red Army with Zepar, when you are under attack, call out to me for reinforcements. Zepar has not earned the trust to be a member of the loyalists and does not bear the mark."

He paused, pressed his lips together, and added, "In regard to Zepar, please alert me of any suspicious behavior."

Michael turned to an angel who had accompanied him on the peak. "As you inspected the forces, what would you require as a formation?"

"Twelve-long, ten-deep chariot units within signaling range of all chariot units both sides."

"How many units?"

"One thousand. We have collected one hundred and twenty thousand charioted angels to fight Satan's massive Legion at either vector attack."

Michael turned his back and walked to the edge of the precipice. "Lord, we honor and praise Your Name." He dropped to his knees and cradled his forehead in his palms. "We don't understand. We just don't understand." His eyes welled up as his spirit sunk lower than he had ever known before. "Why did you allow the enemy to kill off your loyal followers in Sardis, just to subject the survivors to a force much greater?"

He wiped the tears from his eyes.

"We relinquish control to you, Lord, but, we can't help feeling helpless, ineffective, and useless. We know that, if this were up to our wills and our abilities, we would lose. But with you, anything and everything is possible."

He stood up and looked towards the horizon, his fists clenched. "I will not fear, for you are with me. I will not be dismayed, for you are my God. You will strengthen us and help us, and we know that you will uphold us with your righteous right hand. All those who oppose you will be as nothing and perish. Those who wage war against you will be as nothing at all. We pray this in light of Your Word."[253]

Michael heard a chariot approach from behind, its driver calling out to the horses in earnest. The chariot pulled next to him and the other commander, the visitor's face ashen and eyes unblinking.

---

253   Isaiah 41:10-13

"Michael, didn't you hear it through the mark?" Michael looked down and saw his mark fading from a fiery glow.

"No, I must have missed it." He looked up, his face still surrendering to the feelings within him. "What did they say?"

"We are under attack!"

"Attack?" Michael inhaled and marched towards his chariot. "Which one, Malachy or Zepar? We will have to pull all forces and meet the point of that attack."

The messenger froze, eyeing Michael as he accelerated into a jog.

Michael stopped and turned to the angel. "Well, which of the two attacks are taking place?"

The angel swallowed, drilling his eyes into Michael. "Satan's Legion is attacking both of them with…what looks like…millions."

CHAPTER 26

Squatinidale's breathing increased. The pale riders could be lurking in the walls. They appeared to see well in the darkness, an atmosphere that sickened him. He could see his other six scouts, the tips of their helmets piercing the vinifera to the side and rear of him.

The current pushed the seven towards the voices, some of the murmurs subdued, others more jovial. Fortunately, the loyalist's armor didn't shimmer when out of the Lord's Spirit. If they were out of Satan's darkness, their armor would glisten. Here, it just reflected the dark area around it—a morbid, dark grey.

The voices seemed to be around the bend to the left, the echoes jumbling their content. Squatinidale had to drift closer without revealing himself. He motioned for the others to wait at the protruding wall. There would be a smaller likelihood that the enemy would discover them if only one were to drift closer. The six stalled their drifting, leaving Squatinidale to venture alone. He couldn't just shoot them with an explosive arrow. In this closed area, the blast would echo throughout the labyrinth, alerting the enemy far away.

He turned his head and could see that the river meandered around another turn to the left, leaving this occupied beach protruding out like a small peninsula. The enemy sat facing away from a wall jutting out on the other side, but not to the vinifera edge.

Squatinidale remembered another use of the Word weapon that Leihja had taught them, but he would have to draw them to the beach edge and into close range.

Squatinidale submerged himself; fighting the slow current, he returned to his comrades. He motioned for them to swim back out of earshot of the enemy.

They talked and agreed on a strategy.

Squatinidale and five others then drifted, submerged in the vinifera, just beyond the wall on the enemy's opposite side. They emerged out of sight, no lights, Word weapons held in their hands, blades retracted.

Squatinidale and the allies sat with their backs to the wall, listening to the Legion just around the corner. The enemy angels continued their talking, not discussing anything substantive.

Squatinidale peeked around the corner.

"Ssh. What's that?" cautioned one, standing with his spear in one hand.

One of the others stood, gripping his whip. "What?"

"There, floating around the bend—a body."

"It looks like one of the Creator's disgusting soldiers didn't make it back to his army. His armor must have protected him from death. It looks like he is wounded."

"Do you think the loyalists pushed him through the blockage to get rid of him? He's useless to them now."

They all laughed. "I would have," answered one. They laughed again.

The body floated in the middle of the river, his face down, arms spread out to both sides of him. It spun and bobbed as the current pushed it to its unknown destination.

"Who wants the honor of finishing him off?" laughed the large one.

Two guards hurried waist-deep into the vinifera and retrieved the body to the beach by his helmet. Grabbing an arm on each side, two members of the Legion dragged the body to the edge of the shore. The victim remained motionless.

"Lift his head, and I will send it through the Siq ahead of the rest of his body."

"A *head* of the rest of his body!" laughed the other. "Very well put."

Two of the soldiers lifted the head, raising the shoulders from the shore's surface.

A bright light from the stranger's chest blasted out rays as a star fell out of the front of the armor, blinding the assailants.

"Ahh!" yelled the six as they shielded their eyes.

Squatinidale and the others jumped from behind the wall, shields out, their swords detached from their chests and activated. In one motion, the six loyalists grabbed the blades by their tips and cast them like daggers, hitting all but one of the guards, who leaped behind the others. The other five dissolved, sending their remains down the river, searching for a passage to the Siq.

The large guard ran into a dark tunnel, blending into the shadows, twisting, and turning, the passage lined with darkened walls.

Squatinidale dropped his shield and sprinted, his hand converting the Word into a bow, his breath and pounding feet the only sounds escorting him. In front of him was a *Y* in the tunnel.

Which way should he go?

"Show me the way, Lord," he whispered, anxiety reaching beyond his limits.[254]

His feet took him to the right, his eyes searching for any movement, aching for the Holy Spirit's light. He turned the corner. An extended arm knocked him off his feet, his lit star dislodging partially and resting on his chest.

"Die, you slave!"

Squatinidale clutched the star and held it as a shield in front of him, melting the spear's blade, the faces of Satan protruding from it, the shaft, and finally, the menacing angel holding it, cumulating into a fiery blast.

The explosion impaled Squatinidale's ears, echoing through the tunnels.

The battered angel of God staggered to his feet, his hands groping for the wall and his feet tripping over every othelite with the star no longer as his guide. The explosion ravished his bearings.

---

254   Psalm 25:4

He didn't know whether he was backtracking or going deeper into the bowels of Philadelphia. This direction couldn't be the way. He didn't remember any junctions feeding into the path, but he hadn't been focusing on the tunnel design when chasing the enemy.

Squatinidale fell as the wall abruptly stopped on his left. Staggering to his knees, he saw a lighter atmosphere. The hazy room, if it were a room, drew him. He was lost, partially blinded, and unable to stand. He crawled, turning right, then left, and then right again until he hit another wall.

He turned over on his back, his eyes closed, the top of his head butted against a wall. Why couldn't he do anything right? He had been a burden to the Septemviri ever since they had rescued him from Abaddon in the deserted part of Heaven. They were real archangels; he was just a tag-along that they pitied. Gabriel had known he wasn't ready.

"The Lord gives, and the Lord takes away. Why? What did I do to deserve this?"[255]

Squatinidale opened his eyes and looked straight up into the hazy atmosphere.

Staring at him, just a foot away, were a pair of emotionless eyes on an angel dangling upside down against the wall.

It hadn't hurt too much, but Azarias would not have survived and saved Sosthenes if he hadn't raised his shield. The enemy seemed to know of the armor's limitations. Azarias must inform the others that they were vulnerable at their armor's seams. Satan would search for the weakest part of one's faith and character and attack it relentlessly, weakening its resolve. Time would always be Satan's companion and patience, his slow-moving blade penetrating the soft spots of an angel's perseverance.

Sosthenes cried. "I need to arm myself to help you. I should have taken one of the spears at the boat." He picked up one of the

---

255   Job 1:20-22

weapons, the faces of Satan on the guards on both ends. He walked over and grabbed the other spear. Placing the first one down into the leaves, he scraped off the guards on both ends. Satan's faces whimpered a high-pitched sound before dissolving into the black, fluttering particles.

"Do you think the two scouts could have somehow alerted the others remotely?" asked Jael.

"I don't know," replied Azarias. "The enemy could have been alerted remotely or through the noise of all of our explosions. Either way, it eliminates our surprise attack."

Azarias walked to the tree where Leihja had fallen. He picked up the same bunch of leaves that he had spotted during the attack. Their composition had fused into a slab about the length of his arm. But the leaves no longer let the Holy Spirit's light shine through as it did in undisturbed leaves. The side of the leaves that the Word sword touched had turned to a silver color. Azarias flipped one over and saw his face.

"Jael, is this how you built that reflective room where I was held captive?"

She touched the object. "We were able to connect the leaves and lay them on the surface of the profundo. After some time, the profundo would silver coat the side reflecting the Holy Spirit and meld the leaves together, eliminating all seams."

Azarias smiled and looked up. "I praise you, God, because who is like you, Lord God Almighty? You, Lord, are mighty, and your faithfulness surrounds you."[256]

He looked at the others. "I think God just whispered a way we can win this battle against many.[257] It looks like our skirmish wasn't the only violence in this area by the leaves scattered about. Gather the loose leaves and pile them in this area. Leihja, will you remain on guard to make sure the enemy doesn't sneak up on us?"

Azarias, Sosthenes, and Jael gathered leaves, their clearness acting as prisms for the Holy Spirit's light, shooting vectors of

256   Psalm 89:8
257   1 Kings 19:12

colors back up to the trees. The piles grew, covering all available surface space in this part of the forest. Azarias grabbed handfuls and aligned them in a shape fifteen feet long and three feet wide, side by side at his feet. He glided his sword blade over the surface, melding them together into one large, reflective plane. He stood it up and leaned it against a tree. His entire image reflected as clearly as if two angels were facing each other.

He smiled. "Angels, meet your auxiliary troops."

Leihja flew down and stood next to Azarias. A grin grew into a laugh. "Well, Azarias, you are venturing into Satan's domain of altering God's creations. Be careful."

Azarias remained focused on the image. "True, but my alterations are for good, not evil. Besides, I believe God told me to do this, and I had to test His message."

"Sosthenes, we will need you to stand guard since I need Leihja and Jael to replicate what I did here." Azarias was still unsure about Sosthenes's loyalty, but, if he were to build a virtual army, he needed the other two warriors and their swords.

Sosthenes complied and flew to a high branch.

Azarias and the others made another six large reflective planes quickly, improving their efficiency with each one. He placed one mirror by the base of another tree, slightly upwards towards Sosthenes, and two others in the trees behind Sosthenes, catching the rays of the initial mirror and four more in the trees facing Sosthenes. He and Leihja moved to a spot and turned around, facing Jael, standing by the initial reflection. All reflective surfaces, front and back, met them. Azarias could see four Sosthenes in the trees above him and two in the trees behind him. The foliage covered the edges of all reflectors, veiling the reality that they were not actual angels.

"Sosthenes, point your weapon at the mirror at the tree base," commanded Azarias. Sosthenes complied and raised his weapon. A chill ran through Azarias's spirit. If he hadn't known better, he would have thought that four enemy angels were facing him with their weapons. Since Sosthenes was in the tree, it made the images more convincing. In a heated battle, an angel would not see the similarity in the illusion.

Leihja shot Azarias a confident glance.

Sosthenes chimed in. "All I saw were the both of you standing near a tree."

Azarias smiled.

Azarias walked over to a clearing and drew a parabolic arc in the surface with his sword's tip. "I recall when Gabriel was in a rotunda addressing a Council in the Khasneh District, he heard distant voices speaking as if they were standing next to him. We learned that, if designed right, a parabolic arch can deflect energy and sound waves. Light waves are just another frequency of energy, so I believe we can create reflective images greater than reality."

"So, you are saying that we draw the enemy into the parabolic arc where the images are reflecting?" asked Jael.

"Yes."

"How many mirrors do we build?"

"Enough to convince them that we outnumber them."

Leihja pointed with the tip of her sword. "We couldn't make enough of these mirrors to build an army."

"No, we can't, but parabolic reflections can create a small army. We can position enough to mirror other reflections, creating a very deep image of angels standing behind each other. To the enemy, it will look like a disciplined regiment in a formation, with angels lined up behind angels. We can rapidly fire enough arrows to present a show of force. We only need them to panic and think they are escaping the massive attack. I saw countless reflections of myself in the Thyatira mirrored cave. It was compelling."

"Where do you think they will go?" asked Sosthenes.

"I'm hoping some will lead us back to the captured Smyrna angels. Others may panic and leave," said Azarias. "I'm guessing that we are not far from our captured comrades. Does anyone remember how many of our angels Malachy listed on her roll?"

Sosthenes's eyebrows furrowed and then relaxed. "I recall Pollyon reconstructing a list of a few hundred thousand for Smyrna."

"OK, so they would need a big place to incarcerate them. The Paestra Stadium in the district center is the biggest contiguous area and holds about one hundred thousand, I think. That is too small. The only alternative is to imprison the angels outside of the district center. I don't know the area well enough to lure, repel, and then pursue the enemy. If we can observe their patrols, they will lead us to the captives."

"How will we make them panic and run?" asked Sosthenes, his eyes jumping between the three angels.

"That is where you come in."

CHAPTER 27

Asmodeus paced back and forth in a structure overlooking the Paestra Stadium. He stopped and gazed his transparent turquoise eyes over the empty seats that once entertained at least two hundred thousand angels during the Angelus Pennae games.

Zelbeje entered and stood to his side. "I haven't spoken with you since your failure at the games."

"I had them," started Asmodeus, without turning, the back of his long white hair shielding any tension that would be in his neck. "I had Michael and Gabriel in my clutches right here during the games with two hundred thousand angels to support me."

"How did this happen? We cannot make this mistake again. The cost of failure has risen dramatically since your disastrous attempt, and Satan roars more fiercely each time. The last time we failed, he lost his temper and exterminated the messengers. I don't want to be next."

Asmodeus sighed. "Pollyon had informed us of the Septemviri's missions to seek out our friends and offer them the mercy of the Creator."

He chuckled a little.

"Imagine the audacity of that—luring us back to what we rejected. Mercy is adrenalin to the weak-hearted—it is injected into an angel's spirit for a temporary charge, only to evaporate and leave the angel in a worse state than before."

Zelbeje didn't respond.

"Pollyon still hid his betrayal from the other Septemviri and alerted me of when Gabriel and Michael had arrived. I desperately searched for them, with scouts posted everywhere. We had already captured the Smyrna loyalists and moved them out of the way so they could not interfere. If we tried to capture the two by force with a small contingent, they would get away—especially Michael, since he was the brawny one. I had to get them surrounded by thousands of angels to woo them into our world or at least capture them."

Asmodeus exhaled again.

"I rushed to meet them when one of my scouts reported that they had arrived, delaying the Angelus Pennae race as long as I could."

"How did you entice them into the stadium?"

"The plan was fool-proof. I designed it for these two angels since they were the most gregarious of the seven. Their personalities laid the foundation in convincing one of them that God had chosen them to participate in the famous race. Michael wasn't as excited, so I targeted Gabriel. We feigned that God had chosen him to race against Baal Zebub."[258]

Asmodeus pointed to the arena far below. "The two angels started their race, where the Creator set their course routes, leaving only speed as their tool. They could accelerate or decelerate, but they could only win the race if done within the Creator's Spirit. Gabriel was a master of flying in the Creator's Spirit. He was going to trounce Baal Zebub."

"Why did it matter who won? You could have just captured them without the race once they were in your custody."

"I didn't want to capture them, initially. I wanted to convert the two to Satan's belief. At that stage in our rebellion, we tried not to take angels by force unless they resisted. Satan knew their weaknesses and tempted them with greatness, our best weapon.[259] When we forced someone to believe in our philosophy, there was always the risk of the Creator's Holy Spirit wooing them back. By contrast, when they rejected the Holy Spirit, they severed the path

258 2 Kings 1:3
259 Matthew 4:8-9

of forgiveness, not because the Creator wouldn't forgive them, but because they eliminated any route for it to happen. It is, in effect, blasphemy against His Spirit."[260]

"Understood. But you still haven't told me why you failed," shot back Zelbeje, her eyes narrowing.

"Baal Zebub. It was Baal Zebub."

"Why...how?"

"Pride. He wanted to win and be exalted. His pride has always been his downfall. He cheated and finished the race. He then took over my position as race official and exposed all of us as the Creator's enemy right in front of the two I was trying to deceive." His eyes glossed over. "It was like another spirit had taken over his mouth, whipping the crowd into a frenzy."

"Another spirit?"

"Yes, his mouth moved, but his demeanor changed—maybe his voice, too."

Zelbeje pushed her hair from her eyes. "Maybe it wasn't Baal Zebub's spirit that was talking."

The two angels locked eyes for several moments. Finally, Asmodeus asked the question on both their minds. "Satan?"

"He's done it before."

"Done what?"

"Sabotaged a mission with his pride. He probably didn't like it that Gabriel flew well in the Creator's Spirit."

A silence imposed itself again.

"Regardless of the complications, how did they get away from you?"

"Well, I still tried to salvage this plan and acted like I was as shocked as they were. Gabriel believed me and grabbed me. He flew straight into the charging crowd and handed me off to Michael, who was flying towards us. It happened so quickly. Our comrades collided with each other, causing a momentary pandemonium. Gabriel used his speed to blast out of the stadium and away with Michael."

260   Matthew 12:31-32

"So, Gabriel and Michael took you hostage?"

"Yes. I never thought of it that way. Yes, they forced me to abandon the plan by taking me hostage. Yes, that must be it."

Another angel burst into the room. "Our mesa outpost reported blasts in the forest down the slope from it. Our two scouts have not returned, and we fear they might be under attack."

"Our prisoners," replied Asmodeus to Zelbeje. "I hid the Smyrna angels in the mesa caverns under Baal Zebub's command. The Holy Order must have found out."

"How?" screamed Zelbeje. "How could you let their location leak out?"

Asmodeus ran his fingers through his hair. "I don't know. I purposely restricted the number of guards at each mesa exit so there would be a smaller chance of betrayal. None of them could have left without the others reporting it to me. There were too few."

"Maybe one of the prisoners escaped."

"Impossible! The cave exits are only two angels wide. The guards at each one can eliminate an escaping army, two angels at a time. They couldn't have escaped—unless Baal Zebub failed me again. If so, this will be the end of him."

Asmodeus's breathing increased as he turned to the messenger. "Call out three companies and go to the mesa."

What was Satan going to do to the guards at the mesa if the prisoners escaped? What was Satan going to do to him?

BAAL ZEBUB SCANNED THE TREETOPS FOR ANY MOTION, HIS ears sensitive to any sound. "Which directions did the explosions come from?"

The sentry pointed to the distant groves. "In the number two section. Our scouts have not returned."

"How many explosions?"

"We are not sure—two or three. It must have happened below the canopy since we couldn't see anything. I sent a messenger to report to Asmodeus. He will send us reinforcements."

"Asmodeus! I can't let him get the glory of defeating the attackers," yelled Baal Zebub.

Baal Zebub rifled through his options. He could take up a defensive posture and hold them off until the reinforcements arrived. After all, he did have a superior position nestled in the mesa cliffs. No, he couldn't do that. Asmodeus would take all the credit when he led reinforcements to battle the invaders.

On the other hand, if he repelled this attack before Asmodeus arrived, Smyrna's flawed leader would not be able to steal the accolades. Satan might promote him to lieutenant. Though this decision would not be beneficial for the Legion, it would be helpful for him—and that's all that mattered.

"What are your instructions, Baal Zebub? To hold our positions?"

"No. They don't know that we only have a hundred guarding the exits. If we wait for them to attack, they will realize that we are not a big force—our backs will be up against a wall. They will overrun the guards at the cave entrances. We are not large enough to guard them all against an external attack."

"What if we retreat into the caves, sir?"

"And be mauled by hundreds of thousands of loyalists?" shot back Baal Zebub. "It's good that I am in command. None of you can think beyond your self-gratification."

He looked away and then back at his sergeant. "Leave only two guards at each entrance and bring the rest to me to guard the ledges."

The sergeant obeyed and returned with dozens of angels, fully armed.

Baal Zebub chose twenty angels. They departed, heading in the direction of the disturbance, leaving the rest to guard the bluff.

Baal Zebub didn't like the silence. He enjoyed large, cheering crowds hailing his accomplishments and filling his spirit with pride. The quiet forest reminded him of the peace of the Creator—a nagging peace. The loyal angels still held onto that peace and received joy from the Creator because they trusted in Him. It is the main thing that gave them hope—foolish hope.[261]

In formation, he led the company, slowing towards the area where the explosions were said to have taken place.

Baal Zebub motioned and then mouthed, "Let's walk."

The disadvantage in flying to a battle is that you are visible and vulnerable. Aerial attacks only work as support and cover for infantry. By themselves, they give the enemy the advantage during the approach. He should have started running to the area, not flying. Too late now.

The angels landed and grouped into a bunch, their hatchet-spears poised to fire their blades at any moving object. Up in front, a tree stood, split in two. Was this the site of the explosion? Where were the scouts? He walked over to the tree and ran his finger over the devastated trunk. It burned him. The scouts didn't do this. Loyalists had caused the damage. The Creator's Spirit still lingered in it.

Baal Zebub motioned the others to form into a phalanx. If they were to meet the enemy head-on, he wanted depth and strength.

The company inched forward, with Baal Zebub in the front.

Something ahead caught his attention. There, on the surface. He motioned for his comrades to move even slower.

Upon reaching the object, he picked it up, its edges rough, a shiny surface no bigger than four of his hands. He held it in front of his face. The object reflected his face and those standing behind him. A collective gasp filled the ranks.

Baal Zebub released the reflecting surface with a thud, looking up at dozens of armed Legion members, supported by hundreds of soldiers behind each one, their weapons ready to fire. Who were they, and when did they defect to the Creator's army?

From his peripheral vision on both sides, he saw movement. Turning his head quickly from side to side, he recognized others armed as Septemviri, pointing their weapons at them.

He turned to the back, "Fire at will—" Three explosions from different directions rocked the area, destroying several of his

261   Romans 15:13

Legion soldiers. His eyes widened as he landed on his back, black particles fluttering around him, searching for their passageway into the next world.

They had walked into a trap. Angels were screaming as projectiles exploded into their bodies.

The Legion angels tried to fight back, firing their weapons blindly in the directions of the attack. He had to retreat.

Baal Zebub jumped up and ran through the forest, his location visible to anyone in the area. More projectiles landed beside him.

He took flight.

Glancing back, he could see an enemy angel pursuing him. The other enemy angels must be flying to head off his escape. He weaved through the trees, trying to evade the dogged angel, explosions pummeling him from both sides, his eyes open for any movements around and in front of him. He had to retreat to the mesa ledge. The remaining guards would support him.

Baal Zebub, accompanied by several comrades, returned to the ridge, where the violet amborlite hung over its lips, covering the cave openings and the ledge.

He turned to one of his soldiers, the low-level angel's eyes widening. "Collect all guards and report to me. We're under attack."

"But that will leave all of the cave openings on the other side of the mesa unguarded. The prisoners will escape."

"We can always round up unarmed, escaped angels. If we don't repel this attack, we will lose them anyway. We might be able to stall until Asmodeus returns with his company.

"Go scout the forest for my fighters and return," he screamed at another angel. "They must have been pinned down."

The angel returned with three armed angels. Their faces hardened for a fight. "These are all I could find. There may be others still out in the forest."

The platoon lined up on both sides of him, spreading out among this side of the large ledge encircling the mesa, the purple amborlite shielding their location. "We are under attack by a large force. Many of our own Legion have accepted the false calling of the Creator and joined the enemy."

He stopped. How were they to tell which attacking angels were friendly and which were traitors from a distance? They would have to wait until the approaching angels reached the ledge before deciding whether to fight them—and, by then, it may be too late.

No, he can't risk losing the entire battle over some insignificant fellow Legion member. He raised his head. "We cannot identify which of the Legion comrades returning are friendly and which are attackers dressed in our attire and our weapons. Therefore, shoot at anyone approaching us."

Murmurs spread throughout the ranks. "I know this sounds harsh, but we have to sacrifice the few to save the many."

Six Legion angels emerged from the forest canopy in the distance, racing towards the ledge, their hands gripping weapons.

"Exterminate them!" yelled Baal Zebub.

Some angels raised their weapons and then lowered them, puzzled looks framing their eyes.

Baal Zebub raised his weapon and fired three shots into the small group of approaching angels. The explosions dissolved them immediately.

He lowered his weapon and turned to the others. "Now we don't have to worry if they were friends or foes. I had to sacrifice them for the cause, for Satan."

The defense force remained on alert, each picking a niche on the ledge, a dozen cave openings behind and to the side of them. Baal Zebub didn't shift his gaze from the forest. He knew at least one loyalist angel had pursued him. Where did that angel go? He also knew he saw a large company pointing and firing their weapons. Where were they? Why weren't they attacking? The longer they waited, the better it was for him. Asmodeus should be arriving with reinforcements soon. Baal Zebub only had to resist the attack, and he had well-positioned his Legion members to do so.

In light of this attack, he still retained his prisoners. That was another small victory he could brag about to Asmodeus. He kept his prisoners incarcerated without any guards posted on the other side of the mesa. He had just dispatched a patrol of two angels to scan the perimeter a few times for any disturbance. They reported that the only sign of life was the gross singing praising the Creator that echoed from the caves. The angels were still there, too stupid to know that they could escape at any time. Baal Zebub played the odds and won—a story that would reach the ears of Satan and give Baal Zebub the glory. He fought the temptation to smile to himself but failed. So, this was what it was like to feel like a god.

Movement.

He knew he saw something move to the left, in the number ten sector. Three armed figures moved just above the tree line, two in Septemviri armor, one brandishing a Legion weapon—a renegade. Where were all of the other combatants? Baal Zebub had seen a multitude of renegades.

One of the armored angels called out, his voice barely covering the distance between them. "I am Azarias of the Septemviri. Repent of your evil ways and turn to God or suffer destruction."

The Legion guards turned to Baal Zebub. Laughter started to erupt through the ranks, growing to ear-shattering cheering. Baal Zebub looked into the distance behind the three assaulting angels and saw the beautiful darkening atmosphere migrating towards them.

Asmodeus.

"I did it!" shouted Baal Zebub, stepping to the edge of the ledge. "I have beaten the Creator and his attempt to rescue his pathetic followers."

He looked up to God's Throne and shook his fist. "Is this the best you can do? Is this an example of the *all-powerful* God?"

His comrades cheered him on, some shaking their fists, others jeering at the Almighty.

Baal Zebub looked back to Azarias. "You require faith of your followers. Look where it got them. We will execute the prisoners unless they worship Satan and themselves."[262]

Tears filled his eyes, his face flushed as he looked up. "I reject you, Your Word, and Your Spirit. I no longer need you. I am in control of me, in control of you, and in control of destiny!"

Cheers echoed from the ledge, angels throwing their weapons to their sides and shaking two fists in defiance.

A strong gust erupted, blowing the violet amborlite into a frenzy, its particles stirring in whirlwinds into the faces of the Legion. Baal Zebub raised his arms as the stalks blew into his face. Some of the Legion angels turned their backs, hiding their faces in their wings.

The wind stopped, the repulsive scent of the Creator's Spirit assaulting Baal Zebub's nose.

About five wing-lengths away hovered an armored angel with red-starred hair pointing a Septemviri bow and arrow. Gliding behind her were hundreds of thousands of angels, many pointing their weapons towards the ledge, but most forming an enormous wall with their shiny, black armor.

"You have one last chance before we cast you out of Heaven. Do you reject Satan, all of his evil thoughts and deeds, and worship the Lord God?"[263]

"Never," yelled Baal Zebub and the others.

"You may have saved the angels of Smyrna, but you neglected the angels of Ephesus. As I speak, they are being tormented and destroyed," he sneered. "It is much easier to destroy unarmed angels than armed ones."

He laughed and leaned over to pick up his weapon.

A blast of hot light hit him.

He screamed out blasphemous words to the Creator but not from his mouth.

Then, darkness.

Cold darkness—darkness he had never seen before; it pained him. But he still wanted it.

262   Matthew 4:8-9
263   Matthew 4:10

CHAPTER 28

The famous Pergamum Bibliotheca used by angels to seek God no longer glowed with *His* presence, but rather the presence of Satan.

Pollyon glanced at the colored crystal panes, each displaying eighteen seraphim, and then turned to Abaddon. "We have started our attacks at Vectors 1 and 4, spearheading about a third of Heaven. These vector bases border Laodicea and Ephesus, respectively, linking at Sardis between them."

"What about the other districts throughout Heaven, Pollyon? Satan only targeted seven districts surrounding the Siq; our districts don't account for even half of Heaven's angels. The remaining angels could join the Septemviri and fight us."

Pollyon sighed and moved in closer. "That is the beauty about Satan's plan. He doesn't need to engage the other angels to conquer Heaven. He has dominated all seven major districts closest to the Siq. He will use these bases to invade Heaven with the points of his five-pointed star, or pentagram—the vectors numbered 1, 4, 6, 8, and 11. Each point spears the heart of the Creator, dividing Heaven into five major areas. From there, we will close in on the remaining areas and dominate all of Heaven and ultimately, the Creator's Throne."

Abaddon walked over to the index, the passageway to God's mind for all angels visiting the Bibliotheca. He leaned over its walled railing into the large oval and waved his hand through its mist, creating a circling vapor. "This seems ingenious, but angels still can seek God's Spirit in other ways. Take this Index, for example. Angels flocked here consistently, walking into this oval to enter a link to the Creator's mind asking Him anything. Yet, the angels still seemed to find a way to communicate with the Creator. The fact that we confiscated the Index and the rest of the Bibliotheca (and Pergamum) didn't stop their communications."

"That is the best part," shot back Pollyon. "Satan's strategy hits at the heart of the Creator's power with his angels."

"What's that?"

"Faith. The Creator has this ridiculous notion that His angels will do anything for Him because they have faith. This *faith* is a flawed notion imposed on flawed angels by a flawed Creator, ignoring what they hope for and blinding them to what only He can see.[264] After our initial invasion, Satan will increase his most powerful force against the remaining angels: *doubt*. We have already seen the impact doubt has on the loyalist angels. They first start to doubt themselves and then doubt the Creator. Satan exploits this imperfection in the Creator's plan and penetrates each of the angels' spirits and souls. The process torments them by creating desires within themselves, fueled by pride for things and realities they *think* they need. Many millions have come to our side fueled by it. The Septemviri, their armies, the captive angels, and Heaven will join us because of this doubt."

"And angels that refuse to see Heaven our way? I'm sure there will be many," questioned Abaddon.

Pollyon threw up his hands, his voice casual in manner. "We will destroy them. Either way is fine. I don't care about angels who struggle with self-doubt or angels that don't conform. They are expendable, and we will exile them into the material world where we will rule over them as our servants. They will no longer be in communion with the Creator in the material world, making them defenseless. This exile will also sow more doubt, devouring their self-respect, leaving their souls infused with depression. It will be an endless cycle of condemnation initiated by the seed of Satan, fertilized by pride,

---

264   Hebrews 11:1(distorted)

and perpetually watered by their inability to forgive themselves."

A messenger ran into the large gallery, his magenta-hemmed robe swishing, its movement creating a small echo.

"They have been freed!" said the angel, breathing heavily.

Pollyon drilled his eyes into the messenger. "What? Who?"

"The angels imprisoned in Smyrna. Somehow the Septemviri discovered where they were hidden and freed them."

Pollyon tightened his jaw.

The messenger continued. "One of the guards fled before the final confrontation. He said the attacking force distracted the guards and slipped into the mesa caverns, arming the prisoners, who ultimately overpowered the entire regiment."

"Asmodeus failed us," Pollyon said, turning to Abaddon, his comrade's face glum, a dead look in his eyes.

He turned back to the messenger. "What about Baal Zebub?"

"They killed him along with all of the other guards—but one, of course."

"Baal Zebub never fully believed in our movement. He only wanted to be great," replied Pollyon. "The loss of him is irrelevant."

Abaddon stepped up and jeered, "Now what, *great* Lieutenant, another miscalculation on your part?"

Pollyon balked momentarily, his mind reconstructing the events, measuring the price of failure and the adjustments needed to salvage victory before any more losses.

He turned to Abaddon, his voice barely audible. "We may have lost the opportunity to force these angels to join our side, but we haven't lost the district. It's time to unleash all other star invasions."

Pollyon spun back to the messenger. "As far as the angel who fled to protect himself—kill him. It would have been better to die with courage than to live in cowardice."

An invasion? On two fronts?

Michael couldn't fathom a strategy to defend not just one of the fronts, but two? He knew Satan's position, one spearheaded between Sardis and Pergamum, the other between Sardis and Ephesus. With their chariots, the Holy Order may have outmaneuvered either one of these fronts, maybe flanking the enemy on the side. But two battlefronts, with a fraction of angels? Perhaps he misinterpreted the Lord's directions, his pride. Now what could he do?

"Michael? Michael?"

He shook his head and looked at the messenger. "What?"

"Michael, what do we do?"

"Hold our ground," he muttered. "Trust in God."

"Hold our ground?"

"Yes, I need time to think. For right now, I have to save the lives of our comrades and prevent the enemy from taking our chariots."

Michael grabbed his wrist and called out, "Hold fast, but don't advance until further instructions."

Malachy affirmed his message, but Zepar did not have a mark and couldn't hear. Would one of the other angels tell him?

Michael turned to one of his lieutenants, "Fly to assist Malachy. I will fly to Zepar. I don't know if he heard the command. Besides, I still don't trust him. He may lead his company into the arms of Satan just to save himself."

Michael flew his chariot down the Red Army's line, watching as his chariot army held fast, God's flaming chariots at the ready.

Michael had to find Zepar and make sure he was not betraying him, his army, and God. Flying at this high speed, Michael could not distinguish among the angels. He may have already passed Zepar. How could Michael tell them apart in this multitude? He asked the Lord's Spirit to enflame the marks of all angels who bore them so he could see them from above.

As Michael passed along the line, a dark cloud, bigger than he had ever seen, boiled in the distance to his right. The dark mass rolled over the terrain, detonating the amborlite in its path with explosions and wild blazes. It used God's blazing flowers as the forefront of its assault. A chill ran through Michael as he experienced

the destruction of Heaven fueled by hate.

Up ahead, among the thousands of glimmering angels, was one angel not glowing with the loyalists' mark. It had to be Zepar. The defector angel was retreating, riding away from the attack, taking other angel chariots with him.

Michael swerved down, moving up to the side of the flying chariot. Zepar turned, his shoulders tight, hands projecting jerky movements upon his steeds. He shot a glance, still focusing on his horses. "Your God betrayed you, Michael. He provided you with a pitiful army to battle the full might of Satan. What was I to do, stand in the way and let Satan destroy me?"

Zepar whipped the horses, who seemed to want to turn back. "There is another thing, Michael. I'm a traitor. Satan and the Legion make examples out of those who turn by torturing us before death. I have seen these angels experience immeasurable pain in their spirits, crying out to the Creator, who seemed to turn a deaf ear." He turned his head. "You have never seen that happen. Once you do, you will never forget it. I have seen it happen dozens of times. Satan's Legions make a public spectacle of it to deter others from betraying him. I don't have the courage you do to confront evil. I see too much of myself when I do."

Michael didn't know what to say. He struggled over whether to trust this angel. On the one hand, he was a renegade, pitching his loyalty alongside Satan for a long time, condemning, imprisoning, and maybe even executing his fellow angels who refused to betray their God.

On the other hand, Zepar confessed his shortcomings and his fear. He said he realized he was not a "god." He seemed so contrite. Michael had to trust him—for now.

Zepar paused a long while before continuing. "You know what they will do to me when they catch me, don't you?"

"Either reward you or destroy you. You are leading God's army into defeat," scoffed Michael. "The choice is up to you."

"Michael, I don't know what to do to show you my sincerity. I did what you wanted up until the time when Satan charged. Haven't I proved enough to you?"

"Like in Sardis, when you refused to help me turn back and fight the cloud that devoured so many of the angels?"

Zepar didn't respond. He juggled his reins, his eyes focusing ahead.

"I didn't know what to do. I still lack faith in God in times of trouble. I turned my life over to Him but still struggle to trust that He has forgiven me."

"He has forgiven you, Zepar, if you are sincere. You must trust in where He guides you."

Zepar laughed. "Like now, Michael? Do you trust God enough to stand in the way of a deadly wave?"

"I trust but don't always understand. I cannot see how God can take our weaknesses and use them for his purpose. He can take the weak and defenseless and make them triumphant."

Michael could see Zepar shaking his head.

Michael's eyes wettened. He dropped the reins, letting the horse fly unguided, its tact slapping and jingling in careless rhythms. He opened his arms to his sides and looked up, closing his eyes. "Lord, I honor your Holy Name. I trust in you with all my heart and lean not on my understanding. In all my ways, I submit to you, for you will make my paths straight."[265]

A warm wind blew over Michael's face, its soothing touch calming his anxiety. Yes, yes. God was in control, not him. He doesn't retreat. God revives.

He raised his arm and clutched his mark. "Malachy and the angels of the Red Army, drop your reins and give them to God's Holy Spirit to guide you."

Michael opened his eyes and turned to each side. The entire Red Army (as far as he could see) was retreating with him towards the outer limit of this level of Heaven.

"Look! What's that in front of us?" yelled Zepar. "Has Satan's Legion headed us off? How could they cut off our retreat?"

---

265   Proverbs 3:5-6

CHAPTER 29

Squatinidale laid on his back, his head aching, the ringing in his ears subsiding. What was the meaning of this vision—the image of a catatonic angel hanging upside down against a wall? Why did God send such a grotesque picture? Hadn't he suffered enough without a cryptic depiction of death?

It didn't move like the amborlite or Bibliotheca visions. The angel dangled and stared with his mouth open. His arms seemed to be pinned to his side, allowing the head almost to touch Squatinidale's face.

Squatinidale thought it was odd that God would send this to him as he pleaded for his life. Maybe God sent him this vision to show him his future, the future of death—it certainly was an ugly one. Squatinidale thought of crying out for his comrades, who probably had heard the explosion and were looking for him. They may never find him in this labyrinth.

"Help! Anyone! Help!"

His voice echoed in the room but apparently couldn't find the exit. He listened very carefully for voices and then yelled again. "Help!"

His faint "help" returned, but from where? It sounded so quiet, almost as a whisper. These tunnel acoustics played tricks on him, or the explosion had damaged his ears.

He opened his mouth to yell again, but the faint echo returned. "Help me."

Squatinidale muscled his way up to a sitting position. The vision of the upside-down bound angel remained, but now as a full body.

The victim's mouth moved and emitted a very faint sound: "Help me."

Squatinidale jumped up and moved back, his feet still pliable, struggling to keep standing upright. The angel was not a vision but a living angel with hands tied to his side by one of the Legion's golden rings. Oddly enough, the troubled host's feet were tied above by one of the enemy's whips without the usual whip death energy.

Squatinidale remembered the golden ring from when Abaddon had captured him after they had attended the "Great One's" (now called "Satan") Throne. The stout little angel still bore the marks on his arms when he lifted his sleeve—the brand of his former unfaithfulness. He stopped short on the last thought of "once unfaithfulness." He still lacked enough faith.

Squatinidale moved closer to the troubled angel. Different thoughts blazed through his mind. Who was this? Could this be a trap? Why hadn't the whip killed the angel? Fear gripped him; he didn't know what to do. The angel looked ashen, not glorious like other angels. His vacant eyes no longer radiated with the love of God and his Holy Spirit. His hair was still bronze but tarnished with fear and cut very short. Squatinidale had never seen an angel without shoulder-length hair. His forearms were exposed but no longer displayed the radiating channels of God's messenger. The pasty skin covering seemed to obstruct, not transmit, their brilliance. What shocked Squatinidale the most was the angel's hands. The fists were not closed but open. The palms opened upwards, fingers spread, wrists arched backward—an angel's position of worship to God. It was as if, despite this angel's torture, pain, and helplessness, he still resigned to worshipping God. Was his faith so great that he still praised God?

Squatinidale stepped back. Was this some kind of semi-death for an angel? As the angel tried to move, a jolt of energy rippled through his body, creating a moan, casting a flash around him.

Squatinidale kneeled, almost losing his balance again. "I'm afraid to touch you. I don't know who you are. Why are you bound here?"

"Don't be afraid. I am a loyal angel of the Lord. Please untie the whip. It won't hurt you," he said, as each word he emitted seemed to shoot pain through his body.

Squatinidale turned around and staggered to the room's opening to leave.

"Please! Don't leave!" said the distraught angel, his voice trailing off. "God sent you to us. The Lord is gracious and dependable, but he works through His creations. Angels are part of His creations and do his Will. Please do not turn your back on Him and us."

Us?

Squatinidale ducked out the opening and retrieved his star. Holding it to his chest, he whispered, "Lord, you are my light and my salvation—whom shall I fear? You are the stronghold of my life—of whom shall I be afraid?"[266]

The Septemviri member returned to the room he had exited and held the star up. The room wasn't round as he once thought. It wasn't a room at all, but a hallway disappearing as far as he could see. Angels hung on both sides, upside-down, hair cut to obstruct the flow of the Holy Spirit throughout their bodies. Rings bound their arms to their sides. The number of angels strained his estimation because the walls disappeared far away into the dismal atmosphere of death.

Squatinidale walked over to the troubled angel and placed the prisoner's head on his knees. Taking out his sword, Squatinidale cut the whip, knocking the Septemviri commander backward.

Squatinidale rolled over and removed the ring. Sitting the embattled angel with his back against the wall, he looked into the distraught angel's eyes. The angel spoke, "Mai Deus Exsisto vobis." He forced a slight smile onto his face.

"Mai Deus Exsisto vobis," replied Squatinidale. "Who are you, and what happened to you?"

"I am Dionysius, the former Administrator of Philadelphia." He paused.

"Who are you, my courageous friend?"

---

266   Psalm 27:1

Courageous friend. Squatinidale liked the sound of that. The prisoner wouldn't say that if he knew what Squatinidale had thought when he was trying to leave.

Squatinidale raised his sleeve, exposing the mark of the Septemviri. Its uncovering created a slight glow on the rescued angel's face.

Dionysius looked at the Word sword and again back to the mark. "Are you a Septemviri?"

Squatinidale nodded.

Dionysius laughed a little. "This is the second time a Septemviri has saved me. The first was one named Rafaella." His face saddened, and his eyes drifted to the right. "I think I caused her death."

"No, you didn't," said Squatinidale, grabbing his shoulders. "We rescued her, and she is serving as one of the commanders of God's army."

Dionysius smiled a bit. "Thank you. You have taken a heavy weight from me."

Squatinidale stood him up and leaned him against the wall. "Who are all of these angels?"

"Loyal members of Philadelphia left here to die slowly," said Dionysius. "And we would have died if not for you. Help free us, and we will join you in the fight."

"But you are so many," replied Squatinidale, his head still hurting. "The two of us would take too long to free all of them."

"What is impossible for angels is possible with God."[267]

THE LEGION'S SMYRNA FORCES TURNED AROUND AFTER VIEWing the massive Holy Order White Army encircling the mesa. God did not tell Azarias to pursue them, so he held his army back, awaiting other premonitions.

Baal Zebub's words had stabbed him in the heart.

You may have saved the angels of Smyrna, but you neglected the angels of Ephesus. As I speak, they are being tormented and destroyed.

---

267   Luke 18:27

It is much easier to destroy unarmed angels than armed ones.

Was Baal Zebub telling the truth? Had Azarias made a mistake by trying to rescue the angels of Smyrna first? He couldn't be sure. Satan lied; the Legion lied. Every one of them had lost the ability to tell the truth. To Azarias, it seemed that, once this foreign concept of "sin" entered Heaven, all truth vanished from the souls of those who submitted to it. They had lied as easily as Azarias told the truth, with no apparent remorse; they lied to get what Satan wanted and what they wanted. And what about Satan's followers who perpetuated his lies? Did they stop to think if what they were repeating was true? They parroted their leader's lies and tried to use them to advance his—along with their own—selfish agendas.

Azarias shook the thought out of his head and instead thought about Ephesus. The district had always warmed his heart. While other places in Heaven allowed angels to feel God's presence through his creation, Ephesus provided angels a forum to worship God using their artistic gifts. The large amphitheater stood as a platform for angels to sing and recite poetry, all in praise, plea, thanksgiving, or anything else to God. To relinquish it to the enemy was to lose access to the ear of God. His heart ached at the thought.

If Azarias were to battle angels in Ephesus, he would have to have hundreds of thousands to accomplish it, along with Jael and Leihja—he still wasn't sure of Sosthenes.

Azarias called two seraphim. "Please fly fast to scout Ephesus. Let me know if you can find hidden or captive angels and whether there is a force imprisoning them."

Azarias pondered the captive angels' thoughts as he led the White Army infantry between Al Birka and Thyatira towards Ephesus. He hoped that the other Septemviri had rescued angels hidden in the other districts, though he cringed at the casualties he had endured with the Thyatira angel battle. (Jael confirmed that Gabriel saved them).

A dark interruption in the far distance towards Thyatira caught the attention of his left eye. Could that be the enemy? The force didn't seem so large.

Leihja and Jael pulled up next to him. "Do you see it?"
"Yes, it doesn't look as large as our army," said Azarias.
"Follow me."

Leihja flew up into the atmosphere, higher than most angels fly during their missions. She stopped and directed Azarias's attention. "Look."

Azarias swallowed hard. The dark disturbance wasn't a small contingent of angels moving from Thyatira. No. What Azarias saw was the point to a larger force moving behind it. Satan's army spanned as far as Azarias could see, their menacing hate extinguishing remote district outposts dotting its path, killing unknown numbers of angels.

Leihja and Azarias did not have time to stop for a prex précis but asked God to give them a plan. Azarias knew God was in control, but he must muster the faith to hear him.

Something made him turn to his right and gaze at the Al Birka mesas in the distance. A warm feeling engulfed him as he thought about the times in the past he would walk upon their flat tops, hearing the angels sing far above at God's Throne. Life had been so peaceful back then. He'd perform his missions and bask in the presence of God's Spirit. That peaceful time had ended because of one cherub.

The golden amborlite, dripping from the mesas, started to move. Azarias thought maybe he imagined it, but no, it was moving, dissolving, pouring into a large canyon that gouged the level surface of the mesa. The canyon had always been there. Azarias would climb in it at times in meditation. A golden *V* formed as the amborlite dripped down the canyon's edges, leaving the center the usual color. From Azarias's perspective, the golden *V* devoured the canyon from the outside in, leaving the whole canyon layered in gold.

The vision vanished, leaving the canyon and mesas undisturbed.

Azarias looked to the approaching force, to his army, and then to Leihja. "Praise God! I've got it. I've got the plan."

"What is it?" Leihja opened her glowing eyes.

"God's Spirit took me back to my origins, the origins of where I used to seek Him. I always wandered those mesas in the distance calling for Him. I would only hear music sung by the angels at His Throne. He never seemed to answer my questions about why I was doing certain missions—I kept asking."

"Go on."

"I used to climb that canyon, that *V*-shaped canyon, not realizing that I was climbing within the palms of his hands. He had always been there for me, and now he used my memory to tell us what to do."

"Azarias, please!"

"The enemy looks as if it is marching in a ridged formation of small boxes or cohorts. They anticipate a frontal attack and will try to punch through it with the point of their wedge. We will do the opposite of what the enemy is doing and not meet force with force, spear with spear, or arrow with arrow. To do that will create a lot of casualties, and every angel is precious to God and me."

Azarias drew a *V* shape with his finger. "We will lure them. We will use their pride their perverted self-confidence that they are gods, and draw them into the hands of God. Once they are in His hands, He will close them and trap them in a crossfire."

CHAPTER 30

R iding with the Holy Spirit in full control of the entire Red Army, Michael could not understand God's plan. Initially, God had positioned the Red Army in a razor-thin line to confront not one but two of Satan's massive attack vectors. When Michael joined his retreating army, Satan seemed to block their retreat.

Zepar yelled out, "Well, Michael, I thought God was as rational as I in opting for self-preservation over victory, but I guess I was wrong. For some reason, He wants to crush us between the attacking forces."

Michael didn't respond or even glance to the side. He had struggled with understanding God's strategy before. Yet, Michael knew that God worked miracles—of which he had experienced so many. In those times, Michael gave him what little he had to offer. God blessed it and gave it back in a more significant result than he could have imagined.[268]

Michael eyed the mass in the far distance in front of him, which differed from Satan's usual black clouds; it had more of a red tint. Was this another destructive cloud? This force could explain how Satan could conquer places in Heaven where his Legion wasn't present.

Malachy's voice echoed in his head. "Michael. God has turned our chariots around into a retreat and is plunging us towards

---

268   Matthew 14:19-20; John 6:11-13

another attacking mass. Maybe I can plot a map and get each of us to a safe location. I have my maps with me."

"Keep your hands off the reins, Malachy," barked Michael, "and let God's hand do His work."

She didn't respond, the sound of the squeaky chariot reminding Michael that, no matter how much they complained, the power continues forward with the Lord, and He will be faithful to complete it.[269]

"Look on our left horizon," said Zepar, pointing ahead of them.

The massive force approached them with the same pointed attack as Satan's vanguard—not at Michael, but between his and Malachy's companies. "Is Satan trying to divide us by driving a wedge?"

"I don't know. I have never been in a battle this size with the Legion," said Zepar.

Malachy chimed in through Michael's mark. "Michael, do you see the point of the attack to your left? It is on the horizon to our right, driving a wedge between us! They are trying to divide the army and conquer us. I can't see the end of the charge. It is so massive."

"Let God control this, Malachy. I don't know God's strategy, but I do know He loves us."

As the reddish tint grew closer to the left, Michael could see that it consisted of a mixture of flying chariots and infantry angels. Michael gasped when he saw that Satan had colored this Legion red to confuse the Holy Order as to who was their fellow combatant and who was their enemy. How would they distinguish their Holy Order army from the attacking black vector behind him? Michael hated to admit it, but Satan's ability to strategize far exceeded his own.

The red assault passed in the distance between him and Malachy. There seemed to be no end of them. He couldn't believe the size of this force. Had Satan conquered the rest of Heaven without Michael's knowledge? This force seemed almost twice the size of the power attacking them in the black onslaught.

269   Philippians 1:6

The sound grew to a deafening level where he couldn't tell if the noises were from his chariot or the impending army. Whatever the case, he would fight to his death for the right of God to rule Heaven.

The opposing force descended on them. Michael and Zepar yelled as they lead the charge, their sabers waving over their heads.

The red chariots and angels in front of them charged without slowing, apparently determined to bowl over his small red company like they were a field of amborlite.

Michael couldn't distinguish individual riders and angels as the fast-moving mass closed the distance between them.

The enemy parted, creating a hole in their assault, allowing Michael's angels to ride through their ranks untouched. The aggressor army's passage curved to the left and guided Michael's angels in a curved causeway towards Malachy's company. Were they trying to combine them into one massive prison camp? That had to be it.

Michael had no choice but to lead his company into the void opened by the enemy, their massive forces funneling them into their midst. The synchronization of so many angels and horses stunned Michael. How did the enemy communicate with millions of cavalries to channel Michael into their center?

Regardless of how they had managed this, they wanted to surround and capture them.

"Michael. I have to escape. I can't let them take me!" screamed Zepar, shooting glances all around him.

"Give it over to the Lord, Zepar," said Michael. "This is a good time for you to learn what it means to have faith."

Zepar held his place. Michael wasn't sure if it was because of what he said or that Zepar had no exit, as angels passed on either side of them—and now over them—on their way to join Satan's two central attacks.

As the funnel turned them perpendicular to the attack, the enemy's ranks seemed like a tunnel of red fire flying from Michael's right, over him, and descending on his left.

This funneling confused Michael. Was God thwarting the enemy's plan, making them fly above and around Michael's angels? Why would He drive Michael and Malachy's companies into the center? Shouldn't he be directing them away from the center to escape?

The attacking angels in front of Michael ended their arching wave motion, exposing the area between him and the oncoming Malachy, her company of charging chariots in a mirrored formation to Michael's company.

Michael was right. The attacking angels were trying to corral them and lead both companies into the center to contain them in their march through Heaven. Was the enemy planning to conduct mass extermination?

Darkness spiked Michael's spirit as he fought to believe in what God was doing. In his wisdom, God must believe that Michael and his army must be captured and humbled. Michael struggled to accept his fate, but he knew that God shines brightest in the darkest times. He closed his eyes and said, "I believe in you, Lord, with all of my heart, might, soul and strength."[270]

He breathed deep, trying to feel the presence of God that he felt when he was alone.

"Look, Michael," said Zepar.

Michael opened his eyes.

His chariot had slightly changed directions, turning to its left and joining the enemy's movement back towards the center of Heaven and Satan's attacking Legion. Malachy's company had turned to her right, merging the two companies side by side towards Heaven's interior. They accelerated in the center of the point, charging forward.

"Michael," called Malachy, her face still uneasy. "I calculate the center part of this charge is cutting between Satan's two attacks heading towards Sardis."

Sardis? So, the enemy was taking them back to imprison them at Sardis. Why would they need a force twice the size to do it?

---

270   Deuteronomy 6:4; Mark 12:30

An angel with golden wings and a dark bronze face landed on the back of Michael's chariot. Michael turned to strike with his saber. The angel wore God's armor.

"Michael, peace be with you. We are not your enemy. You have shown great faith in the Lord. We are part of the Red Army who will follow you into battle. We have come from the outlying districts in Heaven, those that Satan neglected to infect. God has been waiting for you to trust Him enough to lead his army. You have passed His test."

Both Michael and Zepar froze, their mouths open, sabers at their sides, horse and chariot now glowing brighter—or so it seemed.

Michael felt an upwelling like never before. He had trusted God with every ounce of faith he could muster and thought it wasn't enough, and God came through. He vowed never to doubt God again for even a second, allowing the Most High to fulfill His plan, no matter the circumstance.

The angel departed and spoke to Malachy before disappearing into the massive Red Army. Malachy looked at Michael, her face erupting with a joy he had never seen from her.

He called out. "Malachy. God must want us to start securing Sardis, cutting off the intersecting district of Satan's two charges. We now have a great army to fulfill His purpose."

Malachy nodded.

Michael led the enhanced Red Army of flaming red chariots to Sardis, a familiar district to him now. This time, he would be attacking Satan's forces and not just trying to defend the unarmed.

Was he up to the task?

No.

But God was.

Still dazed from his fight, Squatinidale finished unbinding Dionysius and a few others left hanging upside down in the vinifera caverns between Philadelphia and Pergamum. The moans erupted as those closest realized that their rescuer had arrived. Squatinidale couldn't be sure of how many were hanging since the walls on both sides disappeared into the haze a long, long way down.

A noise startled him as a light found the entry to their hall. "Squatinidale, we found you," said one angel, his face beaming. The other six entered the room, smiles and burning stars accompanying them.

Squatinidale turned to them, staggering as he tried to walk. "I have found the imprisoned angels of Philadelphia. Help me untie some so they can unbind the others."

One of the loyalists looked down the hall. "My Lord. How many are there?"

"We started with a thousand, but I don't know how many are conscious," said Dionysius.

Squatinidale interjected. "We don't have time to untie each of them. Will you and the others fly down the hall and cut the whips and rings binding about one hundred angels? Then the freed angels can help release the others. These angels will be here for some time, helping each other."

Squatinidale clutched two members of his squad, partly to alert them, partly to stabilize himself. "Return to the rest of our strike force and set up at the beach point. We must regroup. If you see other enemy angels, try to evade them until you are at full strength. We have not seen the last of them, especially since they may have heard our skirmish."

"Squatinidale, we must retrieve our horses," said Dionysius, his hand rubbing his forehead.

"What horses?"

"The pale horses. We are the pale riders' company. God provided them to us to use in the war, but, while we were waiting, Satan's forces ambushed us in the hills emerging from the dark lake. They were able to blend their appearances into the horses, evading detection in darkened areas."

The two angel scouts started to depart back to the special forces when Squatinidale raised his hand. "Wait."

"When you return, try to open part of the barricade. Pick two others to go back to Gabriel and Rafaella. Tell them what has happened and that we will not be returning. We must help these captives recover their horses. Tell Gabriel that we are going to the Bibliotheca, where I think the enemy is based. Tell him we will see them in Pergamum or Laodicea."

He paused and then continued.

"Once you do this, bring the rest of our squad along the river to the beach where we skirmished. If we are not there, proceed along the river until you see a narrow dark passage going up to your right. (I hope that was the only passage). We had entered the Bibliotheca that way when we rescued Rafaella and Malachy. We will rendezvous with you at that junction. If you do not find us there, continue along the river to Laodicea. There is a water-rise that Azarias used to defeat a band of angels who were following us. I heard that the Spirit might have reestablished it, allowing it to, once again, surface in the Laodicea public bath. Proceed to there and assess the situation."

He turned to walk away and then turned back. "Above all, be vigilant. We are dealing with skilled adversaries led by a powerful leader."

The two angels departed. A feeling arose in Squatinidale that he may never see them again—a sense that occurred too often.

Squatinidale addressed Dionysius and some of his released comrades. "Do you know of another way out of here that leads to the Pergamum Bibliotheca? I fear that the enemy may be upriver and will ambush us. We must retrieve your horses and eliminate any Legion angels who may trap the rest of the special forces when they return."

"I am not sure," said Dionysius. "Up until recently, I didn't know where the Philadelphia draining fissure led. I only theoretically knew of its existence." He rubbed his jaw, still opening and closing it. "I have a theory."

"What's that?"

"We know that, wherever the Legion goes, the Holy Spirit doesn't dwell, which created a dark and sometimes hazy, morbid atmosphere. I suggest we go back and turn before we get to the beach and head into a large corridor I saw when they brought us here. We can search halls and follow the trails of their morbidity. When we come to a junction, we should walk down the darker way. Their sin and air of rebellion will lead us; we may exit from a place they would least expect."

Squatinidale's mouth erupted in a smile, the first since his fight. "Rafaella told me about your intelligence. She said you had a gift of curiosity."

"Yes, my curiosity dogs me with endless questions and diversions," said Dionysius, shaking his head.

The angels waited until they released the last of the imprisoned angels and exited the hall. It seemed most of the bound angels recovered, but others still needed assistance to walk. They relished in the love of their fellow angels, jockeying for the opportunity to help them.

Dionysius found the large corridor leading towards Pergamum and the Bibliotheca, still some distance from the river. The passage was similar to the last, but a dark haze accumulated as they walked deeper.

Trailed by a thousand angels, Squatinidale and Dionysius reached a three-corridor intersection. The aisle to the right seemed a little darker, but, in the distance, it was much darker.

"We go that way," pointed Dionysius, continuing his lead.

The column of angels behind them, four across, crept down the darkening passage, occasional offshoots meeting them along the way. Squatinidale marveled at God's work in this forsaken place. Since Dionysius hadn't been in the underworld, he wondered who had dwelled down here. Why would God build a complex matrix of passages for nobody?

An arm thrust out from behind the corner at the intersection and grabbed Dionysius around the neck, yanking him to the right, his muffled voice calling for help.

CHAPTER 31

Angels always used the phrase, "in God's time." They mean to project their faith and patience by saying it, but there is a problem with that statement: God exists outside of time. True, angels experience eternity like God while in Heaven. However, in the angel's mind, they live in a linear continuum where one act is followed by another. There is no getting around it. For God, there is no past or future, so everything is in the present. Azarias couldn't explain it, but, since God is always in the present, He is always I *am*—not *I was*, or *I will be*, but *I am*.[271] God's message to Azarias about the dripping amborlite *V* was as timely to God now as when Azarias had walked through the canyon so long ago. But, to Azarias, it was only timely now because he couldn't foresee future events.

Azarias extended his flanks to an equal distance on both sides of him, many angels deep. The angels stood as a substantial force, facing the arrow-shaped charge of Satan. Through his mark, Azarias instructed his army of well over a hundred thousand. Leihja, Jael, Sosthenes, and he met the invaders' point of the charge, shoulder to shoulder. Azarias yelled a command, and, instead of the center army charging forward, it retreated backward. The Black Army retreated, starting at the center, with those on the sides moving with them. The peeling motion of the retreat created an enveloping *V* to Satan's attacking *V*. As the enemy angels moved forward, Azarias's

271   Anselm, *Proslogian*, translated by Thomas Williams, Chapter 22, page 20-21; Exodus 3:14

Black Army flew backward, deepening the giant *V*, with the distance closing between them and their pursuers.

Though he was close enough to hear the insults and cheers of the enemy ranks, he commanded his troops to keep a distance of about one hundred angels standing shoulder to shoulder.

Azarias remained facing the enemy but glanced back at the mesa, closing its distance during his retreat. He thought of himself as running back to God—the God who knew his name, the God who knew his thoughts, and the God who had fearfully and wonderfully made him.[272]

Though Azarias could think of himself as running to God, it was time he stopped and defended Him.

Azarias halted the Black Army, enclosing the two sides of Satan's arrow attack. The enemy's army ceased, too, but now within the eyeshot of his army.

Azarias raised his hand, the sign of the Septemviri glowing brighter than it ever had.

Silence immersed both armies as they stared each other down.

"You have one last chance to throw yourself at the mercy of God—the only true God," he yelled.

Nobody said anything. Azarias thought he could succeed in persuading some converts, but it seemed hopeless.

Finally, one angel from the opposing force stepped out, dropping her spear.

"I will. Lord, I have sinned. Take me back. I don't want to die!"

The angel ran forward, shedding her armor, crying, which brought tears to Azarias's eyes. She had almost reached him, her eyes red with remorse, when a spear pierced her in the back and went completely through her spirit. She fell forward into Azarias's arms, her body dissolving.

Azarias hung onto her, her mouth open and eyes frozen wide. He repeated what he had heard a voice tell him from God's Spirit. "Our God is a gracious God and forgives you."

---

272   Psalm 139:14

She smiled as her body dissolved into a white fluff of particles, her gentle eyes the last to go.

One of the Legion forces started to laugh, which spread to the whole army, going back farther than Azarias could guess.

Azarias clenched his teeth, his eyes glaring. He raised his hand again and said, "May God have mercy on you."

He dropped his hand, the flaming sign on his arm seen and felt by all of his army.

Fiery arrows filled the air like blowing amborlite stalks as the Black Army attacked Satan's forces from the front and the two sides, catching many in the crossfire. The arrows were so thick and went so far back into the enemy ranks that the projectiles partially obstructed the view of the sky. The Legion tried to fight back, but their frontal assault strategy left them few options under this circumstance. Screams from the Legion hurt Azarias's ears. He couldn't distinguish the black particles from the arrow barrage, as the atmosphere seemed to dim the light of the Holy Spirit.

Azarias commanded the army to move forward and inward as Satan's forces relinquished ground through retreat and destruction. The Black Army started marching and then took flight as they pushed the enemy towards Thyatira and beyond.

Farther and farther, they drove the enemy. Some tried to seek refuge in the Thyatira castle, only to be flushed out by Black Army squads who peeled off to search for them. The counter-offensive pushed Satan's forces through the Khasneh Forest and the desolate canyon where Azarias had first discovered Satan's battle strategy.

Azarias's army drove Satan's army without allowing them to rest or regroup until they had reached an area previously unseen by Azarias—the dreaded Siq. He had always imagined it as a large black hole that extended from horizon to horizon. But it was more than that. As the Black Army pushed forward, the black hole became a black sphere with countless galaxies dotting it—the entrance into the material world.

The Holy Order Black Army fired barrage after barrage of arrows at the enemy, forcing the enemy into the Siq. Other angels took flight and exited through the black mass as black particles.

The battle was over for now, and Azarias called to his army. "I pray that Gabriel and Michael have had the same success as we have had in their counter-offensives. We must go to Ephesus and rescue the other captured angels. Once we do that, we will be at full strength to attack Laodicea on the other side of Heaven, freeing those captives. But first, I still have to survey our army and tally the survivors."

Just then, the two scouts returned from Ephesus. One of the scouts stepped up, his face void of emotion. "Nothing, utterly nothing."

"What do you mean by 'nothing'?" replied Azarias, his face on fire.

"Ephesus and its angels do not exist anymore," stammered the angel. "The entire area is in ruins with no life. We looked every place we could find. Ephesus and its angels have been decimated."

Azarias turned and walked away.

He wept.

It's incredible how little Gabriel understood. Satan had attracted his followers by providing "knowledge" that God had "denied" them. What a foolish bargain. They traded their eternal life in Heaven for a piece of dubious knowledge offered by another angel. Why had they done that?

Gabriel got up from the beach overlooking the Philadelphia lake and started to walk up the hill. He didn't want to fly. He wanted to be alone with God in prayer, so he walked.[273] God had spoken to him very clearly to send Squatinidale with only three hundred to find the Philadelphian angels. Three hundred! They may confront thousands.

273   Luke 5:16

Gabriel had never told Squatinidale, but he felt responsible for him—at least as a mentor. He didn't want to see any harm come to that little guy. When he had first met Squatinidale, he felt his pain. Squatinidale's downward spiral had started when he wandered, out of curiosity, to see Satan (called the Great One back then). He learned almost immediately he didn't belong to the renegade angels. Unfortunately, his friend, Abaddon, would not accept that and pursued him into a desolate area. If it weren't for God sending the Septemviri, Squatinidale may not have survived.

Yet, for some reason, Satan had been relentless and attacked Squatinidale again in the Bibliotheca. The prince of darkness imposed himself in the spiritual connection between Squatinidale and God. Squatinidale had explained long afterward that this experience shook him up—so much that he had vowed never to return to the Bibliotheca if Satan were still alive. He said just thinking about it caused him to lose his breath.

Squatinidale had wandered—no—fled from Satan throughout Heaven, eventually settling on Ephesus, not far from where Abaddon first tempted him about Satan. There, he seemed to have changed his outlook of himself and God—at least Malachy seemed to think so. She said the stout little angel burst into a fantastic, energized song, entertaining about a thousand angels, pleading for God to help him. And indeed, God did; He transformed him slowly from the insecure, self-deprecating angel into a warrior.

But was he up to this task?

Lord, please protect Squatinidale and his force and help him to avoid the Bibliotheca.

"Gabriel!" rang out a voice from behind. "Gabriel!"

Gabriel spun. Rafaella and two of the special force angels flew up the hill. *What happened to the rest? Please, God, don't tell me we lost them.*

Please.

Rafaella landed first, her face laced with joy. "These angels have a message for you."

Two angels, whose names that Gabriel couldn't recall, approached. One spoke, his dark skin shining. "Squatinidale found the Philadelphian angels."

Gabriel's heart leaped.

The messenger continued. "They are releasing them now."

Gabriel looked up and exhaled. "Praise God. When do you expect them to return?"

"They can't return. The Special Force will retrieve the pale horses from the enemy upriver but are not able to pass them through the partially dammed wall."

"Pale horses. The enemy's horses?"

"No. God gave them to the Philadelphian angels who lost them in an ambush."

Gabriel motioned for them to sit down. "So, Satan didn't distort God's creations. He stole them."

"Right. And now Squatinidale is leading the Special Force to retrieve them and invade the Bibliotheca.

"Bibliotheca?" asked Gabriel, jerking his head upwards. "Are you sure?"

"Yes. Squatinidale said he knew of a secret passage through the river gorge."

"I recall," murmured Gabriel. "We used it to rescue Rafaella and Malachy, but it was no easy task. Only by God's grace did we make it out alive."

Gabriel rubbed his hand across his forehead, golden channels popping out of his neck. "Look. I don't think he is performing what God wants." Gabriel stood and paced towards the shore, stopped, and turned. "He was instructed to rescue the angels, not lead them into a risky invasion. Squatinidale panicked the first time in the Bibliotheca and almost lost it during the rescue. We have to go get him."

Rafaella walked towards him and turned slightly towards the messengers. "Will you leave us for a moment, please?"

They complied.

She grabbed Gabriel's hand as they walked down to the shore.

"Gabriel. When I was captured by Satan in the depths of the Philadelphian flood, I wondered why God had allowed it to happen. Why would God allow me to be captured, terrorized, and agonized by Satan? I had to realize that, for me to trust God, I had to be tested..."

"But Squatinidale is not you! He is not ready for this type of trial and the temptation that may destroy him. He fell for Satan once, and, under pressure, he may fall again."

Rafaella held up her hand, her face shining with beautiful golden skin with an olive hue, framing her softening eyes. "I almost betrayed God."

Gabriel relented, his mouth slightly open.

She continued. "I look at trials differently, now. I consider trials 'a joy' because, in testing my faith, they produce perseverance. And perseverance leads to maturity in our relationship with God."[274]

The two walked along the ebbing vinifera, silence allowing them to think. Rafaella stopped and turned to the lake. "Have you been asking God to protect Squatinidale?"

"Yes."

"When you ask, you must believe and not doubt, because the one who doubts is like a wave of this lake, blown and tossed by Satan's power. When we doubt, we don't expect to receive anything from the Lord because we become double-minded and emotionally unstable."[275]

Gabriel's eyes teared. He had been God's primary and fastest messenger for a long time and never realized that he would doubt the words that God entrusted him to deliver if put on the spot.

Rafaella was right. He was allowing himself to be tossed on the lake, regardless of what God had proven to him.

"You're right. I must believe in what God's plan will be for me and everyone else whom I command. We have not learned much about this concept of 'sin,' but what I have learned today is that it takes a stealthy form that sneaks up on us."

274   James 1:3-4
275   James 1:6-8

An angel flew in over the ridge and landed in front of Gabriel and Rafaella, his face pale, mouth open. "It has begun."

"What has begun?" asked Gabriel.

"Satan's invasion."

"Where?" asked Gabriel.

"Between here and Laodicea, and here and Smyrna."

"Two invasions? Why don't we see it?

"Because we are at the intersection of the two drives, which have bypassed us on both sides."

"Why would they bypass us?"

"Because we are irrelevant," said Rafaella. "Satan wants one thing. The Throne of God."

CHAPTER 32

Michael led the red charioted army of God towards Sardis's magnificent peak, which rose on the horizon, lording over the troubled district. At one time, it had been the heart of God, allowing the Holy Spirit to sing personalized songs to each angel who sought Him. Michael had recalled when he and Gabriel had ventured there to hear the uplifting music. But that was long ago. Since then, he and Malachy had returned and found it desolate of God's Spirit, His presence, and His love—not to mention meeting Zepar, whom Michael dragged along.

What would they find there, now, after the killer cloud had massacred thousands of his fellow loyalists? The reminder raised a lump in his throat. He would never know if he could have prevented the slaughter.

The Sardis horizon blurred, the peak taking on a life of its own. Michael froze. Was this another of Satan's powers transforming reality? How could this mere angel have so much influence over God's heavenly creation? The peak, still a long way off, started to grow and revolve. Maybe the haze played a trick on his eyes. How could a peak move?

The image divided and divided repeatedly, making up a triangular form of countless pieces. Each piece moved on its own but stayed together as the overall object grew. The individual components moved in the same direction, upwards, pushing the point higher and higher.

Maybe this was from the Lord?

The peak expanded its base to almost a quarter of the horizon, its elements powering its growth and direction. The pinnacle then split, sending one-half of the triangle to the right and the other to the left. These two smaller triangles moved away from each other at the top of the peak, their bases pushing upwards, replacing the tips. The two triangles created another combined point driving up the middle, and then split. With each double-pinwheel revolution, the bottoms pushed up through the center to the tops and swung down on the outside, back to the bases.

A voice came to Michael through his spirit.

THE LAST WILL BECOME FIRST, AND THE FIRST WILL BECOME LAST.[276]

The giant peak disappeared, leaving the actual outcropping standing in its place. Michael turned around and gazed back to the Red Army, which had combined into one big driving wedge with him and Malachy at its head.

He understood. For he and Malachy to defeat Satan, they must move from first to last. The vision created a battle plan and a frame of mind for leading an army—as its servants.

He called out to Malachy, "Move your chariot to the left of me and switch positions. I want to be on the right. I'll explain later."

Malachy complied, replacing Michael as he moved his chariot to the right side of the attacking wedge.

He called out again. "Mimic my maneuvers and keep in communication as we separate."

Malachy nodded.

They were almost at the peak, entering Sardis from behind it. Michael could see the lake he had created to the right, its four geysers still feeding it.

He motioned for Zepar to leave his carriage and join him. He commanded that all angels double up in a chariot, leaving half the

---

276   Matthew 20:16

chariots to run free in their assault.

"Zepar, take the reins and direct the horses to where I tell you."

The dark, hazy cloud reappeared as the massive force swarmed the peak, descending into the central district where he and Malachy stood at the now-collapsed fourteen pillars.

The multitude of angels became clearer as his forces accelerated its velocity.

Satan's army dotted the fallen columns like tiny creatures moving about their tasks, unaware of the imminent attack.

As they began to discover the attack, panic spread, some flew away, others gathered weapons. Michael activated his bow and stood to the chariot's left side, flames now extending about fifteen feet behind as it increased speed.

Projectiles shot up from the columned area towards him, missing their targets badly. The front carriages swooped down about twenty-five feet above the surface, the flaming horses slamming into panicked angels, sending their dark particles to the Siq.

Michael shot arrows over the horses' heads, blasting large holes in the enemy ranks, exterminating them by the hundreds.

"Turn and sweep to the right," Michael barked out.

Zepar guided the horses to the right, moving away from Malachy's section, which veered to the left, both taking their respective cavalry and chariot followers out to the sides.

The rear guard moved up through the center on both sides, firing their arrows "at will."

Some enemy angels managed to get through the barrage and attack Michael, who dispatched them quickly with the saber.

As Michael's division swung right, he and his chariot force faced the enemy on their left. Chariot fighters shifted their shields to their left shoulders, creating a testudo (tortoise) formation.

The spear projectiles bounced off this shielded wall of armor and disintegrated in the chariot's fire protecting the angels. Michael commanded Zepar (verbally) and Malachy (through the mark) to guide the horses back, make a big circle, and bring their sections of the force up through the middle to replace those who had moved forward. These two triangular pinwheels revolved opposite each other, spinning away into the enemy's flanks.

Michael now understood that his force was to whirl away to the right, flanking Satan's attack, whose base stretched from Sardis to Laodicea. Malachy would do the same to the left, countering Satan's other vectors, whose base extended from Sardis to Ephesus. Their Red Army would cut all communications between the enemy assaults.

Up ahead, Michael could see the base of Satan's forces all facing towards the front of their invasion. Their formations and weapons were oriented in front of them, leaving them vulnerable to the side Michael was attacking.

Some of the Legion looked up and to their right and noticed the flanking counterattack. As before, panic spread among the ranks. Michael's attack caught the commanding officers off guard. The Legion tried to regroup a force who seemed less disciplined and prone to thinking about their welfare instead of other angels.

Michael's force smashed into the side of the Legion's division, killing many of their angels. Most were terminated by the fiery horses and chariots, their bodies slipping underneath the hoofs and wheels, exiting as dark particles from the backside.

Michael looked back. He noticed that all of his chariots were towing dark particles behind them as if they were mowing amborlite and casting flowers to the rear. Michael rubbed his forehead. Those particles—those massive volumes of refuse—were once angels who had rejected the Lord.

Michael caught himself. He had to focus on saving Heaven.

The attack kept spinning and spinning, sometimes eliminating the enemy from the right, other times from behind, as the wheel rotated towards Laodicea.

Laodicea would be a landing spot for Michael to invade Pergamum. As tricky as this attack had been, the effort to invade Pergamum and cast Satan out of Heaven would be a monumental task.

He wondered how he could accomplish such a feat. He wondered how God would.

AMBUSHED!

Squatinidale should have walked ahead of Dionysius since he was armed and trained. The Septemviri commander rounded the corner, his armor activated, his sword flaming. His other warriors pushed their way forward, joining him at his side.

In the adjoining passage were six Legion angels brandishing their spears and whips, their faces hardened from battle, their eyes burning with hate.

"Stay back, or he dies," warned the leader, holding his spear blade to Dionysius's neck, Satan's faces revolving slowly on their guards, snarling as each profile turned towards Squatinidale.

How could this have happened? Couldn't the Lord have protected them, giving them a fighting chance?

Dionysius pulled the hand from his face, his voice weak. "Ignore their threats, Squatinidale, for the good of all Heaven."

"We will exterminate him into the material world if you come closer," said the leader, his eyes shifting back and forth among God's warriors.

"I am willing to die for God," implored Dionysius. "Please don't risk any more angels on my account. For me, to live for God is to die in gain.[277] I don't know what will happen to me in the material world, but, if I pass through that barrier, I will still love and serve the Lord, and He will love me."

"Dionysius, I will risk ninety-nine to save one," said Squatinidale.[278]

"Shut up!" yelled another assailant, jabbing his spear into Dionysius's face.

The head Legion soldier waved the other loyalists back and released some tension on Dionysius's throat. "Listen to me. We

277 Philippians 1:21
278 Luke 15:1-7

deserted the Legion during your last attack with your stars. We are hunted, not only by you but the Legion. They are extra hard on those of us who desert the cause. We want no part of you. We just want to escape out of this underworld."

"Are you willing to repent and join the Lord's army?" asked Squatinidale, his face calm.

The Legion members laughed.

The leader spoke, struggling to stifle his laughter between words. "Why would we go back into bondage? We have found ourselves and control our destiny. We don't need the Creator. Even though we have abandoned Satan's majesty, that doesn't mean we will subject ourselves to the majesty of the Creator."

"So, what do you plan to do?" interjected Squatinidale, "Roam Heaven waiting for the moment that members of the Legion or Holy Order will kill you? It seems you have doubled your risk of death with no offsetting benefit."

"We are not alone," said the leader, narrowing his eyes with a more intense gaze. "There are many other renegades throughout Heaven, like us. We will ban together and create our own dynasty—a dynasty without silly rules and obedience to a master."

"But you still are a slave—a slave to your sinful desires," said Squatinidale, not meaning to convince the brute but distract him enough to rescue Dionysius. "As you are slaves of your sin, you are free from the control of righteousness. The benefits you thought you reaped from this freedom after leaving the Creator have now made you ashamed and self-conscious. These false benefits and beliefs will result in death, sooner or later. But now you have the opportunity to be set free from your sin and become slaves of a loving God whose benefits lead you to holiness resulting in eternal life."[279]

The Legion renegades stood silent. Then one of the others spoke up. "Let's leave with our prisoner. We no longer want to be slaves to anyone—Satan or the Creator. Now, move aside!"

The Legion stepped into Squatinidale's corridor and shuffled

---

279   Romans 6:20-22

away with Dionysius as their shield. Squatinidale waved his hand forward as they followed behind the rebellious squad, keeping their distance.

The pace picked up, with the pursuit accelerating into a trot, Dionysius bracketed in by the others who had him by his neckline.

The chase advanced for a long distance, opening into a large hallway supported by thick columns that raised their majestic arms to the ceilings as a form of praise to God. The atmosphere grew darker and darker towards the end of the hall, suffocating Squatinidale with the presence of evil. Were they approaching the enemy and maybe the river? If so, this situation could get worse until the Philadelphian army retrieved their weapons and horses. This could result in carnage.

The renegades stopped in the middle of the room, turning their heads from side to side. About ten exits lined the walls on each side, tempting and confusing the traitors. Straight ahead lay another ten portals opening into a large beach and probably the river somewhere in the darkness beyond.

Many of the former captives from Philadelphia had caught up to Squatinidale and stood in the large hall, looking at their captured leader—quietly praying to God; praying was always the first resort for an angel and, yet, also a perplexing thought to those who didn't believe and felt that these angels were powerless without weapons.

A silence settled in as the assailants' breathing increased, their heads swinging back and forth, eyes puzzled with their options.

Turning to the exits beyond, the renegade leader backed up slowly, using Dionysius as a shield. The six stood at one of the openings, a beachy terrain extending out into the darkness just beyond the doorway.

"Well, we found our river. We can manage without you."

The leader pushed Dionysius to the surface and dashed out of one of the exits, his five partners following behind. The last defector member stopped and turned, his face raising a menacing smile. "I remember what you said, Dionysius. Let me help you."

He raised his whip over his head, its snarling crackle swinging in circles, sparks flying from the tip.

Squatinidale yelled out. "No!" He quickly converted his weapon into a bow and shot an explosive arrow at the assailant. The arrow hit the enemy angel at the same time the whip-end hit Dionysius. Two flashes of light exploded in the room, creating a small blizzard of white and dark particles that funneled through one of the exits. A collective gasp sucked out the remaining spirit, followed by an eerie sound of crying angels.

CHAPTER 33

I rrelevant? Had Satan's two armies passed Gabriel's army to over-
throw God at His Thone? Gabriel couldn't understand how an
angel could have the audacity even to consider conquering God
and taking his Holy Throne. Fighting to take the districts from other
angels was a conceivable feat, but invading God's Throne? Sin had
devoured what goodness might have remained in Satan's soul. He no
longer could think in the light of the truth. The threat had never been
whether he could take God's Throne, but about how many angels he
could convince to reject their Creator while attempting it.

He turned to Rafaella. "Let's enter a prex précis and ask God
how to proceed. I don't want to misunderstand any messages."[280]

The two angels faced each other, heads bowed, hands at their
sides, palms facing upwards. A vision appeared to both of them.

"I think I understand God's vision," murmured Rafaella. "We
divide our army of infantry and cavalry into two main corps. Each
corps will consist of two divisions. One corps will attack Satan's
right wedge at its base, and the other will attack his left wedge at its
base. This strategy will separate Satan's dual attacks, leaving them
stranded."

"I agree," said Gabriel. "I also see the tactics for each corps,
which would split us into two divisions each."

Gabriel called out to the army, who immediately lined up in
two great columns, each ten across, their rear flank disappearing

280   James 1:5

far into the distance. Horses snorted mist as they pounded their hoofs in impatient anticipation for the battle that was to occur somewhere in the distance.

He led one column towards Laodicea, while Rafaella led the other in the direction of Smyrna. Gabriel ran his mounted corps at a high speed towards the black menace which had started as just a line on the horizon and then grown to a dark, intimidating mass as they approached it. He couldn't see the rear end of the invasion, just small districts smoldering in a fire, with white particles swirling like cyclones.

He thought of his fellow angels suffering death, their voices crying for justice from the material world. He raised his head, waved his arm, and then yelled, "Shout! For the Lord has given you the districts."[281] To his surprise, the rest of the corps answered him in the same manner.

Gabriel separated his charging column into two divisions, side by side, each five across. Each column looped out from the other, increasing the distance between them.

Some of the enemy turned, anticipation and panic appearing to overtake them, their attention to those marching in front of them interrupted.

Gabriel gave the command to rejoin the two looping divisions attacking the enemy from two directions.

The two columns veered towards each other as they charged forward. At that last moment, before contact with the enemy's angels, the two columned divisions intersected and crossed each other in a perfectly organized fashion. Though moving at a break-neck pace, not a single rider in one column collided with one in the other column.

The two crossing divisions created a moving X formation just before spearing the enemy's right flank at two angles, stabbing deeply into their disorganized ranks. Gabriel wielded his sword on each side of his horse, cutting the dark menace into a flurry, their black particles, at times, obscuring his vision.

---

281   Joshua 6:16

The two white cuneus military columns cut through Satan's ranks, angling away from each other. One column angled towards the front of the invasion, while the other sliced towards its rear.

Satan had arranged his Legion into blocks of cohorts, with gaps between the blocks of about an angel wing's width. As the two columns cut through them, the perfectly organized Legion angels lost their discipline, cracking their structure. Some members broke ranks and charged the massive white force, trampling their fellow members, while others turned and flew, trying to evade Gabriel's division.

Gabriel's counter-offensive created such a panic that Legion members hid their heads behind their shields, wielding their swords blindly, cutting their fellow aggressors. Black particles filled the area, some falling to the surface, to be stomped by their fellow angels before escaping to the material world. The attack extended for a long time, members of the Holy Order suffering very few casualties.

In the distance, Gabriel noticed an object growing larger as he continued his attack. He couldn't focus on it without taking his attention from the fight, so he ignored it. As he speared the ranks further, he lifted his head again to see the Laodicean arch. He must have been too far away to see the emerald falls cascading through it. His columns had crossed a significant section of Heaven's inner circle and approached the far side of Satan's attacking wedge. He turned and saw that his column had now spread out, no longer five across, but in a single file stretching as far back as he could see.

He called out. "Rafaella, loop the columns back towards each other."

At once, his horse turned to the left and slowly looped back towards Rafaella's column, which was beyond his eyesight. This way, their divisions would corral the remnants of the two vector invasion forces between them.

After some time, the two leaders met, stopping their horses, their combined corps now encircling the last enemy troops.

"Hear me, oh, White Army of God. You are wearing the full armor of God so that you can take your stand against Satan's schemes.

For our struggle is not against things we can see in our visions of the material world or even anything in the spirit world, but against rulers, authorities, the powers of this dark world, and the spiritual forces of evil in the heavenly realms. Today, armed by God, you have been able to stand your ground. Stand firm then, with the belt of truth buckled around your waist, with the breastplate of righteousness in place, and with your feet fitted with the readiness that comes from the gospel of peace. Similarly, take up the shield of faith, with which you can extinguish all the flaming arrows of the evil one, the helmet of salvation, and the sword of the Spirit, which is the Word of God.[282]

With the Word of God held over their heads, the White Army's noose closed against an unrepentant force that hailed its dark leader's name to the end.

Again, the two Septemviri commanders joined their white mounted army together as one power extending from Smyrna, through Philadelphia, and to Laodicea. Gabriel looked into Rafaella's weary eyes as she stepped up to him. She seemed to know what he was thinking. What was the battle going to be like when Satan was personally engaged?

They were about to find out.

THE BARRIER BETWEEN LIFE AND DEATH WAS INVISIBLE TO angels. Even if an angel were to see death approaching, that angel would be powerless to embrace it—not so with Dionysius. He saw the barrier inching closer and didn't flinch. What had he said? *For me, to live for God is to die in gain.*

Squatinidale wanted to think about that, but he had to protect the remaining angels, some on the verge of collapse since losing Dionysius—their beloved leader who didn't hesitate to sacrifice himself for the safety of his fellow angels. He motioned for the squad members to follow through the arched exits after the remaining enemy defectors.

282   Ephesians 6:11-18

Bows drawn, Squatinidale peeked around the opening. The beach loomed dark and deserted. Maybe the renegades had flown up the river. If so, the special forces would intercept them. If they had flown downriver, the traitors could meet their comrades, who would give no mercy.

Squatinidale motioned the others. Following his lead, the other four warrior angels prostrated themselves just inches above the surface and flew towards the beach, their wings mostly collapsed to conserve the power of the Holy Spirit.

Nearing the beachhead, Squatinidale stopped. Sounds of shouting angels seemed to be echoing down river. He couldn't distinguish the words. The angel lowered himself into the grainy silicium, using the power of his wings to bury himself up to his wings, which laid flat. He motioned for two of the others to do the same; they submerged themselves in the middle of the vinifera river, leaving only their heads above its line.

Flashes from two explosions lit up their surroundings as violent confrontations moved closer. The renegade angels rounded the wall, still a considerable distance from Squatinidale and the others. The traitors had confronted their fellow Legion members. The six perched themselves, waiting for their pursuers, their weapons ready.

A massive dark cloud turned the corner, its fingers seeking the living. Squatinidale gasped. The cloud found the traitors and slowly choked them, their eyes bulging out, screams unable or unwilling to exit their mouths. As the fatal clutch tightened its grip, their wings incinerated with black fire and smoldered their only connection to God's Holy Spirit—not that they had felt it recently. The angels' wings did not quench this deadly beast's thirst, as it ate into each angel's body, causing their heads to explode into the black flakes that carried their spirits to the material world. The black fog then evaporated as fast as it had arrived.

Voices filled Squatinidale's ears from other angels appearing from around the corner. "Search for survivors. We cannot let traitors get away. They will contaminate the minds of other Legion members, creating a growing infection."

Ten angels with projectile-firing hatchets shot explosives into the vinifera, raking right to left and then left to right, closing in on the submerged squad. Squatinidale jumped out from the silicium and rapidly fired his arrows at the ten. The reaction stunned them, causing them to drop their weapons. The other squad members leaped out of hiding and fired, destroying the ten Legion soldiers.

Squatinidale's team fled back through the arches as hundreds of Legion members turned the point, poised and ready for a fight. The blast killed two of the squad.

Squatinidale and the other two surviving squad soldiers crouched at the wall, trying to keep the enemy at bay. He had to think of the Philadelphian angels behind him. If the squad continued this fight, they may be captured, tortured, and killed. Alternatively, if they retreated, the Legion would follow them and recapture the Philadelphian angels anyway.

God had to provide a way out. Why would he allow them to come this far just to lose their lives and the lives of those they had rescued? For now, Squatinidale had to trust in the Lord and fight.

The Legion brought up more angels, along with a team of pale horses. The additional troop presence increased the attacker's firepower. The squad was unable to return fire without exposing themselves. They had to retreat into the tunnels. Maybe if they held them off, the other angels could get away. Either way, his squad was doomed to destruction. Dionysius's words of self-sacrifice rang in Squatinidale's ears.

The squad spread out among the large hall, now active with the Philadelphian angels leaping for cover.

He turned back to the enemy forces, now covering the darkened beach. The haze helped and hurt him by reducing the visibility of each of the troops. At this point, it was a standoff, with Squatinidale and his squad having the better position. Luckily, the enemy was unable to destroy the arches.

He had to create a diversion.

A hunch came to him, but he had to use faith to test it.

Squatinidale turned to a Philadelphian angel hiding behind one of the arches. "Is there an exit downriver?

"I think so," screamed the angel, his voice barely audible above the battle noises.

"Lead me there."

Squatinidale spoke to the other two through his mark and asked them to cover him. They would have to hold off the attack until he could draw the enemy away.

Squatinidale and the Philadelphian angel sprinted down a larger corridor that appeared to bypass the beach. Following his guide, Squatinidale turned into a smaller tunnel and headed towards the river. Approaching the exit, he halted.

His hunch was right.

He turned to his companion. "Go back and tell the other two to stop shooting when they see me."

"How will they find you among this pandemonium?"

"They'll know."

Squatinidale snuck out of the small exit, unnoticed by the enemy. In front of him in the vinifera and its surrounding shores stood hundreds of dismounted pale horses. The assaulting forces had made two errors: not returning to mount the horses in their attack and leaving only three angels to defend them.

Squatinidale crept up to the guards, startling them. He wielded his sword, killing all three in three swoops. The killing was quiet and did not arouse the forces fighting upriver.

Squatinidale jumped on one of the horses and herded the rest up into a large, agitated ball. Fortunately, they were already together, so he only had to retrieve a few stragglers.

Squatinidale yelled at the top of his lungs, "Be strong in the Lord and his mighty power!"[283] The horses leaped at the cry and burst around the point and into the attacking Legion. The massive,

---

283   Ephesians 6:10

pale horses stampeded through the vinifera, half running, half flying, filling the river tunnel from side to side, striking panic into the enemy. The enemy reacted too late to fly over the horses. Some flew towards the arches, only to be killed by the other two squad members.

Squatinidale surrounded himself, driving the thundering herd, creating a deafening echo through the canyon.

Projectiles exploded at the sides of the cave as Squatinidale followed the meandering river. He turned back to see the enemy pursuing him by flight. They would catch up to him and pin him between the animals.

Squatinidale yelled out and snapped his horse's reins, moving up through the horses' ranks, ducking at every blast, leaning at each turn.

A blast hit the dipping ceiling just below his head, knocking Squatinidale off the side of his horse, one leg over its back, hands gripping his neck.

Was the enemy gaining?

He couldn't tell.

CHAPTER 34

Squatinidale caught his balance and righted himself. He couldn't evade the Legion much longer. He glanced back to see a massive following of maybe a hundred enemy angels pursuing him, firing their hatchet spears at anything that moved. Some of their shots hit flying horses, who departed Heaven with a frightened whinny that echoed above the clamor. The Legion seemed to not care for the horses, though they were foolishly exterminating their best fighting asset over one angel. Soon their reckless strategy would pay off and hit him or his horse.

Squatinidale remembered Leihja's training. He swung back underneath the horse, arms and legs wrapped around its neck, his cheek pressing against the horse's face. As the horse weaved back and forth, Squatinidale used his wings to coordinate with its gait. This position would give him some cover, but it would not last, as the Legion targeted horses.

Now leading the pack, Squatinidale tipped his head back, eyeing the path ahead upside down. He had to partially retract his wings to avoid the vinifera only a foot away from this flying horse. Nothing laid ahead of them except hazy darkness. Hopefully, he would not collide with other Legion members upriver. How long would they chase him before going back to the beach? He surmised that they would not give up since he controlled their war machines. Yet, he pleaded with God for a way out. His current options would all lead to one conclusion: his death.

In the depth of the haze ahead, a light was hovering just under an overhang. Another light emerged and then another. Squatinidale wrapped one arm around the horse's neck and leaned back, throwing his arm behind his head, almost touching the vinifera. His Septemviri sign lit up, glowing as a reddish fire in the darkness of despair. In front of him, other pinpoints of lights were bearing the same colors—his special forces!

Squatinidale righted himself on the horse, his spirit feeling like it had been reborn. God had heard him and hadn't deserted him.

Like a storm of dislodged Khasneh Forest leaves, hundreds of Holy Order special forces slammed onto the backs of horses, their weapons activated. Squatinidale yelled into his mark, "Attack!"

All horses slid in the vinifera to an abrupt halt. In a massive, coordinated about-face, the electrified cavalry turned and charged the Legion as they rounded a curve. Flaming arrows burned arching trails into the blackness like blowing stalks of amborlite towards the enemy, lighting up the area. No longer able to be on the offensive, the enemy scrambled, trying to evade the oncoming barrage of arrows that blinded and disintegrated them.

Squatinidale called through his mark to his remaining two squad members on the beach. "We are forcing the enemy towards you."

The enemy slipped past a turn and hit a barrage of explosions, the flashes causing Squatinidale to cover his eyes.

He raised his hand and held his cavalry to a walk. Rounding the corner, he met the two surviving members of his squad. The special forces had now reunited, most of them on horseback.

Squatinidale dismounted and hugged his comrades and many Philadelphian angels.

Then he thought of Dionysius. His eyes glossed over as he felt the loss of one he had thought he saved. Only God knows why He would direct Squatinidale to save him, just to lose him.

He had to push the mourning out of him for another time. Now, they must think about terminating Satan and his forces.

He remounted and led the force of over a thousand downriver, his shield up, his eyes alert. A profundo tributary had joined the vinifera river, changing its color to emerald. It narrowed into a tunneled gorge—the site he had remembered when they rescued Rafaella and Malachy. As before, the surroundings made for a perfect ambush. He slowed everyone down to a walk and sent scouts ahead to spy on enemy platoons that had wandered away from the primary division.

One of the scouts returned. "The smaller gorge leading up into darkness is just ahead."

"That is our path to the Bibliotheca. We must be under Pergamum," acknowledged Squatinidale.

As the scout reported, the narrow gorge appeared on their right, leading up into the darkness, just wide enough for one mounted angel at a time. This path may be ideal for trapping enemy angels stationed in the Bibliotheca—but how? They would be defeated if they just filed into the massive hall, one angel at a time.

Squatinidale looked around the gorge, which was still dark and hazy. Up above to his right was a ridge he hadn't seen before in his last excursion. That didn't surprise him, considering his unstable state of mind back then. He motioned for the others to wait.

The ridge was more extensive than he had seen from below. It wasn't a ridge but a ledge. He rode slowly. Nothing else moved, his horse's hoofs clacking noise, the only sound.

He swallowed and continued.

A cave appeared out of the haze.

He paused, ears probing for anything.

He edged up a little more to the cave opening.

He stopped again.

Nothing.

He didn't hear anything. Did this cave empty into the Bibliotheca? If so, where? Could it be another passage that they could enter, or would it take them back downriver and into the gorge like so many others?

A mist slithered out of the cave, hugging the surface, its fingers casually searching for all paths leading to the ledge. Squatinidale backed up and stopped.

The whitish mist snaked around the horse's legs and up to Squatinidale.

He smiled. He knew this mist and where it would lead him.

SOMETHING WAS WRONG. AZARIAS PEERED FARTHER INTO the distance, the Black Army in tow, nearing the end of their journey around the Siq to Laodicea. During his previous flights to Laodicea, a beautiful, bright emerald line would have appeared from this distance. But not now. The profundo falls that leaped from the Laodicean plateau through the large, domed arch to the plains below had vanished.

Azarias recalled when he had temporarily turned the tunnel river against the enemy during their quest to save Rafaella. The river resumed afterward, showing God's beauty once again.

Early in this epic war, Azarias would have recoiled in shock at Satan's distortions, but now, the altered spirits were a common occurrence. The changing and altering of God's creations only disgusted him—beauty turning into evil should repulse anyone.

Upon the plateau, Laodicea spread out over a square kilometer, with gated walls bordering it on three sides, and an archway and bluff on the fourth. A large theater (or stadium) rose to the left, like in Ephesus. He hadn't attended any events there but knew angels who enjoyed a performance after soaking in the spirit at the Spiritual House.

"What do you think?" asked Azarias, who stood with Sosthenes, Jael, and Leihja.

Leihja turned her head, scanning the bluff. "This is the work of Satan. We are now one district away from his evil center outside of Pergamum. He must know that we have defeated some of his forces throughout Heaven and are closing in on him."

"We have to see if there are angels hidden or captured in Laodicea," answered Azarias.

"I have been to Laodicea several times and know it well. I think we should investigate, but carefully," replied Sosthenes. "I can't see the theater from here. If I can get to the theater, I might be able to find clues as to the Laodicean angels' whereabouts."

Jael flew over to Azarias and grabbed his arm. "I told you about him. You can't trust him. He is trying to lure you into a trap."

Azarias smiled. "I understand, but there is still a lot of evidence that he has changed. This will be a test. I'd rather have him betray me when we are alone than during a battle, when he can stick a blade through my back."

Jael looked to the arch and then back. "Send two scouts. Send me!"

"You have already risked your life for me, Jael. You found me when I was adrift. I can't ask you to risk or sacrifice your life again. God's Guardian Cherub gave me this command long before I met you. He made me to lead angels and cast Satan and his followers out of Heaven. I must trust that God will see me through."

Azarias and Sosthenes flew to the plateau, leaving the army ready to support them at any confrontation. As the flat top drew closer, its desolate nature became more apparent. All angels had deserted Laodicea. The angels basking in the Spiritual House were gone, and the cheers or music echoing out of the stadium were now silenced.

Azarias and Sosthenes flew through the arch and landed in front of the portico. Someone had diverted the river. The wonderful liquid that had flowed into the Spiritual House from Philadelphia and Pergamum had ceased to pour over the bluff.

Azarias followed its diversion to the left and stopped short at the theater. A large wall of pillars stood on the stage, offering him no clues.

"Maybe angels are hiding in the seats below. Let's fly to the top of the columns," said Sosthenes. "We can see the whole arena of seats from up there."

The two angels flew to the top, Azarias still searching around for any kind of movement.

Azarias drew his eyebrows together. Profundo filled the bottom half of the theater. Satan had stolen Laodicea's solitude.

The lake waves splashed against the concave seats, the theater devoid of any other motion.

Azarias spoke to Sosthenes, who stood with his back to the arch a short distance away, "What happened? Do you see any clues that may tell you about the Laodicean angels?"

Sosthenes didn't respond.

"We need to rescue those angels, but we need clues. I cannot let the army search aimlessly without a direction. Let's summon some others—"

Azarias glanced up. His eyes teared, and his mouth quivered.

Behind Sosthenes's head were hundreds of angels bound to the great arch's back, facing away from the prairie. They didn't move, their mouths hanging open as if screaming for God.

"Nice work, Sosthenes," said a voice behind Azarias.

He turned.

Zelbeje stood, her hair hanging over one eye, cutting off the corner of her hideous smile. Behind her stood Abaddon and Pollyon, holding spears.

Azarias turned back to Sosthenes.

"I knew nothing of this, Azarias! I am innocent. I am a captive like you. Don't believe her. She lies. She always lies."

Zelbeje laughed. "So, who are you going to believe, Azarias? I didn't ask you to come here."

"You can't seem to keep loyal friends, can you, Azarias?" added Pollyon, shaking his head. He glanced at Abaddon, "Lie? Does she lie?"

"I don't know if she is lying now, but, when she does, it is when she's at her best."

Sosthenes pushed Azarias down. He charged Abaddon, grabbing his weapon, then he leaped towards Zelbeje, pushing her backward over the wall and into the lake.

Azarias regained his balance and donned his armor, activating his sword.

Pollyon stepped forward and shoved the spear at Azarias, who moved in time for it to slip past his face. Azarias returned a jab with his sword.

The two angels sparred on top of the columns, with spear thrusts and sword jabs flashing back and forth. Azarias was able to parry multiple thrusts and a fired projectile with his shield. Each angel flew and somersaulted behind the other.

The unarmed Abaddon backed up and then flew away. This worked as an advantage for Azarias, who didn't want to fight both at once.

The lake's waters seemed to churn more, but Azarias couldn't look to see if Sosthenes had survived the fall.

Azarias lost his balance to his right but supported himself with his sword. Pollyon thrust to Azarias's midsection, but Azarias slipped to the right, allowing the spear to go under his arm. He snaked the spear under his left shoulder and struck it with the sword in his right hand, causing Pollyon's spear to break into two and disintegrate.

Azarias pushed him down and held the tip to Pollyon's face. "You were my friend. You swore allegiance to God and then again as his Septemviri. How can you do this? I can help you return to the Lord! The Lord will forgive you. I will forgive you."

"Forgive?" yelled back Pollyon. "I don't want your forgiveness, nor the Creator's forgiveness. I don't need to be forgiven for living the way I want to live. I'd rather die than go back to slavery."

Pollyon grabbed the tip of Azarias's sword, his hands sizzling, deep red blisters scorching and torturing him. Small, pale creatures burst from open cysts to feed on the many sores now covering his body.

Pollyon's face contorted, and his eyes widened. "Azarias, help me. Help yourself. Don't let the Creator do this to us. We belong here in Heaven in control of our destiny. You're next. You'll see—"

He dissolved into black particles.

A loud boom came from the lake, and a wave almost washed Azarias off the wall as an enormous red dragon exploded out of the depths. It had seven crowned heads and ten horns.[284] On the back of one of the heads was Zelbeje, casting curses at God, singing a siren song.

284 Revelation 12:3

She looked down at Azarias. "Now that I destroyed the traitor, Sosthenes, you will be little challenge. Prepare to die and be defeated, Azarias. Satan is the new king, seventy-seven times over!"[285]

Picture of Satan as a seven-headed dragon

285   Genesis 4:24

CHAPTER 35

The last two times Squatinidale had walked into Pergamum's Bibliotheca, he hadn't been one of the Septemviri and it didn't end well. The first time, Satan had demonstrated his power by interrupting Squatinidale's connection with God. The little angel had panicked and flown out of the structure, thinking Satan had set part of the Bibliotheca on fire, an illusion of the menace's other powers to deceive the mind.[286]

The second time, he had entered with five Septemviri to rescue Rafaella and Malachy out of Satan's hands. Even then, Squatinidale almost fled and jeopardized their rescue mission.

The Septemviri didn't understand how Satan tempted him. Squatinidale had to confront his fears and decide whether he had faith in God. He almost lost all faith when fear consumed him, fueled by Satan's curse of doubt, spiraling into a frenzy. Azarias grabbed him at that moment. His words still rung true.

IF YOU ARE TO BE CONSUMED, ALLOW
YOURSELF TO BE CONSUMED BY THE
LORD'S ETERNAL FIRE. THE LORD DOES NOT
IGNORE THE CRY OF THE AFFLICTED."[287]

Squatinidale returned to his forces down at the river and sent a scouting party up the narrower, dark pathway that he had traveled

286   1 Timothy 2:14
287   Psalm 9:12

the last time he had been here. He instructed them to crawl through the secret entrance and see if the Legion had changed anything. He couldn't execute God's plan in a vacuum. He had to know if the Bibliotheca had changed since being occupied by the Legion.

He explained to the others what he had found on the ledge and what he believed God had revealed to him. The cave served as a better entrance into the Bibliotheca because it was about seven horses wide, unlike the original path where they could enter the Bibliotheca with only one horse at a time.

The two scouts returned. "Squatinidale, you were right. The entrance into the Bibliotheca will still only allow one mounted angel to enter at a time. Once we invade with ten horses, the enemy would be wise to us and block the rest from coming in. The enemy would overwhelm the riders who would enter."

"Perfect," said Squatinidale. "Find eight other angels and move up that passageway. Don't enter until you hear fighting."

"Where will you be entering the great hall?" asked one of the scouts.

"Right now, it's a hunch from God—one that I hope I heard correctly. We are moving towards victory and must keep the pressure on the enemy."

The ten mounted angels rode up the dark passageway leading to the Bibliotheca.

Squatinidale corralled his force of angels and led them up to the ridge. The cave stood wide and dark, reeking with a presence he hadn't felt before. Could he have been mistaken? This path could lead to Satan's lair, where the evil leader had held Rafaella and Malachy. If so, Squatinidale would not be able to reverse a column of so many angels in such a restricted environment. He could be leading them into Satan's hands.

He moved the brigade closer to the cave entrance, the white mist secreting like last time, its wandering arms curling and caressing each pale horse and rider. Squatinidale felt his horse being drawn into the sea of white fog. The mist rose and enveloped him with God's joy—a joy that was quiet and complete.

Yes, he had made the right choice, but the right choice didn't mean survival, just obedience. The angels ventured through the cave; the movement was more fluid than he had expected on a horse.

Squatinidale prayed for success. If not, he would lose the angels God had entrusted to him, in addition to the Philadelphian angels that the Lord had commissioned him to rescue. He could only go where the mist would take him.

The notorious serpent demons that Azarias had fought in Al Birka paled in comparison to what he confronted now. He had never understood how Satan could pervert God's creation using his evil. Azarias had seen visions of reptiles like this on Earth, large and gargantuan, but never a red-headed dragon with seven heads breathing fire. It seemed that the more angels Satan gathered to his side, the more evil increased, and the stronger he got. Evil begets evil and multiplies ad infinitum.

Azarias scanned the area for an escape, his exposure on top of the arena wall not helping. He would have struggled under normal conditions with an armed cherub here, much more now with a cherub who had perverted God's creation to this extent. He had to evade Satan and his rider, Zelbeje.

"I will give you one chance to live, Azarias," said one of Satan's dragon heads. "More than the Creator gave me when he exiled me in Eden, waiting for his *pinnacle of creation* to arrive."

One of the other dragon heads rotated to the front. It exhaled a mist that floated down to Azarias. The fog produced a vision of hills, valleys, and rivers from Earth.

A different head spoke. "All this I will give you if you'll bow down and worship me."[288]

Azarias stayed behind his shield. He could feel the temptation of controlling a part of Earth for himself. No more missions and no more—

288   Matthew 4:9

He shook the vision from his mind.

Satan murdered both angels and truth. When he lied, he spoke his native language, for he was a liar and the father of lies.[289]

The vision disappeared, and Azarias lowered his shield slightly. "The Lord our God is one Lord who I will love with all of my heart and with all of my soul and with all of my strength.[290] You are not God. We will cast you out of Heaven with your followers."

From the corner of his eye, Azarias saw one of the dragon's heads, ridden by Zelbeje, swinging low towards him from his left, her face lit with an evil grin, her staff poised for contact.

Azarias dropped to his stomach as the dragon's head circled to his right.

"You will not escape me now, Azarias," said Zelbeje. She hung upside down under the dragon's chin, her legs wrapped around his neck, the staff held up behind her head for maximum effect.

The dragon's head swung towards Azarias again, his slave's cackling laugh echoing among the theater seats below, the passenger's eyes alive with fire. Azarias rose and stood firm with his sword blazing in front of him.

Swinging closer, they were almost at impact when a blazing red flash entered from his left, grabbing Zelbeje off the dragon's head.

Leihja.

The dragon's head recoiled as the two angels tumbled in flight and over the wall, falling down below towards the Spiritual House.

Azarias looked up through the arch dominating the district center, lifeless angels still bound to their curved display.

He smiled.

The White Army had amassed behind the half-circle arch leading into Laodicea. Azarias flew up and hovered near Jael.

Satan recoiled his fiery mouths, casting their scorching blasts in his general direction.

Azarias looked past the terrorizing reptile and swallowed hard.

---

289   John 8:44
290   Deuteronomy 6:5

A massive force drove through the dark atmosphere, coming to Satan's assistance, spreading across the horizon like Azarias's visions of the Earth's locusts.

The red dragon's heads screeched hideous calls to his army, some diverting to Pergamum, the others accelerating to support their master in the final battle for Heaven.

Leihja and Zelbeje battled on the surface below, each well-trained in the art of spiritual warfare. Azarias wanted to assist Leihja but remembered the angels hanging on the arch. He started at its base, slicing the bindings that held each angel. Some angels regained consciousness and fluttered to the surface, while others did not and crashed with a blast of white particles.

Zelbeje dislodged her spear guards, each consisting of a decaying form of Satan's four faces: lion, ox, eagle, and skull. She threw them at Leihja, who deflected one but not the other.

The horns of the ox pierced Leihja's armor near the seam, its impact sizzling, all four faces laughing in repulsive harmony. She dislodged the heads with her sword and flung them back at Zelbeje, who dodged the blow. The heads rolled on the surface behind her, leaving the lion's face snarling, the skull laughing, and the eagle beak pointing upwards, opening and closing.

Zelbeje found a golden ring and, converting it to a whip, snapped it at Leihja, hitting her shield and sending her tumbling backward.

Regaining her balance, Leihja converted her sword into a bow and blasted a fiery arrow into Zelbeje's shaft, exploding it into white and black fire, throwing the evil angel backward onto Satan's eagle beak. The beak impaled her through the neck, piercing out through her throat, causing parasitical creatures to exit her mouth.

Leihja ran to her, her weapons now retracted. "You can still accept the Lord as your God."

Zelbeje's mouth moved, its sound very slight. Leihja kneeled down as Zelbeje gurgled, "This is not the end."

The evil angel disintegrated, wings first, then legs, face, and last, her delphinium blue hair, all into black particles fluttering to the Siq.

Azarias, Leihja, and what remained of the Laodicean angels retreated to the Black Army behind the arch.

"Look, Leihja," said Azarias, pointing. "Satan's army will soon be here."

"Don't trust your eyes, Azarias, for in hope we will be saved. Hope that is seen is no hope at all. We will hope for what we don't see and wait patiently."[291]

A sound of drums sailed from over the horizons on the far right and then the far left, followed by singing and heavenly instruments. It was a song of battle that Azarias had never heard before. The angels of the Black Army joined in, starting with Leihja and then those around her.

Scan the QR Code to hear the angels sing
as they enter battle against Satan

Sing to our God the praises of His Name [292]
Be strong and fearless.
Forever He will reign

Lord, my God
God, I will sing of your might and your strength[293]
Bear the full armor of God, and stand by truth

Don't fear![294]
For your God will see you through

---

291 Romans 8:24-25
292 Psalm 68:4
293 Psalm 59:16
294 Isaiah 41:10

He will not let you down.
He will not abandon you.[295]

Fight the good fight.[296]
With the breastplate of righteousness[297]
Strong and courageous[298]
Spirit's contagious
He's your God.

When times are troubling
Don't be afraid
Your Lord will be there for you

God is your refuge,
and He's your Strength[299]

Shout out His great Name with Praise!

Don't fear!
For your God will see you through
He will not let you down.
He will not abandon you.

Fight the good fight.
With the breastplate of righteousness
Strong and courageous

Spirit's contagious
He's your God.

Glory to…God
-----------our God

---

295 Deuteronomy 31:6
296 1 Timothy 6:12
297 Ephesians 6:14
298 Joshua 1:9
299 Psalm 46:1

In the highest[300]
-------highest
Praise His Name

Cast all your burdens
Onto the Lord[301]
Your God is marching with you.

Hearts not be troubled.[302]
Your minds at rest.

Open your arms and be blessed

Don't fear!
For your God will see you through
He will not let you down.
He will not abandon you.

Fight the good fight.
With the breastplate of righteousness
Strong and courageous
Spirit's contagious
He's your God.

Strong and courageous
Spirit's contagious
He's your God.

Strong and courageous
Spirit contagious
He's your God.

The music hit Azarias in the heart, his energy surging, his love for God erupting. He turned to the far right and then left. Charging

---

300   Luke 2:14
301   Psalm 55:22
302   John 14:1, 27

over the horizon towards Satan's army were the flaming red chariots of Michael's army and the white cavalry of Gabriel's army, their size dwarfing Satan's army in number.

This was the hour, their hour, God's hour of judgment upon Satan's armies. The pain, the killing of the innocent, the claim that righteousness would always prevail would be embossed into the Satanic angels amounting to about one-third of Heaven.

Satan rose higher out of the flooded theater, his dragon heads spewing out blasphemous vulgarities at God, the crowns now dulling in luster, his size dwarfing the structures all around him.

Azarias commanded the others, "Advance, Black Army, and box in his traitorous army with the Red and White armies."

Leihja turned her head. "Where did Abaddon go?"

"I assume Abaddon escaped to Pergamum, maybe the Bibliotheca," said Azarias. "I don't know why he left—maybe because of cowardness or to regroup another contingent of the Legion to secure their captives. I will take a company of the Black Army and pursue him."

"Do you think he will find reinforcements?" asked Jael.

Azarias exhaled. "Maybe that, or he'll kill the Pergamum captives. That is the last district we haven't infiltrated. We might be too late."

CHAPTER 36

*H*ow could this happen? We were the superior angels, possessing knowledge, finding our free will, and controlling our destiny.

Abaddon tightened his teeth. The Holy Order had not defeated Satan's armies yet. Satan was still the most powerful of all angels and could still rule Heaven and Earth.

The angry commander paced through the great hall of the Bibliotheca.

Abaddon grabbed two of his subordinates who had flown to him, his face rigid with anger. "Did you do it? Did you double the guards at the entrances above? This place has many exits, so we must protect them. We must convince the Septemviri that we are holding the hostages here and not in Satan's throne until the rest of our army joins us."

He drew one angel closer, baring his teeth. "If we are attacked and compromised, you are to go through the tunnel to Satan's throne room, the grotto, and kill the hostages."

He exhaled, his face relaxing into a smile, and, placing his arm around the angel, he spun him around.

"Look up there." He pointed to an arched window of painted crystal panes. "Have you ever looked closely at that before?"

The angel shook his head, his eyes wide with fear.

Abaddon continued. "There are eighteen panes up there, each with the image of a seraph. Satan had designed the panels in three rows of six. Each of the six panes defies the Creator, who insisted

313

on seven as the holy number of perfection. Satan's revolt always expresses in three items of six—six, six, six—to fling rebellion at each person of the Triune God."

The angel said nothing, his face silent with apprehension.

"Now look at the fourth angel on the bottom row," said Abaddon. "Look familiar?"

The angel peered up at the pane and then back to Abaddon. "Yes. It seems to look a little like you."

"A little?" Abaddon sneered. He squeezed the angel's face. "No, it the exact image of me, though the robe border is a different color, and the hair color is slightly off."

He breathed deeply before continuing. "Yes, Satan foresaw me rising in the ranks to be by his side sometime soon. Maybe today? I will be only second to him."

Abaddon's smile fell away. "Of course, there was a slight delay when he promoted Pollyon before me, but I'm sure that was a test of my loyalty. I don't mind Satan testing me, as long as I win." He snickered. "I may have taken care of Pollyon's promotion problem when I left him at the mercy of Azarias. The way I see it, if he can beat Azarias, he should have the lieutenant rank; if not, it belongs to me."

He nodded his head, smiled, and released the angel, patting him on the head.

"Yes, that is how Satan wants it. We have to earn our way into his graces using the tools he provided us—and one of those is betrayal.

"But don't get any ideas," he said, clutching the scared angel, again, by his robe this time. "You are nothing compared to me, understand?"

The angel nodded, his face pallid.

A loud crash exploded above, echoing in the great hall, debris falling among the Index and columns.

Abaddon covered his face and jumped back.

He turned his head towards the sound, his mouth open. The eighteen-pane window had been shattered, pieces strewn around the surface at his feet. Angels scattered in every direction.

Abaddon looked back up. Azarias stood on the window ledge above with about a hundred angels.

"Abaddon," called Azarias. "Prepare to meet the wrath of God!"

The loyalist angels flew down, attacking the Legion angels on the surface. Additional Legion angels flew from the rafters they had been guarding. A large battle ensued, with the rebellious ones adding to their masses, outnumbering the one hundred loyalists ten to one. Explosions echoed, along with screams and blasphemies, through the once tranquil hall. Angels searched for the next victim after sending their opponent to death, the fighting unorganized, white and dark particles clogging the atmosphere and reducing visibility.

Pale riders and horses charged out from the river passage single file, circling the large hall, slicing Legion angels from their advantaged position.

Abaddon noticed Azarias walking towards him through the mayhem, weapons clashing both ahead of him and in his wake, his eyes fixed and a sword held with a tightened grip.

Azarias lunged at him, and the two squared off, each wielding their weapon, the Word sword against hatchet-spear, jabbing and swinging. The two angels weaved between the massive columns, using their feet and wings to gain an advantage.

Moving around the large Index and into a corner, Abaddon swung his staff from left to right. Azarias ducked.

The shaft cleared the shelf supporting three books, *Way, Truth,* and *Life*, spraying them against the wall of three hanging cloaks.[303]

Abaddon speared one of the robes with his point and threw it on Azarias, who caught it with his shield, the hood obstructing his vision. Azarias moved blindly to his right, the Index supporting his back, towards the middle of the hall.

Azarias discarded the robe, but Abaddon thrust at his face, causing Azarias to fall back against the Index railing. Still using the rail as his rear defense, the Septemviri commander circled it,

---

303   John 14:6

making his way into the clear. Another angel attacked Azarias from his right, forcing him back to the railing. He slightly lost his balance.

Abaddon stepped between them.

"No, this one belongs to me," he said, waving off the other angel. He pushed his point at Azarias, whose head and back arched over the rail into the white mist of the Index, its vapors swirling at an agitated rate.

Abaddon wanted to see how far he could get the angel's head into the mist before he removed it. He wanted Azarias to feel his last seconds in the Creator's Heaven. He moved the blade to Azarias's throat, engaging the point but not piercing Azarias's spirit.

"I will enjoy sinking my tip into you very slowly. I love to look into an angel's eyes before killing him and exiling him forever." He placed his knee on Azarias's chest. "I failed twice, Azarias. Now I will—"

A large pale horse and rider jumped out of the Index over Azarias, followed by many others, onto Abaddon. The Legion angel fell backward, sliding into a column, his weapon dislodged from his hands.

He stood and screamed, "Azarias," but the battle had exploded, with a large cavalry regiment filling the hall.

One rider turned and started for him. Abaddon stood and raised his shield as a familiar face drew closer.

Squatinidale.

Abaddon parried the blow but managed to keep on his feet. Squatinidale turned his horse and charged again, knocking Abaddon against a wall. Retrieving a loose spear, Abaddon hurled it at Squatinidale. "You pathetic little imp. You have never been my equal, and you aren't now." Abaddon jammed his blade into Squatinidale's shield of faith, causing the horse to rear back on its hind legs, its front hooves stomping at the air, trying to bludgeon Abaddon.

The horse lowered down onto its front hooves, with Squatinidale flying over the horse's head, his eyes flaming, his face reddened. He drove his sword through Abaddon, impaling him against a wall. The dying Abaddon looked at the inscription on the wall above him—*Seek & Ye Shall Find*. He fell to his knees and then over to the surface, his delphinium blue eyes staring at a book entitled *Truth*.

The other pale riders continued to leap from the Index and the hidden passage, executing God's judgment as death to all who opposed him. The battle continued for a short while, with Squatinidale and the pale riders securing the Bibliotheca.

Azarias noticed one angel fleeing into a hallway towards Satan's lair.

He flew onto the back of Squatinidale's horse. "I saw an angel run that way after the Legion lost the fight. Let's follow. I think we will find the Pergamum angels there."

"Won't we find Satan, also?"

"Maybe. The last I saw Satan, he was about to battle Michael, Gabriel, and the rest in Laodicea. He may come back, so we have a small window to free any remaining angels."

MICHAEL, I CREATED YOU AS THE GREAT ANGEL AND PROTECtor of your cohorts. You will be one of my chief princes in the fight against darkness. I know you are ignorant of the gifts needed to accomplish this, but the Spirit will guide your hands for the destruction of evil. [304]

The message the Word had spoken to Michael never rang more true than now. Commanding God's Black, White and Red armies against Satan was why God had created him.

"Leihja, take a brigade of white horses and attack Satan—low," yelled Michael through his mark, "Malachy, take another brigade and attack Satan—high."

"Gabriel, Jael, and I will close in on Satan's armies from three sides."

Leihja and Malachy jumped onto the back of horses, and each gathered about three thousand mounted angels to follow them. The angels peeled off with the Holy Order armies and charged

---

304   Revelation 12:7

Satan, his dragon abomination now waist-high out of the flooded Laodicea theater.

Malachy and Leihja charged the red dragon, the reptile's fire shooting out of his multiple heads in all directions, exterminating some of God's loyal angels. Malachy's riders circled the dragon clockwise, while Leihja's attackers circled him counterclockwise. The dragon's heads twisted and turned in each direction following the attackers, their necks crossing each other.

Leihja lowered her circuitous attack to the area around the theater, the angels firing their bows at will, arrows bouncing off Satan's semi-armored torso. It appeared that they would have to shoot at close range into a vulnerable area supporting the heads.

Satan's blast almost dismounted Leihja, but she repelled it using her shield. She looped her leg around the horse's back, her torso tucked under its head, firing arrows continuously under the horse's chin to the side.

Michael watched as Leihja and Malachy preoccupied Satan. The enemy armies closed within range. Michael commanded the red, white, and black troops to attack using a three-sided attack. Michael led the Red Army chariots in a direct attack while Gabriel and Jael flanked the enemy at 45-degree angles.

All loyalists fired flaming, explosive arrows while enduring the soaring blades from the enemy's shafts. Casualties mounted on both sides as the atmosphere burst with the white and black particles of deceased angels.

The three sides of God's armies pushed harder and continued to turn the momentum, but the fighting persisted.

Leihja's brigade could not get closer to Satan because of the multiple firing mouths. "Follow me," she commanded.

Her brigade followed her to the theater's seated area as she dove into Satan's profundo lake. Their horses' torsos and tails extended longer, and their coats converted into scales. They rode towards the dragon's two legs, which stood as massive columns, creating powerful undercurrents every time they shifted.

Leihja charged her horse to one of the submerged walls. The rest of the brigade interlocked their horses' heads and tails in front of the dragon's legs.

Michael and the rest of the army had now compressed Satan's army into a tight area, pummeling them with their fiery arrows.

MICHAEL. CORRAL THE LEGION FORCES
TOWARDS SATAN AND BACK AWAY FROM
THESE WICKED ANGELS. THE SIQ WILL OPEN
ITS MOUTH AND SWALLOW THEM UP, WITH
EVERYTHING THAT BELONGS TO THEM,
AND THEY WILL GO DOWN ALIVE INTO THE
REALM OF THE DEAD BECAUSE THEY HAVE
TREATED THE LORD WITH CONTEMPT.[305]

Michael moved Gabriel's line closer and backed Jael's line, directing the warrior mass over the Laodicea structures. He took care to confine Satan's forces into one corpus, pressed in from three sides. The Holy Order expanded the circle wider, leaving Satan's army hovering above his head. Satan continued to cast fireballs from the theater through his heads, sometimes destroying parts of the loyalists' army.

Under the lake, Leihja drew her sword back. Steadying her horse in the current, she fired successive shots into the theater wall retaining the profundo. The barrier shook violently and then collapsed, the columns buckling, releasing the liquid spirit into the streets of Laodicea. Satan, the dragon, fought the deluge, his oversized torso teetering, his mouth screaming obscenities. As he tried to steady himself, his massive legs tripped on the horsetail barrier, toppling him forward.

Satan rocked forward and back, unable to balance himself with his wings. He rose out of the stadium lake, exposing, for the first time, his giant scaled tail. The tail swung back and forth, protecting Satan from any attack on the surface.

---

305   Numbers 16:25-30

Michael flew to where Leihja and the others were washing away in the flood, careening off structures towards the great arch. Their horses flowed with them, neighing loudly, trying to reunite with their riders.

One of Satan's heads pursued the attackers, eyes of rage, its fire incinerating structures. Michael flew behind Satan to divert his attention and confronted another head which bobbed and weaved. He fired an arrow, glancing off the serpent's temple, blowing out one of its eyes.

He returned to Leihja's group, who managed to hold their ground.

Satan lifted himself out of the theater, his tail waving behind him. Michael moved in very close and fired at another head, hitting it in the throat and disintegrating it to the shoulder.

God's holy armies increase their bombardment, compressing Satan's armies into a defensive position, with the Red, White, and Black armies on three sides, their master behind them.

Satan roared with profanity and blasphemy as the remaining heads all craned to attack Michael and Leihja, its rear body surging upwards, his tail sweeping erratically. The tail, pointing upwards, swept a portion of his army in one pass and the remainder of his army in a second motion, sending their remains to dwell on Earth and throughout the entire material world.[306]

The dragon roared again and took flight towards Pergamum, cursing God.

---

306   Revelation 12:4

CHAPTER 37

A zarias didn't like the dark. It had never existed in Heaven until Satan introduced evil, and now it dwelt in many places. The darkness sucked the life out of Heaven and the souls of one-third of the angels. How could they fall for such nonsense?

The dark passage between the Bibliotheca and Satan's lair raised Azarias's anxiety. The last time he had passed this way—walking, not on horseback—was when Pollyon had led him into a trap under the guise of rescuing Rafaella and Malachy.

Pollyon had assumed he had captured Azarias and the other angels by surrounding them with hundreds of enemy angels perched upside down from Satan's ceiling. Fortunately, the Lord implemented a plan that Azarias executed with four other Septemviri, securing all leadership members.

Though the outcome was good the last time, its darkness still stabbed him. It made him think of Uriel and Sosthenes, who now dwelled in it against their wills. He missed Uriel. He wondered what his loyal companion was doing, and how he survived in a universe in which evil dominates.

Sosthenes's death stabbed him also, but in a different way. Azarias still wasn't sure of Sosthenes's allegiance. Had he led Azarias into a trap, only to have a change of heart? Only God knew.

Azarias's mind returned to the present as Squatinidale slowed the horse down, the area pitch black with the stale stench of Satan. Once Satan dwelled in a place, it never returned to the Creator's original luster, or the Holy Spirit's aromatic scent. Evil seemed to leave a lasting mark on anything it touched.

Azarias refocused on this dreary trip. "How are we going to see? Squatinidale reached into his armor and pulled out a shining star. The object oddly had the shape of Philadelphian vinifera branches holding its fruit but with light substituting for the fruit.

The star lit the tunnel walls around them.

Haunting screams reached Azarias's ears, calling out for God to save them. Flashes of light bounced off the distant tunnel walls, silencing the trailing screams, one at a time. Squatinidale kicked the horse into a gallop and with the star leading the way, the angels' swords were activated and laced with God's judgment.

The two Septemviri blasted into the large cavern used as Satan's lair, their light illuminating its entirety. Another scream drew Azarias's attention as an enemy angel executed a bound angel hanging upside down from the curved ceiling. Hundreds of angels dangled upside down, their wings pressed close to their bodies. One thought ran through Azarias's mind. Were these the only angels left in Pergamum? Had Satan's Legion killed the rest of those named on Malachy's report, or had they defected?

Azarias flew off the horse and towards the assailant, the same one he had seen running from the Bibliotheca. The starlight blinded the aggressor, who used his shield to block its glorious rays, the single source of light casting shadows on the walls. The two angels fought, ducking around the defenseless victims hanging from the ceiling, the victims' eyes all wide with horror. Azarias tried desperately to not hit the angels, but the enemy relished in it. When the evil angel didn't need cover, he sliced a prisoner's head off, sending God's host to the other world. Azarias grew desperate, focusing on defending himself, saving the other angels, and killing the executioner.

Squatinidale circled the lair, starting on the far side, cutting the angels' ties and freeing them to fly out of the exit leading to Satan's colossal staging area and throne. Azarias didn't know if Squatinidale should continue to release the angels or help him. If this were Satan's only angel in the area, then Squatinidale should help him—but he didn't know that answer. Others could be joining this menace and kill the remaining prisoners as he and Squatinidale chased this coward.

The two angels continued to battle, Azarias handicapped by choosing not to strike a blow when the enemy angel used a Holy Order member to shield himself.

One last angel hung near the exit to the outside. Squatinidale could not get around the dueling angels to free the poor spirit. Azarias tried to swing the fight away, but the enemy didn't cooperate. He used the hanging angel as a shield, holding onto him with one hand.

Azarias waited until he could position the enemy with his back to the lair exit and the imprisoned victim between them. Like the others, the bound angel looked horrified, squeezing her eyes shut, expecting the unthinkable, lips moving fervently, calling to her God. Azarias grabbed the loyal angel, dangling by her feet, and swung her as hard as he could at his combatant, catching him off guard. The impact hit the enemy under the chin, sending him backward through the exit, where he staggered.

Azarias confronted the enemy angel on Satan's altar. The two angels resumed their fight, weaving in and out of the six obliques lined up on the highest level. Azarias seemed to have the upper hand, the armor of God shielding him from all strikes. As he guided his opponent's back against the cave opening, he hoped that Squatinidale would emerge and stab the menace.

They circled, and Azarias now had him where he wanted him.

The enemy's eyes refocused over Azarias's head. A smile erupted as the adversary cheered and circled again. Azarias moved with the enemy, also positioning himself with his back to the cave.

Squatinidale exited.

"Squatinidale, I need your help in defeating him."

"He is not our biggest worry," yelled Squatinidale. "Look!"

Azarias raised his head. The horrifying body of Satan as a red, mutilated dragon charged through a dark cloud, his eyes burning with hate.

Had the prince of darkness defeated all of the Holy Order armies?

The war wasn't going to be over until Michael drove the evil source out of Heaven. Michael had learned that Satan's evil never rested. Even an angel with a sober mind must be alert and not seduced, because Satan's evil prowled around looking to devour victims.[307] Satan's lies had poisoned the souls and lives of a third of Heaven's inhabitants, sending them into the material world to live in eternity away from intimate contact with God. But, unless the Holy Order cast him out of Heaven, it would happen again because evil could flare-up in an angel, and that usually went undetected until it was too late.

Michael led the Red, White, and Black armies after Satan, flying towards Pergamum. Had they exterminated Satan's army? He had to assume that, because Satan would have unleashed everything to save Laodicea and Pergamum. Ironically, Satan's unbridled temper and hatefulness killed them—the same characteristics that set him apart.

Michael had to account for Azarias and Squatinidale.

His scouts returned. "The Bibliotheca is secured by the Philadelphian pale riders, who are exterminating all known enemies. Satan was not there."

"Jebel Madhbah," he said under his breath.

"What?" responded Malachy.

"You know it by God's name: *Holy Mount of God*. It's now Jebel Madhbah, Satan's Throne. We'll go there."

Michael called out through his mark. "We will go to Satan's Throne to cast him and any of his remaining Legion members, out of Heaven."

Cheers erupted from all corners of the horizons.

A countless number of angels, brandishing their armies' colors of red, black, and white, praised God for the final battle they were about to start.

---

307   1 Peter 5:8

All eternity would rejoice at this victory. Angels (and maybe even creations who may not be angels) would hear of this war—the war between good and evil. They would gaze upon the battles fueled by nothing but faith in God.

Michael saw the dragon far ahead, its heads jerking from side to side, its fire thrusting towards the Holy Mount of God. Some members of the Holy Order must have secured the mount and were fighting to retain it.

Michael closed in. He could see Azarias and Squatinidale moving among the six obliques trying to avoid Satan's blasts. An enemy angel seemed to have joined with Satan in the assault.

Michael called Gabriel, Leihja, Rafaella, Malachy and Jael. "Attack each of Satan's remaining heads and distract the evil one while I assist Azarias."

The five Septemviri flew to Satan's heads, alerting the evil one's multiple eyes as they zig-zagged to move closer. The dragon heads turned and fired blasts of fire.

Michael flew as low as he could, his chest almost scraping the surface, his wings in a flatter glide mode, the blazing Word sword in his hand. He slipped around the arches and landed on the highest platform behind Satan's follower, who was fighting against Azarias. The Legion angel turned and raised his spear at Michael. Michael swung his sword once, cutting the spear in half, and then back again, slicing the angel and killing him.

Azarias and Squatinidale escorted the surviving Pergamum angels, flying low to escape Satan's glare. The dragon fought ferociously against the Holy Order, throwing out curtains of fire in all directions away from Jebel Madhbah.

Michael thought he had one chance to attack the evil leader at the seven heads' base, which the scales didn't cover. All other attacks on the heads seemed to injure them individually or bounce off the scales covering most of the body.

The big angel flew up to the base behind the heads and loaded his bow with seven fiery arrows; his left arm slipped through the straps of his shield. He focused his eyes, thinking he had to hit the base with all points at once to—

Out of the corner of his left eye, he saw a fiery spear projectile. Michael flinched his left arm, causing the fiery point to impale his shield just above his arm. The great angel toppled to his right, tumbling down onto the top of the tholos guarding the staircase.

Michael sat up and saw hateful eyes and a weapon.

Zepar.

The Legion angel fired another projectile, prompting Michael to swing under the tholos roof in time to guard himself. Zepar landed on the steps above him. "Thanks to you and your fellow slaves, Michael, I am now the top angel with Satan. We will rebuild and conquer. This will be just a minor setback, eliminating the weak and half-committed. It won't take long to clean up the remainder of the Holy Order. We already exterminated so many of them. They will be our slaves as we rule the material world."

He walked closer, his spear aiming at Michael, who kneeled under the tholos roof. "You," he sneered, contorting his face, "You and your little band of pathetic, God-fearing, ignorant servants. We gave you your chance. We gave you many chances. You could have been great." He stopped. "But now you are just dead!"

Zepar launched his spear blade at the prostrate angel. Michael rolled over to his right and rose to one knee, firing one arrow into the shocked angel.

Zepar exploded with its impact. The blast knocked Michael back against a small wall supporting two columns, wrenching his weapon from his hands.

He searched for his bow.

He spotted the Word, lying down at the lower level of another six columns.

One of Satan's heads turned in his direction.

Michael looked for any weapon—any at all—but there were none close to him.

Against the wall to his left were six of his remaining arrows.

The dragon head circled above him, blasting fire. The top of the tholos protected Michael and held him prisoner as the fiery shower poured off its roof.

The fire stopped.

Michael looked up as his fellow Septemviri attacked the head, drawing its attention.

He eyed all dragon heads, waiting for the moment when all would turn away from him.

He clutched the arrows and flew straight for the back of Satan. One dragon head spotted him out of the corner of its eye and wailed for the others to turn.

With six arrows in his hand, Michael jabbed them into the back of Satan's conjoined necks.

No penetration. Satan's evil had hardened his heart, his soul, and now even his spirit against any of God's redemptive powers.

Michael tried again—no penetration. He moved his hand closer to the six arrows, just behind their arrowheads, and yelled out, "The Lord thy God is One Lord!"[308]

He jammed them the third time, penetrating the surface as all the dragon heads turned on him.

He pulled away, but it was too late to accelerate; light seeped out of the wound, blinding him.

A passing arm grabbed him by his robe, taking him straight up at a speed he had never known before, his hair streaming behind him as Satan exploded in a cataclysmic cloud of black fire.

Gabriel.

The black fire chased the two up towards God's Throne, its dark fingers stretching for the escaping angels. As the darkness nipped at their feet, Gabriel repositioned his wings and arched their flight higher, leaving the menace behind.

Gabriel loosened his grip on Michael and turned him.

The two wept tears of joy and hugged as the Holy Order blasted a song of praise to God, not only from the Red, Black, and White

---

308   Deuteronomy 6:4

armies but from all over Heaven.

Satan's body dissolved into a giant mass of black particles and blew away in the direction of the Siq.[309] As the particles disappeared into the distance, the Septemviri joined together with cries of joy, jubilation, and praise for the one and only God.

A white, black, and red explosion cast a wave of energy at them. The angels raised their wings to shield their eyes.

"Look!" yelled Azarias, pointing his finger.

Michael looked up. On the horizon rose a giant black globe dusted with the material world's galaxies, nebulas, stars, and comets. Arching over the globe were multicolored bands up to the Lord's Throne.

God had opened all angels' eyes to the true three-dimensional nature of the Siq and the other heavenly layer that God's Throne encompasses. All that was not seen was now seen.[310]

---

309   Revelation 12:7-9
310   1 Corinthians 2:9

CHAPTER 38

Azarias didn't know who or what dwelled on Heaven's third level, now exposed as a beautiful, colorful arch. He went back to the Al Birka headquarters with the others for an extended prex précis. Heaven will never be the same, especially without angels like Uriel and Dionysius.

He looked up at his mesa, the golden amborlite dripping off its edge. He would never have guessed that those beautiful creations would play a role in saving Heaven. How little he knew about what God thought. He cringed about attempting to ask God any more questions.

He walked back to the group and joined in another prex précis with Gabriel, Rafaella, Malachy, Squatinidale, Michael, Jael, and Leihja. They were no longer seven and no longer the leaders of a great mission.

He smiled. He had doubted himself from the very beginning to the last battle.

But not God.

God knew who he was and who he was capable of becoming. He had given God what little he had to offer, and God blessed it and gave it back to him many-fold.

He closed his eyes. The Holy Spirit blew a warm breeze against his face, the smell of amborlite teasing his nose.

All was silent.

A crash assaulted his ears, echoing off the mesas.

Azarias opened his eyes to the stunned faces of his comrades, their mouths gaped open.

"Why are you looking at me?" he asked, very unsettled.

Rafaella pointed behind him.

Azarias turned around.

Uriel.

He didn't look exactly like the Uriel he knew. His square face, now firm, glowed in dark bronze skin, contrasting with his golden hair, violet eyes no longer showing apprehension but leadership. "Mai Deus Exsisto vobis."

Malachy started forward, her eyes wet, her mouth open.

Uriel raised his hand, palm open, his mouth curved in a smile. "The Lord has resurrected all loyal angels who fought for him to return to Heaven. All loyal angels can travel back and forth through the Siq."

"Praise God," hollered Rafaella, throwing her head up to God's Throne. "We missed you and are overjoyed that you have returned to us!"

"God is just," said Squatinidale.

Uriel raised his hand again, but this time, lowered his smile. "I can't stay."

"Why?" Azarias asked. "Heaven has lost one-third of its angels, and we need you."

Uriel turned to the giant global Siq.

"Satan is now ruling the material world. He and his followers have infiltrated the entire universe as dark matter, using their dark energy to pass through all matter, living or not. Everything you are looking at has their presence and they have weighed down all creation, causing it to groan."[311]

"Why is that our concern since we sent him out of Heaven?" asked Squatinidale.

"Satan has established himself in the soul of God's greatest creation on Earth, humankind. This pinnacle of His creation was made in His image. Satan is fighting God and tempting them to follow him to their eternal damnation."

311   Romans 8:22

Michael stepped up. "I'm ready. Let's go to Earth and help them fight."

"No, that is not where we will fight these angelic wars. The human battles on Earth will be just a shadow of the real battles fought for their souls.[312] We will fight the real battles in spiritual warfare that will impact the events and people on Earth."

"So, God will allow Lucifer back into the Heaven that we fought so hard to cast him out of?" asked Malachy. "That doesn't seem right."

"Not exactly." Uriel pointed over their shoulders. "That is where we will fight the spiritual warfare for humans."

Azarias turned. "On the other colorful intersecting layer of Heaven?"

"Yes. It looks like an arch to us but is as complete as the level we are now on. It is the third level of Heaven, where Satan and his now-called demons, can enter. That realm, the intersecting spiral, is where he is fighting God for the greatest and most valuable of all prizes—the human soul."[313]

"When do we start?" asked Rafaella, jumping to her feet.

"Now."

"Humans, like the rest of the material universe, are bound by time, and we have only their short life spans to fight Satan."

Gabriel walked up to the front. "Was our fight for Heaven just a delay of the inevitable?"

"No," said Uriel. "It was just the end of the beginning."

THE END

312   Hebrews 8:5
313   Job 1:6-12; Genesis 28:12; 2 Corinthians 12:2

CUMULATIVE GLOSSARY

Al Birka — Azarias's home residence that adjoins the Al Birka wilderness, where the Septemviri have their base to conduct their activity.

Amborlite — Heavenly stalks of colorful flowers that stand in fields and hang over the mesa bluffs. Amborite flowers have unique and varying petals that are living spirits onto themselves. In Al Birka and some other districts, the flowers are golden; in Smyrna, they are lavender and produce a sweet fragrance.

Bibliotheca — The library-like facility in Pergamum where angels go to learn about the more intricate and mysterious aspects of God and Heaven.

Cherub (pl. Cherubim) — An angel also referred to as a "Living Spirit" or "Guardian Cherub" when residing at God's Throne. Their heads have four faces: lion, eagle, ox, and human. Their legs end in hoofs, and they also have two sets of intersecting wheels, each covered by dozens of eyes. Their four wings are also covered in eyes.

Ego laus a deus intus vos — Translation: "I see (or praise) the god in you." This is the "rebellious" angels' mantra. In angel speak, it proclaims that every angel has the potential to be god.

Ephesus — A district in Heaven where angels perform in the Odeum Theater.

Heaven (layer one) — The outer globe where God's Throne resides. Layer one encases the intersecting second and third layers.

Heaven (layer two) — An internal spiral of Heaven encased by God's Throne globe where angels perform their duties. Early *Angelic Wars* books take place on this level.

Heaven (layer three) — An intersecting spiral encased by God's Throne globe. This is where the future *Angelic Wars'* battles for the human souls take place after Satan is cast out of Heaven's levels one and two.

Holy Order — The organization of God's angels. Later, it refers to angels who remain loyal to Him.

Holy Spirit — Third person of the triune God AKA the Trinity. Usually embodied as light, energy, spiritual wind, internal sensations, and small, tongue-shaped flames.

Khasneh — The record-keeping district in Heaven located in the direction of "six o'clock" on the two-dimensional diagram of Heaven. The district is nestled in the middle of three other districts: Smyrna, Thyatira, and Ephesus.

Khasneh Forest — A multilayer "rainforest" with bountiful colorful and crystal leaves that create an unlimited prism of colors when viewed through different layers. It is located just outside of Khasneh.

Laodicea — A district in Heaven located around "twelve o'clock" on the two-dimensional picture of heaven.

Mai Deus Exsisto vobis –- Translation: "May God be with you" in Angel speak. It is a greeting that all angels loyal to God use.

Mesa — An "outcropping" in Heaven. Mesas, like those on earth, appear as flat-topped mountains. Mesas are found all over Heaven, especially around God's Throne, outside of the district of Al Birka.

Othelites — Small, flat stone-like objects with rounded edges that can fit in an angel's palm. One side is black and the other white.

Pergamum — A district located at the "twelve o'clock" position on the two-dimensional map of heaven, just under Laodicea, closer to the Siq. It is the location of the Bibliotheca.

Philadelphia — An "underground" district in heaven characterized by the melted vinifera spirit. It is located at "ten o'clock" on the two-dimensional map of heaven.

Profundo — The liquid spirit in Heaven that flows like Earth's rivers. Its color ranges from turquoise to emerald, depending on its temperature. The more present the Spirit of God is in the area, the hotter the profundo. An angel can receive a jolt of God's Spirit when soaking any part of its body in it. This spirit flows in ravines like rivers, plunges under the surface like springs, and falls over cliffs like waterfalls.

Sardis — A district in Heaven where structures (buildings) and walkways are animated with personalized music for angels. It is located at "two o' clock" on the two-dimensional map of Heaven.

Seraph (pl. Seraphim) — An angel that resembles a human, except that its height ranges from 12 to 14 feet and it has wings that span 14 to 16 feet. They have six wings, and various "skin" and "hair" colors. Underneath their "skin" are golden channels that circulate God's Holy Spirit throughout their bodies (like our circulatory system).

Sign of the Septemviri — A brand that burns on the Septemviri and, ultimately, on each of the loyal angels' wrists. A picture of this symbol is displayed on the *Angelic Wars'* website and t-shirts.

Silicium — Grainy sediment like Earth's sand that collects in dunes.

Siq — The large dark area that intersects the two spiral levels of Heaven. In the first two books, it appears as a dark hole, however, when the second intersecting spiral is seen, it shows as a large spherical object containing the entire material universe. It is the only gateway to the material universe, where angels fear to tread.

Smyrna — A large district in Heaven consisting of the famous Paestra, the large mountain outcropping stadium that hosts Angelic games. This district is located at "seven o'clock" on the two-dimensional map of Heaven.

Thyatira — A district that is the closest to Al Birka. It functions as a hub for smaller districts. The main castle-like structure sits on a cliff between two intersecting ravines.

Vinifera — A spiritually-potent fruit carpeting the outcroppings (mountains) around the district of Philadelphia. These two-inch spheres grow in bunches on cross-shaped stems, forming a triangular bunch that hangs down. The fruit melts to form brooks, streams, and rivers that pool in Philadelphia, where the angels bask in the Holy Spirit. The spiritual liquid mixes with profundo, the other spiritual liquid, where their unique properties combine.

Water-rise — A profundo (or any other liquid spirit) "waterfall" that "falls" upwards from a river.

Word (person) — The second person of the Triune God (Holy Trinity, Holy Godhead) AKA Priest in the Order of Melchezidek, Jesus Christ, the Messiah, the Alpha and Omega, the Savior, the Good Shephard, Emanuel, Son of God, Son of man, Lamb of God, Logos.

Word (weapon) — The weapon, (as described in Ephesian 6:17. "Take the helmet of salvation and the sword of the Spirit, which is the word of God.") provided to the Septemviri and other members of the Holy Order in the epic battle.

LIST OF ILLUSTRATIONS AND SONGS

ILLUSTRATIONS

SONG LINKS

ACKNOWLEDGMENTS

As always with my novels and music, it took a lot of people and time to realize the publication of the *Angelic Wars: End of the Beginning*. Regarding the novel, the place to start is by acknowledging my lovely wife, Professor Judith Stepan-Norris for her support, editing, and creating of the illustrations as I tried to explain them to her from my jumbled mind. The team at Luminare Press went *above and beyond* to get this into a professional-looking format. Various artists contributed to this book, including Brayden Gardner, who helped design the faces of angels—no easy task. I had a few editors, the best of whom was Ben Dudley, who raked through my sentences tossing out and inserting commas and semi-colons like a master chef with a souffle. Other editors who contributed to the finished project were Hillary Beth Keonig and Nikki Mentges.

Creating the music is a whole project onto itself, in fact five projects. Each song was a production. The first two people to thank are my co-producers, Devin S. Norris (my son) and Lyle Johnson (not my son). These two not only performed on the songs but did a great job lining up other talent to bring these songs to life. All recordings were performed remotely during the pandemic scare which made this even more amazing from an engineering perspective. Without Devin and Lyle, the songs probably would sound like they were played on a Gramophone. I am truly grateful to their dedication to make the music as "heavenly" as possible.

The singers who appeared as the voices of the angel characters really did a great job—again, all remotely and separated from each other due to the pandemic. The four angels who sounded like an angelic chorus at times are: Emilio Tello, Brandijo Kistler, Satya Fuentes, and Andy Wilson. Contributing to the angelic band were also Nate Laguzza on drums, Zachary Ramacier on trumpet, Eddie Pimentel and Kyle O'Donnell on saxophones, Marx Ha on trombone, Devin Norris on keyboards, and Lyle Johnson on guitar and bass. Each of these musicians brought their own style and artistic flare to the songs creating diverse sounds.

Other Books by Rick E. Norris

INTO THE MIND OF LUCIFER
(Prequel to the Angelic Wars series)

ANGELIC WARS:
FIRST REBELLION

If you liked

ANGELIC WARS:
END OF THE BEGINNING,

download the free eBook
novella prequel,

"INTO THE MIND
OF LUCIFER."